SKULDUGGERY
PLEASANT
KINGDOM OF THE WICKED

The Skulduggery Pleasant series

SKULDUGGERY PLEASANT
PLAYING WITH FIRE
THE FACELESS ONES
DARK DAYS
MORTAL COIL
DEATH BRINGER
KINGDOM OF THE WICKED
LAST STAND OF DEAD MEN
THE DYING OF THE LIGHT
RESURRECTION
MIDNIGHT

THE MALEFICENT SEVEN

ARMAGEDDON OUTTA HERE
(a Skulduggery Pleasant short-story collection)

The Demon Road trilogy

DEMON ROAD
DESOLATION
AMERICAN MONSTERS

SKULDUGGERY PLEASANT

KINGDOM OF THE WICKED

DEREK LANDY

HarperCollins *Children's Books*

First published in Great Britain by
HarperCollins *Children's Books* in 2012
First published in this edition in the
United States of America by HarperCollins *Children's Books* in 2019
HarperCollins *Children's Books* is a division of HarperCollins*Publishers* Ltd,
HarperCollins Publishers
1 London Bridge Street
London SE1 9GF

The HarperCollins website address is:
www.harpercollins.co.uk

Skulduggery Pleasant rests his weary bones on the web at:
www.skulduggerypleasant.com

Derek Landy blogs under duress at
www.dereklandy.blogspot.com

18 19 20 LSCC 10 9 8 7 6 5 4 3 2 1

ISBN 978–0–00–826640–0

Find out more about HarperCollins and the environment at
www.harpercollins.co.uk/green

PROLOGUE

It was a beautiful spring day and they were standing on the roof.

"Do it," said Kitana. Her voice was low but urgent, tinged with an excitement that bubbled up from somewhere within her. Her straight white teeth bit lightly on her bottom lip. Her face was flushed. Her eyes sparkled. So eager to learn a new way to hurt people.

Doran turned to the chimney and held out his hand. He grunted, his face going red and the muscles in his neck standing out. It looked pretty funny until his hand started to glow. There was a light under his skin, and it was getting brighter the more he concentrated.

"Oh, great," said Sean. "We have the power of flashlights. Let the world beware."

"Quiet," Kitana said sharply. "Let him focus."

Sean didn't like it when Kitana dismissed him like that. Elsie could see it in his face. Angry, embarrassed, hurt. If Elsie had ever taken that tone with him, she doubted he'd even notice. Not that she ever *would* treat him like that. She wasn't like Kitana, who could spend a whole day mocking him and then, with one smile the next day, would have him back under her thumb.

Elsie wasn't mean like Kitana, but then she wasn't pretty like her, either, or blonde like her, or slim like her. She was fat and ugly and all the dyed hair and black clothes and pierced lips in the world couldn't hide that.

A beam of light shot from Doran's hand, crackling and sizzling, and blasted a hole through the chimney.

Kitana whooped with joy and Sean stared, mouth open. Doran dropped his hand and grinned.

"It was easier that time," he said. "Gets easier the more you do it."

Kitana ran to his side. "Teach me! Oh my God, teach me now!"

Doran laughed, stood behind her, used one hand to guide her arm while the other hand was on her hip. He spoke softly, into her ear, and she nodded as she listened. Elsie looked at Sean. He wasn't looking impressed any more. Now he just looked jealous. Elsie couldn't help it – she was disappointed. Doran was just a thug and an idiot who followed Kitana around like almost every other seventeen-year-old boy in their school. But Elsie had thought Sean was different. She walked over.

Light flared in Kitana's hand and the chimney blew apart. She screamed in delight, hugged Doran.

"That was cool," Elsie said to Sean. He murmured. She smiled. "Maybe we should try it."

"Knock yourself out," he said, and walked away from her.

Her heart did that sinking thing again. Sometimes it seemed like the only reason it ever rose up was just so it could sink back down. She followed Sean over to them, half-listened to the instructions they were given. Doran lost his temper, started calling her names, and Kitana laughed and egged him on. Sean was too preoccupied with figuring out how to do the new trick – she doubted he even noticed they were picking on her again. Maybe that was for the best. If he did notice and he didn't do anything to stop it, wouldn't that be worse?

Finally, after many curses and insults, Elsie began to feel the power in her hand, felt how hot it was getting. Beside her, Sean's arm was trembling.

"Feel that heat?" Doran asked. "Make it even hotter. Make it so that it almost hurts."

They stood in a circle, all four of them, with their arms held up towards the sky. Kitana had already done it twice.

"Feel it?" Doran asked.

"Yeah," said Sean impatiently. "Now what?"

"Now you just push it out of you," Doran said. "All the energy, just push it straight out. Like this."

A beam of crackling energy shot out of his hand. A moment

later, Kitana's beam joined it, a slightly deeper colour that mingled with his.

"This is so cool," she whispered.

Sean gritted his teeth. Sweat rolled off his forehead. But then the light in his hand flashed even brighter, and his own beam of energy raced towards the clouds and he laughed shakily.

Elsie became aware of Kitana's eyes on her.

"Last one, Elsie. You can do it."

Elsie licked her lips. "I'm trying."

"Try harder." Kitana's voice had lost the playful lilt she used with the boys. When she spoke to Elsie, there was always a harder edge to it. "You can't be the only one of us not able to do this stuff. A chain is only as strong as its weakest link, have you ever heard that?"

Of course Elsie had heard that. Who hadn't heard that? But that was part of Kitana's way, to treat her like an idiot. Elsie didn't respond. Instead, she took that frustration and added it to the heat in her hand. It was really burning now. It was like her hand was about to explode.

"Hurry up," said Doran, straining slightly. "Can't keep this going for ever."

Elsie felt that heat and pushed it, tensing every muscle in her body, pushing it up, out of her skin, away from her, and then it burst through, a beam of orange energy, flashing to the sky, joining the others. Elsie couldn't help it, she laughed. It was all so pretty. So beautiful.

Doran was the first to cut off his beam. He lowered his hand with a gasp. Kitana followed soon after, and then Sean, and finally Elsie. She was tired, like she'd poured all of her strength into that beam, but every part of her was tingling. Sean and Doran were both smiling, too. Only Kitana's eyes were narrowed, like she hadn't really wanted Elsie to be able to do it.

A car pulled up on the road below, and a man got out. He looked furious. "Get down from there!" he shouted.

"We're allowed up here," Kitana called out. "We have the owner's permission. Unless you are the owner, in which case get lost or we'll kill you."

"Let's use him for target practice," Doran whispered.

Before Elsie could object, the man swung his arms. A strong wind suddenly blew and he rose upwards like he was flying. Sean cursed and they all jumped back, and the man landed in front of them.

"Do you have any idea how risky this is?" he raged. "You're out in the open, for God's sake. How stupid are you kids?"

"You're... you're like us?" Kitana asked.

"I could see your damn lightshow from miles away. What were you trying to do? Were you *trying* to get noticed?"

"We didn't think there was anyone else," Kitana said.

The man stared. "Anyone else? What? What do you mean?"

"I mean other people like us, people with super-powers."

"What? What are you talking about? Listen to me, all right? You're not superheroes, you're sorcerers, and sorcerers don't use their powers where normal people can see. You've got to be very careful. Secrecy has got to be the number-one rule for you from this moment on."

"We're very sorry, mister," said Kitana.

He sighed. "My name is Patrick Xebec."

"That's a stupid name," said Doran.

"Doran," Kitana said, her tone scolding.

"We don't have time to get into this now," said Xebec, "but you need to take on a new name, otherwise other sorcerers will be able to control you."

"Seriously?"

"I'm always serious. I've never had a very good sense of humour, and I've never been particularly good with children."

"We're not children," said Doran, flipping up his hoodie. "We're seventeen."

"Anyone below the age of ninety is a child to me," Xebec said. "Sorcerers live longer than mortal people."

"Cool," said Sean.

"So your name wasn't always Xebec, then?" Kitana asked.

"This is a name I took. It felt right, so I took it, and it's been my name ever since."

"And if I changed my name from Kitana Kellaway to, like, Kitana Killherway, that would stop me from being controlled?"

"If you want that as your taken name, sure."

Doran grinned. "I'll be Doran Kickass."

"That's the stupidest name ever," Kitana said, giggling. "Sean, what about you?"

"I don't know," Sean said. "How about Sean Chill? Or Sean Destiny, or something? Sean the King." He laughed. "Yeah, I'll be Sean the King."

All three of them laughed. Kitana didn't ask Elsie what her name would be.

"Look," said Xebec, "pick whatever names you want, I don't care. I'm not qualified to take you through this. I don't get involved in any of that Sanctuary stuff. I just live my life and get on with it."

"What's the Sanctuary?"

"It's like our own private government. It has cops and soldiers and they're always saving the world or getting themselves killed. You need to go to them, they'll tell you everything you need to know. But if you want my advice, the moment that's done with, walk away. Don't become part of it. You'll just wind up dead."

"Magic cops," Kitana said. "I don't like the sound of that. Can they do what we do?"

"There are all different disciplines of magic," said Xebec. "I'm an Elemental. What can you do?"

"We don't know yet," said Kitana. "We keep on finding new things. Like, at first we were just strong, but then we could move things without touching them. And now today we can fire beams of energy from our hands."

"I figured out how to do that," Doran said proudly.

Xebec frowned. "You can do all those things?"

"Probably more, as well," said Doran. "Every day there's something new."

"I don't know what you are," Xebec said. "You should only have one of those abilities, two at the most. But even then you'd have to train for years."

"Maybe we're naturals," Kitana said, smiling. "So the cops can't do the things we can do?"

"No," said Xebec. "No one can, as far as I know."

Kitana bit her lip. "Oh, that's good to hear."

"I'll call the Sanctuary," said Xebec. "They'll be able to figure out what's going on. Come on."

He turned, walked to the edge of the roof. Sean went to follow, but Kitana tapped his arm, holding him in place.

"I don't think you should make that call," she said.

Xebec turned. "Listen, kid, I don't know what to do. I wouldn't be of any use to you."

"Actually, you've been a great help already. Thank you so much for everything you've done. But we can't let you tell the magic cops about us."

Doran raised his arm and his hand glowed. Xebec stepped back, eyes wide, didn't even have time to say anything before a beam of energy burned through his leg. He fell, screaming.

Kitana took a deep breath, narrowed her eyes, and Xebec stiffened and collapsed, as dead as anything could get.

Sean looked at Kitana. "What did you do?"

"I squashed his brain with my mind," Kitana said, and she started laughing.

Tyger! Tyger! burning bright
In the forests of the night,
What immortal hand or eye
Could frame thy fearful symmetry?
— *The Tyger*, William Blake

1

THE BUTTERFLY AND THE WOLF

"I'm a butterfly!" screamed the fat man as he ran, flapping his arms like two really flabby, really rubbish wings.

"You're actually not," Valkyrie Cain told him for the eighth time. He ran around her in a big circle, bathed in moonlight, and she just stood there with her head down. He wasn't wearing a shirt, and moments earlier she'd had to drag her eyes away from his wobbling bosoms before they made her feel queasy. Now that his trousers were starting their inexorable slide downwards, she was averting her gaze altogether. "Please," she said, "pull up your trousers."

"Butterflies don't need trousers!" he screeched. A moment later, those trousers landed by her feet.

She took out her phone and dialled. "He's in his underpants," she said angrily.

Skulduggery Pleasant's smooth voice sounded uncharacteristically hesitant. "I'm sorry? Who is in his underpants?"

"Jerry Houlihan," she said. "He thinks he's a butterfly. Apparently they don't wear trousers."

"And *is* he a butterfly?"

"He isn't."

"You're quite sure?"

"Quite."

"He could be a butterfly dreaming he's a man."

"Well, he's not. He's a big fat man dreaming he's a big fat butterfly. What the hell am I supposed to do?"

There was another hesitation. "I'm not sure. You don't happen to have a large net handy, do you?"

"I want to hit him. I want to hit *you*, but I also want to hit him."

"You can't hit him. He's an ordinary mortal under some kind of magical influence. It's not his fault he's acting this way. I assume you have him out of public view at the very least? Valkyrie? Valkyrie, are you there?"

"I'm here," she said dully. "He's started leaping with every third step. It's kind of mesmerising."

"I can only imagine. The Cleavers should be with you in half an hour or so. Can you contain him until then?"

She gripped the phone tighter. "You're not serious. You can't be serious. We've saved the world. I, personally, have saved the world. This here, right now, this is not something I do. This is something other people do and then you and me laugh about it later."

12

"We do what needs to be done, Valkyrie. Once you've handed him over to the Cleavers, meet me in Phibsborough."

She sighed. "Another busy night?"

"It certainly looks that way. I really must go. Sally Yorke has just set fire to her knees."

The line went dead. Valkyrie gritted her teeth and stuffed the phone back in the pocket of her black trousers. This was not how a seventeen-year-old girl was supposed to spend her evenings. She blamed the Council of Elders for making this a priority. Yes, she accepted that it was a major problem that previously unremarkable mortals were suddenly developing magical abilities – aside from the threat they posed to themselves and others, they also risked exposing the existence of magic to the general public, and that was not something that could be allowed to happen. But why, out of all the cases that were popping up all over Ireland, did Valkyrie have to deal with the weird ones who thought they were butterflies? There were a few dozen sedated mortals back in the Sanctuary and not one of those was as weird and unsettling as Jerry Houlihan in his underpants.

Valkyrie frowned, and wondered why she couldn't hear Jerry's footsteps any more. Then she looked up and saw him flying through the night sky, flapping his arms and squealing with glee.

"Jerry!" she shouted. "Jerry Houlihan, get down here!"

But Jerry just giggled and jiggled, unsteady in the air but flying – definitely flying. He reversed course, flapping back towards her. Stupidly, she looked up as he passed directly overhead. The image seared itself into her mind and she felt a little piece of herself die.

Jerry veered off course, drifting from the safety of the park towards the bright streetlights of Dublin City. Valkyrie reached up, felt the air, felt how the spaces connected, and then she pulled a gust of wind right into him, knocking him back towards her. She needed a rope or even a piece of string, just something to anchor him in place like a fat, man-shaped kite.

"Jerry," she called, "can you hear me?"

"I'm a butterfly!" he panted happily.

"I can see that, and a very pretty butterfly you are, too. But aren't you getting tired? Even butterflies get tired, Jerry. They have to land, don't they? They have to land because their wings get tired."

"My wings *are* getting tired," he said, puffing heavily now.

"I know. I know they are. You should rest them. You should land."

He dipped lower and she jumped, tried to grab his foot, but he beat his arms faster and bobbed up high again. "No!" he said. "Butterflies fly! Fly high in the sky!"

He was gasping for air now, losing his rhythm, and no matter how hard he tried, he couldn't keep himself from dipping lower once more. Valkyrie jumped, grabbed him, closed her eyes and tried to send her mind to a peaceful place. Jerry was sweating from all that exertion, and his skin was warm and sticky and hairy. Valkyrie remembered the good times in her life as she pulled him out of the sky, handhold after handhold. He made a last-ditch effort to soar away and she had to grip the folds of flesh on his hips to hold him in place. Then Jerry gave up and stopped flapping, and Valkyrie fell screaming beneath his weight.

"I'm not a butterfly," Jerry sobbed, as Valkyrie squirmed and wriggled beneath him.

The Cleavers arrived on time, as they usually did. They escorted Jerry Houlihan into their nondescript van, treating him surprisingly gently for anonymous drones with scythes strapped to their backs. Valkyrie hailed a cab, told the driver to take her to Phibsborough. They pulled over beside Skulduggery's gleaming black Bentley.

Skulduggery was waiting for her in the shadows. His suit was dark grey, his hat dipped low over his brow. Tonight he was wearing the face of a long-nosed man with a goatee. He nodded up to a dark window on the top floor of an apartment building.

"Ed Stynes," he said. "Forty years old. Lives alone. Not married, no kids. Recently split from his girlfriend. Works as a sound engineer. Possibly a werewolf."

Valkyrie glared at him. "You told me there were no such things as werewolves."

"I told you there were no such things as werewolves *any more*," he corrected. "They died out in the nineteenth century. Unlike certain other creatures of the night that I could mention but won't, werewolves were generally good people in human form. So appalled were they by their carnivorous lunar activities that they actively worked against their darker selves. They sought cures, isolation, whatever they needed to make sure that they didn't spread the curse to anyone else."

"Unlike vampires," Valkyrie growled.

"You mentioned them, not me."

"So if werewolves are extinct, why do you think Ed Stynes is a werewolf?"

"Last night, people in the area reported sightings of a large dog, or a man dressed as a bear," Skulduggery said. "He didn't hurt anyone – werewolves seldom do on their first time out unless they're cornered. But on their second time, things get a lot more violent."

"But if werewolves are extinct..."

"The infection has been diluted down through the generations, but it's still there in a tiny fraction of the world's population. Too weak to ever manifest into any actual transformation – unless the carriers of this infection were suddenly and inexplicably to gain magical abilities."

"So Ed is like my butterfly man earlier."

"Yes. The latest in a worryingly long line of mortals developing magic. Unfortunately in Ed's case, it triggered a long dormant aspect of his physiology. You're going to need this." He handed her a long-barrelled gun.

Her eyes widened. "This is mine? You're giving this to me? This is so *cool.*"

"It's a tranquilliser gun."

Her face fell. "Oh."

"It's still cool," he insisted. "But I'm going to need it back

16

afterwards. It's part of a set. I have the other one, and I like to keep them together. It's already loaded with a single tranq dart, so all you have to do is point and pull the trigger. The dart is loaded with enough sedative to bring down a—"

"Small elephant?"

He looked at her. "What?"

"You know. In the movies, if they're going after something dangerous, they always say their tranquilliser darts have enough sedative to bring down a small elephant."

"What do people have against small elephants?"

"Well, nothing, but—"

"There's enough sedative in these darts to bring down a werewolf, which is exactly what we're hunting. Why would we want to bring down an elephant if we're not hunting elephants?"

"It's just something people say in movies."

"In elephant-hunting movies?"

"No, not particularly."

"If we were hunting a were-elephant, I would understand the reference."

"There's no such thing as a were-elephant."

"Of course there is. There are were-practically-everythings. Weredogs, werecats, werefish."

"There are werefish?"

"They don't generally last very long unless they're near water."

"I don't believe you. I've fallen for this too many times in the past."

"I don't know what you're talking about." He started across the road.

She followed. "Oh, don't you? You'll insist they're real and I'll eventually start to doubt myself, and then I'll ask, *Are there really werefish?* And you'll look at me and say, *Good God, Valkyrie, of course not, that'd be silly*, and I'll stand there feeling dumb. Just like with that colony of octopus people."

"The what?"

"You told me once that octopus people were real."

"And you believed me?"

"I was twelve!"

They reached the door of the apartment building. "And yet most twelve-year-olds don't believe in octopus people."

"I was twelve and impressionable, and I believed whatever you told me."

"Ah, I remember those days," Skulduggery said fondly, then took out his revolver. "There is such a thing as a werefish, though."

She watched him loading the gun. "Those don't look like tranquilliser bullets."

"That's because they're not. They're silver. Only thing guaranteed to kill a werewolf. Apart from decapitation. But then—"

"Decapitation kills most things," Valkyrie finished.

"Exactly."

"Apart from zombies."

Skulduggery slid the revolver back into his shoulder holster. "This gun is just for emergency, last-resort back-up. Ed Stynes is a good man – I have no desire to take his life just because he changes into a wolfman a few nights a month." He took a pair of lock picks from his jacket and started on the door.

"Why don't we wait until morning to do this?" she asked. "Wouldn't that be smarter?"

"And leave him free to roam and kill tonight?"

"It's dark and the moon is full and I don't hear any howling. Maybe it's not as bad as you think."

"He just hasn't transformed yet. All day he'll have felt grouchier than usual. This evening the headaches will have started. Once night fell, the cramps will have kicked in. Judging by the position of the moon, we have about ten minutes before he changes. He'll spend roughly three hours covered in fur, and when the moon slips further away, he'll change back."

"So we tranq him while he's still human?"

"Rarely a good idea," Skulduggery said, opening the door and putting his lock picks away. "Sometimes it works, but most of the time the transformation occurs anyway, and the adrenaline rush clears the sedative from the system. The wolf wakes up angry and it takes a double dose to put it down again."

"So we have to wait until he changes into a monster before we can do anything?"

"Indeed."

"It seems a lot more dangerous."

"It is." He took out a tranq gun identical to Valkyrie's. "Ready?"

"Uh..."

19

"That's the spirit."

They took the stairs to the third floor. The building was quiet, still, like it was holding its breath. They approached Ed Stynes' door and Skulduggery picked the lock silently. He nudged the door open a little. There were no lights on inside. His hand went to his collarbones, pressing the symbols etched there. The false face melted away, revealing the skull beneath.

He entered, and Valkyrie crept in behind him and shut the door with a soft *click*. The tranq gun was heavy. She held it in a two-handed grip, just like Skulduggery had taught her.

So far, no growling.

They stepped into the living room, sweeping their guns from corner to corner, making sure Ed Stynes hadn't lain down to sleep on the couch. It was hard to make anything out in the gloom, but since Skulduggery didn't shoot anything Valkyrie figured the couch was empty. She may have been the only one with eyes, but his night vision was still better than hers. They moved across the hallway, checked inside the small kitchen. The moonlight washed over the headache tablets that were spilled across the countertop. There was a sudden groan from the bedroom and Valkyrie nearly pulled the trigger in response. Skulduggery tilted his head in her direction and she glared.

He moved through the hallway like he wasn't even there. A cat would have made more noise. Valkyrie followed, keeping close to the wall, where the floorboards beneath the carpet would creak less. Skulduggery moved past the bedroom door, took up position on the other side.

Valkyrie edged forward, using the mirror on the opposite wall to look through into Stynes' bedroom. She heard a curse, and there was movement in the darkness, and then the bedside lamp came on. She froze, adrenaline pumping through her, but all Stynes did was push the covers away as he sat up in bed. He was unshaven, pale. Sweating. He looked to be in pain. He groaned as he stood up. Valkyrie glanced at Skulduggery, mouthing the word *Hide?* But he just shook his head and so she stayed where she was, eyes on the mirror.

Stynes took a step, then doubled over.

"Oh, God..." she heard him mutter.

He straightened up with a scream so sudden it made her jump. His fingers curled like his muscles were being tightened on some invisible rack, and still he screamed. She'd never heard anything like it.

The lamplight shone yellow over his skin as thick black hairs pushed through, matting and knotting across his chest and back, his arms and legs. He fell to his knees, his legs changing shape, his bones lengthening and re-forming. He stared in horror and dismay at his hands as his fingernails fell to the floor and sharper, longer claws grew in their place.

"Help me," he gasped. "Somebody help—"

He dropped to all fours, another scream twisting up from his core, wrenching itself from his throat as his jaw dislocated. It cracked and popped and started to balloon outwards, his skin stretching over his newly formed muzzle. Fangs split his gums and his scream turned to an animal howl of rage and pain.

Skulduggery held up three fingers. Valkyrie watched him count down – two, one – and then he stepped into the doorway, tranq gun rising. She took an extra moment to follow his instruction, too stunned by what she had just witnessed to operate with any speed, and so the wolf missed her completely when it came charging out of the bedroom.

Valkyrie fell back, falling in the darkness, trying to make out what was going on just a few metres away. Something broke and something fell and the wolf was snarling and Skulduggery was cursing, and all she could make out was a huge mass of fur on two legs. She looked at her empty hand, wondered where the hell her gun had gone. She swept her arm across the carpet, fingers tapping against something metal. She lunged, gripped the handle and stood, turned, finger on the trigger—

—and something knocked her backwards into the living room. She pushed at it, whatever it was, and Skulduggery clambered off her and the wolf leaped on him again and they crashed into the sofa, turning it over and falling behind it.

Valkyrie got to her knees, started looking around for that damn gun again.

Skulduggery yelled as he was thrown across the room. He hit the TV and glass broke, and he pulled the blinds from the window, and the wolf pounced, pinning him to the floor. It slashed, again and again, and Skulduggery cried out. In the moonlight Valkyrie could see the ferocity with which it struck, its claws tearing through his clothes, raking against his ribs.

She flicked her wrist and shadows wrapped round the wolf's neck, hauling it backwards, but she could feel the sheer strength that fought against her and could do nothing to stop it from tearing free. Its yellow eyes found her.

She bolted, sprinting back into the bedroom, the wolf on her heels. She used the air to smash herself through the window, the glass jabbing at her clothes, but at least now she was outside, falling through space, and the wolf—

—the wolf slammed into her and she lost control of the air and they spun as they fell, the wolf snapping at her, its claws trying to cut through her jacket. The wolf hit the ground with a yelp and they separated, with Valkyrie bouncing away from it and rolling across the courtyard. The wolf stood, shook itself to clear its head, and by the time it looked back at Valkyrie she was already running.

2

THE WEREWOLF OF DUBLIN

alkyrie swept her arms up on either side and the wind lifted her. She cleared the wall easily and came down, stumbling a bit until she regained her balance. She ran across the road, used the air to take herself to a low rooftop and then to a higher one. She jumped a gap and climbed, reaching for a handhold. Grunting with the effort, she hauled herself up and rolled, came up in a crouch. She held her breath while her heart thudded, listening for sounds of the wolf's pursuit.

She didn't hear any. Instead, she heard music.

Staying low, she ran to the other side of the roof. A little bit further on, a line of people waited to gain entry to a brightly lit nightclub, their laughter mingling with the deep beats of the music that throbbed into the night. To a bloodthirsty werewolf cheated of its first meal of the evening, Valkyrie reckoned it would look like an irresistible invitation to feast.

And there it was, concealed in the darkness of the alley across the street. She glimpsed it moving slowly, slipping in and out of shadow. She ran to the edge of the roof and the wind lifted her high over the passing cars. She needed another buffet to carry her all the way across, but she landed on her feet right where she was aiming for. She hurried to the side and peered down. The wolf was directly beneath her. That tranq gun would have really come in handy from this position.

Her finger twitched. To use the shadows from up here, she'd really have to go straight for a killing blow. Anything less would just make the wolf mad, maybe spur it into slaughtering a few people. But she didn't want to kill it. Not like this. Not if there were any other choices to make.

And then the wolf charged across the street.

Valkyrie cursed, flung herself after it, angling through the air until she was on an intercept course. A few people were screaming by now and she propelled herself to ground level, curled up right before she hit the wolf. The impact knocked the breath out of her and she sprawled across the road. She heard screams and shouts, glimpsed faces and saw headlights and then a bus hit the wolf and braked, veered, its back end swinging round and crunching into Valkyrie.

Once more she flew backwards off her feet, the world silent all around her.

She hit the ground. Noise rushed to her ears and she bounced and tumbled way too fast to stop. She was aware that her chin was tucked into her chest and her arms were covering her head.

That was good. It meant she wasn't dead yet.

Her tumbling slowed and she used the momentum to push herself to her feet. The bus hadn't tipped over, thank God. It was parked diagonally across the road, and there were people running about and shouting at each other. She was blocked from view, halfway down the dark street. Her thoughts were returning, too, the more her head cleared. She remembered fur, and fangs. Something growled ahead of her.

Oh, yeah. The werewolf.

She couldn't see it. Everything between her and the lights of the nightclub and the bus melted into an impenetrable darkness. And that's where the wolf moved. She shaded her eyes but it was no use. The glare was too strong. The darkness too thick.

The growling got louder. Closer.

Still dizzy, Valkyrie broke left, ran between two cars, heard the wolf bounding after her. She ran, away from the nightclub and the people, barely managing to keep herself from ricocheting off lamp posts. And then the wolf slammed into her. They rolled, the wolf and her, its jaws clamping round her right arm. The teeth didn't penetrate the armour-weave of her jacket but still she screamed. The wolf shook its head and she kicked out, but it was crouched over her, too heavy to move.

Let me out, said the voice in her head.

Her arm was about to break. The wolf was going to rip it from her shoulder. The Necromancer ring was useless without the freedom to orchestrate the shadows. She tried pushing at the air but the pain clouded her mind. She couldn't even breathe with the weight of the wolf pressing down on her.

Let me out.

The wolf released her arm, went for her throat, and she jerked to the side, grabbed the shadows, turned them sharp like knives and raked them across the wolf's chest. It reared back, yelping, and she pushed at the air and it tumbled. It immediately righted itself and came at her. She threw herself backwards across the bonnet of a parked car. The whole car shook when the wolf crashed into it. Valkyrie scrambled up on to the car roof and brought the wind in to sweep her over the wolf's head. She dropped behind a wall, started running again, saw Skulduggery in the moonlight, flying towards her.

She ducked and he flew past, collided with the wolf behind her. The wolf threw him back and Skulduggery rolled to his feet, the tranq gun in his hand, but he slipped on something in the darkness. He fell and the wolf leaped and something went skittering across the ground.

The tranq gun – mangled.

Fire flared and the wolf howled in pain, and Skulduggery came staggering out of the gloom. His hat was gone and his face was gone. His suit was shredded, and even in this light Valkyrie could see the deep grooves cut along his ribcage. He held his revolver in his hand.

The wolf growled. Skulduggery turned.

It ran straight at him, and Skulduggery brought his other hand up to steady his aim.

"Shoot," Valkyrie cried out. "Shoot!"

But at the last moment Skulduggery dropped the gun and brought both arms down, his knees bending, and a wall of air slammed into the wolf from above, sending it to the ground. It tumbled and yelped and immediately Skulduggery straightened, swinging his arms towards the sky, sending the wolf spinning off its feet. As it was twisting and falling again, he stepped forward and punched, and a column of displaced air struck the wolf in the side and sent it hurtling back.

"Dart!" he yelled as he crouched. He touched one hand to the ground around his feet and it started to crack and buckle. He was almost thrown off as the section he was standing on shot forward like a surfboard, the ground warping and rippling beneath it like waves, and he hurtled towards the wolf as it recovered. Valkyrie grabbed the broken gun, wrenched the dart from the chamber and used the air to send it straight into Skulduggery's outstretched hand. An eyeblink later, he collided with the wolf, stabbing the dart into the creature's shoulder.

The wolf roared and lashed out and Skulduggery went flying, but the sedative was already taking effect. The wolf staggered, shook its head, stumbled against the wall. It looked at Valkyrie and moved towards her, could only manage three steps before its legs gave out and it crumpled. It lay there, tongue out, panting, limbs too heavy to move. Its eyes closed, its breathing deepened, and it went to sleep.

Skulduggery got to his feet. "Victory," he said weakly.

*　　*　　*

When Ed Stynes woke up, he was strapped to a bed in a strange room with strange people looking down at him. Valkyrie almost felt sorry for him.

"Hi," said the blue-haired girl beside her. "I'm Clarabelle. Will you be my friend?"

Confusion etched itself on to Ed's face.

"Hi, Ed," said Valkyrie before things got too weird. "My name's Valkyrie. This is Clarabelle. Clarabelle's a nurse, of sorts, and she's going to be taking care of you."

Clarabelle nodded. "I'm very good at medicine stuff. We had a patient, last week, who came in and I examined him and he had all the signs of bubonic plague, and I healed him."

Valkyrie looked at her. "He really had bubonic plague?"

"Oh, yes. Well, Doctor Nye looked at him and said he just had a splinter, but I was the one who removed it, so... That still counts. Wait until you meet Doctor Nye, Ed. You'll love him, if you love big tall scary things."

Ed whimpered, and turned his head to Valkyrie. "What... what's happening to me?"

"What do you remember?"

"I remember you. I remember... Oh, God, I remember wanting to eat you..."

"Yes," Valkyrie said. "Well, the less said about that, the better."

"I'm going mad, aren't I?"

Clarabelle laughed. She had such a pretty laugh. "Oh, we're all mad around here, Ed!" And then she skipped away.

Skulduggery walked in, wearing a grey trench coat over his shredded suit and a new face over his skull. He didn't want Ed to freak out any more than absolutely necessary. "Hello, Ed," he said. "Feeling better? You're certainly looking better."

"Who are you people?"

"We're experts in this field," said Skulduggery. "We want to help you."

"Help me? I'm a *werewolf*."

"I noticed. Hopefully, however, it's just a phase you're going through. Think of it as a sickness, if you like. A disease. Your dormant werewolf gene suddenly awakening is merely a symptom of the real problem, and while your situation is somewhat unusual, you're not the only person to be afflicted. There are others, normal people like you, suddenly exhibiting unusual levels of power. But you're one of the few cogent ones. Most of the others have been driven beyond sense. You can help us, I think. You just need to answer a few questions. Can you do that?"

"Y-yes."

"Good man," said Skulduggery. "Have you had anything unusual happen to you recently?"

"Yes."

"And that was?"

"I turned into a werewolf."

"Anything apart from that? Have you met anyone new? Have you been abroad, or visited somewhere for the first time...?"

Ed shook his head. "Everything's been normal. It's just been my life, the same as it's always been. Well, apart from breaking up with my girlfriend a few months ago. Do you... do you think she put a curse on me?"

"She's the one who ended it, wasn't she?"

"No," said Ed immediately. "It was a mutual thing. We both... it was decided that... we mutually agreed that she could do better, so..."

"In that case," said Skulduggery, "I doubt she put a curse on you. Has anything else happened out of the ordinary? No matter how trivial it may seem?"

"No. Everything's been normal. Apart from the dreams."

Skulduggery's head tilted. "Go on."

"I was just... I started dreaming about a man, dressed in white. Argeddion, his name was. It's unusual because I never remember my dreams, but Argeddion is as clear as day in my mind."

"What did he want?"

"He had a gift for me. That's what he said. He was so gentle, and warm, and he said he had a wonderful gift to give me. He appeared in my dreams for weeks, telling me to prepare for the Summer of Light, and then the last time I dreamed about him he held up his hand, and he was holding this bright, glowing *energy*, and he put it into my chest. Then he smiled, and said he'd be back for it later. I haven't dreamed about him since then. Do you think that has anything to do with what's happened?"

"Strange men giving you gifts of energy, and soon thereafter you transform into an extinct supernatural creature? I'd say it's a distinct possibility, Ed."

They left him in Clarabelle's dubiously capable hands and made their way out of the Medical Bay. As soon as they were in the corridor, Skulduggery retracted his façade. His skull was still a little dirty from being thrown through the rubbish of Dublin City.

"How are the mortals in the observation ward?" Valkyrie asked.

"No change," he answered. "Every conceivable test has been run on them and is being run again. So far, nothing. Not one clue as to what's going on."

"Will Ed be joining them?"

"He'll be sedated, like the others. They already have a bed waiting for him."

"But at least now we have a lead – even if it *is* just someone's dream. Wow. When you say it out loud like that, it sounds very flimsy, doesn't it?"

"That our only lead is a dream a werewolf had?" said Skulduggery. "Yes, I suppose as far as clues go, it's not the most solid one we've ever had. But we work with what we're given, and we really can't afford to be choosy, not at this stage. With everything that's been going on, we've barely been able to keep this out of the news. Sooner rather than later, the mortals are going to see something that cannot be explained away unless we put a stop to it. And this mystery man in Ed's dream, this Argeddion, might be what we're looking for."

"Any idea what the Summer of Light is? Do you think he means *this* summer?"

"I don't know. But if we're going by the traditional Irish calendar, summer starts on May first, which gives us a week to figure it out."

"The Summer of Light sounds nice, though," said Valkyrie. "Maybe all of this is leading up to some really good weather, in which case we should probably let it happen so I can sunbathe."

"What a marvellous idea. Let's make *that* assumption."

She noticed the way he was holding his side. "You're hurt," she said.

He looked at her. "We *were* attacked by a werewolf."

"But you're actually injured."

"So are you."

"But nothing major. Just bruises and strains and cuts, and I got a doctor to treat them. Your *bones* are damaged, Skulduggery. Why don't you get someone to heal you? It won't take long."

Skulduggery straightened up as they walked. "Doctor Nye tortured my friends to death during the war with Mevolent. I'm not going to it for help."

"Nye's not the only doctor who works here."

"But it *is* the only one who'd have the skill to repair my injuries properly. Besides, I'm not that bad. I'll survive, just like you will."

"You know, there's a distinct possibility that you're too stubborn for your own good. But hey, I'm not going to pressure you. You do what you need to do."

She heard the smile in his voice. "Well, thank you for being so understanding. In return, I'm going to drop you home. It's been a long few days, and you're going to sleep in your own bed tonight."

"Oh, thank God," she said, sighing. "I haven't seen my folks in ages. And Alice has probably learned to walk or something since

I saw her last. She's fifteen months old. What age do babies start walking at?"

"Depends on the baby."

"How about a really advanced one like my sister?"

"Oh, then she should be walking any day now."

Valkyrie grinned. They emerged from the Sanctuary and as they reached the Bentley, Skulduggery's voice softened. "Did you hear her again? Darquesse?"

Her smile faded, and she nodded. "She wanted me to let her out. It's been a year since she's been in control and her voice is getting louder. We need a plan. Something to stop her if she takes over."

He folded his arms on the roof of the car, and lightly drummed his gloved fingers. "You mean something to stop *you*," he said at last.

"I'd much rather you stopped me than let me do what we both know I'm going to do. I don't want to murder anyone, let alone my parents, or my sister, or you. If the time comes and I'm lost and Darquesse is in control—"

He held up his hands. "I'll think of something. Trust me."

Valkyrie glanced over at a limousine parked nearby, with two men in suits standing guard. As good a change of subject as any. "Do we have a visiting VIP or something?"

Skulduggery grunted. "Apparently we do. Here for a meeting with the Council. All very hush-hush and top secret. Only the Elders are allowed to know what they're meeting about."

"But Ghastly will tell us, won't he?"

"Oh, I'd very much expect so."

3

COUNCILS MEET

Ghastly had never been in this room before. It was the same concrete-grey drabness as every other room in the Sanctuary, but this one had a big table in its centre, shaped like a toad. It probably wasn't supposed to look like a toad, it was probably supposed to resemble something grand and inspirational, but in Ghastly's view it succeeded only in resembling a grand and inspirational toad, and that's where he left the matter.

He sat on an uncomfortable chair to the right of Erskine Ravel, the Grand Mage. To Ravel's left sat Madame Mist, her slender frame draped in the Elder robes they all wore, her face hidden by that black veil. They must have looked a sight. Grand Mage Ravel, looking like he should be wearing a tuxedo, flanked by a scarred man and a veiled woman. Ghastly wondered if any of the other Councils around the world looked half as odd as they did. He doubted it.

Right now, he was sitting across from representatives of two of those Councils, and they both looked perfectly normal, if perfectly solemn. Ghastly wasn't even listening to what was being said. Small talk was not his forte. He'd had a boxer for a mother and a tailor for a father – what did he know of the small talk of politicians and bureaucrats? He waited impatiently for them to get to the point of their visit, and when they finally reached it, he wasn't at all surprised.

"You've been having some problems with your sorcerers, we hear," said Grand Mage Quintin Strom of the English Sanctuary. Like most Grand Mages, with the obvious exception of Ravel, he was grey-haired and lined and old. Still immensely powerful, though, and somewhat humourless.

"I'm afraid you've been misinformed," said Ravel. "Our mages are all doing fine."

Strom's eyebrows rose slightly. He was a good actor. "Oh! In which case, I apologise. It's just that we've had reports of disturbances in practically every corner of the country. You're saying these reports are inaccurate?"

"I'm not saying that at all," Ravel said smoothly. "But the problems are not our sorcerers."

Strom nodded. "Ah yes, we heard that, too. Something is affecting the mortal population here, yes? Dreadful, dreadful business. If you need any help—"

"Thank you, but no," said Ravel. "We have it under control."

"Are you quite sure? I don't mean to condescend, Grand Mage Ravel, but I have a lot more experience running Sanctuaries than you do, and there is no shame in accepting assistance when it is offered."

"Thank you for clarifying," Ravel said.

The man beside Strom cleared his throat politely. He was young and American, Ghastly knew that much. "Unfortunately," he said, "things may not be so simple. The purpose of a Sanctuary is to oversee the magical communities and protect mortals from the truth. If even one Sanctuary fails in its obligations, the success of every other Sanctuary will amount to naught. To use a horribly overused phrase, the chain is only as strong as its weakest link."

Madame Mist stirred. "And you are saying that we are this weak link?"

"Oh, heavens, no," said the man. "All I'm saying is that this Sanctuary has had more than its fair share of crises to deal with. Given the pressure you've been under, even the strongest link will strain."

"So you *are* saying we're the weakest link," said Ravel. "I'm sorry, but who are you again?"

"Bernard Sult," said the man. "I'm a Junior Administrator for Grand Mage Renato Bisahalani."

"And why are you here?"

"Sult's here to help," said Strom. "You know the American Elders, they always think they're far too busy to take care of things personally. But what he says is true. It's not something we like to talk about, but the fact is that Ireland has been the source of a great deal of anxiety around the world. It's in our best interests, of course, to make sure you're strong enough to withstand anything that comes your way."

"We don't need to be propped up," said Ravel.

Sult shook his head. "I assure you, that's not what we're saying. But if everything that has happened here in the last ten years had happened somewhere else, say Germany, would you be confident in their ability to handle it alone? Or would you feel the need to lend some support?"

Ravel said nothing.

"The other Sanctuaries are worried," Strom said. "They want reassurances that you are prepared and that you are capable. And so I am among the three they have elected to act as their representatives to—"

"I'm sorry," Ghastly said. "What?"

Ravel was frowning. "They elected you? When? In what forum?"

"It was a private meeting," Strom said, "where we all came together to voice our concerns."

"Without inviting us."

"We didn't want it to seem like an attack. We wanted to voice our opinions, not intimidate you. During the meeting, the decision was taken to approach you with our concerns. Grand Mage Renato Bisahalani of the American Sanctuary, Grand Mage Dedrich Wahrheit of the German Sanctuary and I were elected, and it was decided that I should come here, representing the interests of the Supreme Council—"

Ravel laughed. "That's what you're calling yourselves? The Supreme Council? Well, that's not intimidating at all, is it, Ghastly?"

"Sounds positively cuddly," Ghastly responded. "So here you are, as the spokesman for the Supreme Council, to tell us what, exactly?"

"We're not here to tell you anything," said Sult. "We're just here to offer our help should it transpire that you need it. As Grand Mage Strom was saying, the other Sanctuaries need reassurances."

"That's no problem," Ravel said. "Go back and reassure them that everything is fine."

Strom smiled sadly. "If only it were that easy. Erskine, we have been tasked with verifying, for an absolute fact, that you and your Sanctuary are ready for whatever happens next. And I have to say, this business with the mortals does nothing to boost our confidence in you. I gather a werewolf was on the loose last night. A *werewolf*. We fear, and again we mean no disrespect, that your relative inexperience shows through at times like these."

Ravel nodded. "But I'm still not entirely sure what purpose the Supreme Council actually serves. You want reassurances, but don't appear satisfied when we give them. What more do you want?"

"We need to verify your competence for ourselves."

Ravel looked at Ghastly. "What does that sound like to you?"

"Sounds like they want to watch over us and tell us what to do. Which makes no sense, because as everyone knows, each Sanctuary is its own watchdog, answerable only to itself."

"Times have changed," said Strom. "We can't take the chances we used to take. In the past six years alone you've had Serpine and Vengeous and the Diablerie trying to bring the Faceless Ones back. You've had Scarab's attempt to murder eighty thousand people live on air. You've had a Remnant outbreak which threatened to spread across the globe and, only twelve months ago, the Necromancer's messiah turned up with the intention of killing three billion people. If this Darquesse lunatic really does start her Armageddon here in Ireland, that's seven world-changing events one after the other. How do you expect us to react, after all that? The Sanctuaries are afraid that one of these days your people aren't going to make it in time."

"Before you protest," said Sult, "let me ask you a question. If you didn't have Skulduggery Pleasant and Valkyrie Cain on your side, would we even be alive to have this conversation right now?"

"Detectives Pleasant and Cain work with the full support of this Sanctuary and its mages," Ravel said quietly. "It's a team effort."

"You support them, but they do the work," said Sult. "And they're not always going to be around, or they're not always going to be quick enough. They'll make a mistake. They'll slip up. And when they do..." Sult trailed off, and Strom continued for him.

"Administrator Sult's point is merely that you can't put the security of the world on the shoulders of two people. Sooner or later, it's going to crush them. We're simply offering you support, Erskine. If we feel your Sanctuary is strong enough, then that is what we'll report back and the matter will be forgotten."

"And if you don't feel that we're strong enough?" Mist asked.

"Then we'll help you. We'll supply you with Cleavers, with sorcerers should you need them. There is also, I suppose, the option of sharing responsibility."

Ghastly fixed him with a look. "Meaning you'd take over."

"No, of course not. We're here to help, for God's sake. We don't have an ulterior motive."

"And if we don't want you here?"

Strom looked hurt.

"I'm afraid we'd have to insist," said Sult. "And I mean no disrespect when I say this, but the Supreme Council has been granted certain powers of veto and authority that I'm sure we can discuss at greater length later on."

"Certain powers," Mist said, "that were not agreed upon by us."

"This is true," Sult admitted. "If you want to deny us access, that is your right. However, such a move could cut you off from the rest of the world. You'd be isolated. Alone. With no one to call on for help should you need it."

"That sounds like a veiled threat, Mr Sult."

"I apologise. I only meant to stress the seriousness of the situation."

"I think we're beginning to grasp it," said Ravel. "We'll need to discuss your... proposal before giving an answer."

"Of course," Strom said, and both men got to their feet. "We have sorcerers and Cleavers standing by, ready to help in a purely supportive capacity, but we can only keep them in place for seven days. After this day next week, our offer of assistance must be withdrawn."

"And then?" said Ghastly.

"And then we'll have to take more decisive measures."

Strom and Sult bowed slightly, and walked from the room.

"So not only do we have a threat," Ghastly said when they were gone, "now we have a deadline, too."

Ravel sank back into his chair. "This is going to be trouble."

4

ELIZA

he arrow sliced through the running man's leg, sending him to the mud, screeching.

"Good shot," Eliza Scorn said.

Christophe Nocturnal nocked another arrow in his bow as they walked through the dark forest. "They say man is the most dangerous prey, but the fact is that rabbits are much harder to hit. Still, there's nothing quite like the panicked squeal a mortal makes when they know they're about to die. It's quite relaxing, in its own way."

"I had heard you were quite the hunter, and now I see all the stories are true."

"I've been doing this since I was a boy," he said. "My father used to take us out, me and my four brothers."

"I didn't know you had any siblings."

"I don't. When we reached our teenage years, my father threw us all into a pit and announced that only one of us was coming out alive. I was the smallest of my brothers, but the most ruthless."

"What a charming story."

"It was a different time back then. A simpler time." Nocturnal settled into an archer's stance, pulled the bowstring back, and let fly. The arrow caught the hobbling mortal in the back. The mortal fell, face down. "What do you want, Eliza?"

"Oh, it's not just what I want," said Scorn. "It's what you want, too. We should be allies. Combining the Church of the Faceless with the church you lead in America, we could get this world back on track, you and I."

Nocturnal chuckled. "And there, you see, we have our problem."

"Oh?"

"My church doesn't need you, Eliza. We're strong enough as we are. We're funded and resourced by seventy per cent of those mages who worship the Faceless Ones. Aligning ourselves with your church would not give us the rewards it would give you."

"Ah, but I think you're deliberately ignoring some key facts. We have something you don't – we have a Cradle of Magic. The Diablerie successfully brought through three Faceless Ones only a couple of years ago. We have a track record, as they say. We have credibility."

"But you're weak."

"Compared to your organisation, perhaps. But we're growing

stronger. And I don't say this to cause offence, but at least *I'm* not a wanted criminal."

Nocturnal laughed. "No offence taken. To be honest, though, my renegade status has actually helped my church. The people I represent are nervous by nature, unwilling to proclaim their beliefs for all to hear. They look to me for leadership, as someone who isn't afraid to stand up to the Sanctuaries."

"And they're also, I would expect, more than a little afraid of you?"

"Fear helps things run smoothly."

"I would imagine so," said Scorn. "But you didn't come all this way to turn me down straight, now, did you?"

"No. No, I didn't. I'm interested in your offer, with a few amendments."

"Such as?"

"Your church is absorbed into mine, not the other way around. You would be kept on, naturally, but as my second in command."

Scorn bristled. "I would have thought *partners* would be more fitting."

"My people are nervous," Nocturnal said. "They'd feel safer if they knew I was still in charge. Unfortunately, it is a requirement, not a request."

"Of course. That... isn't a problem."

"And one other thing," said Nocturnal. "Before we go ahead, the mages I represent would like one little favour. A demonstration of goodwill."

"And that is?"

"They've all heard the stories of what happened when the Diablerie brought the Faceless Ones back. They heard about the girl, Valkyrie Cain, and how she used the Sceptre of the Ancients to kill two of our gods, and my people don't think she should be allowed to get away with that."

"What would you have me do, Christophe?"

"I would have you kill her."

"She is under the protection of Skulduggery Pleasant. You know how dangerous it would be to risk—"

"She is the ultimate blasphemer, Eliza. She must be punished."

Scorn considered it, then smiled. "Very well. Cain will die. And as it happens, I know just the person for the job."

5

EARLY NIGHT

alkyrie climbed through her bedroom window, careful not to make a sound. Her reflection sat up in bed, looked at her with her own dark eyes.

"You're hurt," it whispered.

"Oh, yes," Valkyrie replied, keeping her voice low. "But physically all I have are cuts and bruises. Mentally? You just wait till you remember what happened to me tonight. Pay particular attention to Jerry Houlihan. It'll stay with you. Believe me. So how were things here?"

The reflection got out of bed as Valkyrie undressed. "I had an uneventful few days," it told her. "The most exciting thing was an hour-long lecture from the headmaster on taking our studies seriously. He said next year's exams will arrive sooner than we think."

"No, they won't," Valkyrie said, frowning. "They'll arrive next year, exactly when we expect them."

"That's what I told him," the reflection nodded. "I don't think he's comfortable with logic, because he didn't look happy. He sent me to the Career Guidance counsellor, who asked me what I wanted to be after college."

Valkyrie stowed her black clothes. "What did you say?"

"I told her I wanted to be a Career Guidance counsellor. She started crying, then accused me of mocking her. I told her if she wasn't happy in her job then she should look at other options, then pointed out that I was already doing her job better than she was. She gave me detention."

Valkyrie grinned. "You're getting me into so much trouble."

The reflection shrugged. "We keep being asked to fill out the college application forms. Getting thrown out of class is the only way I can think of to avoid it. Have you figured out how to solve this problem over the past few days?"

"Amazingly, no. My folks expect me to go to college and I don't want to disappoint them, but..."

"But how long are you going to have to keep lying to them?" the reflection asked, finishing the thought.

"Yeah. It'd be nice to give them the Stephanie they want while I'm off doing my Valkyrie thing, but let's face it, I can't keep you around for ever, can I?"

"I've already been active longer than any other reflection anyone has ever heard of. I wasn't designed for this."

"I know," Valkyrie said, "and I never meant to spend so much time away from this life. I need to take control again, bring my two lives together. When I'm finished school, that's when I'll do it. Do you think you can keep going for another year or so?"

"I don't see why not," said the reflection. "I haven't been acting strangely lately, and I haven't been blocking any memories or thoughts, like you were getting worried about. I think I'm OK now. I think I've repaired myself. Plus, we're getting along much better, you and I."

"Well," Valkyrie said, "how could I fail to get along with myself? Am I not brilliant company?"

"That I am," said the reflection, smiling.

"Especially since I don't have Tanith or Fletcher any more."

"Or even China."

Valkyrie couldn't help but laugh. "My God, do I have *any* friends left?"

"Skulduggery," the reflection said. "Ghastly, of course, not that you've ever spoken to him about anything other than clothes and hitting people. And me."

"What more could a girl want?" Valkyrie asked, her eyebrow raised. The reflection gave her a smile in return, and stepped into the mirror. Valkyrie touched the glass, absorbing two days' worth of memories. The reflection at school. The reflection at the dinner table. The reflection playing with Valkyrie's little sister. All nice memories. All unexceptional memories. So unlike the two days that Valkyrie herself had experienced.

She checked the time as she climbed into bed. Five in the morning. An early night for a change.

Valkyrie woke but didn't open her eyes, preferring instead to drift slowly in darkness for a while. She loved her bed. She'd slept in others, of varying degrees of comfort, but her own bed in her own room was by far her favourite. It was smaller than was probably practical, narrower, and the mattress wasn't as firm as she'd have liked, and there was a spring by her hip that threatened to jab into her every time she turned, but for the overall experience of a good night's sleep, her bed was definitely the best.

She shifted on to her back, finally letting her eyes open. The ceiling sloped upwards from the wall beside her. When she'd been little, she'd had a load of horse pictures stuck up there, and they'd be the first thing she'd see every morning. She moved her leg from under the duvet, raised it and pressed her foot against the space where the posters had once been. Nothing there now. No horses. China Sorrows had said something once about taking her riding and Valkyrie had been looking forward to it. But that was before Eliza Scorn had told them about China's involvement in the deaths of Skulduggery's wife and child, a slice of history that China herself had always managed to skip over.

Lazily, Valkyrie reached for her phone to check the time. When the screen lit up, she sprang out of bed, cursing. She pulled on her dressing gown, flung open the door and bolted down the stairs into the kitchen, going straight for the cereal in the cupboard.

"Good morning," her mum said as she fed Alice.

"I'm late!" Valkyrie responded, grabbing the milk from the fridge. "Alarm didn't go off! Why didn't you tell me?"

"Oh, I suppose I should have," her mum said, delivering another spoonful into Alice's waiting mouth. "But then I got so distracted by the cuteness of your sister here, and then by the cuteness of your father, and then I saw my reflection in the toaster and I got so distracted by my *own* cuteness, that I completely forgot about you. I'm a bad mother. I'm a bad, bad mother."

"I've already missed the bus. Would you be able to drive me to school?"

"But I'm still in my slippers."

Valkyrie paused, the first spoonful of cereal halfway to her mouth. "Or... you know... I could stay home today. Do some studying at home. There are a few tests I need to revise for..."

"I don't know," her mother said dubiously. "Stay home? From school? Stay home from school on a Saturday?"

Valkyrie dropped the spoon back in the bowl. "What?"

Her mum grinned. "It's the weekend, Steph. You're allowed to sleep in."

Valkyrie shut her eyes and pinched the bridge of her nose. Two sets of memories and neither of them bothered to inform her of this fact. "I'm overworked," she decided. "I'm doing too much in school. I need to cut down on my studying, maybe stop doing homework. I should definitely switch to a three-day week."

"Somehow," her mum said, "I don't see any of that happening.

51

Maybe instead you could try paying attention to what day it is."

Valkyrie frowned. "I don't see how that's going to decrease my workload," she said, and munched on her cereal.

The front door opened, and her father walked in, placing a grocery bag on the table. "The great hunter-gatherer has returned victorious," he announced. "I bring the womenfolk newspapers, fresh milk and bread. The newspapers led me on a merry chase but the bread and fresh milk didn't stand a chance."

"Well done, dear," Valkyrie's mum said.

Her dad sat. "And I've also found Stephanie a new boyfriend."

Valkyrie choked on her cereal and her mum looked up sharply. "You've done what?"

"I know," he said. "You're impressed. You send me out for bread and I come back with a boy. Well, not literally. That would be weird. Even for me."

"Dad," Valkyrie coughed, "what did you do?"

"I met Tommy Boyle in the shop," he said. "You know Tommy Boyle, don't you? About my age? A little smaller than me, with sandy-coloured hair? He always wears these polo shirts. You know him, you do. You've seen him around. He's from Navan originally, so he has this real Navan accent when he speaks. He's married to that woman with the brown hair, who always wears those shoes. You know him."

"I have no idea who you're talking about."

"No, you do," her dad insisted. "He's got sandy-coloured hair."

"Dad, I don't."

"You do. I don't know how else to describe him. Melissa, how would you describe him?"

Valkyrie's mum fed another spoonful to Alice. "He's only got one arm."

"Oh, yeah, the arm thing."

Valkyrie stared. "Why couldn't you have started with that? Wouldn't that be the most obvious characteristic?"

Her dad looked confused. "But his hair is *really* sandy, and he always wears those polo shirts. He's always in them, no matter the weather."

She sat back in her chair. "Right, so that's Tommy Boyle. I've seen him around town. So what? What's that got to do with a boyfriend?"

"His son. His name is Aaron. Very nice lad. He's your age. Tommy was saying that Aaron's never had a girlfriend, and I said he should go out with you, so Tommy's bringing him over to introduce you."

"Oh, Desmond," Valkyrie's mum said. "Oh, Desmond, no."

"What? What's wrong? We're just introducing them, not arranging their marriage. They might like each other."

"Get on the phone," Valkyrie said, "and tell him you're calling it off."

"I can't do that, Steph. It'd be rude. Just meet the boy. Have a chat. No pressure."

"Lots of pressure, Dad! Loads of pressure! I can't believe you did that!"

He folded his arms. "I don't see what you're both getting so upset about. I thought you'd be happy. You haven't had a boyfriend since Fletcher, so any day now you were going to walk in with this strange fella on your arm and say, *Hey, Dad, hey, Mum, this is my new boyfriend.* And then we'd have to get to know him and get used to him, and figure out if he's a good sort. Who knows what kind of lad you'd bring back to us? Fletcher was older than you so the next one would probably be older still, and have tattoos or piercings or ride a motorbike or something. I don't want you going out with someone in their twenties. You're too young for that. I've met Aaron Boyle and he's a nice lad, Stephanie. He's quiet and polite and he's the sort of boy I wouldn't have to worry about, because with all your self-defence stuff you'd probably be able to break him in two."

"Call Tommy," Valkyrie said, "and cancel it."

"Ah, Steph..."

"Des," her mum said, "I know that you're doing this because you love Stephanie and you want all her boyfriends to treat her with respect, but that isn't up to us. We just have to trust our daughter to be a good judge of character."

An image of Caelan popped into Valkyrie's head and she beat it back with a big mental stick.

"But Aaron's a lovely guy," her dad whined. "And I can't call Tommy. I just *can't.* I don't know his number."

"I'm not talking to you until this is cancelled," Valkyrie told him, and went back to eating cereal.

Her father sagged. "But what if I go over there and Aaron

answers the door? Then I'll have to tell him that my beautiful daughter wants nothing to do with him. Something like that, it'd crush a fragile soul like his."

"You should have thought about that when you arranged this whole thing," said Melissa. "And until it's done, I'm not talking to you, either."

He looked at his wife with big imploring eyes, but she ignored him and focused her attention on Alice. Up to that point, Valkyrie's sister had been gurgling away quietly, but even she stopped talking. That was the final straw. Valkyrie's dad got up.

And then the doorbell rang.

"No," Valkyrie said.

"Ah," said her dad, checking his watch. "He's a bit early."

Valkyrie jumped to her feet. "You told them to call round this *morning?*"

"Tommy's got things to do this afternoon. I thought it'd be best. What do you want me to do? Will I tell them to go away?"

"Yes! Tell them I've gone horse-riding, or something."

"You haven't ridden a horse in years."

"They don't know that!"

"Aaron will be very disappointed."

"Dad!"

He went to the front door. Valkyrie heard a murmured conversation, then her dad returned to the kitchen table. "Well, I hope you're happy," he said. "I've just turned away a boy and his father and they both looked very disappointed."

"Well, that couldn't be helped. Did you tell them I was horse-riding?"

"No, I couldn't find a way to make that believable. I just told them you had diarrhoea."

Valkyrie closed her eyes. "Mum?"

"Yes, Steph?"

"Kill him for me, will you?"

"With pleasure, dear."

Valkyrie went upstairs. She checked for messages on her phone, then took a shower. She stood under the spray and closed her eyes. It had been twelve months since she'd split up with Fletcher – a split that hadn't exactly broken her heart, since she'd been the one who'd dumped him. In the weeks that followed, however, she'd been surprised to realise she missed him. She missed the obvious things about having a boyfriend, naturally, but more than that, she missed the friendship he brought.

It was around that time, though, that the reflection had stopped malfunctioning and started behaving the way it should, and Valkyrie began to see other advantages to its continued existence. One of these advantages was simply having someone to talk to, someone she didn't have to hide anything from. Someone she *couldn't* hide anything from. It was liberating, in a way.

It could also be disturbing. There were things Valkyrie didn't want to think about, didn't want to talk about or even admit to herself. Things like Darquesse, and how good it felt to let her take control. But the reflection had no sense of shame, and so it spoke without fear until Valkyrie told it to shut up. Which it did, immediately and without any feelings to hurt.

Valkyrie dried herself off, walked to her room with her dressing gown bunched in her hand while her mother continued to scold her father downstairs, and touched the mirror. The reflection stepped out, smiling. Valkyrie knew it wasn't a real smile, that the reflection wasn't *actually* amused, but it was doing what it was made to do, pretending, and so she didn't mind that much.

"Poor you," the reflection said. "What *is* your dad like?"

"He's something else," said Valkyrie as she dressed. "Definitely doesn't live in the same world as the rest of us." She pulled on her boots and zipped up her jacket. "There. How do I look?"

"Amazing."

"You're not biased?"

"That's entirely possible, but you still look amazing."

Valkyrie laughed, and jumped out of the window.

6

BACK IN THE SANCTUARY

Roarhaven sat beside a dark and stagnant lake, and was surrounded on all sides by barren lands of coarse grasses and dead trees. Nothing ever grew in Roarhaven. No birds ever sang.

The Sanctuary squatted on the edge of town, a low, circular building like a rusted hubcap that had come spinning off a passing car and then had just fallen over. The building itself went five floors beneath the surface, and was riddled with tunnels and secret passageways. Everything was dark and damp and smelled vaguely of mould. On the third floor down there was a large room filled with cabinets, and it was to this room that Valkyrie and Skulduggery were headed, to look for information about this Argeddion guy the werewolf had dreamed about.

"I'm so excited right now," Valkyrie said as they neared.

"Stop complaining."

"Finally, a reason to go into the fabled Mystical Hall of Magical Cabinets."

Skulduggery looked at her. "That's not what it's called."

"A chance to sort through millions of files and really do some good old-fashioned detective work. This is where the job gets glamorous. This is where I come alive."

"You can stop being sarcastic any time now." He led the way through the doors, and they walked along the rows of cabinets.

Valkyrie sighed. "Wouldn't it be simpler if this was all on a computer somewhere? It'd take up a bit less space, for a start."

"Computers crash," said Skulduggery. "Electronic information can be hacked. Sometimes, hard copy is the way to go."

"But there's so much of it," she whined. "Please tell me that there's some sort of cool magical search system where the name we seek will suddenly appear to us."

"Yes," said Skulduggery. "It's called Alphabetical Order." He opened a cabinet, skimmed over the files, then opened another one.

Valkyrie thought about helping, then decided against it. She'd probably just get in the way. "Is Argeddion really a problem?" she asked.

"You don't think everything that's happened has been a problem?"

She shrugged. "It's been an inconvenience, and it's been unfortunate, because of the people who have been hurt or killed. But if Argeddion was really going to affect the world, or if this

Summer of Light thing is bad news, the Sensitives would have seen something, wouldn't they?"

"They don't see everything," Skulduggery murmured, and looked up. "In fact, they see very little. In the past they have missed huge, world-changing events. In 1844, a psychic called Ethereal Ethel – yes, she chose that name herself – had a vision. She saw into the future, to Sunday the twenty-eighth of June, 1914. Do you remember why this date is significant?"

"Did Ireland win a big football match that day?"

"You would have learned about this in school. I also went over it as part of your close-protection training."

"Oh, was this about Ferdie?"

"Please don't call him that."

"Archduke Franz Ferdinand, then."

Skulduggery returned his attention to the cabinets. "Go on."

"He was assassinated in Sarajevo. There was an attempt on his life with a grenade that didn't kill him but injured the people around him. He wanted to visit the hospital on his way back, so he deviated from the agreed route and promptly got himself killed like an idiot, which basically kick-started World War One. So Ethereal Ethel had a vision of his assassination?"

"No. She had a vision of a woman in Greece who would invent a new kind of shoe."

"Oh."

"Every psychic missed the assassination. It changed the world, and they all missed it."

"What about the shoe?"

"The Greek woman invented the shoe, then was run over by a train. Ethel missed that bit as well."

"She wasn't a very good psychic."

"No, she wasn't," he said, searching through another cabinet. "But that's what you get when you rely on prophecy to highlight oncoming threats – you're going to be caught by surprise nine times out of ten. It's a trap you must not fall into."

"But psychics saw Darquesse's arrival, and look at me, here I am."

"You're talking about it like it's a self-fulfilling prophecy, like the only reason you're Darquesse is because they had a vision about you. That's not what happened. Self-fulfilling prophecies don't exist. The threat you pose as Darquesse did not come about because of what they saw. You didn't learn your true name because of a vision. You learned your true name from the Book of Names, and once you became a threat, they started having the visions. When a psychic does have a vision, they are rarely wrong. The problem is they don't see *everything* that's going to happen."

"Right."

"You look confused."

"I feel confused. The Death Bringer—"

"Was a scientific inevitability, not a prophecy. You're not the Chosen One, Valkyrie. There is no Chosen One, there never was and never will be. The very idea is ridiculous. You're your own person, independent and free to choose."

"But we saw Darquesse. We saw what she does."

"We saw a possible future, and if we're very unlucky, that future will happen. But you're not going to destroy the world just because people have *seen* you destroy the world. You're going to destroy it for your own reasons."

"That really fails to make me feel better."

"I realised that halfway through. Sorry." He slid the cabinet shut and stood there, tapping his fingers. "Nothing here. No files on Argeddion, no notes or cross-references or mentions of the Summer of Light. How annoying. We walked all the way in here and now have nothing to show for it. What a waste of walking. We could have walked somewhere else and be having a great time by now."

"Yeah," said Valkyrie as they started back, "it's a real tragedy, all right. Maybe we should get the word out that we're looking for him."

"Already taken care of, but it could be days or weeks before we hear from anyone – if anyone out there *does* know him."

They climbed the stone stairs into the main corridor network. "Do you think the Sensitives would have any information?" she asked. "Maybe we should call in on Finbar."

"Finbar is out of the psychic business, Valkyrie, you know that."

"But he'd do it for us. He *likes* us."

"I'm sure he adores us, but it's not that he *won't* use his powers, it's that he *can't*. The Remnant possessing him like that, it overloaded his mind. And the mind is a delicate thing. If he tries opening it up to the psychic highways and byways, he may well never get it back. Besides," Skulduggery continued, "I've already alerted a Sensitive to be on the lookout."

"You *have* been busy."

He shrugged. "What do you think I do at night while you're sleeping? I asked Cassandra Pharos to let us know if she senses anything."

Valkyrie's smile faded. "Oh."

"Do I detect reluctance? What's wrong with Cassandra? You've only met her once."

"Nothing. Nothing's wrong with her. It's just... You know that dream whisperer she gave me? I burned it."

"You did what?"

"Oh, come on!" she exclaimed. "It was Blair Witch creepy and you know it! A little man-shaped bundle of sticks that *whispered* to you at night? How could you *not* burn something like that?" She quietened again. "But the problem is, with Cassandra being a psychic and all, the next time she sees me she'll know instantly what I did."

"She can't read minds, Valkyrie."

"She'd be able to read mine. I just know it."

"I'm sure she'd understand."

"Well, of course you think that. You have no idea about presents or what they mean. The last present you gave me was a stick."

"You wanted a weapon."

"It was a stick."

"It had a bow on it."

"It was a *stick*."

"I thought you liked the stick. You laughed."

"I laughed because I thought the stick was a joke and you were about to give me my real present, but then you went home and I was standing there with a stupid stick with a stupid bow on it."

"You're welcome, by the way." Skulduggery stopped, turned his head. "Hear that?"

"What?"

He didn't answer, he just changed direction and she followed. Gradually she heard the rhythmic slap of flesh on leather, and they walked into a sparse room with only a punchbag hanging from the ceiling. Ghastly Bespoke moved around it, wearing jogging bottoms and nothing else, sweat running over his scars as he made the punch bag regret the day it had come into existence. They stood watching him until he saw them, and he finished with a flurry and stepped away, breathing hard.

"Hello, underlings," he said.

"Elder Bespoke," Skulduggery responded, leaning against the doorframe. "Did that bag do something to upset you in any way?"

Ghastly wiped his face with a towel. "It was mocking my choice of friends."

"Aha, so you were defending our honour."

"Actually, I was trying to make it shut up before someone passed by. I'm a respected member of the Council of Elders, I can't be seen to be taking advice from large bags of sand."

Skulduggery shrugged. "I can see how that might give the wrong impression."

"I heard you've the word out for someone called Argeddion," said Ghastly. "Any luck?"

"None so far."

"Any idea how he's mixed up in all this? We're getting a lot of pressure from the international community to get this solved and squared away."

"Is that who the VIPs were last night?" Valkyrie asked.

Ghastly looked at her. "That was official Sanctuary business. I'm sorry, but I can't be talking about that with you. I can't say, for instance, that Quintin Strom turned up on our doorstep as the voice of the Supreme Council, elected by a virtual conglomerate of other Councils around the world, to voice their concerns over matters of Irish security."

Skulduggery tilted his head. "Simply to voice their concerns?"

"Oh, yes," Ghastly said. "No other agenda than that, he assured us. And please ignore the fact that he brought a small army of mages with him as bodyguards, an army that stands ready to act at a moment's notice, or that we have a week to resolve this situation with the mortals or something unspecified will happen."

"Ah," said Skulduggery. "An unspecified threat. The worst kind."

"Indeed," said Ghastly. "Thank God we're all friends, that's all I can say. A more suspicious man than I might grow paranoid with all these foreign agents hanging around, especially with most of our own operatives spread out around the country to try and contain this magical outbreak. Why, if the Supreme Council got it into their little heads to launch an attack, we'd be completely defenceless."

"It's a good thing we're all friends, then," Skulduggery murmured.

"Indeed it is. So you see how finding this Argeddion person is suddenly very high up on our list of things to do and do quickly."

"Then we'll get back to it," Skulduggery said. "Oh, did you get that jacket I left in to be repaired?"

Ghastly's eyes narrowed. "I told you to be especially careful with that suit, didn't I? I told you I was especially proud of my work on that suit. And what did you do? You wore it werewolf-hunting."

"I only did it to help you, Ghastly. I fear this job robs you of the simple pleasures of tailoring that you need to remain true to your roots."

"You're so thoughtful."

Skulduggery doffed his hat. "Always thinking of others, that's me."

They left Ghastly and headed for the main doors. Valkyrie chewed her lip a moment before asking, "Are we in danger?"

"Constantly," Skulduggery replied.

"I mean from the Supreme Council."

He looked at her. "Why would we be in danger from them?"

"Something Ravel said last year. If the other Sanctuaries try to take over, you and me would be the first people they'd kill."

"Ah, yes, because of our wonderful propensity for causing trouble."

"So? Are we in danger?"

They passed a Cleaver standing guard. "I honestly don't know," Skulduggery said. "If they do want to take over, and I'm confident they do, there are different ways to go about it. If they had chosen a hostile takeover, then absolutely, one of their first moves would be to have us killed. But the route they appear to have chosen is far more insidious – they're using logic and reason against us. The fiends."

"But they *do* want to take over?"

"They've wanted to for some time now."

Valkyrie kept her voice down so passing sorcerers wouldn't hear. "So do you think they're behind this Argeddion stuff? If they wanted an excuse to stick their noses in, mortals turning magical would seem to be a great one."

"I don't think so. This is far too uncontrollable. One mistake and magic is revealed to the world. That's too much of a risk for them to take. No, I think they're doing what every good invading force does – simply taking advantage of an obvious weakness."

"Do you think we'll go to war with them?"

"I hope not," Skulduggery said. "War doesn't exactly bring out the best in me."

"Detectives."

They turned as the Sanctuary Administrator approached.

"There's a woman here to see you," Tipstaff said, "one Greta Dapple. She claims to be familiar with this person you're looking for."

Valkyrie raised an eyebrow. "She knows Argeddion?"

"Knows him?" Tipstaff said. "From what she says, she used to date him."

7

THE STORY OF WALDEN D'ESSAI

Greta Dapple was old. Valkyrie was used to old people – Skulduggery was somewhere over 400, after all – but very rarely did she meet someone who *looked* old. Greta had white hair, tied in a bun. She was small and frail and it was like she'd been left out in the sun too long. She sat in the interview room with her hands folded across her purse, and smiled at them when they entered.

"Miss Dapple," Skulduggery said, "thank you for coming in. We were told you know a man named Argeddion – is this true?"

"Yes, it is," Greta said, "although he was Walden D'Essai when I first met him. Lovely man. Had the kindest eyes I ever did see. We fell in love one summer. The kind of love you have to hold on to. But I didn't, because I was young and I didn't know any better. I've never regretted anything so much."

"Walden D'Essai," Skulduggery murmured. "Can't say I've ever heard of him."

"I'm not surprised, Detective – aren't the people you *do* hear of mostly criminals or terrorists or troublemakers? Walden was none of those things. He was a pacifist. He was so gentle, he'd never hurt another living thing. That's what I loved about him most. He believed in the goodness of people. That's probably what got him killed."

Valkyrie frowned. "He's dead?"

"Of course he is. Isn't that why you want to talk to people who knew him? To solve his murder?"

"That's exactly it," Skulduggery said. "We just want justice. Tell us what you know."

"Magic was never that strong with me," said Greta. "I'll be two hundred years old this week and I look one hundred. My magic has never been strong enough to slow my ageing to any great degree. Not that I have any cause to complain. I've lived twice as long as I should have, and I'm grateful for it. But Walden was strong, and he loved magic. Not in a bad way, though. He didn't get like some people get – it wasn't the power he loved. It was simply the magic. He said it was the most beautiful thing in existence. Well, actually, he said that *I* was the most beautiful thing in existence, but magic came a close second." She chuckled and Valkyrie smiled.

"When we weren't together," Greta continued, "he was studying. Reading. Researching. He went on vision quests, looking for answers. He wanted to find the source of magic – where it came from, how it worked. He wanted to know why Ireland was a Cradle of Magic, and Australia and Africa. He wanted to know if there were any other Cradles that we didn't know about. Oh, the things he discovered. The secrets he learned."

Skulduggery tilted his head. "Did he happen to tell you any of these secrets?"

Greta laughed. "A few. But it's not my place to repeat them. These answers came to him after years of searching – you'll forgive me if I don't cheapen his achievements by simply blurting them out."

"Annoying," Skulduggery said, "but completely understandable. Go on."

"Thank you. One of Walden's overriding beliefs was that our true names are not actually the source of our magic, but rather they are directly *connected* to the source – it is through them that magic flows."

"Flows from where?"

"He was never that specific, I'm afraid. He talked about the source as a place, but didn't explain how it fitted into his theory. I suppose he would have, if I had asked, if I had even pretended to understand the things he got excited about. But as I said, I was young, and my mind was elsewhere.

"He became obsessed with learning his own true name. He poured all his energies into it. Vision quest after vision quest. He withdrew from the world. Withdrew from me. I know now that I should have fought him, that I should have refused to let him go, but... I didn't. He grew more distant and I left. I don't think he even noticed I was gone for the first few weeks."

"Argeddion was Walden's true name," Skulduggery said slowly, and Valkyrie's mouth went dry. Argeddion was like her – a sorcerer who knew his own true name. The most dangerous thing imaginable.

Greta nodded. "A year after I left him, he got in touch. He told me he'd finally discovered it, that he was now Argeddion, and that all the answers were within his reach. But something else had changed, apart from what he called himself. He wasn't the obsessed man that I'd walked out on. He had a new name, but he was his old self again. Full of wonder and joy. I was so happy to see that his gentleness had returned, but I was also nervous. Only a handful of people had ever discovered their true names. I didn't know what would happen, what he'd become. I wasn't... You must understand, I wasn't scared of him, but I was scared of what it might *mean*."

Greta was silent for a moment, and when she spoke again, her voice was sad. "I wasn't the only person to feel that way. Somehow, they heard about what was happening, and they came to my door asking questions."

Valkyrie frowned. "They?"

"Sorcerers. There were four of them, three men and a woman, but I only remember one name, the leader's – Tyren Lament. The woman was a Sensitive. Lament said she'd had a vision of the future or some such rubbish. I'll tell you honestly, I've never trusted those people."

"But this Sensitive," Skulduggery said, "she saw a future where Walden had done something wrong?"

Greta looked flustered. "She saw nonsense, that's what she saw. Walden D'Essai was a pacifist. He'd lost his mother to violence at an early age and it affected him deeply – he couldn't stand to inflict pain on anyone. But this Sensitive, this psychic, had a little nightmare where there's violence and death and suffering and Walden is apparently the cause of it all. After they'd left, I called Walden, told him they were looking for him. He told me not to worry, he'd explain everything and they'd understand that he wasn't a threat. That was the last time I ever spoke to him."

"You think they killed him?"

"I do. Can you arrest them?"

"Tyren Lament disappeared thirty years ago," Skulduggery said. "If Walden *is* dead, it sounds like he wasn't the only one to die that day."

"If they died," said Greta, "it was their own doing. Walden would never raise a finger to hurt anyone."

"Maybe not directly," Skulduggery said, "but we've been dealing with a lot of unexplained phenomena where people have been hurt and killed – and someone called Argeddion would seem to be behind it."

"Wait. You think my Walden is *alive*? No. I'm sorry, but no. If Walden were still alive, he'd have contacted me long before now. He's dead. I know he is."

"And theoretically that would be enough to keep him down," Skulduggery said, "but in our line of work death is seldom an obstacle."

The Council of Elders had never convened faster. They dropped whatever it was they were doing and immediately met Skulduggery and Valkyrie in the throne room. Ravel and Mist wore their traditional robes, but Ghastly was fresh out of the shower and sat there with his shirtsleeves rolled up. Skulduggery filled them in on what Greta Dapple had told them.

"So you think Argeddion is still alive," said Ravel, "just hiding somewhere, and has unimaginable power from discovering his true name, which allows him to enter people's dreams and give them magical abilities?"

"In a nutshell," said Skulduggery.

"Well, now I'm conflicted. On the one hand, it sounds like things are progressing quickly, which is wonderful news. On the other, it means that there's a sorcerer out there who could kill us all with a wave of his hand – which dampens my mood somewhat. I'm assuming that Ghastly has already broken with protocol and told you about the Supreme Council and their deadline?"

"He has," said Skulduggery.

"Then let's focus on the positive. A quick solution is what we need to get them off our backs. Whatever you need from us, just ask."

"That's why we're here, actually," said Skulduggery. "We need to know about Tyren Lament."

Ravel nodded. "All right, then. Good."

Skulduggery waited. "So?"

"So what?"

"So what can you tell us about him?"

Ravel laughed. "Me? I knew him as well as you did, which wasn't very well. Why don't you look up his file?"

"We did. His files are missing."

"Missing? Then why would you think I'd know anything?"

"Because you're the Grand Mage," Skulduggery said. "You have access to the Elders' Journals."

"Oh," said Ravel. "Oh, yeah."

Skulduggery tilted his head. "You *have* read them, haven't you? One of the requirements for taking a seat on the Council is you have to read the Journals of those who have gone before."

"I was getting around to it," Ravel said, a little defensively. "I was about to start, but... Listen, being an Elder is not an easy job. I rarely sleep, did you know that? I go to bed late, I get up early. Every day I'm in meetings or briefings or I'm doing this or that. I would *love* the opportunity to take a few afternoons off and read those Journals, I really would. The chance to learn from the wisdom of past Elders... It would be an honour, and I'm looking forward to it."

Skulduggery nodded. "There are three hundred and forty-four Journals."

Ravel blanched. "Seriously?"

"All big leather-bound books, a thousand pages long. Single-spaced."

"Dear God."

"It's going to take more than a few afternoons to get through them."

"So it would appear." Ravel scowled. "OK, you caught me out, I haven't read the dusty old diaries. Big deal. I'll get to it. Ghastly, you've read them, what can you tell us about Lament?"

"Uh," said Ghastly.

Skulduggery shook his head. "Oh, not you, too."

"One of them is on my bedside table," Ghastly said quickly. "I started it. I did. But my God it was boring. It was all 'forsooth' and 'verily' and 'forthwith'. Did we really speak like that back then?"

"So no one has actually read the Journals," Skulduggery said. "Is that what you're trying to tell me?"

Ravel and Ghastly both looked sheepish. Finally, Madame Mist spoke.

"I have read them."

Ravel looked startled. "You have? You didn't find them... boring?"

"I find many things boring," Mist said in that quiet way of hers. "It does not mean I'm going to forsake my duty."

"Well, good," Skulduggery said, "at least someone here is doing what they're supposed to. What can you tell us?"

Madame Mist observed him through her veil. "Nothing," she said.

"Lament wasn't mentioned?"

"He was mentioned, but I cannot tell you in what context. Only Elders are allowed to know what those Journals contain."

"Well, we can tell Skulduggery and Valkyrie," Ravel said.

"No. We can't."

Ghastly sat forward so as to look at Mist better. "Yes, we can. They've earned that right."

"It is not for us to decide," said Mist. "It is a rule."

"We're breaking the rule," said Ravel. "Today that rule is broken.

I'm Elder Mage, I decree it. The rule is no more. So tell them what the Journals said."

"If we want to change the rules, we must vote on it. It need not be unanimous. A simple majority would suffice."

"So you're looking for a two-to-one majority," sighed Ghastly, "when you know exactly how myself and Ravel are going to vote? What's the point?"

"It is the rules, Elder Bespoke."

"Fine. All in favour of telling Skulduggery and Valkyrie what the Journals say, raise your hand." Ghastly and Ravel voted. "There. Two-to-one. We win. Now, if you would be so kind – what did the Journals say about Lament?"

"Tyren Lament was a detective under Meritorious," Mist said, "specialising in science-magic."

"That much I know," said Skulduggery.

"There were others, but their names weren't mentioned and a definitive number was never given. Lament and his colleagues were a specialist group, tasked with dealing with global threats in as quiet a manner as possible. Meritorious and the Elders spoke very highly of them, but provided few details as to their assignments. There were notes on some low-profile arrests at the beginning of Lament's Sanctuary career, but even that tailed off."

"What about Argeddion?" asked Valkyrie. "Was he ever mentioned?"

"No. Neither was the disappearance of Lament and his group."

"So they vanish off the face of the earth," Skulduggery said, "and none of the Elders even bother to make a note of it. It sounds like Lament and his friends were Black Ops, the same as our Dead Men, or Guild's Exigency Mages, but in peacetime. The dirty jobs that have to be done. They went in to take down Argeddion and whatever happened has been wiped from official records. Meritorious covered it up."

"Not the first time," Ghastly murmured.

"But wouldn't that mean Argeddion is dead?" asked Valkyrie. "If they went in and failed, Meritorious would have just sent someone else. He'd probably have sent you. But he didn't."

Skulduggery nodded. "Which would seem to indicate that it was mission accomplished."

Ravel shifted in his chair. "So if everyone who knew about this mission *is* now dead, where does that leave us?"

"Maybe not everyone," Skulduggery countered. "Lament may have been killed, maybe most of the others, but there's no reason to think there wasn't a survivor who reported back to Meritorious when it was done."

Valkyrie looked at him. "So we need to find out who else was in Lament's group. How do we do that?"

Skulduggery put his hat on. "In order to find a man's friends, who are the best people to ask?"

Valkyrie smiled. "His enemies."

8

GAOL TIME

ammer Lane Gaol was, to all outside appearances, a small house on the border of Laois and Offaly that stood with its front door open. There were a few dead trees out front, and a garage in the back, and plenty of mud all around. And inside was one of the last men arrested by Tyren Lament.

The Bentley splashed through puddles on the uneven road and pulled up. They got out, and Skulduggery didn't bother with his façade as an old man wandered over.

"Hi there," the old man said. "Lost, are you?"

"You really think we're lost?" Skulduggery asked. "You really think we're civilians just passing through, one of whom happens to be a skeleton?"

"Oh, yeah," said the old man. "Yeah, that kind of gives the

whole game away, doesn't it? Suppose you're wanting to visit the prison, then."

"I suppose we are."

"Stay right here, I'll put the call through. What'd you say your names were?"

"Skulduggery Pleasant and Valkyrie Cain."

"Pleasant and Cain," said the old man, nodding. "And you have an appointment?"

"Yes, we do."

"Be right back."

He shuffled off into the garage, and Valkyrie looked at the little house with its open door. It shimmered slightly, like it was caught in a heat haze.

"Why's it doing that?" she asked.

"I'm not sure," Skulduggery said. "It could be some kind of projection, or it could be an energy shield of some description."

"It's a little small and, I don't know, *accessible* to be a prison, isn't it? Unless it's a prison for really tiny criminals who aren't too bright and who don't really want to escape."

"Just the regular-sized criminals, I'm afraid. And the house would merely be the entrance – the prison is underground."

Valkyrie sighed. "Everything is underground. I'm sick of things being underground. Sanctuaries are underground, gaols are underground..." She faltered.

"Wow," said Skulduggery. "Two things that are underground. That's a pretty exhaustive list."

"Shut up. All I'm saying is, it'd be nice if there were a base or a headquarters of something that had big windows and a nice view and maybe even a little sunshine every now and then."

The old man wandered back. "The warden is ready for you," he said. "You ever been to Hammer Lane before? The only tricky bit is getting through that front door there. The important thing is not to touch the sides as you walk through. For slender people such as yourselves, this should pose no particular problem. But for other people… " He shook his head, like he was remembering a personal tragedy.

"What happens if we touch the sides?" Valkyrie asked, but he was already walking away. She looked at Skulduggery, and motioned to the open door. "Age before beauty."

"So kind," he said, and walked through. He looked back at her. "Well? Are you coming?"

Valkyrie hesitated. The doorway shimmered. She licked her lips, then turned sideways and inched forward into the house.

Skulduggery stood watching her. "What are you doing?"

"Being careful," she said under her breath.

"You walk through doorways every day and manage not to bounce off one side or the other."

"Stop distracting me."

"You could walk in with your hands on your hips and you still wouldn't touch the sides."

She took a deep breath and took the last step as a hop, then gasped in relief.

"You puzzle me," Skulduggery said.

It was a one-room house. There was a tattered armchair and a tattered rug and peeling wallpaper. Something beeped, and the floor started to descend.

"Cool," Valkyrie whispered.

They left the peeling wallpaper above them and descended through a brightly lit steel shaft, picking up speed as they went. Just as Valkyrie was beginning to enjoy the experience, it was over, and a door slid open to reveal a man in a suit and tie and a smile.

"Hi," he said. "I'm Delafonte Mien, I'm the warden here. Can I get you folks some lemonade?"

Their tour through Hammer Lane Gaol took them through gleaming corridors and steel doors. The main body of the prison was a vast cylinder, at the base of which was the mess hall and social area. There were five levels of cells built into the walls, each one with a circular perimeter walkway that was bordered with a clear material that sounded like glass when Valkyrie knocked on it. They were standing on the Observation Deck, the sixth and highest level, allowing them to overlook the whole structure.

"It sounds like glass," Mien told her, "because it *is* glass. Reinforced, of course. It'd take a rocket launcher to even make a crack in one layer of this thing – and it's four layers thick. Impenetrable." He waved his hand along the metal barrier, and a section of glass retracted. They leaned over, looking straight down. Valkyrie felt a touch of vertigo.

"Your prisoners are very well behaved," said Skulduggery. Far below them, the convicts sat in their bright orange jumpsuits at their tables in perfectly ordered groups.

Mien chuckled. "Ah, I wish I could say they're always like that, but any minute now one of the inmates is going to be rejoining them from a month in solitary confinement. He's a bit of a troublemaker, so I have extra security down there to deal with any messing.

"You know, before I came here, this was the worst gaol in Europe. Disruptive behaviour, riots, inmates escaping... I was assigned here seventeen years ago, I looked around at what we had at our disposal, and I made changes. Within two years, this place had become a fortress. No prisoner has escaped in fifteen years. Even *attempted* breakouts have dropped to almost zero."

"How did you manage it?" Skulduggery asked, stepping back from the barrier, casting his eyeless gaze to the pipes that ran in crazy zigzags across the high ceiling.

Mien waved his hand again, and the glass sealed over. "You may have noticed a slight flickering on your way in. That was the entire building oscillating between dimensions."

Valkyrie looked at him. "I'm sorry?"

"As we're talking here," Mien said, "we're travelling through eight dimensions a second. Forty dimensions in all, and then back again. A continuous loop. If anyone were to breach the walls, they'd be torn to pieces and scattered through half a dozen realities. There really is no escape except through the front door. The inmates know this. They know it's hopeless. Because of that, I've been able to cut back on the amount of sorcerers and Cleavers needed to run this facility. We operate with a skeleton staff, if you'll excuse the expression, Detective."

"Expression excused," Skulduggery murmured. "So how do you do it?"

"Ah," Mien said, laughing, "I'm afraid I can't tell you." They started walking back the way they'd come. "Every warden of every gaol around the world has tried to find out, but I'm keeping it to myself for now. It won't be long before I'm assigned to one of the bigger prisons, though, and maybe then I'll share the secret of my success."

Skulduggery looked at him. "An ambitious man, are you, Mr Mien?"

"I suppose you could say that. Nothing wrong with ambition, is there?"

"Absolutely nothing," Skulduggery said, "so long as it's channelled the right way."

"I assure you, all of my ambition is channelled to enable me to better perform my duties."

They passed through another steel door, and a uniformed man handed Mien a touch-screen device the size of a brick.

"Excuse me for a moment," Skulduggery said, taking out his phone and stepping away.

Mien took the opportunity to show Valkyrie the device in his hand. "I control the entire building with this," he said, his fingers tapping and sliding over the screen. "My own design, actually. I hope to get it smaller, but with the amount of power it has to generate this is the best I can do at the moment."

"Isn't that dangerous?" she asked. "To have everything centralised in something someone could run away with?"

Mien smiled. "I'm the only one who can operate it, and it's kept here, within the confines of the main facility. I never bring it outside that door. Security is my business, Detective Cain. I know a thing or two about it."

Skulduggery came back. "It all looks very impressive, I have to say. It's certainly a unique set-up. Were you told which prisoner we're here to see?"

"I wasn't," said Mien, "but it doesn't matter. With the protocols I've installed, any inmate can be accessible within minutes. Just give me a moment to call up the proper screen... OK. Name of prisoner?"

"Silas Nadir."

Mien's fingers hesitated over the device.

"N," he said. "N... where's the N? I can't... can't find the... Oh, here we are. Nadir. And what was the first name?"

"Silas," said Skulduggery.

Mien nodded, tapped the name in, and waited.

"Oh," he said.

Skulduggery tilted his head. "Oh?"

"I'm terribly sorry, it looks like you've had a wasted trip. Silas Nadir died two years ago."

Skulduggery stopped walking. "What?"

"Oh, this is awful," said Mien. "I'm terribly sorry. He had a heart attack. The staff here weren't even aware he had a medical condition. He died in his sleep."

"So why wasn't his death reported?"

Mien blinked. "It was. I... I'm sure it was. It would have had to have been. Our Chief Medical Officer would have been required to process all of the appropriate paperwork."

"Can we speak to him?" Valkyrie asked.

Mien looked sheepish. "I'm sorry. Doctor Taper no longer works at this gaol. Can I ask why you wanted to speak with Nadir? Maybe someone else could help you?"

"We needed Nadir," Skulduggery said curtly. "Do many prisoners die while in your custody, Mr Mien?"

Mien's look of embarrassment faded quickly as his mouth set into a straight line. "No, Detective Pleasant. They do not." He started walking again. Skulduggery and Valkyrie kept up.

"How many prisoners have died here in the last year?" Skulduggery asked.

"None. The inmates may be convicted criminals but they are nonetheless entitled to the best care we can provide."

"How many prisoners have died here in the last ten years?"

Mien bristled. "Three. Nadir and two others – Evoric Cudgel and Lorenzo Mulct. Should I have personally informed you of *their* deaths as well?"

"Mulct and Cudgel," Skulduggery said. "Never heard of them. What were they in for?"

Mien turned to them, jabbing irritably at the device. "Mulct was... Mulct was found guilty of multiple counts of robbery. Cudgel was one of Mevolent's men. Just another low-level sorcerer."

"And yet," said Skulduggery, "you remembered the names of these unexceptional inmates without a problem. But when you heard the name Silas Nadir, a notorious serial killer with murders in the double digits, you had to look him up."

"After a hesitation," said Valkyrie.

"Indeed," Skulduggery nodded. "After a very *telling* hesitation that seemed for all the world like you were frozen for a moment at the mere mention of his name."

"I'm sorry," said Mien, "I have no idea what either of you are talking about."

"What happened to Silas Nadir, Mr Mien?"

"I told you what—"

"And I think you're lying."

"This is preposterous. Why would I lie? I'm not a criminal. The criminals are the ones in the *cells*."

"The *prisoners* are the ones in the cells," Skulduggery corrected. "Criminals can be anywhere."

"I'm very sorry but I can't help you," Mien said, his voice tight. "If you'll excuse me, I have a gaol to run. The way out is just ahead of you, but I'll have the Cleavers escort you just to be sure." Mien turned, started walking away.

"What happened to Nadir?" Skulduggery asked after him.

"Good day, Detectives."

"Where is he, Mr Mien?"

"Good day."

"How about the Summer of Light?"

Mien froze. Turned. "How do you know about that?"

"You know what it is?"

"No. No, I don't have the first idea what it is. But the inmates...
Our more psychologically disturbed inmates have taken to screaming
about a man named Argeddion. They say he comes to them in
their nightmares. Some of them have written his name, in their
own blood, on the walls of their cells, along with that phrase. The
Summer of Light."

"What do they say about Argeddion?"

"Nothing. Absolutely nothing. Just his name and that he appears
in their dreams."

Skulduggery considered the gaoler. "We'd like to speak to one
of these inmates, if you wouldn't mind. Preferably one of the more
lucid ones. Do you have the list there?"

Skulduggery walked up to him, Valkyrie following behind.

"What does any of this have to do with Nadir?" asked Mien.

Skulduggery didn't get a chance to answer. An alarm rang out,
so sudden and so loud it made Valkyrie jump. She looked around,
looked back, and a wall of glass slammed down in front of her,
sealing her off from Skulduggery and Mien. At that moment, sigils
faded up along the walls, and she felt her power dampen. On the
other side of the glass, Skulduggery looked at her, then spoke to
Mien, who was clearly agitated. Valkyrie couldn't hear a word of

what they were saying. Mien hurried away, and she raised an eyebrow at Skulduggery.

His jaw moved up and down. She pointed at her mouth.

His hand went to his collarbones, and a false face spread over his skull. This time, she could read his lips.

Don't panic, he said.

I'm not, she mouthed back.

He knocked on the glass. *We can't break through this. We'll get you out in a second.*

Cool.

Mien appeared behind Skulduggery. He looked even more agitated than before. Skulduggery exchanged words with him. A lot of words. Still the alarm rang out. Finally, Skulduggery turned back to her. *Good news*, he said. *You can start panicking now.*

She glared. He took out his phone and rang her.

"It seems that a riot has broken out," he said when she answered. "That prisoner who was released back into the general population evidently started some trouble. Now, before you begin to worry, the section of the gaol that I'm standing in is completely secure. No problems here. I'm not in any danger whatsoever."

"And the section I'm standing in?"

"Well," he said, "the important thing to remember is that *I'm* perfectly safe."

Valkyrie sighed. "I'm stuck in here with the bad guys, aren't I?"

"Or you could be glass-half-full about it and say that *they* are stuck in there with *you*. Which might make you feel better."

"It really doesn't."

"Mien's working on a way to isolate this corridor from the rest of the gaol in order to get the door open, but it might take – oh, do you mind holding on for a moment? I have another call coming in."

She stared. "What?"

The line went silent, and she watched Skulduggery talk into his phone. She knocked on the glass. He held up a finger as he spoke.

She stood there and fumed.

Finally, he nodded to her, and she raised her phone to her ear.

"You look angry," he said.

"You put me on hold."

"For a very good reason."

"You put me," she said very, very slowly, "on hold."

"And judging by the look on your face, and what a pretty face it is, I'm going to be very sorry about that later on. Back to now, though, that was Ghastly. A few moments ago I called him, asked him to get a Sensitive to run a remote scan of the facility, just out of curiosity. I wanted to know where the power was coming from to keep this place oscillating between dimensions. It's coming from deep down in the lower levels."

"Yay," Valkyrie growled, still glaring.

"Before his apparent demise, Silas Nadir was a Dimensional Shunter. He could move himself, or other people or objects – such as the bodies of his victims – into different realities. They call it shunting."

"I gathered that. You think he's still alive and he's being kept in the basement, where he's constantly shunting this whole building around."

"Yes, I do."

"And you can't get to the basement, can you? But I can. And that's where you want me to go. You want me, a seventeen-year-old girl without any magic or protection, to wander through a prison while the convicted murderers and God-knows-whats are running around having a riot. Is that what you want me to do, Skulduggery?"

"It is."

"And is this a safe thing for me to do, Skulduggery?"

"It isn't. But there are two very good reasons why you should do it anyway. Reason number one, it's our chance to look around without Mien's interference. Reason number two, the corridor you're standing in will soon be filled with convicts."

"How do you know?"

"You heard Mien. The front door is the only exit. This is the only corridor to the front door. There are bound to be some convicts who are going to try and take advantage of the distraction the riot provides."

"So I should go now, before they get here."

"Indeed you should. Keep your phone to your ear, I'll guide you."

"How do you know the way?"

"I glanced at the schematic on the way in."

"You *memorised* it?"

"Glancing, memorising, it's the same thing. You should really, really go now."

She took a deep breath. "Get this door open and come after me."

"Count on it."

Valkyrie looked at him, then turned, ran down the corridor and round the corner.

"At the junction," Skulduggery said, "turn right. Can you see anyone?"

"No," she said, moving fast, "not yet."

"Hopefully, we'll be able to keep you out of sight. You won't be in the prison area as such – but then neither will the prisoners, so..."

"I have to admit," she said, "I'm worrying."

"Perfectly understandable. I'm heading to the security room. I'll be able to see you on the monitors soon enough. You should be seeing three doors ahead of you."

"Yeah, I've just reached them."

"Take the second one to your left."

She tried it. "It's locked."

"Kick it open."

"It's a sturdy door, Skulduggery."

"But it's not reinforced. It's not designed to keep any prisoners in or out, it's designed to keep unauthorised personnel from going places they don't have clearance for. It's just a simple door with a simple lock. And you've got very strong legs."

She looked at the door. "See, this is where a gun would come in really handy." She kicked. "Ow! Oh, God!"

"Are you OK?"

"Kicking doors hurts! Even with Ghastly's boots!"

"Put your weight behind it. Pretend the door is someone who has really annoyed you recently."

"Can I pretend it's you?"

"I really don't see how that would—"

She kicked it, and the door burst open. "I'm in," she said, closing the door behind her. "And that really hurt my foot. I'm in a room with machines along the walls. Lots of blinking lights."

"Do you see the ventilation duct along the floor?"

She froze. "Please tell me I don't have to crawl through that."

"I'm afraid you do."

"No. I can't. It's too small."

"The measurements are—"

"I get claustrophobic! You know I do! Especially after the caves last year, with all those things and I couldn't move my arms and they were in my hair and—"

"Calm down."

"I'm not getting in there, I'm just not."

"You'll be able to fit," he said, his voice gentle. "You will have space to move. You won't be trapped."

"I can't."

"Valkyrie, listen to my voice. I know you don't want to, I know you don't think you can, but you don't have a choice. I'm in the security room now and I can see the monitors. The prisoners are swarming the building. You can't let them catch you."

She dropped to her knees at the duct. "How do I even open it? It's screwed in place."

"You're going to have to prise it open. Is there anything you could use?"

She looked around. "There's a bench here with things on it, bits of machinery and stuff. And some tools. There's a screwdriver! I could use the screwdriver to prise it open!"

"Yes," Skulduggery said, "or you could use it to unscrew the screws."

"Oh, yeah," she muttered. She grabbed the screwdriver, hurried back to the duct and got to work.

"The Cleavers are doing a good job with the riot," Skulduggery said, "but there are prisoners running everywhere. How are you doing?"

"One almost... OK, it's out. Three left."

"The prisoners have reached the security door."

The screwdriver kept slipping out of the groove. "The glass door?"

"Yes."

"So they're really close."

"Yes."

Her mouth was dry. "The moment they realise they can't break through that door they're going to turn around, find their way through here."

Skulduggery hesitated. "They've turned around, Valkyrie."

Two screws left.

"They're heading towards you."

The screwdriver slipped again.

"Valkyrie..."

"I'm going as fast as I can." Her heart hammered. The third screw fell. "One left."

"Valkyrie," Skulduggery said, "you're going to have to be really, really quiet."

She heard voices, and running footsteps. She turned, screwdriver clutched like a knife, waiting for the door to burst open.

The voices passed the door, started to grow distant.

"They're carrying on to the end of the corridor," Skulduggery said. "There's no way out there. They'll have to double back. You don't have long."

She spun, screwdriver working, twisting and twisting until—

"Done," she said, the last screw joining the others on the ground. She dug the screwdriver in at one corner and prised the covering loose, then got her fingers in there. She bit her lip and pulled, ignoring the pain as the metal dug into her skin. It came free all of a sudden and she lifted it away. She looked at the square hole. It was dark, and looked too small to fit in.

"Are you sure I won't get stuck?" she asked.

"You don't have a choice," Skulduggery said. "They're on the way back to you. You're going to be crawling to your left. Move!"

Valkyrie took a deep breath, and plunged in.

9

HUNTED

It was tight.

It was small and tight and dark. She couldn't even raise herself up on to her hands and knees. She shuffled forward on her elbows.

"See?" Skulduggery said. "I told you you'd be fine."

She kept shuffling until she froze. She closed her eyes, turned her head so she could whisper into the phone. "Get me out of here. It's too small. How am I going to get out? I can't turn around."

"It won't do you any good to panic."

"I'm going to get stuck in here, I know I am."

"Shh. They're in the room behind you."

She quietened. She could hear them, their raised voices, arguing among themselves. One of the voices got suddenly louder, and she twisted to look back. A head appeared in the shaft, examining the space. He couldn't see her, lying there in the dark.

"Valkyrie," Skulduggery said, very softly. "There aren't any cameras in the room. I can't see what they're doing."

She didn't answer. The head ducked back out and the voices started up again. Valkyrie crawled on, as fast and as quietly as she could. There was a series of loud noises behind her.

"They're in here with me," she whispered. "They're following me."

"Just keep going," she heard Skulduggery say. "You're going to pass four more covers like the one you just opened. The fifth one will overlook a stairwell that should be empty. That's where you're getting out."

The first ventilation cover was up ahead. Already her muscles were burning. Her hair fell over her face but she didn't have room, or time, to tie it back. She crawled on, phone in one hand, screwdriver in the other.

The closer she got to the vent, the louder the alarm sounded.

She didn't want to glance back, didn't want to see anyone moving back there. She kept her eyes front, kept her elbows working. She reached the vent and glanced through into a dark room. She moved on. She could hear voices behind but she did her best to block them out.

There was another vent ahead. Light streamed in through the slats. There was some movement outside. People running. She reached the vent and shuffled onwards, but a voice behind her drifted up.

"You see that?" the voice said. "There's someone up there."

She froze.

"No there's not," said another voice. "Just keep going, will you?"

"Just look. See? They were moving just a second ago. Hutchinson, get up here. See that?"

"Yeah," said the third voice, the one they called Hutchinson. "Hey there! Hold on a sec!"

Valkyrie took a deep, deep breath and started crawling again, as fast as she could, without caring about the noise she was making. The men behind her shouted but she couldn't hear the words. She didn't want to hear the words. They were far behind her and there was no way they were going to catch up.

Her muscles burned and she stopped for a moment, heard frantic movement close behind her and glanced back, saw a grinning face moving through the slotted light.

"Hey!"

It was the one called Hutchinson. He was small and thin and squirming through the ventilation shaft like a rat. She started crawling again but it was no use. She felt his grip on her boots and tried to stamp her foot back into his face. His soft chuckle echoed as his hands wrapped round the back of her knees. He hauled himself forward, moving over her kicking legs centimetre by centimetre. He got another handhold, the waistband of her trousers this time. She squirmed, reached behind her and tried to keep him away, but he pushed her hand down and now he was squeezing in on top of her. He wasn't heavy but he was filling every space now, and she couldn't even move her arms.

"It's OK," he whispered as he crawled up her back. "I'm not going to hurt you." She could hear the smile in his voice. He tried to slip his right arm round her throat but she tucked her chin down. His fingers worked beneath her jaw. "It's OK," he whispered. "Shhh..."

He pulled her hair with his free hand, but didn't have the space to make it unbearable. He abandoned that tactic, tried to make her loosen up by jabbing at her, but she kept her chin down. Even so his right hand was getting in there. He was going to get in eventually. She readied the screwdriver.

His hand slipped through and suddenly his arm was round her throat. She jabbed blindly over her shoulder with the screwdriver and he squealed, started thrashing as she heaved herself ahead of him. He didn't try to stop her. He fell against her legs and she grunted, kicking back to shove him off. She'd lost the screwdriver but it had been worth it, and now he was an obstacle to the men crawling behind him.

But his screams had attracted attention. There were shouts from up ahead, and someone started kicking the vent. If they got it open, she'd be trapped.

She stuffed her phone into her jacket pocket, and crawled faster.

The men behind were shouting now, trying to make themselves

heard over Hutchinson's screams. And then there was a horrible cracking sound, and the screams stopped. Valkyrie didn't have to look back to know what they'd done.

"Kick it in!" one of them shouted. "She's trying to get by!"

The kicking resumed. Intensified. The covering started to buckle.

Valkyrie reached it, didn't even glance through the slats.

"There she is!" a man shouted. "Get it open!"

Multiple boots, kicking. She got by but the ventilation cover burst open behind her and a man reached in, grabbed her ankle.

"Got her!"

She kicked, kept kicking, kept slamming her heel on to his hand, even as she was hauled backwards. She looked over her shoulder, saw more hands reaching in, grabbing her, and now her feet were out of the duct, and she was dragged out after them.

She slid across the floor, men in prison uniforms staring down at her. She got her legs free and scrambled up, burst through them into the corner of the room then turned, hands clenched, teeth bared. Exhausted, sweating, terrified.

The men formed a semicircle, cutting her off from the open door. Four of them, and now two more crawling out of the duct. All the shouting had ended. All the cursing. Now they looked at her, and she looked at them, and none of them said anything.

One of them, the biggest, started to grin. It started small, then spread across his face. "I haven't killed anyone so pretty in years." He stepped forward.

Another man, a skinhead with facial tattoos, put a hand on his arm. "No," he said. "We use her as a hostage. She's our ticket out of here."

The big man tried to shake the hand off. The skinhead held on. A scuffle broke out, and then a fight, and suddenly all six men were slamming into each other. One of them, a man with yellow teeth, reached for her, grabbed her wrist, and yanked her through the gap he had made.

"Run!" he shouted, and cried out as the big man snapped his neck.

Valkyrie ran, kept running, found herself skirting the top tier of the Observation Deck. Two convicts were sitting against the wall up ahead, just talking, looking like they'd opted out of all the violence going on down below. She ran past them and they stared at her, but didn't try to follow. There was a shout and she glanced back. The big man was coming.

She saw an AUTHORISED PERSONNEL ONLY sign and followed it, sprinting through a narrow corridor that ended with a door. A convict was on his knees by the door, trying to pick the lock. He gave a little cheer and stood up, opened it and turned with a smile on his face that she wiped off with a flying elbow. She didn't even see him crumple to the ground, and now she was in a stairwell, jumping down the steps.

The big man was hurtling down after her.

There were no cameras in the stairwell, but surely Skulduggery had seen where she was heading. She jumped and slammed against the wall, pushed herself off, almost falling down to the next level.

Speed was one thing, but if she twisted her ankle trying to get away, she'd never leave this stairwell alive.

She heard the big man stumble and fall, his curses ringing out, giving her a boost of hope. She was going to make it. Five more floors to go before she reached the basement. He was, what, maybe three levels above? She was going to make it. She was going to get to the basement level and burst through the door and Skulduggery was going to be there, gun in hand.

He'd better be.

Valkyrie got to the basement, all cold walls and leaking pipes, flickering lights and gloom stretching into shadows. She lunged out through the door, into a small maze of corridors. Skulduggery wasn't there.

The big man came through the door like a bull and she took off. He was right behind her, and gaining. Valkyrie dodged left so he overshot, then took the adjoining corridor, glancing back to see him stumbling to correct his course. There was a door ahead, marked MAINTENANCE. She ran into the tiny room, slamming the door shut behind her. She spun, planted her left foot forward, her right leg ready. His footsteps and his curses got louder and as he burst in, she was already kicking.

Her boot hit the door, the door hit his head.

Valkyrie fell back from the impact and he dropped to his knees, hands clutching his face. She sprang up, grabbed a mop, smacked the handle on to the top of his skull. He howled, started moving away. She jabbed him in the face with the handle until he knocked it from her hands, and she jumped out after him, swinging kicks into his side. He caught her leg, held it to him as he struggled to his feet. He was panting heavily from the exertion, blood running from his nose. He slammed her back against the wall, one hand still holding her leg, keeping her off balance while the other hand wrapped round her throat.

She went for his eyes, digging her thumbs in. He tried turning his head, then took her violently to the ground. Kneeling between her legs, both hands now at her throat. Unable to breathe, her head suddenly pounding, Valkyrie squirmed into position then turned on to her hip, bringing one leg in to press against him. He pushed forward and she scissor-swept his legs, flipping him on to his back. Now she was on top and she rose up, started raining down palm shots and elbows. Four of them were all she needed, but she kept going, just to be sure. When he sparked out, unconscious and limp, she rolled off, breathing hard.

She forced herself to her feet. Her arms and legs were drained. She couldn't get her breathing under control. She staggered away from him, turned a few more corners before she let herself stop and bend over, hands on her knees, panting. While she was down there, she noticed a series of pipes free of rust or wear. She started following them, all the way to a door.

Once she was breathing properly again, she wiped the sweat from her forehead, and stepped into the room. "Ah," she said. "Found you."

10

NADIR

Her magic returned to her the moment she set foot in there but she almost didn't notice it, what with the man lying flat in mid-air, suspended off the ground by dozens of cables and wires that stretched taut from his wrists and ankles to the four corners of the room. The cables pulsed with an energy that emanated outwards. The man's eyes were open but unseeing. Some kind of helmet was strapped to his head. Thick bundles of wires cascaded from the back of it, disappearing through a small hole in the floor. Valkyrie stared at Silas Nadir and wondered if he was even aware of what was going on.

The door burst open behind her and Skulduggery ran in, gun in hand. He saw her. Froze. "Are you OK?"

She nodded.

"They didn't hurt you?"

She shook her head.

"The Cleavers are taking back control. The riot has been subdued. The last stragglers are being rounded up. You're sure you're OK?"

"I'm grand. You can probably put your gun away."

He looked at it. "I think I'll keep it out, actually. In case I want to shoot someone. I see you've found the dearly departed Mr Nadir."

"Mien's been using him to shunt the prison through realities. Look at all these wires. The whole place is hooked up to him. It must be awful."

Skulduggery joined her. "Don't forget, the man *is* a serial killer."

"He still shouldn't be used like this."

"The alternative is to keep him in a cell, being of no use to anyone."

"Are you actually in favour of this?"

"Not at all," Skulduggery said. "But I understand how Mien justified it to himself. Of course, I doubt either of us would be so morally righteous if Nadir had murdered anyone we knew."

"That's not the point," said Valkyrie. "So what do we do now?"

"We unhook him," Skulduggery said, examining the cables. "Hopefully, he'll wake up and we can question him about Lament. Once we have our answer, we throw him back in his old cell."

"Do you know how to unhook him?"

"I'm assuming we just take off the helmet."

"Just like that? Will he be harmed?"

"If we're lucky, it might sting him a little. If we're unlucky, it might cause irreversible brain damage. I'm feeling lucky, though, aren't you? It's a Saturday. Saturdays have always been lucky for us."

"I hadn't noticed. Look, we should probably find someone who knows what they're doing."

"Probably," Skulduggery murmured. "However..."

His gloved fingers skipped lightly over the helmet, then gripped a wire and yanked it from its slot.

Valkyrie's eyes widened. "Are you *sure* that's a good idea?"

"I think I've worked it out," he said. "I just need to disconnect the Emergency Valve Regulators one at a time. Once that's done, removing the helmet shouldn't result in any significant trauma."

"Emergency Valve Regulators," she repeated. "So you *do* know what you're doing?"

"Not really," he said, yanking another wire. "I made that term up to keep you happy. I'm just pulling all the red wires because they're the pretty ones."

Before she could protest, he'd yanked another three, then nodded. "That should do it."

"Oh, dear God."

He started undoing the helmet straps. "If this works, you're going to be mightily impressed with me."

"And if it doesn't work, you could kill him."

"For the chance to see the look of sheer awe on your face, Valkyrie, I'm willing to risk it." He removed the helmet and let it fall. Nadir's head lolled back and his eyes closed.

Valkyrie frowned. "When will we know if he's OK?"

"When he wakes up, I should imagine. Help me unstrap him."

They worked together to free Nadir of the wires and cables holding him off the ground, and together they laid him on the floor.

Valkyrie stood quietly for a few seconds, and asked, "Can we wake him now?"

"Patience has never been your strong suit, has it?" He slapped Nadir's face. "Excuse me. Excuse me, could you wake up now, please?"

Nadir moaned, and frowned, and Skulduggery slapped him again. His eyes snapped open and he looked at them, glared at them, and scrambled up.

"Mr Nadir, my name is Skulduggery Pleasant, and this is my partner Valkyrie Cain. We're here to—"

Whatever those cables were they must have been exercising his muscles as he slept, because there was no sign of atrophy as he lunged forward. He grabbed Valkyrie's arm and she cried out and he tried grabbing Skulduggery but Skulduggery just punched him. He staggered into the wall and Skulduggery cuffed his hands behind his back, then looked at Valkyrie as she rubbed her arm. "Are you OK?"

"Fine," she growled. "Just static electricity, gave me a little shock."

"What the hell is going on?" Nadir raged. "What is this? What are you doing to me?"

"We're actually helping you," Skulduggery told him. "You've been napping down here for the last fifteen years, Mr Nadir. You must be well rested."

"Fifteen years? What are you talking about with your fifteen years? I was just in my cell this morning!"

"I don't generally have much time for serial killers, so I'm going to explain this to you once and then immediately move on. You were sentenced to seven hundred years for multiple counts of murder. You were sent here, to this pretty shoddy gaol. When Mien took over as warden, he connected you to the building and began using you to shunt the entire facility through dimensions. It's the ultimate security system. No one can break in or break out because the prison travels to eight different realities every second, and it's all thanks to you. Are you with me so far?"

Nadir gaped at him. "Fifteen years?"

"Indeed. Now then, we are here for an entirely different reason – but if you help us, we will ensure that you spend the remainder of your prison sentence, all six hundred and seventy-eight years of it, in the comforts of your duly-appointed cell. Understand?"

"Fifteen *years?*"

Skulduggery looked at Valkyrie. "Oh, dear. I think he might be brain-damaged."

The door burst open again and Mien ran in.

"You!" he cried. "What are you doing? You can't be here! This is a restricted area!"

"Valkyrie," Skulduggery said.

She walked up to Mien, and the prison warden turned his attention to her. "This is *my* gaol and when you are here you operate by *my* rules, and this is not—"

Valkyrie smacked her palm into his jaw and he went backwards, his legs giving out. He crumpled to the floor where she cuffed him, binding symbols glowing on the narrow shackles. "Mr Mien," she said, kneeling on his back, "you're under arrest for, uh..." She looked to Skulduggery for help.

"Improper use of inmates," he suggested.

"There you go," she nodded. "You have the right to remain unconscious."

Mien did not respond.

"Very well done," said Skulduggery. "What do you think, Silas? Do you think that was well done? How does it compare to the way you were arrested all those years ago? Tyren Lament, wasn't it, the man who arrested you?"

"Lament," Nadir said, and spat. "It's his fault I'm here. His fault I'm—"

Skulduggery interrupted him. "Actually, it would be your fault. You know, for killing all those people. Speaking of Lament, as we were, I need to know the names of his associates."

Nadir glared. "Go to hell."

"Silas, now really. Is that any way to speak to the person who has just liberated you from the void? Lament's colleagues. Who were they?"

Nadir licked his lips. "And what if I tell you? What do I get?"

"You get unhooked, Silas."

"You say I've been here for fifteen years? The last thing

I remember is being in my cell. OK. OK, I'll help you, but in return you hook me back up."

Skulduggery tilted his head. "I'm sorry?"

"You hook me back up to this thing. Let me serve my sentence here. If you do that, I'll help you."

"See?" Mien said from beneath Valkyrie, his voice shaky. "He *wants* to be here…"

"Shut up," Valkyrie said. "He wants to be here because fifteen years went by and he didn't even notice it. But he wasn't sent to prison just so it could pass in the blink of an eye. He has to suffer."

"That's my condition," Nadir said. "I know a few of Lament's buddies. He called in three or four of them when he was hunting me. I can help you. I know what you need."

"OK," Skulduggery said, "you have a deal. Give me the names."

Nadir laughed. "Call me cynical, skeleton, but I don't trust you. I want this deal on paper and signed by the Grand Mage himself – by the end of the day. And I want it on that special Sanctuary paper I've heard about, the kind that can only be written on by the Elders. You're not going to cheat me out of this."

Skulduggery was quiet for a moment. "We'll see what we can do," he said.

Nadir was sitting behind a desk when a Cleaver escorted them in three hours later. Skulduggery slapped the page down in front of him. Smirking, Nadir ran his finger along the embossed header.

"Official Sanctuary paper," he breathed, then laughed as he

started reading. Valkyrie watched him. His lips moved, forming the words. When he'd finished, he looked up.

"It's already signed," he said. "I wanted the Grand Mage to sign this in front of me."

"That's not going to happen," Skulduggery said. "He's a busy man. Too busy to be visiting prisons. You know it's genuine – only the Grand Mage can write on that paper."

Nadir tipped a finger to his lips. "And what about dear old Delafonte Mien? How is he going to be punished for his blatant abuse of power?"

"Mien is already in a cell in the Sanctuary. His punishment is yet to be decided."

"You be sure to throw the book at him, you hear me? I feel violated, Detective. Violated."

"I'll throw this table at you if you don't give us the names we're looking for."

Still smirking, Nadir lounged back in his chair. "Lament was a scientist, so he never went anywhere without his muscle to back him up – Vernon Plight. That woman was with them too sometimes, the small one, the psychic. Lenka Bazaar, that's her name. And someone else."

"Who?"

"Can't remember."

Skulduggery reached for the contract but Nadir snatched it back. "Kalvin Accord! That was it! That's all I know."

Skulduggery looked at Valkyrie. "Vernon Plight is missing

presumed dead. Same with Kalvin Accord, and I've never heard of this Lenka Bazaar."

Nadir shrugged. "That's not my fault. I fulfilled my side of the deal."

"Yes, you did," said Skulduggery. "There's no one else you remember? No one else they mentioned?"

"I wasn't really taking much notice of what they were saying in between hitting me. Those are the names I've got for you. That's all."

"OK. It's something to go on, at least. Cleaver, could you escort Mr Nadir to his cell, please?"

Nadir stared. "What? You said you'd hook me back up. You said you'd take me back to that contraption!" The Cleaver hauled him to his feet and shackled his wrists. "We had a deal! We have a contract!"

"Yes, we do," Skulduggery said, picking it up off the desk. "Unfortunately for you it's not binding."

"But the Grand Mage signed it! Eachan Meritorious himself signed it!"

"The Grand Mage did sign it," Skulduggery nodded, "but Eachan Meritorious is dead – which you wouldn't have heard about, what with being hooked up to that thing for the last fifteen years. And unless Erskine Ravel, the current Grand Mage, signs this contract with his own name, well... It can hardly be considered a legal document, now can it?"

"You cheated me!" Nadir screeched as the Cleaver dragged him to the door.

"You're a serial killer, Mr Nadir," said Skulduggery, tearing up the page. "You deserve to be cheated."

11

SCENES FROM A
COFFEE SHOP

Coffee. That's all she wanted right now. Just coffee. Sunday morning coffee. Lovely Sunday morning coffee. Just the thing to take her mind off the dull throb that was making her arm ache, right where Nadir had grabbed her the day before. Just the thing to take her mind off the mystery surrounding Argeddion and Lament. Coffee, in fact, was almost a wonderful enough experience to take her mind off the fact that her next port of call would be a murder scene.

Valkyrie didn't like murder scenes. The more she'd visited, the less she'd liked. If they were more along the lines of the murder scenes that her gran watched on TV, where elderly detectives tut-tutted around beautiful countrysides and manor homes, she might have changed her opinion. But the murder scenes she tended to visit belonged in horror movies or police procedurals, where the emphasis was on blood splatter and defensive wounds and, occasionally, finding the head.

Skulduggery had warned her that this morning's murder scene contained blood, and lots of it. But that was ages away. Skulduggery wouldn't be picking her up for another half an hour or so. If she were a mayfly, that would be practically a *lifetime* away. So here she was, in a nice bright coffee shop in town, standing in line like a normal person.

She gave her order, paid and stepped back to wait. A middle-aged woman in the queue behind her stopped rooting through her handbag long enough to look at the selection available and annoy the people behind her by taking ages to make a choice. She smiled at Valkyrie and Valkyrie smiled back politely. She looked like a nice enough person. She probably had a nice enough name, like Helen, or Margaret. Seven people stood behind Margaret, getting increasingly irritated. An eighth person walked in, joined the queue at the end. A big man in a long coat with a shaven head, looking straight at Valkyrie.

She met his gaze and he looked away. He was broad-shouldered. Looked strong. Margaret finally handed over her money and then stepped away to let the next person place their order.

"I always take so long," she said.

Valkyrie took her eyes off the big man. "I'm sorry?"

"To choose," Margaret said. "I always take so long to choose."

"Oh. I wouldn't worry about it."

"And I can always feel the daggers being stared into my back," said Margaret, chuckling. "I suppose I'm just not cosmopolitan enough for somewhere like this."

Valkyrie gave her another polite smile, then took her coffee from the girl behind the counter and went to an empty table by the wall. Weird woman, being all chatty to a complete stranger. She blew on the coffee to cool it down and let her eyes drift. The big man wasn't looking at her any more. Margaret was now chatting to the girl at the till. Music played. A young man sat by the window. He was dark-haired, heavyset, wearing a suit. Bad tie. He smiled at her. What was this, Be Nice To Strangers Day? She gave him a curt nod, which he mistook for an invitation. She groaned silently as he picked up his coffee and his pastry and approached.

"Mind if I sit?" he asked, a twinkle in his eyes.

"Something wrong with the table over there?"

"It's a lonely table. All the beautiful girls are at the tables over here." His smile widened and he sat. "Hi. I'm Alan."

"Hi, Alan."

"Can I get your name?"

Valkyrie. "Stephanie."

"Beautiful name for a beautiful girl. So, Stephanie, what do you do?"

Catch bad guys. Save the world. "I'm still in school, Alan."

He laughed. "No, you're not. Seriously? Wow. How old are you?"

"I'm seventeen."

"Seventeen. Wow. You look older. I don't mean you look *old*. You don't look *old*. Oh, God, I've probably insulted you now, haven't I?"

He really did like to laugh, this Alan.

114

"I just saw you sitting here," he continued, "dressed all in black, standing out from the crowd, looking like a girl who was worth getting to know. Are you a girl worth getting to know, Stephanie?"

"Nope," she said, "not me."

"I think you're being modest."

She took another sip of coffee.

"Well," he said, "in case you were wondering, I'm twenty. I work in Boyle Solutions, around the corner there. It's a pretty good job. Pays well."

"Good for you."

"I only started a few months ago but already my boss is lining me up for a promotion. I mean, here I am on a Sunday, on my way in for a few hours when everyone else is at home. They appreciate that kind of dedication, you know? In fact, there's this office thing, some kind of get-together, next week, and I was wondering if maybe, if you're not doing anything, you'd like to accompany me? It'd only be for an hour or two, but we could grab something to eat afterwards if you'd like."

"I don't think I'll be available."

"But I haven't told you what day it's on."

"That really doesn't matter."

Alan laughed. "Oh, I like you. I like your style."

"Excuse me," she said when her phone beeped. She took it out. She didn't recognise the number, but she read the message.

ONE OF THESE PEOPLE IS HERE TO KILL YOU.

She put the phone away, took another sip of her coffee. Alan sat there and smiled. Six people standing in line, the big man at the till. Margaret sitting in the corner. Another five people sitting around the shop. Four coffee shop employees behind the counter. Seventeen people in all.

"Good news or bad news?"

She looked back at Alan. "Sorry?"

"The text message. Good news or bad news?"

She shrugged. "Just news."

He leaned closer. "Really? You're not going to say it's from your boyfriend or something? Maybe use it as an excuse to get me to go away?"

"I don't have a boyfriend, Alan."

"Now *that* is a crime."

The big man passed behind Alan and Valkyrie tensed, but he walked on and sat at a table without making any suspicious moves. His boots were slightly scuffed, his jeans worn. The coat had seen better days but had character because of it. He wore a thick watch. No jewellery.

Now that the conversation had stalled, Alan hid his awkwardness by taking a drink and looking at something interesting on the wall. Valkyrie glanced at him. Out of shape but not obese. Soft hands, though. A watch that looked expensive but wasn't. Off-the-rack suit, badly ironed shirt, bad tie. She leaned back, her eyes flickering to his shoes. No laces, no grips.

"Don't you just love awkward silences?" he asked, and she smiled as he chuckled, and looked over his shoulder at Margaret. Her coffee lay untouched on the table before her. Her bag lay open, within easy reach. Anything could be in that bag. She was casually watching the people queuing up, like she was keeping her eyes away from Valkyrie's side of the room on purpose.

And those were only the three people who had paid attention to her. There were over a dozen more in here who hadn't even glanced her way. There were the men in suits and the harried-looking women and the dude in the jeans and the idiot in the—

Margaret glanced at her and looked away immediately. Valkyrie settled her gaze. Another few seconds passed and their eyes met again. Margaret gave a cheerful smile, and when Valkyrie didn't return it, that smile faded into a straight line.

They stared at each other across the coffee shop.

Alan was saying something and the people to her left were laughing, and a new song came on the radio and Valkyrie looked at Margaret and Margaret looked at her. She watched her right hand slip into the bag. Valkyrie's own left hand raised her coffee cup to her lips. Her right hand flexed.

Alan was still talking. About what, Valkyrie didn't have the slightest idea.

"Alan," she said softly, without taking her eyes off Margaret, "would I be unforgivably rude if I asked you to go back to your table?"

He didn't answer right away. "No," he said. "Not at all. You'd be honest. And I appreciate that."

"Thanks for understanding."

He gathered up his pastry and his coffee. "It was very nice to meet you, Stephanie."

"Same here," she murmured.

She didn't watch him as he walked away. Margaret gave her a nod of acknowledgement. Valkyrie nodded back.

Moving very slowly, Valkyrie stood up. So did Margaret, who took her hand from her bag. She wasn't holding anything. Three chatting teenagers passed between them.

Valkyrie stepped towards the door and Margaret stood in her way.

"Leaving?"

Valkyrie nodded.

"But you haven't finished your coffee."

"My friend's waiting for me outside."

Margaret smiled. "I don't think so."

Margaret took a step towards her. She was wearing a ring she hadn't been wearing before. She grabbed Valkyrie's arm. Valkyrie tried to pull away but Margaret wouldn't let go. Margaret was smiling. And then she frowned, looked down, looked at Valkyrie's jacket.

In the movies, spies killed other spies by jabbing them with poisoned spikes concealed in rings. Valkyrie grabbed Margaret's wrist, pulled her hand away, saw the spike that had failed to puncture her sleeve. Margaret twisted, locking Valkyrie's elbow, tried to grasp her bare hand. While people chatted and laughed around them, Valkyrie manoeuvred to the side, teeth gritted, trying to turn the ring away from her. They were being noticed now, conversations dying down. The spike drew closer to her bare skin.

Valkyrie bit Margaret's face and Margaret turned and dragged Valkyrie across her hip and flipped her. Valkyrie slammed down on to a table, people jumping back and shouting, but all Valkyrie cared about was keeping that spike away from her face. Margaret pressed down. She was stronger than she looked.

The big man stepped in, tried to separate them, and Margaret jabbed him in the eye with her free hand. He fell back, cursing, and Valkyrie tried to get a knee between them. Margaret raised her up then slammed her down again, the table almost toppling, the spike almost nicking her chin, but now Valkyrie had one leg wrapped round Margaret's head. She dragged the hand with the ring to one side, then hooked her other leg over her foot, caught Margaret in a triangle choke. People stood and stared. The only sounds were the music, the table rocking on its struts and the older woman's strangled grunts.

Margaret heaved herself to one side and they both fell to the floor. But Valkyrie kept the choke on. Margaret's face was bright red. She was sweating. Spittle flew from her lips. She was close to passing out. She brought her legs in, got her feet under her. Any second now. Any second now she was going to pass out. Margaret lifted Valkyrie off the ground. Any second. And then this frumpy, dowdy, middle-aged woman straightened her back, lifted Valkyrie high in the air, turned around, and dropped face down. Valkyrie hit the ground and her legs flew apart and Margaret rolled out, sucking in lungfuls of air.

Valkyrie focused on a shocked face staring at her. Poor Alan, frozen where he stood, probably vowing not to chat up another girl in a coffee shop ever again.

Still trying to get her breath back, Margaret grabbed Valkyrie's leg, going for the ankle. Trying to find bare skin. There was a commotion, and then two men in luminous yellow jackets were there, pulling Valkyrie and Margaret to their feet. Guards.

Even as the Guard holding Valkyrie was telling everyone to just calm down, Margaret swung an elbow into her cop's throat and ran, barging through the onlookers.

"I'm really sorry," Valkyrie said as she turned and drove her knee between the legs of the cop holding her. He doubled over and she let him fall. The crowd parted for her as she hurried to the girl behind the counter. "Where are the security logs? I don't have time to argue, just tell me where they are."

"Backroom," said the girl, her eyes wide. "To your left."

Valkyrie rushed in, found the monitor hooked up to the CCTV. She clicked her fingers and fried the hard drive. Then she ran out into the street, scanning the faces of the people passing by until she saw Margaret's scarf by an open door. Obviously a trap.

She crossed the street, passed through the door into what had once been a shop. Now it was just empty, with a ladder and a few tins of paint. There was a sound behind her and she turned. Margaret stepped in, a gun aimed directly at Valkyrie's head.

"Do not raise your hands," she said. "Keep them by your sides, away from your face. Those clothes of yours are bulletproof, I take it? Pretty fancy, but I suppose I should have expected that. Only the best for Skulduggery Pleasant's favourite little pet."

"Who are you?" Valkyrie asked, backing away slowly.

"You won't care what my name is when you're dead. I just want to say that I had planned to do this low-key. You wouldn't have felt even the *tiniest* of pinpricks. And the poison? It wouldn't have hurt. You'd have gone to sleep tonight and just not woken up in the morning. Painless. Subtle. But what happens instead? A fight in a coffee shop in front of dozens of witnesses. And cops! There were even cops!"

Wherever Valkyrie moved, that gun tracked her. "And you're blaming me for this?"

"Yes, actually, I am. I'm a professional. I fly under the radar. A fight in a coffee shop is not under the radar. I have a reputation to maintain, for God's sake. If I can't take care of one teenage girl, what use am I?"

"Funny," said a voice behind her, "that's exactly what I was thinking."

Margaret turned and a blade flashed. She dropped the gun, took a step and crumpled face down. Her last breath escaped her body and then she was completely still.

The woman standing over her wore boots, brown leather trousers and a brown leather waistcoat. She was blonde and pretty and her arms were strong, her shoulders wide. Tanith Low wiped the blood from her sword and smiled. "Hey, Val. Missed you."

The fallen gun sped towards Valkyrie's outstretched hand but a man in a suit and sunglasses shot out of the wall, snatching it before it reached her.

Shadows wrapped round Valkyrie's fist but Billy-Ray Sanguine backed off.

"We're not here to fight," Tanith said, hands up. "Well, we are, but not here to fight *you*. Her, your would-be assassin there, that's another matter entirely. Although you were pretty much taking care of business without us. Up until the end."

"You sent me the text," Valkyrie said.

"What are friends for?"

"You're not my friend. You're a Remnant."

"That doesn't mean I'm not a good person," Tanith said. "Well, hold on, no, actually that's exactly what it means, but that's no reason why we can't still be mates. I miss talking to you, Val. I miss all the gossip. How's Fletcher?"

"What do you want, Tanith?"

"Just to save your life, Val. Some Americans want you dead. Christophe Nocturnal and his funky little church of idiots demanded that this lovely lady be sent after you. Seems they didn't appreciate you killing their gods."

"What? That was years ago. They're just getting around to revenge now?"

Tanith shrugged. "I think they might be lazy."

"And how did you hear about it?"

"We were hired to protect you," said Sanguine. "Someone over on Nocturnal's side, and I ain't sayin' who, figured that the skeleton would hunt down whoever killed you, and whoever paid them, and everyone they knew, and probably their dogs and cats too for good measure, and this someone figured it just wasn't worth the hassle and eventual death. So we were called to swoop in and save your little life. You're welcome, by the way."

"But none of that's important," Tanith said. "What's important is that we're back, Val, you and me. We heard what's been happening with mortals getting magic. Need any help with that? I'm stronger and faster than I was before, and I was plenty strong and fast back then."

"You can't help, Tanith."

"Sure I can help," said Tanith. "Just point me at the bad guys."

"You can't help because you *are* a bad guy."

"One of these days, you're just going to have to get over that little fact."

"If you want to come back, then come back. Come back to the Sanctuary, let the doctors figure out a way to cure you. I miss you."

"I'm right here."

"No, you're not. You look like my friend and you sound like my friend but you're not her. You're someone else. Do you have any idea what that's like, to look at a face you know so well and not actually recognise the person behind it? You used to say we were like sisters, Tanith. Prove it. Do this for me. Get cured."

"There is no cure, Val. There's no getting the Remnant out. It's bonded to me now."

"I miss you. Ghastly misses you."

Sanguine slung an arm round Tanith's shoulders. "And he can go on missin' her. We are, in case you've failed to notice, what you might call an item."

"Billy-Ray," Tanith said gently, "don't embarrass yourself."

Sanguine took his arm away.

Tanith smiled at Valkyrie. "Ghastly is a lovely guy. He is. And if none of this had happened, yeah, we'd probably be together right now. But there's no point living a life of regrets."

"He really wants to see you."

"Tell him I said hi."

"We should go," Sanguine said.

"Right. Yes. Val, you might want to send a few Cleavers after Christophe Nocturnal before he sends another assassin after you. Just a thought. Last I heard, he was staying somewhere in Killiney. It was great seeing you again. You look amazing, by the way."

She held Sanguine's hand, and they sank down through the ground.

Valkyrie allowed herself a moment, then went back to the door. There were squad cars all over the place, Guards milling around the street and barking orders into walkie-talkies. The poor guy she'd kneed in the groin stood hunched over by an ambulance, and the cop that Margaret had struck stood nearby, glowering.

The Bentley pulled up, and she waited until the cops had stopped admiring it before stepping out and running over. She jumped in.

Skulduggery looked at her, then looked at all the cops. "Your doing?" he asked. She nodded, and he sighed as they pulled away. "OK then, who tried to kill you this time?"

12

THE BEDROCK OF INVESTIGATION

From one scene of violence and death to another – Valkyrie didn't know how she managed to be so lucky. The house was cordoned off with official Garda tape, but the men and women in the uniforms who were standing around were not Guards.

Skulduggery led the way up the garden path, talking on the phone as he did so. He was arranging for a squad of Cleavers to comb through Killiney with a Sensitive leading the hunt. He was confident that if Christophe Nocturnal really was staying there, they'd bring him in. Valkyrie was only half listening. She nodded to a mage she knew at the door, and went in through the hallway. It was a nice house, small but well maintained. Skulduggery put the phone away and they stepped into the living room.

"My God," he said.

There were recognisable body parts in the mess, but not many. Valkyrie lunged back out of the door and threw up in the flower bed. When she'd finished, she leaned against the doorframe and closed her eyes. A few moments later, Skulduggery joined her. He was quiet.

He spoke to the other mages, then they both got in the Bentley and Valkyrie wiped her eyes.

"The house belongs to a Gary and Rosemary Delaney," he said, "both of whom are confirmed to be at work at the moment. They have one son, Michael, eighteen years old. We're waiting on the test results to get back, but it would appear that Michael is the one in the living room."

"That's weird," Valkyrie said. "I'm crying. Look. I'm crying. I don't feel like I'm crying but look at my eyes. Those are tears. Why am I crying?"

"Because you know that somebody did that," Skulduggery said. "Somebody, a human, not an animal, purposefully ripped that boy apart. You're crying because you can't understand how anyone could do such a thing."

She took a deep breath and let it out. "You didn't spend long in there."

"I got what I needed."

She looked at him. "You know who did it?"

"No. But I have enough information to start narrowing it down. So do you."

"I just glanced in."

"And what did you learn?"

"Skulduggery, please, I'm really not in the mood for this."

"Which is why it's important."

Valkyrie sighed. "The whole place was covered in blood. There were pieces of him everywhere."

"How was he killed?"

"Ripped apart, like you said."

"But how, Valkyrie? Claws? Was he ripped apart by the killer's bare hands?"

She pictured the scene and shook her head. "No. There were no footprints in the blood. If there had been someone in there, physically attacking him, there'd be footprints. There'd probably be drops of blood leaving the house, too. I didn't see any."

"What does that tell us?"

"Whoever killed him did it remotely. From a distance of more than two or three metres, I'd say."

"Very good."

"Apart from all the blood, the room was tidy. No signs of a struggle. There was no scorching, either."

"Why does that matter?"

"If he was killed with an energy blast, you'd expect it to go through him and out the other side to get a result like that."

"Then that's not how he was killed."

"The killer could have a power like Baron Vengeous. You told me about that friend of yours. Vengeous just looked at him and his whole body ruptured."

"It shares similarities, yes. But there are a dozen ways to kill someone like that."

She hunted around in her pocket, came out with some chewing gum that she popped in her mouth to get rid of the horrible taste. "Can we leave this to someone else? We have enough to be dealing with, and there are other detectives. Let's give this case to them."

Skulduggery considered it. "We do have a heavy workload."

"Hell yeah, we do. We should be concentrating on Argeddion, pouring all our energy into that. Forget this horrible murder and forget people trying to kill me and forget Tanith hooking up with Billy-Ray bloody Sanguine... Let's just solve a problem. Summer starts next Saturday, so we have until then to figure out what's going on. Let's get this thing solved and put it away and forget about it, and then move on to the next."

"Sounds like a lovely idea."

"That's because it is. And we let the Cleavers arrest Nocturnal and deal with him. I know his people want me dead, but I really don't want to have to deal with religious fanatics today."

"Understandable. Then how about we return to the Sanctuary, open some files, and do a little research on the names that Nadir gave us?"

She made a face. "Research?"

"It's the bedrock of any investigation."

"Isn't that punching?"

"It's the bedrock of *most* investigations."

"Most?"

"Some. Listen, we're doing research and that's that."

"Blood-splattered crime scenes and musty old filing cabinets," she said. "My life is beyond glamorous."

They got back to Roarhaven and Valkyrie trudged after Skulduggery on their way to the Magical Hall of Mystical Cabinets, which she insisted on calling the file room, mainly because it annoyed Skulduggery. They walked down the steps, turned the corner, and a man in a black suit was standing there.

"Name, please," he said, holding up a hand. He was big and strong with a Newcastle accent, one of Quintin Strom's heavies.

Skulduggery tilted his head. "I'm sorry?"

"Name, please," the heavy repeated. "I have a list of people authorised to pass beyond this point. What are your names?"

Valkyrie frowned. "We always pass beyond this point. We're *allowed* to pass beyond this point."

The man nodded. "And so long as your names are on my list, you are free to do so again."

Skulduggery took a moment to observe him, then spoke. "I have to say, without any sense of false modesty, that I am a unique and distinctive person. Look at me. I'm a skeleton in an exquisitely tailored suit. I would even go so far as to say that I am somewhat famous in the circles in which you, Valkyrie and I all move. So the question *do you know who I am*, which I *could* ask, is immediately made moot. Of *course* you know who I am. I'm me. And of course you know who Valkyrie is. She is she. Neither of us knows who you are, but we seem quite comfortable with the lapse."

"My name is Grim. I am the bodyguard to—"

"The point I am making, Mr Grim, is that since you know who we are, and since you know what our role is in this Sanctuary, then you are either impeding our progress because you have been ordered, specifically, to keep us out, or because you have taken it upon yourself to do so. Which is it?"

"You're not—"

"Never mind, I don't really care. Move aside."

Grim puffed out his chest. "By order of the Supreme Council, no one gets by here without—"

"The Supreme Council has no jurisdiction in this country."

"You'll have to take that up with them. I just do what I'm told."

"Oh, good," Skulduggery said, "that'll make this much easier. Move aside."

He went to walk past and Grim moved directly into his path. "You're not getting through."

"I actually think we are."

"I'm giving you this one and only warning."

"How nice of you," said Skulduggery. "By the way, the sparrow flies south for winter."

Grim frowned, opened his mouth to form a question and Skulduggery swung his hand up, catching him in the side of the jaw with his palm. Grim went down like a sack of rocks.

"Do you think we'll get into trouble for that?" Valkyrie asked.

"I might," Skulduggery said, walking on. "You probably won't, unless there's a new accessory-to-slapping law that I don't know about."

"What are they doing acting as security men?"

"I don't know, but I doubt Ravel approved this."

There was a man talking to Tipstaff as they approached, and when he caught sight of them, he shook Tipstaff's hand and walked over. Tipstaff, for his part, looked unimpressed.

"Mr Pleasant," the man said in an American accent, hurrying over to shake Skulduggery's hand. "I am such a huge – forgive me for saying this – a huge, huge admirer of yours. I've followed all of your cases, scoured the archives. Huge, huge admirer. Oh, heavens, sorry, my name. I'm Bernard Sult. I'm one of the Junior Administrators at the American Sanctuary. And Miss Cain, very lovely to meet you. We all owe you a gigantic debt of gratitude for the service you've done in a few short years. Thank you, Miss Cain. Thank you."

Valkyrie shook his hand. "Sure," she said. "No problem."

"No problem!" Sult repeated, almost spluttering the words as he laughed. "No problem, she says! Defeating Serpine and Vengeous and the Diablerie, defeating gods, recapturing the Remnants...! No problem to Valkyrie Cain, maybe, but for the rest of us, it would have been a great big problem indeed!"

He laughed again, had to wipe his eyes he was laughing so hard. Valkyrie glanced at Skulduggery and he shrugged.

"You're here with the Supreme Council, then," Skulduggery said, walking on. Sult kept up with them. "We met one of your friends back there. He didn't want to let us by."

Sult looked horrified. "He tried to stop you?"

"He definitely tried. You might want to check on him when you have a spare minute."

"Well," said Sult, "I must apologise most profusely if he offended you in any way. Some of our people, they're so eager to make a good impression that, well, sometimes they're a little too stringent with the rules."

"And what rules would they be, Bernard? As far as I'm aware, you and your associates have no duties whatsoever in this Sanctuary."

"You're absolutely right," Sult said, nodding. "But we were just talking with your Cleaver commander about lending a hand if a hand was needed, all in a very unofficial capacity, you understand. Could I ask, was the gentleman who interrupted you from the English Sanctuary?"

"Indeed he was. A Mr Grim."

"Ah, the bodyguard. That explains it. We had different briefings. I can assure you that such a misunderstanding will not happen again. You have my word. It's all very embarrassing."

Now that Sult was focusing on Skulduggery, Valkyrie gave him a quick once-over. Looked to be in his thirties. Dark hair, cut short and neat. Nice suit, tasteful tie. Shiny shoes. Gold wedding ring. Apart from that, there was nothing distinctive about him at all.

"Do you work closely with Bisahalani?" Skulduggery asked.

"With Grand Mage Bisahalani, indeed I do," Sult said, nodding again. "Well, I say closely, but really I'm just one of his many aides. Still, I'm honoured that he chose me to represent him here."

"I would say so. The Supreme Council and all that. It all sounds so very important."

Sult laughed again. "It does, doesn't it? To be honest, I wish they'd have chosen a less grand name but, well... what sorcerer doesn't love a grand name, eh?"

"Very true," chuckled Skulduggery. "I suppose that's one crime we're all guilty of. At least the Supreme Council is upfront about its intentions. It'd be so much worse to be stabbed in the back by something called the Nice and Friendly Council, wouldn't it?"

"Stabbed in the back?" Sult laughed. "I'm afraid I don't get it."

Skulduggery and Valkyrie stopped walking. "Oh, come now, Bernard. The Supreme Council want nothing more than an excuse to come in here and take over, isn't that right? What are they looking for? What excuse do they need before they'll be happy?"

Sult's smile wavered. "I... I don't know what you—"

"A huge admirer, are you?" Skulduggery said, talking over him. "Is that why your mouth keeps turning down in contempt? Is that why you practically sneered when you said Valkyrie's name?"

Sult stepped back. "I assure you, you're mistaken. I'm—"

"Just because I don't have a face to call my own does not mean I can't read other people's," said Skulduggery. "You don't like us, Bernard. In fact, you hate us. You despise us. You're here to take this Sanctuary down. And as for this administrator thing, this unimportant aide to Grand Mage Bisahalani story, well, I think we can both agree that that's not entirely true, can't we? Who are you? You're not one of his detectives – I'd know you. You don't step into the light much. You prefer working in the shadows. Is that who you are, Bernard? Bisahalani's invisible enforcer?"

Sult smiled, and for the first time Valkyrie believed the smile was genuine. Cold, unfriendly, but genuine.

"We're not here to take over," Sult said. "We're just here to help. And I don't dislike you, Detective. You've saved the world. Both of you have. The problem is, you've mainly saved the world from your own mistakes. Time and again, this Sanctuary and its Council of Elders have endangered the lives of the people it is supposed to protect. And in doing so, it endangers the lives of everyone else on the planet. And speaking for everyone else on the planet, that isn't exactly fair."

"And yet," Skulduggery said, "by interfering, you're breaking the international Sanctuary code. What's next? We don't solve the latest crisis in six days, and you take the decision out of our hands entirely? Purely for our own good, of course."

"If we have to," Sult said. "And it's five days."

"That's what I thought," said Skulduggery. He went to move off but Sult put a hand on his arm.

"Don't act like we're the villains," he said. "We have been forced to step in because this Sanctuary is incapable of handling its own affairs. This isn't our doing. It's yours. And you know it."

Skulduggery didn't say anything, he just waited until Sult removed his hand, and then he walked away.

He gave Valkyrie an armful of files and told her to go through them while he went off to find Ghastly. She wanted to be there as they discussed what had just transpired, but reluctantly accepted that she'd probably be able to offer very little insight into what their next move might be. So she found an empty room and settled down and started reading.

It took twenty minutes before she threw the first file back on to the desk in disgust. Nothing was going in. She'd read the words and seen the words but there was a room full of blood and a middle-aged woman with a poisoned ring to keep the words from sinking in. And if that wasn't enough, there was also the man who'd tried to stop them coming down here and there was Sult, impossibly smug Sult and his stupid face. And her arm still throbbed. She didn't know what Nadir had done to her, but whatever it was, it was irritating.

She put her feet on the desk, pushed the chair back on to two legs and stared up at the ceiling. She thought about poor Ed Stynes the werewolf man and poor Jerry Houlihan the butterfly man, and how they were both downstairs, sedated, being poked and prodded by the Sanctuary medical staff. How many were down there now? Forty-three? Forty-three mortals lying in beds, bubbling over with magic they didn't understand and couldn't control. Sooner or later, one of these outbreaks was going to take place right in the public eye where there'd be no denying what had happened, and then what? Then everything would change.

She went for a walk. She passed sorcerers and Cleavers and didn't speak to any of them. There were a group of American mages who quietened down when she walked by. Things were tense enough as it was without the Supreme Council and their little army wandering around whispering to each other.

She went outside, looked out over the dark stagnant lake to the wasteland beyond, to where dead trees clawed at the sky like the land itself was screaming. Valkyrie wondered if the whole world would end up looking like that when she was through with it. Would there even be dead trees? Would she leave any sign of life, even as a memento? She didn't think so. If and when she ever did give in and allow Darquesse to take over completely, she imagined that she'd just burn the planet to a crisp. Do the job and do it properly, sort it out and put it away, then move on to the next thing. Whatever the next thing was. Maybe hunt down the Faceless Ones.

She smiled. She liked that idea. After she killed everyone here, hunting down the Faceless Ones would be the logical progression.

Her smile faded.

There was a shout and she turned. A mage was on his back next to a Cleaver van, and a man was running into the streets of Roarhaven, his hands shackled. Valkyrie recognised him as Christophe Nocturnal, the man who'd tried to have her killed. A Cleaver walked after him, not in any hurry.

Nocturnal grabbed a woman, spun her around, started shouting threats, issuing demands. The woman he'd grabbed was unimpressed, and Nocturnal didn't notice that the street behind him was beginning to fill with Roarhaven citizens.

The woman waved her hand casually and the air rippled, flinging Nocturnal backwards. He scrambled up and a man stepped out of the crowd, laid a hand on Nocturnal's shoulder and made him scream in absolute agony.

An old lady shuffled by, took hold of him and hurled him to the ground with astonishing strength. Valkyrie couldn't hear his words as Nocturnal crawled back to the waiting Cleaver, but she imagined he was doing a lot of apologising.

Roarhaven was not a town to make trouble in.

She stayed out of sight as Nocturnal was hauled to the Sanctuary. She just wasn't in the mood for yet another confrontation, not with the day she was having. Even so, she was pleased to see him in shackles.

Just as the Cleaver and Nocturnal reached the main doors, Skulduggery emerged. Nocturnal turned to glare but Skulduggery completely ignored him, and strode up to Valkyrie.

"Did you talk to Ghastly?" she asked.

He waved the question away. "Forget Ghastly. Forget Sult. Forget all that. I've just figured it out."

"Figured what out?"

"They're not *dead*."

She raised an eyebrow. "Who aren't dead?"

"Lament and his missing sorcerers. They're not dead, Valkyrie. Neither is Argeddion. Maybe they couldn't find a way to kill him, maybe for some reason they didn't want to, but they knew how to imprison him. That's where they are. They're guarding him."

Valkyrie didn't say anything, and he continued.

"Tyren Lament was, above all else, a scientist. Some of his

research remains in the archives, enough to tell me that he had been working on a containment system. From the levels recorded, his theory was that it could contain something – or someone – of immense power. I think he was designing a prison for Argeddion. A prison capable of holding a sorcerer who knows their own true name."

"But you said that wasn't possible."

"Lament found a way, I'm sure of it."

"Then this is it," she said, excited and nervous at the same time. "This is what we need to hold Darquesse. We could build one for me."

Skulduggery looked at her. "Exactly. It's for *you*, Valkyrie. Don't forget we're talking about building a prison to contain *you*."

She swallowed. "But what choice do I have? Go to a prison cell until I learn how to control myself, or kill my own parents and probably my little baby sister? Not to mention the rest of the world? I think I'll choose the prison cell, thank you very much. Are you sure about this?"

"It's the only thing that answers all the questions. Why were their files destroyed? Why weren't their disappearances mentioned in the Journals? Meritorious was doing his best to hide Argeddion's existence from anyone who might go looking."

"So where are they?"

"I don't know yet, but it would be somewhere out of the way. Isolated. Somewhere without a magical presence."

"Do we have any leads?" she asked.

"Just one. A freight company that Lament used was mentioned in the notes. There are companies all around the world, either run by or owned by sorcerers, that operate for both the mortals and the magical. Their dealings with other sorcerers are, as you can imagine, completely under the radar. Dagan Logistics is one such company."

"So we just talk to them about their dealings with him, where they shipped whatever supplies he needed, and we have where he's keeping Argeddion. Right?"

"Right."

"Right. So why aren't you looking pleased?"

He tilted his head. "How do you know I'm not?"

"I just know. What's the catch?"

Skulduggery sighed. "Dagan Logistics is not the most reputable of companies, or the most co-operative. I'd imagine that's the reason Lament used them – they're used to keeping certain dealings secret. It's owned by one of Mevolent's old supporters. Arthur Dagan."

"Oh," Valkyrie said. "*Him*. He doesn't like me."

"He's not too fond of me, either. He didn't fight in the war, he was always far too timid for that kind of thing, but he worshipped the Faceless Ones as fervently as any fanatic, and he aided Mevolent whenever he could."

"I can't really see him helping us."

"Me neither. His son, on the other hand..."

"Hansard? Would he be able to help us?"

"He's in the family business. He'd have access to his father's files. And you two seemed to really hit it off at the Requiem Ball."

"He *was* very hot," Valkyrie murmured. "But why would he help us?"

"Hansard Kray is twenty-two years old. He wasn't around for the war, and he's been brought up in a very pro-Faceless Ones environment. Do you know what happens to people like that? They tend to rebel against their parents' beliefs. Besides, he seems to have a good head on his shoulders, and if you ask him really nicely, how could he refuse you?"

"I *am* very hot," Valkyrie murmured.

"We just have to get you close to him without his father finding out. I made a few calls, asked a few people, and it seems that Hansard will be personally overseeing the transport of a large cargo on the invisible railroad tomorrow morning."

"The invisible railroad?"

"I never told you about the invisible railroad?" Skulduggery asked, walking to the Bentley. "Then you're in for a treat. So long as you like trains. And invisible things."

"I love invisible things."

"What are your feelings towards trains?"

"Meh."

"That's good enough for me."

13

MANIPULATIONS

Despite all the setbacks and hardships and obstacles in its path, the Church of the Faceless was growing.

It was a small growth, but a steady one, and it made the Church stronger with every passing month. For Eliza Scorn it was a point of pride to be now in a position of some influence. Certainly, from the moment she had taken control from the weak-willed and ineffectual Jajo Prave the Church's fortunes had started to lift, so much so that now representatives of Nocturnal's church were calling her, pleading with her, begging her to help them. And of course she felt compelled to do so. Were they not all followers of the Faceless Ones, after all? Were they not all brothers and sisters? Granted, Nocturnal's people were a notoriously conservative bunch of prim and proper puritans who sought to drain the fun out of living, but their hearts were in the right place, all things considered.

She heard Prave's voice on the other side of the door, insisting quite strenuously that Miss Scorn must remain undisturbed. Unsurprisingly, he was completely ignored, and Tanith Low and Billy-Ray Sanguine walked into her office like they owned the place. Prave trailed behind them.

"Some people here to see you," he whined.

"Tanith," said Scorn, rising from her desk, "Billy-Ray. So good to see you. Would you like some tea?"

"Thank you, no," Tanith said. "We don't do time-wasting, Miss Scorn. We are a busy, upwardly mobile kind of couple. Things to do, people to kill, that sort of thing."

"Of course, of course. Prave, you may leave us."

He wanted to stay. Of course he wanted to stay. But he backed out of the room and closed the doors after him, because of course he would do as he was told.

"Mission accomplished," said Tanith. "Valkyrie Cain saved, would-be assassin eliminated. A good day, all in all. And now comes the bit where you hand over our reward."

Scorn sat. "I'm afraid I don't have it."

Tanith fell silent. She looked at Sanguine, who took out his straight razor.

Scorn smiled, and held up her hands. "Now, now, before we say some things or kill some people that we might regret, I don't have the information you're looking for but I do know someone who does."

"That," said Sanguine, "reeks to me a little of time-wastin'.'"

Tanith nodded. "Indeed it does, honey-bunny. Miss Scorn, I am prepared to cut you a little slack, seeing as how you beat the hell out of China Sorrows and blew up her library. When I heard that, I have to admit, I laughed. But that is the only thing preventing Billy-Ray from sliding his razor across your pale little throat."

"Your understanding is appreciated," said Scorn. "But our initial arrangement was not that I hand over the information you were after, only that I find it. And I did find it. I just don't have it."

"Semantics," Tanith said, unimpressed. "How I love semantics. OK then, Miss Scorn, you tell us who does know where the dagger is and we'll leave you with all your blood on the inside."

Scorn smiled. "Christophe Nocturnal."

Sanguine took off his sunglasses to wipe them. The holes where his eyes used to be seemed to drag in the darkness of the room. "The same Christophe Nocturnal who is now in Sanctuary custody?"

"The very same."

"You've made things awkward for us," Tanith said. "I don't like awkward."

"It was necessary, I'm afraid," Scorn told her. "Nocturnal is the head of a very large church in America, a church that I want absorbed into mine. And now that he's in shackles, his congregation is worried he might start naming names. So all of their money, and all of their power, and all of their influence, might all be snatched away from them, along with all of their freedom."

Tanith folded her arms. "So they've gone running to you," she said, "begging you to silence Nocturnal before he has a chance to rat them out. In return, I expect they've agreed to join the Church of the Faceless?"

"Indeed they have."

"And you want us to break into the Sanctuary and, when Nocturnal has told us where the dagger is, you want us to kill him."

"Naturally," Scorn said, nodding. "Of course, you'd be doing this job for free."

Sanguine laughed. "Now why in tarnation would you think that?"

"Because once he told you where the dagger was, you'd be killing him anyway, wouldn't you? To stop him from telling Skulduggery Pleasant or some other investigator what you were looking for?"

Sanguine's laugh died on his lips. "Dammit," he muttered.

"You," said Tanith, "are a very cunning woman. Even more cunning than China Sorrows, I'd say."

"Oh, you flatter me."

"And just for that, I don't think we'll kill you."

"Thank you very much," said Scorn. "Now, without wanting to be rude, I have a lot of work to do. By the end of the week my Church will be one of the most powerful and well-funded organisations on earth, and I have arrangements to make."

14

KRAY

It was a little past nine on Monday morning. The Bentley was parked in a field, and Skulduggery and Valkyrie were standing in long grass.

"Welcome," Skulduggery said, "to the invisible railroad."

Valkyrie looked down at the rusted old railway tracks. "Two things," she said. "First, it's not invisible. Second, it's still not invisible. That's two things immediately wrong with something called the invisible railroad. I could go on."

Skulduggery dipped his hat lower so that the sun wouldn't get into his eyes. She didn't know why he did that. Force of habit, probably. "The invisible railroad was used a lot during the war," he said. "It'd ship people and supplies all over the country, then link up with other railroads around the world. Some of these tracks go underwater – and I don't mean in a tunnel, either. The trains run along on land and then they get to the shoreline and they go down and continue along the seabed."

"You promised me invisible things."

"Did you hear what I just said?"

"Trains that travel underwater. Brilliant. You promised me invisible things."

He checked his pocket watch. "And I keep my promises," he said. "It should be along any moment now. We should step back."

They walked away a little, and Valkyrie looked up the tracks. "Are we waiting for an invisible train?"

"Yes, we are."

"How do we know when it's here?"

"We'll know. The train isn't invisible itself, but rather it's encased in a series of bubbles."

"Cloaking spheres?"

"Exactly."

"And where does the train stop?"

"Pardon me?"

"The train station, where is it?"

Skulduggery laughed. "There isn't one, Valkyrie. It's an express service."

"So what are we supposed to do? Hop on a moving invisible train?"

He looked at her. "Of course. What did you think we were going to do?"

She felt the air shift, pressing against her cheek. To her eye, though, the track was still empty. "It's coming," she said.

"Yes, it is," Skulduggery responded, wrapping his arm round her. They lifted off the ground, moved over the tracks, and started picking up speed. Below them, the long grasses were suddenly blown back by something huge, travelling fast.

They dipped lower, passing through the bubble, and suddenly the train was right there below them and the noise was deafening. They landed on the roof of the last carriage, Skulduggery diverting the rushing air around them.

"I should go in alone," Valkyrie said, speaking loudly to be heard. "If we both go in, it'll look too official."

"So I'll just stay out here?" Skulduggery asked. "But what'll I do? There's no one to talk to. It's boring."

"You're standing on the roof of a speeding train," Valkyrie pointed out. "If you find this boring, you really need your head examined. Just wait here. I'll do what has to be done and I'll be right out."

"Fine," he said, sounding grumpy. "Don't be long."

She grinned and stepped away from him, bringing up her hand to deflect the air. Her movements were too casual, however, and the sheer force of the rushing wind took her by surprise. It hit her like a truck and she cried out as she was taken off her feet. Skulduggery reached for her but she was already tumbling backwards, the train whipping beneath her. She threw out a hand, grabbed a ladder rung, almost yanking her shoulder from its socket as her legs dangled over the blurring track. She got her other hand on to the ladder, and her feet, and clung on to the rear of the train, her entire body trembling.

She looked up and saw Skulduggery standing there, perfectly straight without even his tie being upset by the wind. He shook his head and she managed a shaky smile to reassure him she was OK. *Here lies Valkyrie Cain, who died heroically after falling off a train.* At least it rhymed.

She climbed down the ladder, kept a tight hold of it as she slid open the rear door of the carriage. She lunged in, slid it closed behind her, shutting out the noise and the wind. She took a moment to fix her hair and calm down. Oh, that was stupid. Skulduggery wasn't going to let her forget that one in a hurry.

Her composure regained, she made her way forward. Whatever they were transporting, it wasn't cargo in the traditional sense. These carriages had windows but no seats. Large canisters were held in place by thick, heavy webbing and nets on either side of her. She slid open the door at the other end, the wind once again threatening to snatch her away, and stepped over the link to the next carriage. In here it was more of the same, dozens of unmarked canisters, clinking together with the rhythm of the train.

She emerged from the other end just as the track went into a tunnel, throwing everything into darkness. She stretched out, her hand closing round the door handle of the third carriage. Still surrounded by pitch-black, she jumped the link, slid open the door and stepped in. She had to struggle a little to get the door shut, but she managed it and turned. Her instinct was to click her fingers and summon a little light, but if those canisters contained some kind of gas, then a naked flame would probably be a bad idea. So she stood there and waited, rocking back and forth with the train, and then the track emerged from the tunnel, the darkness went away and sunlight flooded in, and she found herself in a carriage packed with Hollow Men.

Valkyrie froze. Papery skin, slumping shoulders, arms weighed down by those heavy fists, they all had their backs to her, their featureless faces turned away. She swallowed, reached behind her for the door handle. One of the Hollow Men, the one closest to her, started to turn. Valkyrie darted forward, ducking behind it. Another turned, and another, shifting their slow, clumsy bodies as they looked at the space she had just occupied. Seeing no one there, however, didn't make them return to their previous positions. Now there were half a dozen Hollow Men with their blank gazes focused on her escape route. There was no way she was getting back there without being seen. She crouched lower, looked the other way, up the carriage.

Scowling to herself, she got on her hands and knees, and started to crawl.

She moved slowly through this forest of softly rustling legs. The train rocked, and while the Hollow Men swayed with it, their feet were so heavy it was like they were anchored in place. Valkyrie accidentally brushed against one or two of them and she froze, waiting for those hands to grab her, but they didn't seem to notice.

Not one of them was looking down. Not yet, anyway. She was almost to the other end when the forest of legs suddenly became impenetrable. No gaps. No way through. She gathered her feet under her, took a deep breath to calm herself, and counted down from five.

At *three*, her fingers curled, drawing in the air around her.

At *one*, she straightened up and flung her arms wide, throwing Hollow Men back and clearing a space all around her. She sprang forward, ducked a grab and snapped her palms at the air, flinging another Hollow Man into its brethren. One of them caught her, snagged her arm as she passed. She flicked her right hand and a shadow raked across the Hollow Man's chest, but it didn't let go. Panicking now as more hands reached out, she did it again, making the shadow sharper, making the cut deeper. She brought it around in a great swathe, slicing through four necks at once. Their heads lolled back, green gas billowing from their wounds, their bodies deflating.

Valkyrie tripped, coughing, eyes streaming, throat burning from the gas. Hands on her and she tried to shake them off but the grip was tight, and she felt herself being pulled backwards, out into the rushing air. Then she was beyond it, and the wind shut off. The hands again, pulling her up, leading her forward. She didn't fight them. She was bent forward, and water splashed her face and someone was talking to her.

"Don't rub your eyes," he was saying. "It makes it worse. Just let the water do the work."

She moaned something, unable to speak. Acid burned in her belly. She wanted to throw up. Again, the water splashed. Not much, just cold drops, working to drive away the stinging. She tried pressing her face downwards, to submerge her whole head, but the hands stopped her.

"You're going to be fine," said the voice. "Try to breathe. You're going to be OK."

Slowly, gradually, she began to relax. At the voice's instruction, she stopped screwing her eyes shut, and let the water cool her eyelids. When she was finally able to open them, Hansard Kray handed her a towel and stepped back.

"Your nose is running," he said.

Valkyrie covered her face with the towel, hiding her embarrassment and drying off at the same time, then used it to blow her nose. When she looked up, Hansard was holding out a tissue.

"Oh," Valkyrie said. "Sorry."

"Never mind," said Hansard. "You can keep the towel if you want. We have lots."

He stepped out of the washroom and she followed him. The carriage they were in was long and luxurious. There was a table, a bar, and even a bed down the other end. No one else in it. She glanced out through the glass in the door, back into the carriage filled with Hollow Men.

She turned to him. "What are you doing with them?"

"I'm sorry?"

"Hollow Men. What are you doing with a train full of Hollow Men? I thought you weren't like your father."

Hansard leaned back against the bar. "Meaning what, exactly?"

"You know what," she said. "Why do you need them? What are you planning? What are you a part of?"

"I'm a part of the family business," he replied. "As for what I'm planning to do with eight carriages of Hollow Men, I'm planning on delivering them to the people who placed the order."

She frowned. Her eyes still stung. "What?"

"They're not for my use, Valkyrie. This is a freight company. Transporting things is what we do."

"Then who ordered them?"

"I'm afraid I can't tell you that. Confidentiality is a big part of why people choose us. From your reaction, though, I can tell you're thinking the worst. I know that Nefarian Serpine was fond of using Hollow Men, but not everyone who does has evil schemes in mind. Mostly they're used as cheap labour or security, if Rippers can't be afforded."

She looked at him, her hostility dampening. "Oh," she said.

Hansard smiled. "Not that I don't enjoy being accused of terrible plots against humanity, but may I ask what you're doing here? Aside from insulting me, of course, and damaging property that isn't mine."

"I'm sorry," Valkyrie said. "I didn't know they could be used for... other things. But they attacked me."

He shook his head. "Without specific orders, Hollow Men don't do anything on their own initiative. If they attacked you, you must have attacked them first."

She hesitated. "Maybe," she said. "Oh, God, I'm really sorry. But they're different from the other ones."

Hansard nodded. "These Hollow Men are tougher, their skins more expensive. You should see the new ones they've come out with – you'd need a chainsaw to cut through them."

"I really don't like the sound of that."

"You didn't answer my question, Valkyrie."

She cleared her throat. "I'm actually here to ask you for a favour."

He laughed. "A favour? After this?"

"Yeah. I know. Sorry."

"And what's wrong with using a phone? Or calling by the office, or the house? I'm sure you'd be able to find out where I live without much trouble. Aren't you a bona fide Sanctuary Detective now? And where is your partner? Don't tell me he let you stow away on a strange train alone?"

"I didn't stow away," she said. "I just dropped in. And as for where Skulduggery is, well, if you look outside your window..."

Hansard turned, saw Skulduggery flying alongside the train in a standing position with his arms crossed.

"Now that," Hansard said, "looks like fun." He looked back at her. "You didn't want to run into my father again, did you?"

"Not really."

"You've got to remember, he was extremely drunk when you met him. He's not normally like that."

"He's not normally a worshipper of the Faceless Ones?"

"No, he is always that... He just isn't usually so mean."

"He threatened to spank me."

"I'll refrain from commenting," Hansard said, showing that smile again. "So what's the favour that you have gone to such great lengths to ask me?"

"You've heard about those ordinary people who've suddenly developed powers?"

"I have. My dad is by turns amused and horrified at the prospect. What about it?"

"We think the answer lies with a man named Tyren Lament, who hired your company thirty years ago to ship materials to an unknown destination. We need to know that destination."

Hansard exhaled. "Thirty years ago? You mean before computers were as commonplace as they are now? When every little bit of information was recorded in ledgers and on paper in dusty old cabinets? You're looking for an address in all of that?"

"Yep."

"So you obviously didn't hear me earlier when I said that confidentiality is a big part of why people choose to do business with us."

"But this was thirty years ago."

"That doesn't make it any less confidential."

"But Lament is dead. You can look it up. He's listed as missing, presumed dead."

"That's really sad."

"It really is, but he's not around any more, so why keep his secrets?"

"Keeping secrets is one of our policies."

"We really need that address, Hansard. People are dying. And the longer this goes on, the greater the chance that the mortal world will find out the biggest secret of all."

He smiled. "Nicely done."

"Thank you. And, well... if you help us, I would personally be ever so grateful."

"Would you now?"

"I would."

The train rocked and she let herself stumble slightly. He caught her, his hands round her arms, her own hands pressing against his chest.

"I really would," she said softly.

He looked at her, and chewed his lip thoughtfully. "Fine," he said at last, leaving her standing there and walking to the table. He sat, opened up a laptop, started tapping the keyboard. "Lament. What was the first name?"

"Tyren," she said, walking over. "But I thought you said all this information was in a dusty old cabinet somewhere."

"It is," he said, nodding. "And I spent an entire summer transferring it to computer when all of my friends were out having fun. That's the disadvantage of a family business – you've really got no choice in the matter." His fingers flew over the keys, and he sat back. "Tyren Lament," he said. "Going back over fifty years, he used this company three times in total. Twice shipping materials from New York to Dublin, and once shipping from Africa to Switzerland. The Switzerland job was the last time he used us."

"Then that's the one I'm interested in," Valkyrie said. "Is there an address?"

Hansard scribbled a few numbers on a piece of paper, and handed it to her as he stood.

She smiled. "Your phone number? Do I have to call you before you'll tell me?"

"They're co-ordinates, Valkyrie. The materials were delivered halfway up a mountain."

"Oh," she said. "Thanks."

He shrugged. "What harm can it do? The guy's dead, right?"

"Exactly." She smiled. "But really, thank you. And I'm sorry about, you know, accusing you of whatever. And sorry about the damage. I don't have a happy history with those things."

"That's understandable," Hansard said. "And don't worry about it. I'll put it down to travel damage, we'll reimburse the owner, and my father will never know you paid me a visit."

"Cool. Thanks. Well, I should probably get going."

He nodded, and she smiled awkwardly and walked to the carriage door. Right before she opened it, she turned. "Do you want my number?" she asked quickly. "My phone number, like. Do you want it?"

He looked at her as if she'd asked him to list off mathematical equations. "Why would I need it?"

She blinked, and felt the heat rising. "No. No reason. Just thought. OK, cool, thank you so much for—"

"Oh," he said, his eyes widening slightly. "Ah, of course. Sorry, I'm a bit slow sometimes. Certain things, you know, it takes ages for them to reach my brain."

She laughed. "I know the feeling."

He smiled. "But no, I don't want your number."

Her laugh died. "Er… OK then."

She waited for a little more information, maybe a reason or the name of a girlfriend, but she didn't get either of those things.

"No problem," she said, sliding open the door and leaning out into the wind and noise. She gave him a forced smile and stepped out, letting the wind catch her. She adjusted the current and propelled herself upwards, passing through the cloaking bubble that took the train from her sight. Skulduggery swooped in, caught her, one arm encircling her hip.

"Did you get it?" he asked as they hovered there in the light breeze.

"I am morto," she mumbled.

"Sorry?"

"Mortified. Oh, God, I want to die."

"What happened?"

She buried her head in his bony shoulder. "I don't want to talk about it."

"You brought it up."

"I don't want to talk about it."

157

"Well, we *weren't* until you—"

"I have the co-ordinates," she interrupted. "It's in the Alps."

"Marvellous. I love the Alps. Why are you mortified?"

"Don't. Want. To talk about it."

"Your eyes are red."

"There were Hollow Men in there, being taken to someone who wants to use them for something. Is that illegal?"

"Owning Hollow Men is not illegal, no. It's unsettling, but not illegal. Hansard didn't happen to tell you who they're going to, no?"

"He was tight-lipped."

"Ah," said Skulduggery. "Then I can see why you were mortified."

She glared. "Shut up."

"How could anyone possibly resist the fabulous Valkyrie Cain?"

"Shut up."

"Unrequited love is nothing to be ashamed of. Many people have crushes. It's all perfectly natural."

"What, like you and Grace Kelly?"

Skulduggery turned his head away. "Don't talk about Grace Kelly."

"Oh, so it's OK for you to make fun of *me* for having a crush but not the other way around?"

"No, I mean don't talk about Grace Kelly when I'm flying. I need to focus, and talking about one of the most beautiful women who ever lived makes me inclined to drop you."

"I've seen her photo, you know. She wasn't *that* hot."

Skulduggery looked at her. They floated in mid-air.

"OK, fine," Valkyrie said at last, "she was. But she had skinny arms. I could totally have taken her."

"You may be stronger than she was," Skulduggery responded, "but I dare say she'd have cut you to ribbons with her elocution."

"She had electric powers?"

"I swear to God—"

"I'm joking. I know what elocution means."

"Sometimes I wonder about you, you know."

"Yeah," she said. "Sometimes I wonder about me, too."

15

KILLING CHRIS

The Sanctuary buzzed with activity, and Tanith didn't like it. She had no idea why there were so many mages here from America and the UK and Germany, and she had no idea why there was so much tension. She didn't care, either. She just knew it was there, and it annoyed her, but she struggled through, because that's what she did.

It could have been worse, of course. There could have been new mages in every part of the Sanctuary, which would have made sneaking in so much more difficult. But there were rooms in the Medical Bay that hadn't been disturbed in months, and so this was where they stepped into, the wall closing up behind them. Sanguine waited until he thought she wasn't looking, then wiped the sweat from his brow. But of course she saw it. That last trip had hurt him, and it wasn't even a particularly long one.

It just confirmed what she'd already known – something had to be done.

They waited until Doctor Nye was alone, and Tanith walked across the ceiling so as not to make a sound. Then she dropped down behind him and politely cleared her throat.

Nye turned, and she pressed the tip of her sword against its long throat. It raised its arms slowly. "You don't have to kill me," it said. She hated its voice. It was too high-pitched and too soft. Everything about it screamed weakness. "I can help you," it continued. "Whatever you need, I can help you."

"Of course you can," Tanith said. "And you're going to."

"We need access to a prisoner," Sanguine said, joining them. "One Mr Nocturnal. You're gonna have him brought here, say you have some tests you have to run."

"Actually," Tanith said, "there's been a slight change of plans as far as Nocturnal goes." Sanguine frowned at her from behind his sunglasses, and she continued. "I've decided that I'll kill him in his cell. I know the way there, it won't be a problem."

"You're gonna do it yourself? What am I meant to do – play chequers with the doc here?"

She hesitated. How to say this so as not to offend him? "You're useless, Billy-Ray. Sometimes your power works fine and everything's great, but then you have a bad day and every time you try to burrow somewhere it hurts. And then you complain, and gripe, and sulk, and really, I've had enough of you acting like a child."

He stared at her, and Tanith wondered if her plan not to offend him had actually worked. Regardless, she pressed on. "I can't rely on you, and I need to rely on you. You're a huge part of my plans, and I can't continue without you. But this injury you've been carrying around... it just won't do. So Doctor Nye here is going to patch you up."

"I told you," Sanguine said, "no one can patch me up. It was a botched operation the first time round, and no amount of repair work is gonna fix it."

"Oh, I'm aware of that. So Nye isn't going to try and repair the damage. He's going to rip you open and start all over again."

"He's gonna what?"

Tanith looked up. "Doctor Nye, you're not the bravest of creatures, are you?"

"I have been known to run from my fair share of conflicts."

"And you're not the most noble of creatures, either, isn't that right?"

"Nobility is a crutch for the ethically stunted."

"That's what I thought you'd say. Or something like it. And given your history, and you do have a history, I would go so far as to say you hold no particular loyalty to the Sanctuary as it stands."

Nye gave a disturbing little giggle. "These people? Oh my, no."

"Then what will it take for you to fix my friend Billy-Ray here without alerting your colleagues?"

Nye's tongue flickered over the thread that punctured its thin lips. "A favour," it decided. "Someone I might need killed when this is done."

"You have a deal. Can you operate now?"

"I can. From what I know of the injury, it will take some time."

"Well then," Tanith said, "you'd best get started. I'll be back in a bit."

She ignored the look on Sanguine's face as she left the Medical Bay. It was disappointingly easy to move through the shadows, passing mages of great reputation, coming so close she could have whispered in their ears. They were all too preoccupied to look up. They talked fast, walked faster, and there was that delicious tension again. It would have been all so very intriguing, if she cared about such things.

She got to the detention area, slipped by the mage on duty and strolled past the doors, reading the names of the prisoners inside. When she found the door she was looking for, she pressed her palm to the lock, and it clicked as it opened. She stepped into the small cell, and felt her powers dampen. She hated that feeling, but pushed it away. Christophe Nocturnal was sitting on his bunk.

"You're a little early with the food, aren't you?" he said, rolling his eyes. "And you've forgotten the food. Well done, idiot."

The door closed behind her and Tanith smiled. "You are a charming man, aren't you?"

"My charm is reserved for those who warrant it."

"I don't warrant it?"

"Only those who accept the Faceless Ones as the true masters of their souls warrant a kind word from me."

She walked slowly so that she was standing directly in front of him. "And how do you know I'm not a fan of the Dark Gods?" she asked.

"Your apparel, for one thing."

She raised an eyebrow. "What's wrong with the way I'm dressed?"

"What's wrong is that you are *barely* dressed. True believers pride modesty and humility above all other attributes save obedience. We do not try to overshadow or outshine our lords and masters by wearing tight or revealing clothing."

Tanith looked down at herself. "Are you saying I'd make the Faceless Ones feel inadequate?"

He glared. "You are unclean."

"But I showered before I came here."

"You are tarnished by vanity."

"I'm tarnished by a lot more than that."

"Cover yourself up, repent for all the harm you've done, do penance and accept the Faceless Ones as your lords and masters. Maybe then your soul will not be burned upon their return."

"Covering up, repenting, doing penance... I'm sorry, but your church really doesn't sound like it's my kind of thing. I'm not here with your food, Chris. It has been brought to my attention that you know where a certain dagger is. I need to know what you know, Chris."

"Who are you?" he said, frowning.

"According to you, I'm a sinner."

"You work with the Sanctuary?"

"*With* them? I don't know if I'd say *with* them. *With* them makes it sound like they know I'm here. I'd say more alongside them. Or possibly against them. Yeah, actually, I work against them. Kinda like you, except obviously in a more successful fashion."

"What do you want?"

"I told you. The dagger."

"I don't know what dagger you—"

"Pish posh, Christophe. Of course you know what dagger I'm talking about. The only dagger *worth* talking about. You know who has it. That's information I need."

"Get me out of here and I'll tell you."

"You tell me, and I'll get you out of here."

"Once you have the information, what's to stop you from leaving me in this cell?"

Her eyes widened, all innocence. "My word is my bond."

"I'll tell you once I'm free."

"But what if you're killed while we make our escape? Then after the weeks of crying and wailing and mourning your death, and thinking of what might have been between us – because there's a connection here and you can't deny it – then I'll be left with nothing, not even the location of the dagger. Do you see my dilemma, my sweet pumpkin? Please spare me the heartache and tell me now."

"You mock me."

"Only because I care. Oh, Christophe, our moment is now. You and me, baby. Once I get you out of here, my boyfriend will be there, and of course Eliza will be waiting, and she's so pretty, and I can't stand the thought of you leaving me for—"

"You're working with Eliza Scorn?"

"But of course."

"Why didn't you tell me that? Take me to her, damn you. Why waste time with this ridiculousness?"

"Because you're the one paying me to rescue you, Christophe. You're paying me with the location of the dagger I want, and I always get paid *before* a job. Not after."

Nocturnal grabbed his coat, put it on. "You could have said that when you came in," he snarled. "The dagger is in the possession of Johann Starke."

"Starke... One of the Elders in the German Sanctuary?"

"Yes, him. Can we go now?"

"Thank you so much, Christophe. You've been a great help."

"Take me out of here."

"No. I'll be killing you now."

He froze. "What?"

"I'm afraid Eliza doesn't want you rescued. All your friends, back in your church? You know those people who really wouldn't approve of me, or my clothes, or how I wear my clothes? Remember those good and decent people? Yeah, they want you dead."

"You're lying."

Tanith drew her sword. "They're worried you might start talking, maybe mention a few names."

Nocturnal backed away. He'd gone quite pale. "I haven't said a word. I haven't said anything!"

"But your modest and humble friends can't take that chance. They've decided it would be best for everyone, apart from maybe yourself, if you were to be killed."

"No, no. I can get you the dagger."

"I'll take care of that."

He dropped to his knees. "Please..."

"Don't beg. It cheapens the moment."

"Have mercy."

She smiled with black lips, and showed him the veins beneath her skin. "I'm all out."

16

THE OTHER HERE

n their way into Dublin City, Skulduggery made a call, arranging for a plane to take them to Switzerland. When he hung up, he told Valkyrie that Ghastly had sounded especially harassed. The Supreme Council was making its presence felt yet again, it seemed, and new calls were coming in all the time about unusual disturbances. He took the next right.

Valkyrie sighed. "Not another incident."

"No," Skulduggery assured her. "Well, maybe. A missing person, one Patrick Xebec. Elemental. Last seen Friday afternoon."

"So? People go missing all the time."

"I think we should meet his wife, see what she has to say. This may tie in with what's going on."

"Why? What did Ghastly tell you?"

"Something about streams of energy in the sky. A public display of power like that could very likely be another mortal developing magical abilities. Does that pique your curiosity?"

She considered. "No. But then I'm not easily piqued. I'll reserve judgement."

"That's all I ask."

They parked near the city centre and walked for a few minutes until they came to the apartment complex where Patrick Xebec lived. They were let in by Xebec's wife, a Frenchwoman with tired eyes.

"I was on the phone to him," she said. "We were talking about something, the neighbour's cat, and then he said there were these lights in the sky. He said they were energy streams. I told him to call the Sanctuary but he said you wouldn't get there in time. He said someone was going to notice and realise it wasn't just a light show. He told me he'd ring me back once he figured out what was going on. I... I haven't heard from him since."

"Do you know where he was when he saw all this?" Skulduggery asked.

"He was driving through Monkstown. But he said the energy streams were miles away. He didn't say what direction. Patrick has never gone more than a few hours without checking in, let alone three days. Something bad has happened to him, I know it." Her hand went to her mouth. "Please, Detective, find my husband."

"We'll do our best," Skulduggery said.

They walked back to the car and Valkyrie's arm started to ache.

Skulduggery was talking about something that had just occurred to him, something to do with Greta Dapple.

"She mentioned that her birthday is this Saturday," he said, "which means it's May the first – the start of summer. Coincidence? I don't think so. But what does Argeddion's old girlfriend have to do with mortals developing magic? What does she have to do with the Summer of Light?"

The ache was spreading, turning to a dull but persistent throb that Valkyrie could feel in her chest. The world flickered and she stopped walking, suddenly dizzy. "Whoa."

Skulduggery took her arm, steered her round the corner. "Valkyrie, look at me."

He flickered and the whole world vanished, just for the blink of an eye. Valkyrie staggered back against the wall. "What the hell is going on? Skulduggery? Everything's disappearing. What's wrong with—"

And then Skulduggery was gone and the building behind her was gone and she was falling backwards, splashing into a puddle. It took her a moment to figure it out.

"Fletcher!" she called. He didn't answer. She was sitting in a puddle in a filthy alleyway.

She didn't recognise her surroundings.

Skulduggery was gone.

She was alone.

She got up. It had to be Fletcher. He was the only Teleporter left alive. No one else could have done that. She took out her phone.

Impossibly, it told her she didn't have a signal. But this phone always had a signal.

She walked out of the alley. The buildings were all old, old and dirty and small, made of brick and stone and wood. A man passed, dressed in dark brown, the colour of mud. A woman walked the other way, wearing the same colour. Valkyrie followed the woman to a wider street, but then stopped at the corner, hung back. Everyone here wore brown. Brown trousers, brown shirts, brown coats. They didn't wear it as a uniform, though – it was just as if the only clothes available were all the same colour.

Valkyrie stepped into the street and suddenly people were turning around, changing direction, looking up at the sky or down at the road as they passed her. She started to feel very self-conscious dressed all in black. Two women approached, and Valkyrie walked over.

"Excuse me?"

They hurried by, heads down, pretending not to see her.

"Hey," she said. "Hey, hello. Excuse me."

"You should go."

She turned. A man in his forties, in those same brown clothes as everyone else. Balding and unshaven.

"Where am I?" she asked.

"Not where you're supposed to be," he said. "Do yourself a favour, do us all a favour, and leave. Please." He started walking. She followed.

"I don't know where I am. Tell me where I am."

"Pageant Street," he said brusquely.

"I mean what city."

"Dublin."

She frowned at him. "This isn't Dublin. I know Dublin, and this isn't..." A thought struck her. A horrible, amazing thought. "What year is this?"

"Year?"

It made sense. The old-style buildings. The fact that there were no cars, no technology. She'd travelled back in time. "Tell me what year this is."

He stopped suddenly and looked at her, fear in his eyes. "You're a sorcerer," he said.

Valkyrie blinked. "Uh..."

He backed away. "Oh, my... Oh, you're one of them. Please don't kill me. I only wanted to help. I didn't mean anything by it."

She followed, keeping her hands up, trying to calm him down. "You know about sorcerers?"

"I don't know anything, I swear. I'm no one."

She clapped her hands in front of his face and he jerked his head back. "Hey! Listen to me. I'm not going to hurt you. I just need to know some things. I'm not from here and I don't know how anything works. You say this is Dublin? What century?"

He looked at her like she was crazy. "Century? The twenty-first."

Oh. So she hadn't time-travelled. Fine. "What happened to it?" she asked next.

"What do you mean?"

"I mean what happened here? Where are the cars and the streetlights and how come everything is so old and dirty? Why is everyone wearing these clothes?"

"I don't want to get into any trouble."

"Answer my questions."

"But I don't know what you mean. It's always been like this."

"No," she said, "it hasn't. Dublin is brighter and bigger and flashier and... and OK, it's not a whole *lot* cleaner, but the people wear better clothes, that's for sure. I don't know what you're trying to pull but this isn't the Dublin that I know, all right? This..." And then it dawned on her. Nadir, the Dimensional Shunter. The throbbing in her arm. Whatever he'd done to her, this was the result. "I'm in a different reality," she said softly.

The balding man looked at her. "I'm sorry?"

"I'm not from this world," she told him. "You understand? I'm from one like it, but... different. We have cars and electricity and... Why is it like this? Why don't you have cars?"

"I don't know," the man said, distressed. "Is a car like a carriage? We have carriages. Horses pull them. I can show you where they're kept."

Valkyrie looked around. "Never mind. There are sorcerers here, right? Maybe they can help me."

The man paled. "You don't want to go to them."

"Why not?"

"If you don't know them, you don't want to know them. You should leave. Now. You should run."

A woman hurried by, waving a handkerchief by her side. The man turned.

"They're coming."

"Who are?" Valkyrie asked. "What's wrong?"

He took her hand, dragged her off the street. They ran between two buildings. He jumped a wall and she followed.

"What's going on?"

He didn't answer. He led her into a sagging house. The door was open and the floorboards were rotten. She followed him up the stairs and he crossed to the window.

"The Sense-Wardens are patrolling," he said. "Some of them can read your mind. When you see them, you have to just think of nothing, just focus on being empty, or they'll see something in your thoughts and they'll come for you. They got my wife, seven years ago. She didn't know they were there and they grabbed her off the street, took her away. I haven't seen her since."

"That's terrible."

"The ones in white," he said, "they're the Sense-Wardens."

Valkyrie joined him at the grime-covered window. Nine people passed below, three of whom wore white robes with hoods obscuring their faces. They walked slowly, hands clasped. Forming a circle around them were six people in robes of deep scarlet. Beneath the robes, black boots and loose garments. On their backs, scythes.

"They send the Redhoods after us," the man said bitterly. "There's no point in running. They're too fast. There's no point in fighting.

They're too strong. And those blades of theirs... I once saw a man cut in two as easy as cutting paper."

"Cleavers," said Valkyrie. "They're called Cleavers. Or that's what they're called where I'm from. And they're dressed in grey, not red."

"Well, here they're called Redhoods," said the man, "and if one is coming for you, you surrender. Save yourself the pain."

He stepped away from the window but Valkyrie stayed where she was, watching. There was a symbol on the breast of their robes – two circles, the smaller one barely bisecting the larger. She watched the Sense-Wardens and their guards move on, watched the people slow down to a stop as they approached. To suddenly turn and walk the other way would be a sign of something to hide, so instead the people paused, lowered their heads and closed their eyes. Probably focusing on being empty.

One of the Sense-Wardens turned his head, his hood shifting slightly. He stepped from the circle, slowly nearing a young woman with short cropped hair. Her eyes were closed but she could undoubtedly hear his footsteps. She stiffened, and even Valkyrie could see her face twitch with panic.

The Sense-Warden walked slowly round her. The young woman's shoulders started to shake. She was crying, but her eyes remained closed.

Another Sense-Warden broke from the circle, joining the first. A pale hand emerged from a voluminous sleeve and lightly touched the woman's head. She flinched and sobbed, and her legs gave out and she fell to her knees. She looked up at the Sense-Wardens as they backed away, and a Redhood came forward. He gripped the young woman's arm and pulled her to her feet.

"They have someone," Valkyrie said, her voice quiet. "A girl. Not much older than me."

The balding man, from somewhere behind her, spoke without emotion. "She'll be taken to the Palace. Whatever secrets she's hiding will come spilling out of her, and if they're bad enough, she'll be killed. If not, imprisonment."

"There must be someone who fights against this."

"There is," said the man. "At least, I think there is. For all I know it's just another legend, a story to tell our children at night. I wouldn't be surprised. Every sorcerer I've ever met has hated mortals. I suppose it's childish to think there are some out there who fight for us."

"I'm a sorcerer," said Valkyrie, "and I'll fight for you. For as long as I'm here, anyway."

The man shrugged. "Then by all means, go down there and save that girl."

She hesitated. "There are nine of them."

"And it's only one mortal girl," said the man, nodding. "She'd hardly be worth the risk."

Valkyrie glared at him. "That's not what I meant. I meant you've got to pick your battles. Charging in head first would only get me killed, and what use would I be to anyone then?"

"What use are you to anyone now?"

"I'm not going to die for someone I don't know in a reality I don't understand. This isn't even my dimension, for God's sake."

"Fair enough. No one could expect you to bother yourself."

"I wouldn't stand a chance anyway. If your Redhoods are the same as my Cleavers then their clothes are resistant to magic. I wouldn't last two seconds against nine of them." As she spoke, she looked out of the window. The Redhood was taking the young woman, who was now wearing shackles, back through the streets. The others, including the Sense-Wardens, had continued on in the other direction, out of sight. She looked at the Redhood and the young woman. "However..." she murmured.

"However what?"

"However, I might stand a chance against one of them."

She moved to the door but he stood in her way. "No."

Valkyrie arched an eyebrow. "No?"

"You can't."

"You were just saying—"

"Because I didn't think you'd try anything. If a Redhood is attacked, do you have any idea what that would mean? They'd tear through these streets looking for whoever did it. They'd torture and kill and take their anger out on innocent people. You can't interfere."

"But that girl—"

"Is one of a countless number who are taken off the streets every week. You can't save them all, and saving one would make it worse for everyone else."

"So no one does anything? How do you expect things to change if you're not willing to make a stand?"

The man laughed. "But I *don't* expect things to change. This is the way of the world. Those with magic rule and live for ever, and those without magic work and perish. You think it's any different in France? Britain? In what's left of America? Everywhere's the same." His voice softened. "Look, thank you for wanting to try. Even though I'm starting to doubt that you are a sorcerer and not just some lunatic, it's appreciated."

Valkyrie clicked her fingers and the balding man recoiled slightly from the fireball.

"OK," he said quickly, "you're a sorcerer."

She let the flames go out.

"If you're not from here," he said, "then you should try to go home as soon as possible, before you do something that has repercussions for those of us who have to live here."

She sighed. "Yeah. I suppose you're right. I'm going to need help, though. A Dimensional Shunter sent me here, so I'm going to need another one to send me back."

"I don't know what that is, but maybe you should track down the Resistance, see if they have one."

"Are they the sorcerers who are fighting for you?"

"Yes. I don't know where they are, though."

"Wow," she said. "You're a great help."

He frowned. "I'm not really."

"Yeah. That was sarcasm. Don't you have sarcasm in this reality?"

He didn't answer and she paled. "Oh my God. You don't, do you? Oh, you poor people."

"I don't know what that word means."

"Sarcasm? It's a kind of joke, where you say one thing and mean another."

"I... still don't fully understand."

"It's OK, you don't have to." She patted his arm. "It just means that, right now, I'm the funniest person in the world."

They walked back to the stairs, Valkyrie taking the lead this time. The whole building creaked around them. She got a hand on the banister, about to take the first step down, when she heard the man gasp behind her.

A Redhood was standing at the foot of the stairs.

17

KEEPING THE DEMON DOWN

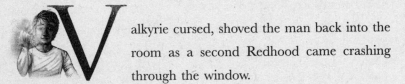alkyrie cursed, shoved the man back into the room as a second Redhood came crashing through the window.

Valkyrie pushed at the air but he moved through the ripples, his scythe flashing. The blade cut through the balding man's neck, severing his head. Valkyrie pushed at the air again, catching his body as it crumpled and slamming it into the Redhood, taking him off his feet. She felt the air shift behind her and she ducked, barely dodging the other Redhood's scythe. She threw herself forward, rolled and sprang for the broken window. She leaped through, falling to the street, hands out to slow her descent. But her thoughts flashed with pain and she tumbled through space and hit the ground hard.

The three Sense-Wardens stood before her, attacking her mind, driving needles into her brain. Her vision blurred. Figures in red approached from her left. She tried to get up but couldn't.

Get out of my mind, said the voice in her head.

The pain doubled and she cried out. The pain, the agony, wasn't just in her brain any more, it was all over. It was in her *self*. It was in her *being*. She could feel them, with their psychic needles, poking and prodding and gouging. They were attacking who she was. So who she was attacked *them*.

GET OUT OF MY MIND.

The Sense-Wardens staggered and the pain went away, and Valkyrie fought to keep Darquesse trapped within her. She brought her hands in, the wind snatching her from the street just as the Redhoods reached her. She rose into the sky, dropped to a rooftop and immediately started running.

As she used the air to leap from rooftop to rooftop, she tried making sense of where she was. This was still Dublin, although a different Dublin to the one she knew. Somewhere along the timeline of this reality, something significant had happened that hadn't occurred in her own dimension. But there should still be landmarks she recognised, some clue to help her get her bearings.

She swooped up to a higher roof, and almost stumbled in astonishment. The River Liffey coiled before her, but on its far banks lay a wall like she had never seen. It coiled with the river, looming over the water forty storeys or more. O'Connell Bridge seemed to be the only entry point, leading to a pair of massive gates. And beyond all that the towers and steeples of what looked like a cathedral or a palace rose above even the wall.

"And who might you be?"

Valkyrie whirled. A man stood on the rooftop, smiling. He was good-looking, with a thin moustache that actually twirled. His clothes were beautiful, his shoes polished to a gleam. He looked like he had never done a day's work in his life.

"I'm Valkyrie," she said at last. "And you are?"

"Alexander Remit, at your service." He even bowed. "May I enquire as to the nature of your visit to this neck of the proverbial woods?"

"I took a wrong turn."

"Oh, I see. This is all a big mistake, then?"

"Something like that."

"Then I should just leave you to go about your business?"

"If you wouldn't mind."

She started walking across the rooftop. He followed on a parallel course.

"And you have absolutely nothing to do with the Resistance," he said, "or the sorcerer who leads it?"

"Nothing at all."

"Valkyrie, and that is a lovely name, I'm finding it hard to believe you, I'm afraid to say. I think you might be fibbing. I think you might be here as an agent of the Resistance to spy on us, or possibly even attempt an assassination."

"Not me."

"In that case, you would have no objection to accompanying me to the Palace, as my guest?"

"I actually would have an objection."

"Such a pity. Here I am, extending an olive branch, and you refuse to take it. I don't have to be so polite, you know. You attacked Sense-Wardens and Redhoods. Such criminal acts are punishable by death."

"I'm just trying to get home, Alexander."

"Where is home, Valkyrie?"

She shrugged. "Not here."

They each stopped walking, and he took a pair of shackles from his jacket. "You look like an intelligent girl. Do the smart thing, and put these on."

"That's not going to happen."

"That makes me sad."

"You're about to get a lot sadder."

Remit vanished. Teleporter. The instant that word registered in Valkyrie's mind she was twisting, swinging her fist. She'd spent enough time with Fletcher to know that his first move was always to teleport behind his enemy. She swung blindly and was almost surprised when her arm struck Remit's jaw. He spun, eyes rolling in his head, his legs collapsing beneath him. He crumpled to the rooftop.

Valkyrie cuffed his arms behind his back with his own shackles, and waited for him to wake up. Her arm, the arm where Nadir had grabbed her, started to throb again.

"You're under arrest," Remit said weakly.

"Hush now, or I'll tell people that I cuffed you with your own shackles."

The throbbing got worse, just like it did before she shunted over here in the first place.

"Your head'll be on the block soon enough," he said, trying to get to his knees. "No one dares assault a—"

His voice dimmed for a moment. *He* dimmed for a moment. In fact, *everything* dimmed. Valkyrie stepped back, suddenly dizzy. The world flickered. Remit was too busy sitting up to notice.

"You'll be tortured first," he was saying. "We'll prise every little secret out of your pretty little brain."

He got to his feet, a little awkwardly, and she didn't stop him. "You'll beg for mercy. Every sorcerer we capture renounces the Resistance, and they all beg. You'll be no different. I'd say you wouldn't last more than a few hours, in fact." He stumbled, still groggy. "I bet everything I own that the day you're captured, you'll be swearing your loyalty to Mevolent before the sun goes down."

Valkyrie looked up, eyes wide, and then the world flickered again and it was gone, and she was in a room and falling, crashing to the ground and smacking her head.

A mop and bucket. Cleaning supplies. A storeroom.

She got up, rubbed her head. Moving quietly, she opened the door and stepped out into a hotel corridor. It was bright, and clean, and normal. She hurried to the nearest window and looked out across Dublin City. Her Dublin City. She took out her phone. Four missed calls, all from Skulduggery. She pressed RETURN CALL and waited for him to answer.

"Hi," she said. "I'm back."

* * *

As if the Elders didn't have enough to deal with, now they had Valkyrie's adventures in Bizarro Land. She felt strangely guilty as they convened, like she was pulling them away from other, more important matters. Ghastly rushed over immediately, asking how she was, if she was hurt. Ravel looked like he wanted to do the same, but he forced himself to sit in the Grand Mage's chair and act like a professional. Only Madame Mist didn't seem like she cared.

Valkyrie told them what had happened, the exact same story she had told Skulduggery, minus a few swear words and sidebars. She had almost reached the point where Remit had mentioned Mevolent's name when Tipstaff entered, apologised unreservedly, and hurried over to whisper in Ravel's ear. Ravel listened, sighed, and thanked him.

"I have to go," he said. "Pressing matters, all that stuff. Valkyrie, I'm glad you're OK, I really am, and I need to hear the rest of the story, but for the moment, business calls. Ghastly tells me you have a plane waiting to take you over the Alps."

Skulduggery tilted his head. "We're not going."

Ravel frowned. "You're not?"

Valkyrie frowned. "We're not?"

"We can't," Skulduggery said. "We need to get Nadir to reverse whatever he did."

"The search for Argeddion takes precedence," said Ravel. "We have to stop whatever he's doing, before any more mortals acquire magical powers. You said yourself that Xebec was probably killed by one of them. This is the priority."

"For you, maybe. But Valkyrie could be pulled back into that other reality at any time, and we need Nadir to stop that from happening."

Ravel shook his head. "Don't make me pull rank on you, Skulduggery. Behind all the jokes and amusement I am still the Grand Mage. You persuaded us to take this job, remember? It's because of you that I'm here, and it's because of you that I'm forced to order you to keep Argeddion as your priority. If Valkyrie gets pulled back in, she can take care of herself. She came back here once, right? She'll do it again. Valkyrie, all you have to do is stay out of trouble."

"There's something we haven't told you yet," Skulduggery said, "about where she went."

"Over there," Valkyrie said, "Mevolent is still alive."

Ravel's eyes widened.

"Their timeline could have been identical to ours," Skulduggery said, "right up to the point where Mevolent died. Obviously, over there, he survived. And now he's in charge."

"You should have seen it," Valkyrie said. "Sorcerers control everything over there. The mortals are terrified. People disappear and are never seen again. There's torture and executions and Sensitives patrol the streets, listening out for guilty thoughts."

"What if Valkyrie is pulled back over there," said Skulduggery, "and she's captured? What if Mevolent questions her? And when she returns, *if* she returns, what if he's touching her, and she brings him back with her? Do we want Mevolent walking the streets of our reality? We got rid of him once, but now he's had another hundred years to grow even more powerful."

Ghastly sat back. "He could invade," he said, his voice quiet.

"He could set up an Isthmus Anchor between dimensions. He could open and close a portal any time he wanted."

"And he already has a Teleporter," said Valkyrie.

"He wouldn't need one," said Mist. "The Diablerie required Fletcher Renn to open their portal because their Anchor stretched between this world, in this dimension, and another world, in another dimension. But Mevolent's Anchor would only need to serve as a link between alternate versions of the same world."

"Which means," Ghastly said, "it would be easier. Which means he could transport whole armies at a time."

Ravel hesitated, then shook his head. "We're talking about possibilities," he said, "but Argeddion is a certainty. We only have a few days before the Summer of Light begins, whatever that is, and even less time to prove to the Supreme Council that we can handle things without their 'help'. I'll arrange to have Nadir transported here so you can talk to him when you get back, but Argeddion is our most immediate threat, and he must be dealt with using everything and everyone we have. Skulduggery, Valkyrie, I'm sorry, but we can't do this without you."

Skulduggery started to speak, but Valkyrie put her hand on his arm. Finding Argeddion meant finding his prison, and finding his prison meant Valkyrie's family had a chance of survival.

"We understand," she said. "We'll take care of Argeddion first."

Skulduggery looked at her, and didn't say anything.

18

A JAR WITH A VIEW

ife was simple, for a head in a jar.

Scapegrace didn't need trousers, for one thing. Or shoes. Or shirts. In fact, clothes as a concept were now completely irrelevant to his wants and needs – with the possible exception of hats. He could wear hats. He could wear an assortment of hats of different shapes and styles. Boater hats, cowboy hats, bowler hats. The list went on. Pork-pie hats, bucket hats, trilbies and panamas. Top hats, straw hats, trapper hats. Wide brim, narrow brim, stingy brim. He could wear a fez. Fezzes were cool. Hadn't someone once said that fezzes were cool? He was pretty sure they had. And they were. They were cool. And he could wear them. He could wear them all.

Not while he was in the jar, of course. It was far too narrow, and filled with a formaldehyde solution to stop what remained of his flesh from rotting away. He could wear a woolly hat, he supposed, or a beanie, if he didn't mind getting it wet. He decided he wouldn't wear baseball caps. Zombie Kings, he reckoned, should not wear baseball caps or trucker caps. Such hats were beneath them. As it were.

As a head, he would have also had the option of wearing sunglasses were it not for the fact that he only had one ear still attached, and his nose had fallen off. That had happened only recently, while Thrasher had been away, so Scapegrace had been forced to watch his nose drift around his head for three hours. It was unsettling, to say the least. No man should be forced to see his nose like that.

When Thrasher returned, he had been all apologies, of course. He wept with shame as he struggled to scoop the nose out of the jar with a little fishing net he'd picked up at a pet store. Every time he'd jabbed Scapegrace he'd let out a howl of anguish. Not for the first time, Scapegrace wished he'd chosen someone else to be the first zombie he'd ever turned.

To make matters worse the jar had been sitting on a table, which meant that Scapegrace was forced to look straight at Thrasher's belly while all this was going on. Several months earlier, the idiot had somehow disembowelled himself with a can opener. The accident, while at first highly amusing, soon became hugely distressing to Scapegrace, as Thrasher's guts kept falling out. In an attempt to keep himself in one piece, Thrasher had tied a sheet round his midsection, and now seemed completely oblivious to how stupid it made him look. Aside from anything else, it wasn't even very effective, as a small piece of dried and shrivelled intestine had escaped its confines and swung merrily every time Thrasher made a move.

Walking up to the Sanctuary, therefore, made it swing with a rhythm that was almost hypnotic – a fact that Scapegrace could attest to as the idiot was carrying him the wrong way round. They stopped suddenly.

"What the hell are you?" asked a sorcerer.

"I'm a zombie," said Thrasher, "and this is my master."

"Your master's a jar?"

"No, my master's *in* the jar."

Scapegrace tried to look up, but all he could see was Thrasher's belly.

"Oh, God, that's disgusting," said the man. "What are you doing here? Why did you come? Do you want us to put you out of your misery?"

"No!" Thrasher said, startled. "No, sir, thank you, we're quite happy with our misery. We just want to speak with Clarabelle. She works with Doctor Nye? She's its assistant?"

"I know who she is. She's that crazy one with the hair. She expecting you?"

"Not really," said Thrasher, "but we're old friends. She'll be happy to see us."

"I doubt that. You smell really bad. But fine, whatever, you can go in. But don't cause any trouble and don't try to eat anyone."

"Thank you," Thrasher said, and suddenly they were moving again, and that piece of intestine was swaying back and forth, back and forth…

They walked through a set of doors and then Scapegrace heard Clarabelle's voice.

"Gerald!" she cried. There was the sound of running feet and then darkness loomed as Thrasher was wrapped up in a hug. It was a tense few moments of sloshing about, but at least the motion turned Scapegrace in his jar, his head lodging diagonally against the glass. Now he was looking at her belly instead of Thrasher's, and that was a definite improvement. Her top had ridden up, and he could see the piercing in her navel. It was a little love-heart.

She released the hug and stepped back. "I thought you were dead! Well, you *are* dead, but I thought you were properly dead, the kind of dead where you don't walk around afterwards. Valkyrie said you'd probably been eaten by monsters down in those caves. I'm really glad you weren't."

"Thank you," said Thrasher, sounding pleased. Idiot. He eventually remembered his job, and put the jar on a table.

Scapegrace had to wait for the liquid to settle before he could talk. "Hello," he said. His confines didn't do him any favours as far as his voice went. Every word he spoke sounded like he was blowing bubbles.

Clarabelle looked around. "Who said that?"

"I did," said Scapegrace. "Look down. No, too far. Look up. At the table. See the jar?"

Clarabelle peered through the glass, and a huge smile broke out. "Oh, wow! Scapey! You're alive, too! Oh, I'm so happy!" She clapped her hands in delight. Scapegrace would have done the same if he'd had any hands.

Clarabelle hunkered down to eye level, and frowned. "There's something different about you."

"I'm in a jar."

"That's probably it. Did you get a haircut?"

"No. I'm in a jar, though."

Clarabelle murmured, not entirely convinced. "I think you're shorter than you were," she said.

"Yes," said Scapegrace, "because I'm in a jar. I'm just a head."

Clarabelle shrugged. "We're all just heads, when you think about it. The only difference between us is that we have arms and legs and bodies and we don't live in jars like you do. It's a nice jar, though. Where did you get it?"

"I got it," Thrasher said. "It was filled with sweets, but I emptied them all out."

"You're very clever."

Thrasher giggled. "Thank you."

"Clarabelle," said Scapegrace before the giggling grew too much, "we need your help."

"Do you need another jar?" she asked. "I don't think I have one that size. I have a flowerpot. Would you like to live in a flowerpot? It's got a hole in the bottom but apart from that it'd be perfect."

"Clarabelle, my situation is dire. I am a bodiless man. If my enemies were to attack, I'd be defenceless."

"Do you have enemies?"

"All great men have enemies."

"But do you have enemies?"

"I... yes. I'm a... I'm a great man."

"Oh."

"And I'm the Zombie King, and many people would love to kill the Zombie King because they fear me and my army of the dead."

"You have an army of the dead?"

"It's... more of a metaphor."

"A metaphor for what?"

"A metaphor for..." Scapegrace hesitated. "...Thrasher. But they still fear me, and without a body I am a... a..."

"A head," Thrasher said helpfully.

"Shut up, you fool."

"Sorry."

Clarabelle sat back on her haunches. "So what do you need me to do?"

"I need to speak to Doctor Nye."

"You already asked it to help you ages ago. It said no. And Doctor Nye doesn't change its mind a lot."

"I told him we shouldn't come back," Thrasher said quietly.

Scapegrace would have swung around to him if he'd had a neck. "Thrasher!"

"Sorry, Master," Thrasher said quickly, "but it's just not a very nice creature, and I don't trust it. I heard it tortured people during the war. I also heard it conducted bizarre human experiments."

"I heard that, too," said Clarabelle in a whisper. "I heard it once turned a man into a goat. Or a goat into a man. Or a goat into another goat. I don't know, I can't remember."

Now Thrasher came around to squat beside Clarabelle and peer into the jar. It wasn't a pretty sight. "You see, Master? This might be a mistake, coming here. We asked it for help once before and it told us to go away."

"That was before I was a head in a jar."

"You think the doctor would reattach your head to your body?" Clarabelle asked.

Scapegrace took a moment to seethe a little bit. "I don't see how, since a horde of rat-things ran away with my body and we've never seen it again. And we know whose fault that was, don't we?"

"Mine," Thrasher said meekly.

"Yours," Scapegrace confirmed.

"But, Master, I couldn't carry both your body *and* you."

"Did you try? Did you even attempt it? No. You didn't."

"Because the White Cleaver was there in the caves, and Skulduggery Pleasant and Valkyrie Cain, and Valkyrie Cain has a history of damaging you."

"Enough excuses!" Scapegrace roared in bubbles.

"Sorry, Master," Thrasher mumbled, head down.

"Scapey," Clarabelle scolded, "don't be mean to Gerald. He does his best, don't you, Gerald?"

"I do," Thrasher whimpered.

"And I don't know if Doctor Nye will even see you. It's very busy right now. It's back there working on top-secret things that it won't tell me about because it thinks I talk too much and it can't trust me. I'm not allowed to even peek. I heard a voice and it was an American accent, and he said a bad word. Do you want to know which one it was? It started with F. It's not the one you're thinking of, though. It's the other one. The one that ends with P. Do you want to know what it was? It was froop." She frowned. "Wait. That's not a word."

"Clarabelle," Scapegrace said, "you're absolutely right. I asked him to help us and he did say no, but that was before. That was when I was merely a zombie. And even though he said no, I could tell he was intrigued."

"Doctor Nye is an it, not a he."

"Then *it* was intrigued. The chance to bring life to a zombie was almost more than it could handle."

"And yet," came a high, raspy voice from behind, "I still managed to say no."

Scapegrace scowled. He could see Thrasher's reaction to Nye's entrance, but the idiot didn't think to turn the jar around.

"Of course you said no," Scapegrace said loudly, "and I couldn't blame you. Bringing life to zombies? How boring. How pedestrian. That's not a job worthy of your talents."

Doctor Nye's knees came into view. Its legs were impossibly long and impossibly thin, the smock it wore grubby and bloodstained.

Those knees bent and Nye's body contorted as it leaned down. That scab of a nose, those small yellow eyes, that mouth, its thin lips punctured by broken thread, twisting into a smile.

"And now you have a job that is worthy of me?" it asked.

"Of course," said Scapegrace. "I'm a zombie head in a jar, I'm unique. I'm a challenge."

"What would you like me to do?"

"I want you to attach me to a new body, Doctor. I want to live again."

Nye laughed, and straightened, immediately towering out of Scapegrace's view. "I think not," it said, and turned to walk away.

"I can pay you," Scapegrace said.

Nye hesitated. Scapegrace could see its long fingers, contorting like a huge spider. Nye swung its head back, its small eyes magnified as it peered in.

"How much?"

"I won't be paying you in money, Doctor. I'll be paying you in something far more valuable."

"I am not a patient creature, zombie-head. Tell me what you have or—"

"The White Cleaver," said Scapegrace. "I have the White Cleaver."

Nye observed him through the glass. "The White Cleaver is destroyed. Lord Vile tore him apart."

"And even then, he was alive. Little bits of finger, twitching on the ground in all of the blood. His right eye was intact, and it was

196

looking around. So I got Thrasher to pick up the pieces – every single little piece – and put them in plastic containers."

"He is functional?"

"You just have to put him back together," said Scapegrace. "So you can do that, and take ownership, after you've attached my head to a new body."

"And mine," Thrasher said.

"We are not sharing," Scapegrace said quickly.

"I mean a new body of my own, Master. This one rots, and my intestines keep falling out."

Scapegrace sighed. "Fine. You find us new bodies, Doctor Nye, and you get to keep the White Cleaver. Someone like you, with your history, I'm sure you could find a use for him."

Nye smiled. "I'm sure I could, zombie-head. Very well. But you should know – this idea of transferring your heads to fresh bodies is ridiculous. Your heads would continue to rot, after all. Instead, I will be transplanting your brains. You will have to say goodbye to what is left of your face."

"I barely *have* a face any more, Doctor. Do we have a deal?"

"Yes, zombie-head. We do. I will arrange for your idiot companion to bring me the remains through a private entrance, and once that is done, I will make you live again."

It was a very dramatic moment, spoiled only by Thrasher saying, "Yippee."

19

JUMPING FROM AIRPLANES

alkyrie was halfway to the Bentley when Ghastly called out to her. She turned, waited as he approached.

"Here," he said, handing her a small box, "this is for your journey."

Valkyrie opened it, pulled out what was inside. "A mask?"

"It should keep you warm," Ghastly said. "Unless you'd prefer a woolly hat and earmuffs?"

She smiled. "This will do fine, thank you."

"It's the same material I used for your clothes, but don't get too carried away. It'll absorb impacts and dissipate the effects, but you're still going to feel it and it's still going to hurt."

"But it's still bulletproof, right?"

Ghastly hesitated. "Yes," he said slowly, "it is bulletproof. Just do me a favour and don't get shot in the head. The mask won't let the bullet through, but the impact alone might be enough to kill you. Valkyrie, please – view this as something to keep your head warm. Nothing more."

"Right," she said. "Thanks."

"There are also some gloves in there."

"You're the best, Ghastly."

"Call me Elder Bespoke when we're in public."

She blinked, and he chuckled and walked away. "I'm so funny," he said.

She grinned and got in the car beside Skulduggery, and they drove to the private airstrip the Sanctuary owned. Their transport was a huge cargo plane that looked like it had seen action in a world war – which one, Valkyrie couldn't be sure. It was big and loud and cold, and they had the entire body of the thing to themselves. She put on her new gloves and tried to go to sleep against the netting, eventually falling into a fitful doze. She was woken, hours later, by Skulduggery.

"We're here," he said over the roar of the engines.

She sat up. It had gone from cold to freezing. Moving a little stiffly, she crossed to a porthole and looked out over the snow-capped peaks of the Alps.

"Wow," she said. "It's just like watching TV."

Skulduggery shook his head. "Yet again, you manage to drain the wonder out of the most impressive of spectacles."

Valkyrie grinned at him. "Are we close to the airport?"

"Airport?"

"Sorry, airstrip. The landing thing. Runway. Whatever."

"Ah," he said. "I'm afraid we won't be landing. This is a round trip for the pilots, no rest stops in between."

Her eyes widened. "We're going to parachute out? Oh my God, I've always wanted to try that!"

"Parachutes," Skulduggery said. "Yeah, they'd probably have been a good idea."

She frowned. "We don't have parachutes?"

"Why would we need them?"

"Because… we're jumping out of a plane."

"You jump out of your bedroom window all the time."

She stared. "That's a little different, Skulduggery. My bedroom window isn't thirty thousand feet off the ground."

"But you still use the air to slow your descent, yes? So do the same here. I don't know what you're so worried about."

"I'm not worried about the jumping," she said. "I'm worried about the falling. I'm worried about the splatting."

He patted her shoulder. "You amuse me," he said, and walked up to the cockpit.

Valkyrie pushed the nerves down, and found herself grinning. She took the mask from her pocket and pulled it on. It covered her whole head save for her eyes and mouth, and there was even a hole in the back for her ponytail to hang from. Like everything Ghastly made, it fitted perfectly, and it warmed her immediately.

Skulduggery came back, holding a GPS device. "Sixty seconds to our destination," he informed her.

She put on her gloves. "What do you think? Do I look amazing?"

"You do indeed."

"Do I look like a ninja?"

"Not a million miles away."

She looked around for a reflective surface, actually found a mirror tied into the netting. Probably there for when paratroopers applied camouflage to their faces or something. She ducked down to see how fantastic she looked, and her grin dropped.

"Oh my God," she said. "I look like a freak."

"You look great," Skulduggery assured her.

"Ghastly made me a freak mask."

"It actually looks rather fetching."

"Yeah, if you're a freak."

"Nonsense. You look perfectly normal. Come on, it's time to jump out of a plane without a parachute."

Still frowning, she followed him to the door. They looked at a light bulb. Waited. Valkyrie's frown left her and she started to grin again.

The bulb lit up, and Skulduggery opened the door and threw himself out. The wind took him, whipped him away. Grinning ever wider beneath her mask, Valkyrie took hold of the bar above the doorway, and with a roar of pure adrenaline she launched herself out after him.

Immediately she was lost in rushing wind. The mountains were unimaginably vast, devastatingly beautiful, stretching to a horizon that flipped around her as she fell. The freezing wind shot up the sleeves of her jacket, down past her collar, up through her trousers. She whooped as she spun through the cold.

Skulduggery was below her, his hat in one hand, the GPS device in the other. She followed where he went, both of them diving down, twisting and arcing. He was more graceful than her, but Valkyrie didn't care. She'd just jumped out of a plane without a parachute. Beneath her mask, she laughed.

She levelled off, arms and legs outstretched, copying Skulduggery. She brought the air in to correct her course, angling for the side of a peak. She didn't want this to stop. Out here, up here, she was as free as she had ever been. The only time she'd approached this level of pure abandonment was when she'd been Darquesse, flying over Dublin City. She remembered the joy, wallowed in it for a moment, then shut away the memory, covering it with shame.

Skulduggery was slowing, the air around him rippling. Valkyrie brought the wind in to buffet her descent, trying to do it gradually, straining to catch the currents. She lost control and spiralled away, reached out to snag something, anything, brought in a gust that flipped her head over heels towards the mountain face. She pushed back against the air and fell, tumbling, calling for help, and then there was a surface approaching and she managed to slow herself enough so that when she slammed into it she didn't break any bones. She rolled, grunting, found something to grab. She hung on, trying to get her bearings, trying to figure out which way was up, and then Skulduggery was there, looking down at her.

"Well," he said, "that was needlessly dramatic."

He walked off, and after a moment, Valkyrie sat up. She looked out over the ledge, at the great expanse of the snow-covered Alps. The beautiful, pristine Alps that had very nearly killed her.

She was sore. The cold was seeping through the eyeholes in her mask, giving her a headache. Her neck was freezing, making her shiver.

"I hate this place," she said loudly. Skulduggery didn't hear. The stupid alpine wind had snatched her words away. Stupid Alps.

She got up stiffly, hurried after him. The plane was already looping around, disappearing into the clouds.

"These are the co-ordinates," he said. "They should be close by."

"I'm cold."

"Then you should have worn a coat."

"I thought my jacket would be enough. It's really cold up here. Why don't you ever bring me somewhere nice? Somewhere warm and sunny? Somewhere I could sit by the pool?"

"You're talking about a holiday."

"No, I'm not. I'm just talking about a case where I have to sit by pools and be warm and get a tan. How hard would it be to find us a case like that?"

"Our next case," he said, "I'll be sure to look out for poolside opportunities for you."

"That's all I ask."

"Hmmm..."

"What?"

He crouched. She crouched, too.

"What?" she asked again.

He pointed ahead of them. "See that?"

"What, the snow?"

"Beyond that."

"More snow?"

"Stop looking at the snow."

"I don't know what you're pointing at. Are you pointing at the mountain? Yes, Skulduggery, I can see the mountain. It's kind of hard to miss. It's a mountain." Something moved in the distance, something with dark fur. Her eyes widened. "Oh my God. Is that an Abominable Snowman?"

"It would appear so," Skulduggery said.

It was hard to make out, but it was big and furry. Valkyrie leaned closer and kept her voice low. "Can I ask you a question? You know with vampires and werewolves and goblins and things, is there any mythological creature that *doesn't* actually exist?"

"Of course," he replied. "The unicorn and the leprechaun would be the two main ones. The Loch Ness Monster isn't real, either, that's just someone called Bert. Any more questions, or can we get back to the situation at hand?"

"Please do."

"Thank you. The Yeti, or the Kang Admi as it is otherwise known, is not indigenous to these parts. In fact, I don't think I've ever heard of one straying from the Himalayas."

"Maybe this one got lost."

"Or maybe Tyren Lament brought it along for security purposes."

"Is it dangerous? It looks dangerous. On a scale of one to ten, how dangerous would it be?"

"Well, if one is a kitten, and ten is a Yeti, then I'd say it's a ten."

"Dear God, I want to hurt you so bad."

"Yetis are strong and fast and fierce. If you see one running at you, it's already too late. We'll have to stay out of sight. By the way, dressing head to toe in black is not the best camouflage when you're in the snow."

"Says the man in the navy-blue suit."

"Ah, but all I have to do is remove my hat and my head blends into the background."

"So then it looks like there's a navy-blue suit running around on its own, which is way less suspicious." Valkyrie looked around. "If Lament did bring the Yeti to act as a doorman, that means the door *must* be somewhere around here."

"Look for anything that seems out of place."

"You mean anything that isn't a rock or a snowflake."

"Exactly."

He stopped suddenly, and Valkyrie looked down at the massive pawprint in the snow.

"So what?" she asked. "We already know it's there."

He shook his head. "I'm not altogether sure that Yeti made this track. At the rate the snow is falling, this should have been covered up by now."

"Which means?"

He looked at her. "Which means there is more than one Yeti."

From behind them there came a growl and Valkyrie whirled, fire filling her hands as the creature charged, and she prepared for the fight of her life.

"Well," Skulduggery said once the fight of her life was over, "that was bracing."

Valkyrie wheezed, and sat up. "It tried to eat my head."

"Yes, I saw that."

"It literally had my head in its mouth."

"What was that like?"

"Smelly. Wet. Horrible. Exactly what you'd expect if a Yeti tried to eat your head. My freak mask saved me."

He helped her to her feet. "You handled yourself admirably."

"You think so?"

"Your constant screaming definitely made it hesitate."

"Yeah, it's a new tactic I'm trying out. Pants-wetting fear. Do you think its mate heard me?"

"I wouldn't say so. The wind carried your screaming in the opposite direction. But we should probably get moving before it comes back. I'd imagine it would be quite irate."

"If you threw me off a mountain, I'd be irate, too."

She walked beside him across the snow, her gloved hands tucked under her armpits. She kept her mouth closed. Her lips were freezing. Her eyeballs, too. The snow was sucking at her boots, trying to pull her down. It didn't take long before her legs got tired.

"Are we nearly there?" she asked, looking around at him for the first time since they started walking. "Hey. You're cheating!"

The snow curled around him but didn't touch him, and the snow on the ground parted for his feet. "Snow is water," he said. "I've been waiting for you to realise this for the past five minutes."

She glared. "My brain is frozen."

"Manipulate the snow just like you would water and you'll be fine."

The gloves Ghastly had made for her were the same as Skulduggery's, meaning she could click her fingers to generate a spark or feel the air to move an object. But for something like water, an element she hadn't spent much time practising with, she needed a bare hand. She took off her right glove, the cold closing round her skin and robbing it of its warmth. She did her best to ignore all that, and focused on making the compacted snow under her boots roll backwards like a wave. But nothing happened. The dynamics were totally different than with free-flowing water. She gritted her teeth and poured her magic into it, and the snow surged, whipping her feet out from under her.

"Found it," Skulduggery said from up ahead.

Growling, Valkyrie struggled up and clomped through the snow to where he was standing. Once, maybe, it had been a cave, but now it was just a mass of snow-covered boulders and rocks. "This looks just like everything else around here," she said. "Are you sure this is it?"

"There's evidence of a bridge out there," he said, nodding his head towards the ledge. "It must have connected this peak to the one next to it. Once all the equipment was shipped in, the bridge was destroyed and the entrance collapsed."

Valkyrie stamped her feet. "So how do we get in?"

Skulduggery pressed his hands against the rock. A moment later, Valkyrie heard a low rumbling. Dust fell. The wall of rocks shifted violently, tearing a hole in itself. Skulduggery stepped back.

"There," he said. "That's as much as I can do while still maintaining the integrity of the wall."

The hole was a narrow gash of an opening, slanting almost at a horizontal angle. Valkyrie was not a fan of tight spaces. "You want us to climb through there?"

"I'll go first," he said, "to make sure it's safe. Hold my hat."

She did so, and watched him crouch by the hole. He slipped his head and shoulders in first, manoeuvred around, then pulled himself through. She watched his shoes disappear.

"How is it?" she called. "What's on the other side?"

"A tunnel," he called back. His hand came through, fingers wiggling. "My hat, please."

She passed it to him, and crouched. She eyed the gap uneasily. Another tight space. "Are you sure I'll be able to fit?"

Skulduggery's face appeared on the other side. "Of course you will. I did."

"But you're a skeleton," she pointed out.

"Yes, but I'm big-boned. You'll be fine."

She looked behind her, at the swirling snow and vast empty whiteness of it all, and sighed. She put her arms through first, getting a good grip, and then put her head and shoulders through. The other side of the cave wall was warm – much too warm to be natural. Skulduggery held fire in his hand so she could see what she was doing. Grunting slightly, she climbed in further, her chest scraping along the rock. When she was halfway through, she slipped sideways a little, down the slant. She tried to pull herself through.

"I'm stuck," she said.

"No, you're not," Skulduggery told her. "Just wriggle, you'll be fine."

"I'm stuck," she insisted, and started laughing despite herself.

Skulduggery tilted his head. "I thought you didn't like tight spaces."

"I don't. I'm kind of panicking, but my bum is jammed. How can you not laugh when your bum is jammed? Help me."

He took her hands and pulled.

"Oh my God," she said, doing her best to stop giggling, "that's doing absolutely nothing. Could you *please* get me out of here?"

"But of course, dear." He reached in, gripped her waistband and pulled her out of the narrower end. He hooked his hands under her arms and dragged her the rest of the way through. Once back on her feet, she brushed the dust from her clothes and took off her mask, grinning at him.

"Never mention this to anyone," she said, stuffing the mask and gloves into her jacket.

"Your secret is safe with me."

They walked down the sloping tunnel, holding fire in their hands until the darkness shifted to mere gloom, and then brightened. They let the flames go out and proceeded cautiously.

The ground turned into a metal grille. Thick support struts criss-crossed overhead and glowing orbs hung from them, as if someone had caught handfuls of daylight and brought them underground. They passed through corridors of rock walls. The air was fresh, and carried a scent of cut grass and flowers. It was a warm summer's day down here in this mountain.

A bird flew past, disappearing around the corner.

"Well," Valkyrie said, "that's just unexpected, is what that is."

They walked on until the corridor widened, and in this widened corridor a man wandered by. Valkyrie recognised him from his file. Kalvin Accord. Adept, specialising in science-magic. Now dressed in what looked like a bathrobe and sandals.

"Kalvin," Skulduggery said gently.

Kalvin whipped around, eyes wide. Stared at them.

Skulduggery took a step forward. "Sorry. We didn't want to startle you. How are you?"

"Oh, this isn't good," Kalvin murmured. "Oh, this isn't good at all."

He turned and ran.

Skulduggery glanced at Valkyrie, and they started jogging after him.

"Kalvin," Skulduggery called. "There's nothing to be worried about. Please, just stop and talk to us."

But Kalvin kept running. Granted, it wasn't a very impressive run – there's only so fast a person can move wearing sandals. He stumbled and one of the sandals came flying off, and he went on without it. Valkyrie picked it up on the way past.

Skulduggery caught up to him and they ran side by side. "Hi, Kalvin," he said.

Kalvin whined.

Valkyrie appeared at his other elbow. She held the sandal out as they ran. "I picked this up for you."

Kalvin was panting. "Thank you," he said, taking it from her.

"Why are you running away from us?" she asked.

"I'm not sure," he answered. "But now that I'm doing it, I may as well keep going."

"Except you're not really running away from us," Skulduggery pointed out.

"True," he gasped. "But I don't think I can stop. I want to stop. I do. But I don't think I can."

"Just slow down," Valkyrie said. "Come on, just slow down. That's it. A little more."

They slowed the run back to a jog, and Kalvin's legs started to wobble. He veered away from them and ran into the wall, then collapsed and rolled across the floor, clutching his side.

"Stitch," he explained when they looked down at him.

"You don't get an awful lot of exercise down here, do you?" Skulduggery said.

"Not really..."

"Do you want a hand up?"

"If it's OK with you... I'll just stay down here... for another moment."

"No problem."

"Why... why are you here?"

"It's about Argeddion."

"Then you're going to want to talk to Tyren." Kalvin took another few breaths, and sat up. "He is *not* going to be happy to see you."

20

LAMENT'S SORCERERS

Tyren Lament was definitely *not* happy to see them. Skulduggery and Valkyrie sat at the long table in the dining hall, and Lament stood looking at them with his arms crossed. He looked to be around forty, with long fair hair. He had a long nose and sharp, intelligent eyes. He was dressed identically to Kalvin. From the glimpses Valkyrie had snatched of the other sorcerers on the way here, robes and sandals seemed to be the uniform for mountain-dwelling mages.

"How did you find us?" were his first words to them.

"It wasn't easy," Skulduggery said.

He looked annoyed. "It was *supposed* to be impossible. We didn't go to all this trouble to be 'hard to find'. We did it to disappear."

"We'd never have come looking for you if it wasn't for Argeddion," said Valkyrie. "He's doing something to ordinary people, giving them magic."

Lament shook his head. "Impossible. No one can transfer magic in any way to anyone who doesn't already have magic within them."

"For all we know," said Skulduggery, "these mortals *did* have magic within them. But if they did, it was dormant. They didn't know anything about it."

"And what do you think Argeddion has done to them? Because whatever you suspect, I can assure you, he didn't do it. He's been resting in a coma-state for the past thirty years."

"You're sure?"

"Quite sure. He is closely monitored at every moment. The slightest increase in neural activity would be picked up on. Whoever is doing this to the mortals, it's not Argeddion."

"If it's not," said Skulduggery, "then it's someone connected to him somehow. We'd like to see him, all the same."

"I'm afraid I can't allow that."

"Why not?"

"Because I don't want to. You've already breached our outer perimeter – I can't allow you to breach the inner one. I knew you thirty years ago, Skulduggery, but a man can change in thirty years."

"You don't trust me."

"I don't. And I don't even know your companion."

"We've saved the world," Valkyrie said.

"And on behalf of this little part of that world, I thank you," said Lament. "But you're still not getting close to Argeddion, I'm sorry."

Skulduggery sighed, and sat back. "Can we ask about the facility here?"

Lament sat opposite them. "Of course."

"How many can it hold?"

"I'm not sure what you mean."

"If there were another sorcerer like Argeddion, someone who found out their true name, could they be kept here, too?"

Lament paled. "There's another?"

"This is just hypothetical."

"Hypothetical questions are a prelude to actual questions," Lament said. "You told me that once. There is another?"

"There might be," Skulduggery admitted. "Hopefully, there won't, but there might be. Maybe your psychics here have picked up on it. A sorcerer named Darquesse."

Lament nodded. "We've heard of her. We didn't know that's how she got her power, though. Do you know anything about her?"

"No one does," said Skulduggery. "All we have is the vague promise that she will eventually turn up. How would you stop her?"

"If she hasn't realised who she is yet, I'd use her true name against her."

"And if she's already sealed it?" Valkyrie asked.

Lament exhaled slowly. "Then you're in trouble. You want to know how we subdued Argeddion, don't you? You want to use this technique against Darquesse? I'm afraid you travelled all this way to be disappointed."

Skulduggery tilted his head. "So how did you stop him?"

"There really was nothing to stop," said Lament. "From what I've been told, Darquesse will be a force of destruction. How she comes to be this way, no one knows. But Argeddion was not like that."

"We spoke with Greta Dapple," Skulduggery said. "According to her, Walden D'Essai was a pacifist. When he became Argeddion, this didn't change."

Lament nodded. "This is true, but... Up until D'Essai, eight sorcerers over the course of human existence have learned their true names. Eight that we know of, anyway. Three of these were killed soon after, before they could exploit what they'd learned. Two of them couldn't control their power and ended up killing themselves. Two more had their true names used against them and became virtually powerless. And the eighth one simply vanished. We presume he obliterated himself. No one who has ever learned their true name has been able to live peacefully."

"So while Argeddion was a pacifist and showed no inclination towards violence, you didn't want to take the chance that he could change his mind."

"It wasn't an easy decision to make. I liked Walden. He was a good man. I trusted him. I couldn't trust Argeddion. How could I? All it would take is one bad day. Maybe that's what sets Darquesse off. Maybe she's a normal sorcerer, doing good work, but sometime in the near future she's going to have one really bad day, and she'll make the world suffer for it."

"So what did you do?"

Lament hesitated. "Argeddion enjoyed talking about the things he was learning. Every day he'd develop a new ability, or he'd understand a new law of magic that no one else had even guessed at. He talked about the Source. He talked about the Cradles of Magic and how they related to each other and how they affected everything around them. He was a fascinating man. He was starting to view things in a completely new way."

"And then you ambushed him."

"We did. The problem with adopting a radical new perspective is that you lose your old one. We couldn't afford to let him abandon his humanity. We couldn't let him start to value magic over people."

"Was that where he was headed?"

"Possibly. Very possibly. The moment I realised this, I knew we had run out of time. So we ambushed him."

"How?" asked Valkyrie.

"When Walden was a child, his mother was murdered right in front of him. Her killer, a man who was never caught, turned to Walden and spoke to him. He said three words to a traumatised little boy, and ran. We found out what those three words were, and we used them against him. He froze, and we struck. We didn't use violence. We just trapped him, sent him to sleep. He hasn't woken up since."

"How did you send him to sleep?"

"We targeted his brainwaves. Took them over, regulated them... He was asleep within moments."

"Could we use that against Darquesse?"

"I don't know. Argeddion underestimated us. Maybe it was his new power, making our attempts against him look harmless. Whatever the reason, he didn't view us as a threat, and so he was already calm when we struck. Darquesse, from what I've heard, is not going to be calm. If you tried this against her, she'd fight it and win easily."

"But if we managed it," Skulduggery pressed, "could she be contained in here?"

"Here? No. This entire facility is equipped for only one patient. But if you were to build an exact replica of this place, I don't see why not. She would need constant monitoring and supervision, however."

"If she was trapped in somewhere like this," Valkyrie said, "that'd be it, though, wouldn't it? There'd be no chance of talking to her, of getting her to control herself or anything like that?"

"That would be impossible. The only reason Argeddion hasn't escaped is because he's been kept in an artificially induced coma. We can't allow him to wake up – ever. With Darquesse, it would be even more important to keep her sedated. If you give someone like that a moment of consciousness, she'd kill you and everyone else."

"Well," Valkyrie said, frowning, "that sucks."

Lament looked surprised. "You'd prefer the alternative?"

"No," she said quickly. "No, I was just thinking, from her perspective that sucks, not from our… Never mind. Could we have a copy of the plans?"

"I don't see why not," said Lament. "But do you have enough

people to monitor her? Do you have anyone who'd be willing to give up the rest of their life to spend with her?"

"I would," Skulduggery said.

Valkyrie looked away.

A girl rushed in. Petite, blonde hair, huge eyes, somewhere in her twenties. "People," she gasped. "But…"

Lament smiled. "It's OK. They're not our enemies. Lenka Bazaar, this is Skulduggery Pleasant and Valkyrie Cain."

Valkyrie stood to shake her hand and Lenka jumped on her, wrapping her up in the biggest bear hug Lenka's little arms could manage. "People!" she screamed. "There are people here! New people!"

Valkyrie couldn't help but laugh, and finally Lenka released her.

"Hi. I'm Lenka. Will you be my friend?"

"Uh," said Valkyrie, "sure."

"Tyren," Lenka said immediately, "I only have room for a certain number of friends in my life, so you're not my friend any more. I'm really sorry."

"I'm sure I'll survive."

Lenka grinned at Valkyrie. "I don't want to alarm you," she said, "but there's a skeleton in a hat standing behind you."

"Don't worry, he's supposed to be there," Valkyrie said with a smile.

"Very pleased to meet you," Skulduggery said, shaking her hand.

"Lenka is the youngest of us," said Lament, "a Sensitive and a gifted engineer in her own right."

"I never thought I'd ever meet someone new," Lenka said, her eyes still wide. "I thought that the three people I'm down here with were the only people I'd ever know for the rest of my life. And now look. Two more people! And one of them's the coolest person I've ever seen!"

"Thank you," said Skulduggery.

"I was talking about her," Lenka said, and Valkyrie laughed.

"Have you seen the Arboretum? Tyren, have you shown them the Arboretum?

"They've only just arrived—"

"Then it's high time they saw the Arboretum!" Lenka announced, seizing Valkyrie's hand. "Come! The tour!"

Valkyrie cast a look back as Lament turned to Skulduggery. "Do you want me to hold your hand?"

"I'd rather you didn't."

"Perfectly understandable," Lament said, and they followed Lenka and Valkyrie out of the door.

They met Vernon Plight on the way. He was a narrow, dark-skinned man with a warm smile. Valkyrie had read his file. He was almost 300 years old and an Adept, with a reputation as a fierce soldier. He knew Skulduggery and they exchanged a few friendly words before Lenka dragged them on.

"This is a momentous occasion," said Lament. "When do we ever get the chance to show someone the Arboretum for the first time? Skulduggery, Valkyrie, welcome."

They stepped through a wide doorway into a vast cavern, and

in this cavern a rainforest sat. The heat, the humidity, the sounds of streams and waterfalls and birds and insects met them and enveloped them.

"Oh my God," Valkyrie said.

Even Skulduggery was impressed. "This is remarkable."

Lament smiled. "This is our very own biosphere, maintained by Lenka and Kalvin. There are adjoining caverns, each with a different kind of environment, but this is definitely the biggest. We've had to forgo a few luxuries, but we grow our own food here. Whatever we need. Whatever we want, really. We even have our own coffee beans. It's actually quite good."

"Are those monkeys up there?" Valkyrie asked, craning her neck.

Lament nodded. "We have animals, birds, insects... It's a self-perpetuating ecosystem. It helps to make life interesting."

"I imagine boredom would be a major problem," Skulduggery said.

"It is, but we have access to the outside world thanks to Kalvin. When he isn't helping me maintain the facility's essential systems, he's building relays and whatnot to view films and read the latest books... I don't understand technology at all, to be honest, but Kalvin... Kalvin can access the world without leaving a trail that leads back here. He is invaluable."

"That must be difficult," Skulduggery said, "to view the world but not be a part of it."

"That was the big debate we had when we first started," Lament told them. "Do we cut ourselves off completely? I was in favour of total informational shutdown. I thought the alternative would be too hard to handle. But now I see the value in being open to it all. It reminds us of why we do what we do."

A butterfly landed on Skulduggery's finger. "I have to say, you have my admiration," he said. "What you're doing is astonishingly good and decent. I tend to forget there are people like you out there." The butterfly flew away again.

Lament smiled. "We're not saints, Skulduggery. We argue and squabble like the most ill-tempered family you've ever seen. But that's what we've become. A family."

"It's a shame no one knows what you're doing," said Valkyrie.

"They can't know." Urgency entered Lament's voice now. "You can't tell *anyone* about this place. It's bad enough you're here – and I mean that in the nicest possible way. But there are sorcerers out there who would tear this facility down with their bare hands to get at Argeddion – either to find out what he knows, or simply to unleash him into the world. They would ignore the simple fact that controlling him is impossible, and focus only on the rewards they think he would bring. Can you imagine what would happen if a Sanctuary were to send its Cleavers in here? Once we were all dead, they'd start their experiments, and Argeddion would inevitably awaken."

"There are people out there you can trust," said Skulduggery. "Starting with us."

Lament looked at him, looked at them both, and didn't respond.

21

ARGEDDION

At night, the orbs that lit the mountain facility grew gradually dimmer, and deep hues of orange and red began to sneak through before being replaced by the silver, grey and blue tones of moonlight.

They spent the evening in the living room. Lenka explained that they had gone through phases of calling it the common room and the social area, before deciding that living room just sounded more comfortable. There were sofas and armchairs and tables and pictures on the walls and a massive screen down one end.

"How do you pass the time here?" Valkyrie asked when Lenka had finished explaining everything.

Vernon Plight laughed. "It can get quite boring at times," he admitted. "We watch television and we play music, but mostly we've found ways to amuse ourselves."

"Really?" Valkyrie asked. "Like what?"

Plight's smile faded. "Like human sacrifice."

He grabbed one arm and Lenka grabbed the other and Valkyrie cried out.

Then they both let go, laughing.

"Naw," Plight said, "we just play board games."

Lenka doubled up with laughter. "Your face!" she squealed. "Your face when you thought we were going to kill you!"

Valkyrie glared at them. "That," she said, "is not funny."

"It's a little funny," Lament said, passing the door.

"It's not funny at all," Valkyrie insisted. "Skulduggery, tell them."

"I wish I'd had a camera," he said, shaking his head.

"I hate all of you. Every single one of you."

Kalvin Accord came in.

"She fell for it!" gasped Lenka. "She fell for the human sacrifice bit!"

Kalvin chortled, he actually *chortled*, and turned around and walked out again.

"I hate you all," Valkyrie said miserably.

It may have been the mountain air, but Valkyrie awoke refreshed the next morning, full of energy, thinking good thoughts and feeling positive. She showered, dressed, and met Lenka for breakfast. They had freshly picked fruit and freshly squeezed orange juice.

"And now," said Lenka, rubbing her stomach, "we have freshly slaughtered pig."

Valkyrie made a face. "You kill your own animals?"

"It's not like we can pop out to the nearest supermarket," Lenka said, laughing. "Pig. Pork chops. Bacon. Oh my God, bacon..."

She closed her eyes and smiled. Valkyrie frowned.

Then Lenka sighed, and looked up. "We don't have pig," she said sadly. "We have the animals and the birds in the Arboretum but we don't touch them. We can't. Those monkeys are too cute."

"So why didn't you bring some pigs? When you started, I mean."

"Oh, we did. But they escaped. They're loose somewhere in this mountain and every year, their numbers grow. Sometimes at night you can hear them, calling to each other. It's quite spooky, in an oinky sort of way."

"I... don't know whether to believe you or not."

"Probably wise. But then we all decided it would just be easier to become vegetarians, so we did. Do you eat meat?"

"Yes."

Lenka sat forward, eyes sparkling. "What was the last piece of meat you ate?"

"Uh," said Valkyrie, "I don't know, it was... It was before I got on the plane. I brought a sandwich with me. Chicken and stuffing."

"Chicken!" Lenka exclaimed. "How was it? How did it taste?"

"It was OK. It tasted fine. Like chicken."

"Wow," said Lenka. "It tasted like chicken. I envy you so much, being able to eat chicken and being able to do... things. I'd love to spend a day in the world. Just walking around. Going into shops. Going to a concert. Sitting in an office."

"An office?"

"Oh, yeah. And everyone's wearing shirts and ties and arguing about annual reports and the photocopier not working... That'd be heaven."

"Are you sure?"

"The hum that phosphorescent lights make – is it as comforting as I remember?"

"Uh..."

"I miss that sound so much." She looked away, and after a moment Valkyrie became aware of a very low hum that was coming from Lenka's direction.

Valkyrie cleared her throat. "Can I ask you something?"

Lenka stopped humming. "Sure."

"Why did you come here? I mean, I can't imagine making that decision, to leave everything behind just to watch over one person that you don't even know."

Lenka smiled. "Tyren asked. How could I refuse? I'd just started working for the Sanctuary, and I was full of ideals and pure thoughts. Once you start working there, you give yourself over to a higher duty, don't you? You become a protector. You're ready to give your life to ensure the safety of others."

"That's a very dramatic way of looking at things."

"I'm a very dramatic person. But I'm sure you're the same."

"Dramatic?"

"Willing to give your life for the safety of others."

"Eh, I don't think so. Have you met those others? Most of them are idiots."

"So there is no one you would die for?"

Valkyrie went quiet for a moment. "I'd die for my parents and my sister."

"See?" Lenka said. "Out there, in the world, there are people I would die for. They are the reason I'm here. They are the reason I've sacrificed a normal life. I do this to keep them safe."

"I hope they appreciate it."

"Sadly, they will never know. They think I just disappeared one day. I couldn't even leave them a note."

"My God. That's the most... selfless thing I've ever heard."

"Then you should talk to the others," Lenka said with a little laugh. "They've all sacrificed just as much as me, if not more. But we do what we do to make the world a safer place. When it gets cold here, really cold, that thought keeps me warm."

"I... I want to hug you."

"Hugging also keeps me warm."

Valkyrie hugged her and Lenka laughed again.

"When you're quite finished," Skulduggery said, walking by.

Valkyrie got up. "See you around?" she said to Lenka.

Lenka held up her hands. "It's kind of inevitable."

Valkyrie caught up to Skulduggery. "These people are really nice. I'm not used to nice people. I'm used to you."

"I'm nice," he said.

"I can't believe that *you* are what I now think of as normal, so that whenever I meet nice people they seem like weirdos."

"I'm very nice."

"You insult everyone you meet."

"Not every *single* person. I don't have time to insult every *single* person. And have I insulted anyone since we got here? No, I have not, because I am, as I said, nice."

"I don't think I'd be as nice as these guys if I'd been stuck here for the last thirty years. What kind of person do you think you'd need to be in order to spend thirty years in a mountain?"

"I don't know," Skulduggery said. "The kind of person who loves mountains, perhaps?"

"I don't think I'd be able to handle it."

"Me neither. I'd say you'd be quite cranky. But Lament picked them for a reason. They each have the right temperament. They each have a little thing called patience."

Valkyrie snapped her fingers. "See, that's why I'd be useless in here."

"It's definitely one of the reasons."

She scowled at him.

The corridor split and they veered left until they came to the only room in there that didn't have natural rock for walls. The laboratory was all stainless steel and polished surfaces, as precise and detailed as anything Valkyrie had ever seen in the Sanctuary. It was sleek and so compact that she almost missed the fact that the room was packed full of machinery and monitors. Lament sat in the corner, drinking tea.

"Hi," Valkyrie said as they approached.

"He can't hear you," Skulduggery told her. "See his eyes? See the way they move? He's working."

"He's drinking tea."

"His body is drinking tea. His mind is in the circuitry."

She looked around. "What, in all this?"

"Why bother looking at a computer when you can *be* the computer?"

"That's... kind of creepy."

Lament stood up. "Indeed it is."

"Oh! Sorry..."

"No need to apologise. When I was your age, my mother did her best to persuade me to study a more conventional discipline of magic, but science was always too dear to my heart. Thanks for waiting. I just had some tests I needed to finish up. Did you sleep well?"

"I did," said Valkyrie. "Thank you."

"I have to ask your forgiveness, actually, for last night. You caught me unawares, as you can imagine. You came all the way here to see how we managed to contain Argeddion, and it would be churlish of me to deny you. Please, this way." He led them through a door, standing to one side and presenting his creation with a flourish.

The room was a mass of alloy and wood, with magical symbols

carved on every surface. Four steel arms protruded from the corners, stretched towards the middle where they almost met. Hovering between the tips of these arms was a cage of energy that crackled with power, and within that cage was a man. Dressed in a white bodysuit, Argeddion rotated gently in mid-air, his eyes closed and his expression peaceful. He looked young, maybe around thirty years old. He had black hair, cut short, and a clean-shaven face. He didn't look like the kind of man who would destroy the world if he woke up.

Directly beneath the cage was a metre-high glass pyramid, in which raged a small storm of energy. The pyramid had wires and cables running from its base to a padded chair set into a metal arch, decorated in sigils and circuitry.

"Six hours every day," said Lament, "one of us sits here, strapped in and hooked up."

"What's the pyramid for?" Valkyrie asked.

Skulduggery answered instead of Lament. "Their magic is drawn out of them and stored in there, am I right? Presumably to power Argeddion's cage."

"Very good," Lament said, clearly impressed. "We call it the Cube, though. A cage is something you keep an animal in. The pyramid is called the Tempest. Our magic is collected inside it, pretty turbulently but not dangerously so, and then siphoned off to maintain the Cube's integrity."

Skulduggery nodded. "And is one person a day really all it needs?"

"A *lot* of power was required when the Cube was first created,"

Lament said, "but only a minimal amount is needed to keep it going. That's the beauty of it."

"And what if something goes wrong?" Valkyrie asked.

Lament nodded towards a big red button. "This," he said, "is the Big Red Button. If there's an emergency, I press this and the Tempest empties itself into the Cube, reinforcing it. It means it wouldn't have to be recharged for three days. Hopefully, that would give us enough time to fix whatever emergency had occurred and get back to our normal routine. We haven't had to use it yet. Hopefully, we never will."

"This is quite a machine," Skulduggery said, examining the chair. "If all gaols had this level of technology, there'd be no more break-outs."

"But then we'd have the Nadir problem," Valkyrie said. "What's the point of sending criminals to prison if they're going to sleep their way through their sentence?"

Lament shook his head. "They wouldn't have to be asleep," he said. "Roughly a third of the power we collect is dedicated to making sure Argeddion stays in a coma-state, but he could just as easily be conscious. Naturally, with Argeddion, that would be a bad thing, as the Cube itself wouldn't be enough to contain him. But for anyone else it would be more than sufficient."

Skulduggery approached the Cube. "Has there been any ageing?" he asked. "That long without magic should have had some effect by now, no matter how slight."

"He doesn't *appear* to have aged," said Lament. "We didn't expect that, to be honest. Maybe it's because of his evolved state of being or maybe it's a side effect of keeping him in a coma, but according to our tests he hasn't aged even one day."

"So what's your plan? You're going to keep him contained until *you* all die of old age? Then what?"

"We're still trying to figure that out."

"You've obviously considered killing him."

"That is not an option."

"Destroy the brain, Tyren. Destroy it before his survival instincts kick in."

"We didn't go to all this trouble just to end the life of the man in our care."

"It may be mean-spirited but it's a practical solution to a problem that has precious few."

Lament shook his head. "There is always another way."

"But there's not always a *better* way."

"Skulduggery, even if we wanted to end his life, I'm not even sure that we could. His mind is asleep but his body could still heal itself. And someone of Argeddion's power... I'm not sure there's any wound we could inflict that would be enough to kill him instantly."

"Then how do we stop him from spreading the infection? We had a *werewolf* in Ireland, Tyren. It has to stop."

"We're not even agreed that Argeddion is responsible. The man is comatose."

"The subconscious is more powerful than you know, Tyren. I've seen it myself, firsthand. It's possible that Argeddion's subconscious is infecting the minds of those susceptible and actually transferring magic to them remotely. And if this did all start a few weeks ago, then it leads me to only one possible conclusion."

Lament frowned. "Argeddion is waking up."

"His mind is becoming active."

"Impossible. No, I'm sorry, Skulduggery, but there has been no change in our readings. No unusual brain activity, nothing like that. Lenka is in here every day, scanning his mind. If anything was going on, surely a Sensitive would pick it up?"

"Not necessarily. It's possible to throw up a false reading. It's been done before."

"But only by the most powerful of psychics."

"And is Argeddion not the most powerful of everything right now?"

Lament hesitated.

"You're right," Skulduggery said. "There has not been one single Sensitive around the world who has even heard of Argeddion. But we visited a prison where the more unstable inmates, those more susceptible to this kind of thing, were scrawling his name on the walls. He visits people in their dreams, Tyren. He's doing something to the mortals, something to do with a Summer of Light. We have less than four days to figure out what that is. He has to be stopped."

"And I told you, I don't know how to do that."

"What about telling the Elders?" Valkyrie asked. "I know it wasn't safe in the past, but now Ghastly Bespoke and Erskine Ravel are in charge, and you can trust them."

"And can we trust Madame Mist, a Child of the Spider?"

"Well," said Valkyrie, "no, but she can be kept at a distance. You can get back-up there. The Sanctuary can support you. It'd mean you wouldn't have to live here any more, you could go back to your lives. We could all share the responsibility and, I don't know, maybe make the Cube stronger."

"That's an idea," Skulduggery said slowly. "If we do make the Cube stronger, it would block Argeddion's subconscious from wandering off and infecting anyone else. I've seen the blueprints, and it seems to me that there's absolutely no reason why the Cube couldn't be reinforced two, three times over."

"Now, just wait a second," Lament said. "You're both speeding on ahead."

"It's possible, though, isn't it?" Skulduggery asked.

Lament hesitated. "Yes."

"And a reinforced Cube would mean Argeddion does not wake up."

"But the risk involved with acknowledging his existence..."

"Would immediately be overshadowed by the risk of Argeddion opening his eyes."

"I don't know. You're asking us to abandon our plan."

"The moment you realised he wasn't ageing, that plan became null and void. The Cube can be reinforced, right?"

"Yes, of course it can, but the power needed to maintain a

reinforced Cube would kill anyone who charged it. The Tempest would drain them in an instant of both their magic and their lives, and then you'd need another mage to charge it. No, sorry. It's impossible."

"I don't see how the process would be any different to the way it is now. The Tempest is just a storage chamber, after all."

Lament shook his head. "Not when you're dealing with this level of power. There'd be no more storage – everything would be instant. The magic would be donated, sucked through the Tempest, and within nanoseconds it would be crackling around the Cube. In order for your plan to succeed, the Cube would have to be hooked up to a constant source of massive, massive power. And I'm sorry, but that cannot..."

He faltered.

"What?" Valkyrie asked.

"Nothing," Lament said. "It can't be done."

"You were going to say something. What was it?"

Lament looked away. "I need to talk to my colleagues." Without waiting for an answer, he walked out.

Valkyrie looked at Skulduggery, and shrugged. "*That's* promising."

22

CONVERSATIONS WITH MY KILLER

Plastic containers full of body parts threatened to nudge Scapegrace's jar over the edge of the table. They were stacked six high and still Thrasher was bringing them in through Nye's secret entrance. Scapegrace wouldn't have thought that a human body would have so many little pieces to collect, but apparently it had – unless Thrasher had accidentally scooped up a load of pebbles when he'd collected the White Cleaver's remains. Which, knowing Thrasher, wasn't exactly unlikely.

Through the liquid all around him, Scapegrace heard the idiot's slow, plodding footsteps, back with another few containers. Nye was going to have some job putting all this back together. Still, if there was one creature who'd probably appreciate a new hobby like that, it was Doctor Nye. And then suddenly Scapegrace was sliding over the edge of the table.

"Hey!" he screamed. "Stop!"

The jar started to topple, the liquid tilting him upside down, and then Thrasher was there, diving to catch him.

"Oh, Master!" the idiot wailed, clutching the jar to his bosom. "I'm so sorry! Are you OK? Oh, Master, please speak to me! Please say something!"

"I will," Scapegrace growled, "as soon as you shut up."

Thrasher was practically weeping with joy. "Oh, thank heavens. Oh, thank heavens."

"Find somewhere else to put me," Scapegrace said, "as far away from you as possible."

Thrasher looked around, eventually deciding on a room in the back of the Medical Bay. There was an area that was curtained off, but beside that was a table. He put the jar there, and then plodded off, probably to cry. Scapegrace bobbed around a bit before coming to a stop. The curtain wasn't pulled over all the way, and he could see a patient lying on a bed, his midsection wrapped in bandages and soaked in mud. He was wearing sunglasses indoors. Even before he turned his head Scapegrace knew who he was.

Billy-Ray Sanguine looked at him without expression, so Scapegrace returned the favour. He wasn't going to be intimidated by the man who'd killed him. He was beyond that now. He'd changed. Grown. He was the Zombie King, and who was Sanguine?

Just some annoying American with a stubble-covered jawline and good muscle tone. So what? At least Scapegrace had *eyes*, and one of them even worked.

He looked right at Sanguine and Sanguine looked right at him. Neither man looked away. It was a matter of pride now. It had become something more than a mere staring contest. Now it was about dominance. It was about superiority. It was about strength. And Scapegrace was damned if he was going to be the one to look away first. Although he did feel that wearing sunglasses was technically cheating.

Moving slowly, Sanguine sat up. Pressing an arm to his bandages, he got off the bed. He groaned slightly with the effort, pulled the curtain open wider, and walked the few paces to the table. Scapegrace's mind churned with possible insults and comebacks. The first words out of Sanguine's mouth were going to be nasty, he knew that much.

Sanguine leaned down and they looked at each other, face to face. Then Sanguine tapped the glass with his finger. "Ugly little critter, ain't ya?"

"Takes one to know one," Scapegrace retorted triumphantly, and Sanguine screamed and leaped back, hit the bed and fell backwards over it, collapsing into a heap on the other side.

Scapegrace stared.

Nye and Thrasher rushed in and immediately went to Sanguine's aid. They picked him up and laid him back on the bed. He was obviously in a great deal of pain.

"What happened?" Nye asked, checking the bandages. "I told you no movement."

Sanguine pointed. "You got a head in a jar."

"So?"

"It spoke to me!"

"What did you think it was going to do, shake your hand? You could have pulled your stitches. You must remain still while you heal. I explained this to you."

Sanguine grabbed Nye's coat, pulled the creature in close. "Why," he said through gritted teeth, "is there a goddamn head in a jar talkin' to me?"

"You talked to me first," Scapegrace pointed out.

Sanguine lay back. "Somebody shut it up. It's freakin' me out."

"It's your own fault," Scapegrace said.

"On principle alone, I refuse to have a conversation with a decapitated head."

"You're the one who killed me!"

Sanguine looked around. "I make it a point of rememberin' who and how I killed, and I ain't never chopped someone's head off."

"My head was on when you killed me. I am Vaurien Scapegrace."

"I'm happy for you."

"You murdered me and your father turned me into the walking dead!"

Sanguine frowned. "Hey, I remember you now. You're that guy..."

"Yes."

"The idiot."

"What? No."

"You're the moron who pretended he was an assassin, and then you lost control of your own zombies."

"I didn't lose control of them," Scapegrace said. "They lost control of me."

Thrasher stepped forward. "He's the Zombie King now."

"Good God," Sanguine said. "It's another one. How many of these things do you have here?"

"Two too many," Nye said absently.

"Well, at least this one has his head on. But how do you stand the smell?"

Nye pressed its fingers against Sanguine's stomach. "I don't have a nose. Does this hurt?"

"Yeah."

"Good."

"Why is *he* here?" Scapegrace asked. "The last I heard, this man was wanted for a variety of crimes. At the very least he killed *me*."

Nye looked up. "You and I have a deal, zombie. You give me what I want, and I give you what you want. I have the same sort of deal with Mr Sanguine here. I expect discretion from all my patients."

"I think we should flush him down the toilet," Sanguine said.

"Don't you dare!" Thrasher screeched, jumping in front of the jar so that now all Scapegrace could see was the way the back of his trousers sagged.

"Oh, God," Sanguine said, disgust in his voice. "Is that his intestine? It is, ain't it? Look at it swingin' there. For God's sake, man, put it away. That's disgustin'."

Scapegrace closed his eyes in embarrassment.

"I am who I am," Thrasher proclaimed proudly.

"Hey, you go fly your freak flag high, but you just tuck that little bit of yourself back in so you don't scar no minds. Have some dignity."

Thrasher turned away dramatically, hands on his hips, and his little piece of shrivelled intestine slapped against Scapegrace's jar. "You don't tell me what to do. Only Master Scapegrace, the Zombie King, can order me around."

"Put it away, Thrasher," Scapegrace said.

Thrasher blinked down at him. "Sir?"

"Tuck it in, you idiot."

Thrasher's lower lip quivered, and he rushed out of the room. Scapegrace sighed, and looked at Sanguine and Nye as the doctor finished its inspection.

"You're lucky," it said. "But if you move off this bed again, I'll snip every last one of your stitches myself."

It walked to the door, and Sanguine frowned after it. "Hey, you just gonna leave this head talkin' to me? Hey, Nye, at least turn it so that it's lookin' the other way or somethin'!"

But Nye was already gone. Sanguine glowered, and lay back.

Minutes ticked by. Finally, he looked over. "So what happened?"

"What happened when?"

"I mean how'd you lose your head?"

"I didn't lose my head," said Scapegrace. "I lost my body."

"How'd you lose your body, then?"

"The White Cleaver cut it off."

Sanguine nodded, and it went quiet again. Then he said, "Wanna play I spy?"

Scapegrace would have shrugged if he'd had shoulders. "Sure," he said.

23

THE PLOT

"How much do you know about Roarhaven?"

Valkyrie and Skulduggery sat in the mountain facility's living room, around the large table with Lament, Plight, Lenka and Kalvin on the other side.

Skulduggery sat back, hands clasped over where his belly would have been, tapping his fingertips together. "The very fact that you ask us that leads me to believe there is something important that we *don't* know about Roarhaven. Valkyrie will tell you what we *do* know."

"Uh, OK," said Valkyrie, doing her best to remember. "Most magical communities establish themselves in towns or cities and kind of blend in and go unnoticed. But the people of Roarhaven built up their town in the middle of nowhere. They isolated themselves on purpose, and because of that their hostility towards normal people grew. They didn't agree with official Sanctuary policies – they believed sorcerers should be ruling the world, not hiding in it. So they hatched a plot to destroy the Sanctuary and steal control."

"And what was the plot?" Lament asked.

"No idea."

Skulduggery looked at her. "I told you this."

"No, you didn't."

"Yes, I did. I told you about the bomb that didn't go off and the failed coup and the arrests."

"Oh," she said. "Yeah, that sounds familiar."

Skulduggery sighed.

"The coup was only the start of it," Lament said. "From what we've gathered, the Roarhaven mages had much bigger plans. Did you know that since the war with Mevolent ended, hundreds of sorcerers from all over the world have gone missing?"

"Sorcerers go missing all the time," Skulduggery pointed out. "*You* went missing, after all."

"Very true," said Lament, "but we didn't meet with representatives from Roarhaven right before we disappeared."

Skulduggery's chin tilted downwards. "So what happened to these missing sorcerers?"

"We don't know," said Plight. "This is just another sliver of information we picked up about that town and its people. They had big plans, and I doubt those plans have been abandoned. After all, they got what they wanted, didn't they? The Sanctuary is now in Roarhaven."

"But that wasn't because of a coup," Valkyrie pointed out. "That was because Davina Marr destroyed the old Sanctuary. The Elders chose to move there."

Plight shrugged. "We've been tucked away for thirty years, we don't know the ins and outs of the situation. But however it happened, it happened. The Sanctuary is now in Roarhaven, and so is the Accelerator."

Lament sat forward. "Scientists talk. We share ideas and discoveries and theories. I would never have been able to build something like the Tempest or the Cube without talking through aspects of it with other people far more intelligent than I.

"As an extension of that, scientists love to gossip. I heard about a colleague of an old friend of mine. This colleague, a man named Rote, was working on a project so secret he wouldn't tell anyone what it was. But he discussed aspects of it with different people to get their advice and input. Purely by chance, some of these people got together, started talking about Rote and his odd questions. They each had a different piece of the puzzle, but when they put them together, it began to take shape. The project he was working on, the Accelerator, appeared to be a machine capable of boosting magic, amplifying it to an incredible degree."

"It may even correspond with Argeddion's own discoveries about the source of magic," Kalvin said. "Maybe Rote found a way to channel that power, to draw it out and use it."

"Unfortunately," said Lament, "we don't know enough to come to any definite conclusions."

"What were they going to use it for?" Valkyrie asked.

"A hostile takeover. Every sorcerer around the world would get this massive boost of power, enough to turn bullets into dust and missiles into rainbows. Mortal civilisation would be overrun within weeks. Then the Accelerator would be shut down, power levels would return to normal, but the world would be completely different. Sorcerers would be the dominant race."

"I've seen what that's like," Valkyrie said. "It's not fun."

"And this Accelerator exists?" Skulduggery asked.

"I think so," said Lament. "And I think it's hidden somewhere in Roarhaven. Even if it's half finished, we could work on it, bring it online."

"Why?"

"Because it doesn't have to be used for its original intention," said Lament. "It could be altered, used to charge the Cube indefinitely. Skulduggery, you were talking about increasing the Cube's power by two or three times? The Accelerator would increase it a hundredfold, and we wouldn't even need the Tempest hooked up to it. Argeddion would never wake up, never escape. And if this Darquesse really is as powerful as everyone thinks she will be, she can be held in a Cube alongside him. We're talking about a maximum security prison strong enough to hold *gods*."

"In that case," Skulduggery said, standing up, "I think it's time I made a phone call."

Valkyrie followed him to an empty room. His phone was in his hand but he didn't dial.

"What do you think?" he asked.

"About what? The idea? I think it's great."

"What do you think of building a prison that could hold you? This isn't theoretical any more – if we go down this road, it's a reality. We'll be building a Cube for you, Valkyrie."

She shrugged. "That's what we want, isn't it?"

He folded his arms. "Are you really going to stand there and tell me this whole thing doesn't scare you?"

She laughed. "What do you want me to say? 'Don't build a Cube for me?' Then what? I kill everyone?"

"All I want you to do is admit how you feel."

"What good is that going to do us?"

"You need to be absolutely sure about your motivations for going along with this."

"So you want me to be honest? Because the two of us have always been really good with honesty, yeah? Because we've never hidden the truth from anyone? You know what? Fine. I don't want a prison built for me, OK? I don't want to sleep for an eternity in a Cube. I want to be free and stay free and be happy and alive. But I'm not going to get that chance."

"We don't know that yet."

"Of course we do. My God, every time I give in and Darquesse comes out things start making sense. Nothing scares me and nothing worries me. I'm pure. I'm content. Do you know how wonderful that is? To feel that? And the more it happens, the harder it is to push it back down again. I... I like being Darquesse. I think I might like it even more than I like being me."

They looked at each other for the longest time, and then he took a single step and hugged her. He was cold and bony, but when she rested her head against his sternum, that didn't matter.

"Of course you do," he said softly.

She stepped back. "What?"

"I told you," he said. "Power is addictive. Why wouldn't you love being that strong? Why wouldn't you love being able to bring yourself back from the brink of death?"

"It's not just that. It's the way I'm starting to think. It's the thoughts I have. I don't even realise I'm thinking them and then suddenly it hits me. It's not that Darquesse is taking over, it's... It's that I'm becoming more like her with every single day that passes. I don't want to spend the rest of my life in a Cube, Skulduggery, of course I don't. But we need it. We need to build it."

"OK then," he said. "Just as long as we're both ready to admit what it might mean." He dialled a number, put the call on speaker.

"Finally!" Ghastly said when he answered. "You do remember I asked you to call in every four hours, yes? And that was twenty hours ago?"

"I was going to call," Skulduggery replied, "but I was too busy being brilliant. Tyren Lament says hello, by the way."

"They're all there?"

"All four of them, in a secret base built into the side of a mountain. You'd love it. It's very James Bond."

"And Argeddion? He's alive?"

"He's being kept in an artificially induced coma, yes. There might be a way to reinforce the cage that's holding him, which should cut off whatever influence he's having on the world. But in order to do this, we need another machine located somewhere in Roarhaven. Probably in the Sanctuary itself."

"What is it?"

"It's called the Accelerator. I'll send you a file as soon as I have one, just to let you know what you're looking for. It was part of the Roarhaven coup attempt, so it's probably well hidden. It might not be wise to involve any Roarhaven mages in the search for it – or, in fact, any other mages at all, apart from Ravel."

"You're sounding awfully paranoid."

"I have reason to be. In the wrong hands, the Accelerator could be the most devastating weapon the world has ever seen."

24

SEARCHING THE SANCTUARY

"Grand Mage, Elder Bespoke, I was wondering if I could have a word."

Ravel talked as he walked. "You, Mr Sult? Are we no longer important enough to warrant direct communication with Grand Mage Strom? Instead, they send a Junior Administrator to speak to us?"

"We'd almost be offended if we cared," said Ghastly.

"My deepest apologies," Sult responded. "I assure you, we mean no disrespect. It's just, with the murder of Christophe Nocturnal in this very building, Grand Mage Strom has been advised to move to a more... secure location. But I am fully authorised to speak on behalf of the whole Supreme Council on all matters."

"They left you behind, then?" Ravel said. "They must really like you, to leave you in such dangerous territory."

Sult smiled politely. "They have faith that I will be well protected by your Cleavers and operatives, all of whom are beyond reproach in their duties. Personally, I do not feel in danger in the slightest."

Ghastly glanced at Ravel, and stopped walking. Sult almost collided with him, then backed off with a chuckle as Ravel kept going. Ghastly looked him in the eye. "What can I do for you, Mr Sult?"

"Ah, yes, to business. It has come to my attention, Elder Bespoke, that there has been some tension arising between our people and yours."

"You mean the fight that broke out last night."

"Yes, sir, I do. I wish to apologise on behalf of the Supreme Council. It is not our intention to make trouble."

"OK."

"However, the incident has resulted in three of our operatives needing medical attention."

"And two of ours."

"Yes, sir, but, without wishing to offend, it was your men who started the fight."

"That's not how I heard it."

Sult smiled. "I have no wish to contradict you, sir. But we have our report, in which a verbal disagreement escalated into a physical confrontation when one of your men punched the leader of our security team."

"Who had been making some pretty derogatory remarks."

"For which he will be disciplined. However, a verbal assault and a physical assault are completely different things."

"They're both assaults, are they not?"

"Yes, sir, but—"

"And a physical assault is usually preceded by a verbal assault, and our people are trained to spot this and act accordingly. So while my man may have thrown the first punch, he did not actually start the fight. That was your man."

"Elder Bespoke—"

"Mr Sult, I have neither the time nor the inclination to stand here and argue this with you. Your guys had a fight with my guys. That's it. It happens, and that's the end of it. But if it happens again, we'll be kicking your guys out of the country."

"What? You can't be serious."

"Tempers are frayed. Patience is short. We have a huge problem that we're trying to deal with and a prisoner has been murdered while in our custody. I don't care about a fight in which nobody was seriously injured, and neither should you. There are other things to worry about. Give my regards to your bosses."

Ghastly walked away. Sult, to his credit, didn't even try to follow.

Ravel was waiting around the next corner. "Thanks," he said. "I really don't like that guy."

They took the stairs to the lower levels. Cleavers stood to attention when they passed. The corridors got darker and colder and Ghastly had to take out a map to keep track of where they were going.

"Isn't this beneath us?" Ravel asked as they walked. "This is probably beneath us. We're Elders. We're not supposed to look for things. We're supposed to get things handed to us."

"It amazes me how quickly you've become spoiled."

"I never liked looking for things," Ravel grumbled. "You remember looking for clues with Skulduggery? I always hated that. I never knew what was a clue and what wasn't. I'd look at a room and see a room and he'd look at it and solve a mystery."

"I wouldn't worry about it," said Ghastly. "You might not be as good a detective as Skulduggery is, but you're good at other things. Like wearing a robe and complaining."

"I'm *amazing* at those things," Ravel said. "And I order people around really well. This morning, Tipstaff came over with a cup of tea and I told him no, I don't want tea I want coffee. That was great. I really asserted my authority."

"Did he go and get you a coffee?"

"No, he said he'd already made a pot of tea so I took the tea because, you know, he'd already made it, but my authority was still firmly asserted."

Ghastly nodded. "He'll think twice before making tea again."

"That he will, Ghastly my friend, that he will. What are we looking for, by the way?"

"Seriously? I gave you the file half an hour ago."

"Yes, you did."

"Did you read it?"

"No, I did not."

Ghastly sighed. "It's called an Accelerator. It's a big machine type thing."

"Great. What does it look like?"

"I don't know."

"Is that it?"

"No. That's a wall."

"It could be disguised."

"You're really *not* very good at looking for things, are you?"

"I'm good at looking for walls. Look, I found another one."

They came to a junction and Ghastly stopped walking, and frowned. "This is odd. That corridor isn't on the map."

Ravel folded his arms. "Maybe it isn't there."

"Maybe the corridor isn't there?"

"Maybe it's an optical illusion. Or it's like Schrödinger's cat. Until you look at it, it's both there and not there."

"But we're looking at it now, Erskine, and I'm pretty sure it's there. It just isn't on the map."

Ravel shrugged. "It's an old building. There are tunnels and secret passageways all over the place."

"But the first thing we did when we moved the Sanctuary was send a team of mages down here to check for things like this. I'm holding the map they made."

Ravel looked at him. "We sent a team of Roarhaven mages."

"They left out this corridor on purpose," Ghastly said, putting the map away. "Skulduggery was right. We can't trust them. So what's down here that they wanted to keep secret?"

"Hopefully, it's the Accelerator, and not just some bathroom they wanted to keep private. We should probably get a squad of Cleavers to go down first, make sure it's safe and clear of booby traps."

"Yeah," said Ghastly. "We probably should. We could go back up and sit on our thrones and drink tea while we wait."

"Good idea. Safe, too. Tipstaff would approve."

"He really would," said Ghastly, and they both started down the corridor.

They found a series of rooms without doors. Those that weren't empty were stacked with building materials and supplies, and a thick layer of dust covered everything. The power down there hadn't been connected, so they each held fire in their hands to light their way. Rats scuttled in corners and water dripped into large, cold puddles, and the shadows played as they walked. Ravel stopped.

"I think I've found it," he said.

They stepped into a large room. Most of it was empty space, as dark and as damp as the corridor outside. The Accelerator stood in the exact centre like a giant vase that had burst open from within. Its curved wall bent gently back, the jagged tips almost scraping the ceiling. The front section was open, allowing access into the thing itself, where a white disc rested on its base, forming a slightly raised platform. Circuitry ran like dull veins through the skin of the machine, which seemed almost translucent under the flickering firelight.

Ravel knocked his fist against it. The sound suggested a strange mixture of metal and rubber. Ghastly stepped through the opening, on to the white dais. Hemmed in on three sides, he got an odd feeling of claustrophobia.

"Can't see how to turn it on," Ravel said.

Ghastly stepped out before Ravel hit something he wasn't supposed to. "Let's leave that to the scientists, OK? We'd probably break it if we tried."

"I'm sure we could figure it out," Ravel said, peering at it. "We're intelligent enough. We may not be scientist-smart, but we're smart in other ways. We're street-smart, is what we are."

"And what street is that, exactly?"

Ravel shrugged. "Probably one of the dumber ones, to be honest. Maybe you're right. We'll tell Skulduggery we found it, and Lament can come over and get it working."

"That's a really good idea, Grand Mage."

"I sometimes have them."

They left the Accelerator and retraced their steps, eventually finding their way back to a corridor they recognised. It was cold and damp and the lights flickered overhead. They passed a corner that should have been guarded by a Cleaver. There was no Cleaver there now. Ghastly checked his watch. Early shift-change, maybe – although he wasn't aware of any Cleaver who'd ever left his post unguarded in their entire history.

Three mages hurried their way. Ghastly didn't know any of them particularly well. Brennock was the big one, and the woman was Paloma. Tevhan, the third, was the strong, silent type that liked to glower at everyone.

"Grand Mage," said Brennock, "Elder Bespoke. I'm sorry to interrupt, but there is an emergency call from Detective Pleasant."

Ravel quickened his pace. "What happened? What's wrong?"

"I'm afraid I don't know, Grand Mage. He will only talk to you."

Brennock and Paloma fell in on either side of Ravel, and Tevhan waited on Ghastly to catch up. All three of them Roarhaven mages. Ghastly took out the map as he walked, scanning the fine print until he found the names of the sorcerers who'd been assigned to draw it up. He found them, and nodded to Tevhan as he passed. Three names. Brennock, Paloma and Tevhan.

"Grand Mage," Ghastly said, as he put the map away, "did you know that the sparrow flies south for winter?"

"What an odd thing to say," Ravel said, and as he turned, he snapped his palm against the air and Paloma slammed into the wall.

Ghastly spun, catching Tevhan with a right cross that buckled his knees, making him drop the knife he was sliding from his sleeve. Ghastly hit him again, and again, never giving him a chance to get his bearings. Tevhan was an Adept, but Ghastly didn't know what discipline he'd trained in. He wasn't going to take any chances.

When Tevhan went down, Ghastly turned back to Ravel in time to see him sweep Brennock's legs from under him. Brennock's head smacked into the ground and Ravel gave him an extra kick to make him stay there.

"What do you know," Ravel said, breathing a little faster, "Skulduggery's silly little code actually works."

25

THE INEVITABLE RETURN OF FLETCHER RENN

Lament showed them to a small room with four large sigils engraved on the walls. He left them and Valkyrie stood beside Skulduggery in the centre of the room. After a moment, the sigils started to glow, and hazy images of Ravel and Ghastly appeared before them.

"Sorry for the extra trouble," Ghastly said, "but we needed to talk to you over a secure line, as it were." His image was transparent but he sounded like he was actually standing right there in front of them.

"I should get this for my phone," Valkyrie said.

"Trouble with the Supreme Council?" Skulduggery asked.

"No, actually," said Ravel. "Well, yes, but this isn't because of them. We found the Accelerator. It's in good condition but it doesn't work."

"Don't worry about that," Skulduggery said. "Lament is confident he can get it running. What's the other problem?"

"We were attacked," Ghastly said. "Roarhaven mages. People who have been working beside us for the last year. We've managed to keep it quiet so far. Our own people trying to kill us is not something we want to explain to Strom and the others right now."

"So far, our would-be assassins haven't given us any answers," Ravel said. "Our Sensitives have tried breaking through but they know how to block psychic probes."

"Do you think they attacked because of the Accelerator?" Skulduggery asked. "How did they even find out you were looking for it?"

Ghastly glanced at Ravel, who chewed his lip. Eventually he said, "We think our phones have been tapped. And that's not the only problem. It seems that every Cleaver in that area had been reassigned minutes before, to give our attackers a clear chance. We've talked to a few people and no one can explain to us how this happened."

"I can," said Valkyrie. "It was Madame Mist."

"We don't know that," Ravel said quickly. "And even if she *had* wanted to kill us, this is much too clumsy for someone like her."

"She might be getting desperate," said Skulduggery. "If she

already knew about the Accelerator's existence, then she wouldn't have wanted you stumbling upon it."

"And if she didn't know of its existence?"

"If she just found out about it by listening in to our conversation, then she may have simply seen her chance and latched on to it, however clumsily."

"Maybe," Ravel said. "But I'm still not convinced."

"Even so, an attempt on your lives is a major step for anyone to take. If they've gone this far, they'll go further."

"We need greater control over the Cleavers," Ghastly said. "They don't question orders. If Mist – or whoever – used them against us once, she might do so again, and I don't fancy going up against those scythes."

"Agreed," said Skulduggery. "Erskine, you should take direct control from now on – the Cleavers take orders from the Grand Mage and that's it. Mist has Roarhaven on her side. We need the Cleavers on ours."

"But their numbers are still depleted," Ravel pointed out. "If Mist *is* behind this and we go up against her, even with the Cleavers and whatever mages are loyal to us, we can't be guaranteed of winning. We need more. We need an advantage."

All three fell silent. None of them wanted to state the obvious.

"We could ask the Supreme Council for help," Valkyrie said.

"Let's change the subject before I hit someone," Ghastly said, and Ravel's image immediately shifted away from him slightly. "What do we need to do to get this Accelerator working?"

"Lament will have to take a look at it," Skulduggery said. "Can you get it shipped up here?"

Ravel shook his head. "It can't be moved. From what we understand, the Sanctuary itself acts as a kind of lightning rod. If you want to use it to power Argeddion's cage, you're going to have to bring the cage to Roarhaven."

"OK," said Skulduggery, "it shouldn't take too much convincing to get Lament to agree to that. I also think Valkyrie's ex-boyfriend will come in handy here."

Ravel frowned. "The dead vampire?"

Valkyrie glared at him. "I think he means Fletcher."

"Oh. Sorry."

"Caelan was never my boyfriend."

"I didn't mean to—"

"We don't talk about Caelan," Ghastly muttered.

"I'm really sorry, Valkyrie," Ravel said. "Fletcher's great. He's wonderful. I'm sure he'd be delighted to help, and having a Teleporter here will certainly solve some problems. We'll arrange that, we'll get him over to you, start the ball rolling, as it were. Once again, sorry about bringing up the vampire."

Ghastly shot him a look, whispered, "Why do you keep talking about him?"

"I can't help it," Ravel whispered back. "Now he's all I can think about."

"You realise," Valkyrie said, "that we can hear you both perfectly well."

Ghastly shut up immediately. Ravel nodded slowly. "Right. Righto. You sure you heard everything, now? Did you hear the bit where I complimented you and called you amazing?"

"I must have missed that part."

"Oh, that's a shame. That's a real..." He looked off to his right, eyebrows raising. "What's that? I'm needed elsewhere? Important business?"

Ghastly sighed. "There's no one there."

"Valkyrie, Skulduggery, we'll talk with Fletcher and get back to you," Ravel said, and glared at Ghastly as their images faded to nothing.

Four hours later, the same huge plane that had flown them to Switzerland appeared as a speck over the mountains. Valkyrie held fire in her hand to warm herself while she waited. She knew Fletcher wasn't onboard. He rarely suffered through the indignities of travel any more. Because Teleporters can only teleport to places they've already been, or places they can actually see, he had devised a tactic to be used on planes and trains and boats.

First, he'd have teleported to Ireland, where he'd have introduced himself to the pilots and stepped on to the plane. Then he'd have teleported home to Australia and spent the next few hours doing whatever it was he did when he was over there. When the plane had reached its destination – roughly where it was now – the pilot would call him and he'd teleport back to the plane, look out of the window, see her, and teleport down. It was a simple and effective way of visiting places all around the world without having to actually waste time getting there. And it was typical Fletcher.

The plane got closer and she took off her mask, then sent a fistful of shadows curling along the snow to attract their attention. A moment later, Fletcher Renn appeared in front of her.

"Oh my God!" was the first thing he said. "It's freezing!"

Valkyrie grinned. "That'd be all the snow. Come on, it's warmer inside."

He frowned at the hole in the rocks she'd squirmed through to get out there. "Haven't these people heard of doors?"

"It keeps the Abominable Snowmen out."

He stared. "Seriously?"

"Two of them, yeah. One of them tried to eat my head."

He held out his hand and she took it, and he crouched down, peered through the gap, and suddenly they were on the other side of the rocks, in the warmth. These days, teleportation didn't even result in a twinge of nausea, much less puking her guts up like it did in the early days. Fletcher straightened, and smiled at her.

"Hi," he said.

"Hi." She smiled. "You look well." He did. She'd forgotten how cute he was. "Your hair's still stupid."

Fletcher nodded. "Thanks for that. Should've known better than to expect you to stay nice for more than a few seconds."

She laughed. "Sorry. Bad habit. You really do look good, though. Australia agrees with you."

"Australia has good taste. And it's taken a while but you've obviously decided that you can't live without me, either. I have to say, coming up with this whole Argeddion thing just to have an excuse to see me again? I admit it, I'm flattered."

"You're such a goon. Why do you have to be such a goon? You're cute and you're hot and if you'd just stay quiet, you'd be perfect."

He shrugged. "My mouth gets me into trouble. As you well know."

"And now you're a dope. You're both a goon and a dope. Well done."

"I try my very best." He suddenly frowned. "Should we hug, or something? I think we should hug, after not seeing each other for so long."

"Why not?" she said, and hugged him. For a moment Valkyrie remembered how good it felt, and then she stepped away.

His eyes flickered over her shoulder, and he stood a little straighter as Skulduggery walked up.

"Skulduggery."

"Fletcher."

Fletcher stuck out his hand. Skulduggery observed it for a moment.

"I'm sorry, what are we doing now?"

"Shaking hands," Fletcher said. "Like adults. I just want you to know that this past year has changed me. I've grown, as a person. I'm not the same Fletcher you used to know."

"You look a lot like him."

"Well, yeah, but—"

"And you have the same ridiculous hair."

"Can we just shake hands?"

"Of course we can," Skulduggery said, and they shook. "Now what?"

"I, uh... I don't really know. What do adults usually do after they shake hands?"

"Generally, the first thing they do is let go."

"Oh, right," Fletcher said, and Skulduggery took his hand back. "So, Skulduggery, how've you been? You're looking well. That's a really nice tie."

"It's blue."

"And such a nice shade."

Skulduggery looked at Valkyrie. "You promised me he wouldn't be annoying."

She glared. "And you promised you wouldn't be mean."

Skulduggery sighed, turned back. "Fletcher, how is your training progressing? As the last Teleporter, it's important that you take your responsibilities seriously."

"I am," Fletcher said. "I do."

"When I was your age, I met the last Kineticist. Do you know what that is? He had the ability to absorb kinetic energy and store it as pure strength. Essentially, the more he was hit, the stronger he became. When he died, all the secrets of his discipline died with him. A few years ago a young sorcerer decided to train to be the first Kineticist in four hundred years. Do you know what happened?"

"No," Fletcher said. "What?"

"He was really rubbish at it."

Fletcher frowned. "Oh."

"Let that be a lesson to you," Skulduggery said, and walked back the way he'd come.

Fletcher edged closer to Valkyrie. "I thought that story would have a more dramatic ending," he whispered.

"Yeah," she whispered back.

She took him on a tour. Kalvin was there to meet them at the Arboretum, and he explained what they needed to keep in mind when transporting the birds and animals. It was decided to just take everything, trees and all, to empty plots of land around the world according to the needs of whatever was being transported. Valkyrie stood by and let them talk, becoming quietly impressed with Fletcher as he steadily got all the information he needed.

When they were done, Valkyrie took him to see Lenka, whose reaction was, as she had expected, one to treasure. Fletcher walked in, and Lenka laughed so hard she fell off the table on which she'd been sitting.

"His hair!" Lenka gasped from the floor. "Oh my God, his hair!"

Fletcher sighed.

Lament came in, shook Fletcher's hand and asked him to ignore the hysterical girl rolling across the ground. He took them to the Cube, and Fletcher peered in at Argeddion.

"You're sure he's asleep?" he asked.

"We were," Lament said, frowning slightly. "These days, we're not so sure. And so time is of the essence."

Fletcher nodded, and looked at the machine. "So you need all of this moved at the same time?"

"Yes," said Lament. "The Tempest, that's the pyramid there, won't be needed once we've attached the Cube directly to the Accelerator, but that will require a day or so of work. In the mean time, we'll need everything just as it is – but in the Sanctuary. Do you think that would be a problem?"

"Wouldn't say so," said Fletcher. "It's all hooked up and everything is connected, so it doesn't look like anything will be left behind. Should be a clean teleport right into the room Ghastly showed me."

"You've seen the Accelerator?"

"Yep," he said. "Weird-looking thing."

Lament smiled. "Thank you very much for doing this, Fletcher. I don't know how we'd manage it without you."

Fletcher shrugged. "Just doing my bit to help out," he said, and walked from the room with an extra bit of swagger. Valkyrie rolled her eyes, and followed.

The clearing-out of the mountain facility took a few hours. Valkyrie stayed with Fletcher for most of it, having a laugh and chatting while they waited for the next shipment of equipment or animals or whatever to be made ready. Lenka had tears in her eyes when it was time to say goodbye to some of the monkeys, but Fletcher transported them to nice safe places, and this helped her sniffling. The last thing to be moved was Argeddion himself and all the machinery that held him in stasis.

Fletcher looked tense. Valkyrie felt for him. If this went wrong, they'd be releasing a sorcerer on the world who was more powerful than anyone else alive.

Lament and his three sorcerers came together and joined hands.

"This place is our home," said Lament. "We came here thirty years ago to protect the world from a threat, and in doing so we found a new place to love. It certainly hasn't been easy living here, isolated and alone, but we got through it. We didn't think we'd ever return. But now, thanks to these people standing beside us, the impossible is possible, and we have a second chance at life. I'll miss this place." He smiled sadly. "But I won't miss it a lot."

There were a few laughs, then everyone linked arms and Fletcher placed a hand on the chair, and in less than an eyeblink, much quicker and more easily than seemed to befit the gravity of the situation, they were in a large room deep within the Sanctuary, beside a machine that could only have been the Accelerator.

It was done. No explosions, no screaming, no all-powerful sorcerer suddenly loosed upon the world. It was, if Valkyrie was being honest, a bit of an anticlimax.

Ravel came in to welcome them, and Lenka turned and threw up all over his shoes.

Valkyrie and Fletcher sneaked away while the introductions were going on. They left the Sanctuary and took a walk around the lake. The stagnant water wasn't very pretty, but it was the only walk available.

"Good job," Valkyrie said. "Thanks."

He shrugged. "It's not easy being the one you all run to in an emergency, but I cope admirably well."

"That you do," she said with a laugh. "Are you heading off now?"

"Unless there's something else I'm needed for."

She stopped walking, and looked at him. "Well," she said, "I'm not doing anything for the next few hours..."

He looked back at her, and his smile dimmed a little. "Oh."

Valkyrie laughed. "Wow. Now that was *not* the reaction I was expecting."

"No, sorry, I didn't mean it like that. I just meant..."

She held up her hands. "Fletcher, relax. It's no big deal."

"No, Val, it's just, I'm kind of seeing someone."

Now it was her turn to say, "Oh."

"She's really nice," he said. "We've only been going out for two months or so, but she's dead cool. You'd like her, I think. Here, hold on."

He vanished.

Valkyrie blinked. *He* was going out with someone? He had found someone before she had? While not having any kind of plan or timetable arranged, she was still pretty sure that she was supposed to move on before he did. She'd dumped *him*, after all.

Fletcher reappeared before her, holding hands with a pretty girl.

"Valkyrie," he said, "this is Myra."

Myra had light brown hair and a nice smile and Valkyrie wanted to punch her in her stupid face. "Hi," Valkyrie said.

"Pleased to meet you," said Myra, and they shook hands. Valkyrie was pretty sure she'd be able to crush that little hand in hers. When Myra spoke, she spoke with an Australian accent. It was annoying. "Fletcher's told me all about you. To be honest I was starting to think he'd made you up. I reckoned no one could be as great as the way he described you."

Valkyrie found a smile somewhere and put it on. "I have my moments," she said. "So how did you two meet?"

Myra wrapped an arm round Fletcher's waist. "He saved me. There was a fire at my college and he got me out. My knight in shining armour."

Valkyrie blinked. "You're mortal?"

Fletcher laughed. "I thought you hated that term."

"What? Oh, yeah, I do, I meant you're not a sorcerer, then?"

Myra shook her head. "Depressingly normal, I'm afraid. But don't worry, I can keep a secret. Fletch was telling me about all the things you can do and what a kick-ass fighter you are and all that. That is so cool. I couldn't fight my way out of a paper bag, if I'm being honest. I'd love to be able to do magic, but I reckon having a boyfriend who can do magic is almost as good."

Valkyrie didn't want to hit her any more. Myra was too nice a person to hit. Valkyrie wanted to hit *someone*, though. Maybe Fletcher.

"I've been wanting to introduce you two for a while," Fletcher said, "but I didn't know how to do it without making it look like I was trying to prove a point. Like, *Look at me now, Valkyrie, I have a new girlfriend and a new life.* But... well, here we are. I just want you to know that there are no hard feelings about what happened and how it ended and I'm glad we're still, you know, friends."

"Yeah," Valkyrie said. "Me too."

They stood there, the three of them, all friends, in awkward silence.

"We should get going," Fletcher said. "I grabbed her just as she was about to take the muffins out of the oven."

Valkyrie looked at Myra. "You make muffins?"

"Not very well," Myra said. "I used to make them with my mum all the time. It's such an old person thing to do, isn't it? Make muffins?" She laughed. "Anyway, it was so good to meet you, Valkyrie."

"Good to meet you, too."

Myra smiled, and Fletcher gave her that grin that used to make Valkyrie's heart beat faster, and then they both vanished.

"Well," Valkyrie said aloud, "that sucks."

26

POOR TOMMY PURCELL

Elsie O'Brien wasn't a brave girl. She wasn't an especially bright girl, or an especially talented girl, and she definitely wasn't an especially pretty girl. But these things she already knew about herself. These were the honest, inescapable facts that formed the basis of who she was. As for bravery, she'd never given it a second thought. She'd more or less assumed that she'd be the type of person to do the right thing in a bad situation, but here she was, trailing from bad situation to bad situation with no idea what the right thing to do was any more.

Kitana and Doran certainly didn't know. They were lost. They were drunk on this power they'd been given. There was no hope for them. She didn't know if there was any hope for her, either, but she didn't much care about that. The only person she cared about was Sean, but he was slipping away every day, becoming more like the others.

"Keep up," Kitana said, and Elsie dutifully trotted along after them a little faster. All she wanted to do was turn and run. But she didn't. She kept following, because that's what she did. She was a follower.

They got to Doran's house. His dad was out. His mum was gone, having abandoned the family years ago. Doran never talked about it and Elsie had never asked. Not that he'd have answered her if she had. When Doran was ready, they went inside, into the living room, where his older brother was playing a video game.

"Hey, Tommy," said Doran.

Tommy looked around. His scowl turned nonchalant when he saw Kitana. She had a habit of making guys act differently.

"Hey," he said, sitting a little straighter.

Doran was trying not to grin, and doing a really bad job of it. "What's the game like? Is it good? Are you good at it? Are you good at playing your little video game?"

Tommy put the controller on the coffee table and slowly stood up. "What's this?" he asked. "Acting tough in front of your friends? You weren't so tough last week when I twisted your arm so much you started crying, were you?"

Whatever reaction Tommy was expecting, a wider grin was not it.

"No, I wasn't," said Doran. "Wasn't nearly as tough as I am now, big brother. You want to try that again?"

Tommy's eyes flickered to Kitana, then back to Doran. "You really want that? You really want me to embarrass you in front of your girlfriend?"

"Oh, I'm not his girlfriend," Kitana said sweetly. "I prefer older men. What age are you, Tommy?"

"Twenty," he said, squaring his shoulders.

"Twenty," Kitana breathed. "That's the perfect age for me."

Tommy had a grin of his own now, and he looked back at Doran. "Why don't the rest of you run along? Kitana, you want to hang out for while?"

"Actually," said Kitana, "I'd really like to go somewhere private. Maybe go for a drive."

Doran laughed so suddenly it was like a gunshot. "Yeah, Tommy," he said. "Take her for a drive. Take her for a drive in your car. How is your car, anyway? Is it in good shape? Is it roadworthy? Have you seen it lately?"

"What the hell are you talking about?"

"Your car," Doran said, laughing again. "Have you seen it in, say, the last few minutes?"

Tommy frowned. "You better not have done anything to it."

Doran shrugged. Tommy barged past him on his way to the window. Doran stumbled back against the wall, still laughing.

Elsie didn't need to look out of the window to know what Tommy was seeing. He was seeing his prized car – the car he had so lovingly restored – dismantled and in pieces in the driveway. He was seeing the dissected engine and the sheared body and the shredded tyres. He was seeing what it had taken Doran five minutes to accomplish.

Tommy sagged so quickly he had to grip the windowsill to stay upright. His eyes were wide, his mouth open. He had gone a dangerous shade of pale.

Doran was doubled over he was laughing so hard. Tommy spun, face contorted with utter, utter hatred. He ran at his younger brother, fist arcing downwards to catch Doran full in the face. Doran fell back, still laughing. Tommy started lashing kicks in, and with every kick Doran would just laugh harder. Tommy straddled him, began raining down punches. Doran howled like he was being tickled.

Finally, Tommy fell backwards, panting hard, upset and confused as Doran sat up like he hadn't a care in the world.

"Oh," Doran said, wiping the tears from his eyes, "oh man, that was funny. The look on your face. I'm going to remember that for as long as I live."

He got to his feet without any hurry. Tommy scrambled up.

Elsie felt sorry for Tommy. She didn't like him, she never had. Any time she'd seen him he was beating up Doran, humiliating him in front of everyone out of some need to be seen as strong. Sometimes he beat him up just out of sheer meanness. Tommy wasn't a nice guy at all, but she felt sorry for him all the same. He didn't have the first idea what was going on or what he was dealing with.

Tommy shoved Doran again. "What did you do to my car?"

"Same thing I'm going to do to you," said Doran, grabbing him.

And just like he had pulled apart the body of the car with his bare hands, he pulled apart poor Tommy's body.

By the time Doran was done, Sean was so still and so pale he looked dead. Kitana laughed as Elsie hurried from the room. She burst out of the back door and threw up in the garden. Tears ran down her face but her mind was strangely calm. Despite the horror of what she had just witnessed, her thoughts were clear.

There was a low wall at the other end of the garden. Elsie climbed over it and walked away. She didn't bother running. It'd be another half an hour before they even noticed she was gone.

27

MAYHEM

"Remember that sorcerer who went missing?"

Valkyrie raised her head off the pillow even as she woke. For a moment she didn't know where she was, then she recognised the house on Cemetery Road and blinked a few times before croaking out, "Who?"

"Patrick Xebec," Skulduggery said, standing in the morning sunlight that streamed in through the window. "The Elemental who went missing. He was passing through Monkstown when he saw those energy streams in the sky. Michael Delaney, the poor chap who was torn apart in his own living room, lived in Woodside. That's practically next door to Monkstown."

Valkyrie sat up, bleary-eyed. "So the lights in the sky have something to do with whoever killed Michael Delaney."

"And probably something to do with whoever killed this latest victim."

"There's another one?"

"In Ballinteer. Wheels up in fifteen."

He left the room and Valkyrie sighed, swung her legs out of bed. She took a quick shower, dressed, and Skulduggery had a bowl of cereal waiting for her when she emerged. When she had first visited his house, all those years ago, every room had been a living room. Now she had her own bedroom, there was a bathroom with a huge shower and a kitchen with a fully-stocked fridge. Sometimes she wondered how much money she'd cost him with her insistence on refurbishment, then realised she didn't much care. Money wasn't a big deal to someone like Skulduggery.

By the time they were both in the Bentley, her wits had woken up, too.

They arrived at the house in Ballinteer. As usual, there were Cleavers disguised as Guards making sure no one got too close. Philomena Random was talking to a news crew that had arrived. By the time Valkyrie got out of the Bentley, the news crew were packing up and heading away without filming a single frame.

Valkyrie let Skulduggery go inside. She didn't need to see any more blood. She waited at the door until he came back out.

"Same killer?" she asked.

"The method is different but the result's the same," he said. "This one was done by hand. The victim was thrown about the place like a rag doll. Plenty of footprints. Sloppy. Angry. Sadistic."

"Does that mean we have two killers?"

"If this murder is connected to the others, then I think we have at *least* two people working here, maybe more. This has all the hallmarks of a gang urging each other on. Each murder is more savage than the one before. Each time it gets more personal."

"Any idea why there's a car spread out like a jigsaw in the driveway?"

"None whatsoever."

"We have to find the link between the victims," Valkyrie said. "What was his name?"

"Thomas Purcell. Tommy. Twenty years old. Apprentice electrician. Mother absent, father works the nightshift, isn't home from work yet. Younger brother Doran, seventeen."

"Maybe he could help us," Valkyrie said. "If Tommy had any enemies, anyone who'd want to hurt him, his brother ought to know, right?"

"Maybe. That is if his brother is in any fit state to talk."

"Is he here?"

"Geoffrey's talking to him in the garage. See if he can be of any help. I'll take a look around outside."

Valkyrie nodded, walked to the garage and looked in. Geoffrey Scrutinous was sitting on a crate talking to a boy dressed in baggy jeans and a hoody. Geoffrey's hair was its usual wild and frizzy self, but he looked exhausted. These last few weeks had seen him rushing all around the country, convincing people they hadn't seen what they thought they'd seen.

"You can feel yourself calming down," Geoffrey said. "You're calm and you're clear. Oh, hello, Valkyrie. Valkyrie Cain, this is Doran Purcell. Doran lost his brother today."

"I'm very sorry," Valkyrie said.

Doran looked up at her. Geoffrey's routine had worked wonders. Doran looked remarkably calm.

"It's OK," he said. "Thank you."

"Do you mind if I ask you a few questions?"

Doran smiled. "You're my age. What are you doing, acting the detective?"

"I just want to talk to you, see if you can help us find out who did this terrible thing."

"Right," said Doran. "Terrible. Yeah. Sure, ask away."

"Thank you. Do you know who might have wanted to hurt your brother?"

Doran nodded. "Oh, yeah. Yeah, I got a good idea. Everyone who ever met him."

Valkyrie blinked. "I'm sorry?"

"My brother was a tool. He was a bully. He'd bully whoever he could get away with bullying. He had loads of enemies. Everyone wanted to hurt him. I'm telling you, there'll be a load of happy people today once this gets out."

"Are you happy, Doran?"

"Me? No. He may have been a bully but he was still my brother."

"Did he ever bully you?"

"Yeah."

"That must have been tough."

A shrug.

"Do you know who did this?"

"No. I got home late last night, came in the back door, went straight up to bed."

"Do you have any suspects?"

"Like I said, he had lots of enemies. Could have been anyone." A sliver of a smile played across his mouth, so quick Valkyrie wasn't sure she'd actually seen it. "You know who it could have been?" he asked, leaning forward. "Mark Boyle. He was Tommy's best friend, ever since they were little. Boyle was as bad as Tommy. They might have had an argument about something, and it got out of hand."

"It got out of hand?" Valkyrie said doubtfully. "Doran, have you actually seen your brother's body?"

"What there is left of it, yeah."

"And how do you think Mark Boyle would have done that?"

"I dunno. Knife? Maybe a chainsaw."

"That's a possibility," Valkyrie said. "Listen, will you be OK here for a moment? I'll have to start a search for Mark Boyle. If he's running, we'll have to act fast."

"Go get him," Doran said.

Valkyrie walked out, approached Skulduggery.

"I think we have our killer," she said quietly.

Skulduggery's false eyes flickered over her shoulder, looking back at Doran.

"He might be in shock," Valkyrie said, "so I might be reading this completely wrong, but he's practically dancing with joy now that his brother's dead. He also smells of soap."

"He'd need to have a shower to wash off all that blood," Skulduggery murmured. "Then it's another one of Argeddion's infections, you think?"

"Only this time the mortal with the magic is a psychopath."

"It was bound to happen. We can't take him down here. Someone that powerful, it'd be too unpredictable in a public place. We need to get him isolated."

"What'll we do?"

"Let him go, and follow him. Hopefully, he'll lead us to his accomplices. We'll assemble a team, take them all down at once, and no one needs to get hurt."

"What a lovely plan."

"Thank you."

"How likely is it to actually work?"

"With our luck? Not very."

Three hours later, her arms were folded and her brow was furrowed. "I hate this car."

Skulduggery dropped into a lower gear. "What's wrong with it?"

"It's orange."

"But a nice shade."

"It's horrible. It's an Orange-mobile. We're driving around in an Orange-mobile trying to be inconspicuous."

"We *are* being inconspicuous," Skulduggery said. "The Bentley, while the height of good taste in and of itself, is not suited to tailing somebody. This car, with its thoroughly unexceptional bodywork and engine capacity, blends in with the other cars on the road."

"Blends in?" Valkyrie repeated, looking around them. "Do you see any other orange cars out there? Do you? I don't. This doesn't blend in, it sticks out."

"And yet instantly fades from memory."

"I doubt it'll fade from *my* memory," she grumbled.

"Has Doran Purcell noticed us yet? No, he hasn't. Do you know why? Because the people he passes are not pointing at a beautiful black Bentley as it follows him slowly up the street. You should learn to appreciate the unexceptional, Valkyrie."

"But why does the unexceptional have to be such an awful colour?"

He shrugged. "It amuses me."

Doran Purcell walked into a café, and the Orange-mobile pulled in to the side of the road.

"I could do with some coffee," Valkyrie murmured.

"He might be meeting someone in there."

"I'll check," she said, reaching for the door handle.

"He knows you," Skulduggery said. A fresh face covered his head. "He doesn't know me. Stay here."

"Get me a coffee."

"No."

"Get me one."

He got out, crossed the road and entered the café. Valkyrie yawned, turned on the radio. An Imelda May song was playing

– 'Big Bad Handsome Man'. Valkyrie started singing along. She'd just got to the bit about his rugged good looks when Skulduggery came crashing out through the café window.

Valkyrie cursed, slid over to the driver's seat, started up the car and swerved out on to the road. Skulduggery staggered to his feet, ignoring the shocked looks from the people around him. Doran Purcell and two others – a boy and a girl – stepped out through the broken window behind him, grinning.

Valkyrie snapped her palm against the air, shattering the glass on the passenger side door. She sped past him and Skulduggery lunged at the car, using the air to take him to the window. He slid in and a stream of sizzling energy took out the wing mirror. Valkyrie cursed again, glanced in the rear-view and saw the three teenagers step into the middle of the road. The girl raised her arm and there was a flash of light and the car flipped and the world tilted and spun, then the car hit the road and flipped forward again. Everything blurred and roared.

When the world quietened down, the car was on its side and Valkyrie was in the back seat with blood in her mouth. She'd bitten her tongue.

Skulduggery's false face came into view. "Are you OK?" he asked, his voice distant.

She murmured, and nodded. Her clothes had absorbed the multiple impacts.

"We need to get out," Skulduggery said. "Move, Valkyrie. Now."

She turned over, noticing the pieces of glass embedded in her blood-drenched hand. Just cuts. Painful but not serious. She crawled out through the open door, on to the road. Her head ached. It buzzed. Doran Purcell and his friends were approaching, walking up the middle of the road, laughing to each other. Skulduggery appeared beside her, gun in hand. He fired, and the boys went to run but the girl stopped them. She gazed at the air, which had turned a hazy shade of blue – a protective bubble to keep the bullets out. The girl giggled.

Skulduggery grabbed Valkyrie, dragged her behind the wreck of the car. She heard him fire again. She made herself sit up. Gunfire and energy blasts in the middle of the day in the middle of the street. She saw the faces of the people as they hid and peeked. She took a deep breath.

"Valkyrie," Skulduggery said. "I need you with me."

"I'm here," she said. She risked a glance around the bonnet, then ducked back to avoid an energy stream.

Skulduggery shook his head. "We need to get away. People are going to get hurt. If we're gone, they'll stop attacking."

"Can you fly us?"

"We'd be an easy target in the air. We have to break their line of sight first. Can you run?"

"I'm fine, I'm good."

"Well, OK then."

There was a boarded-up bookshop next to them. Skulduggery put his gun away and snapped his palms against empty space. The air rippled and the boards exploded inwards. He clicked his fingers, summoning flame.

"Ready?" he asked.

She nodded.

Skulduggery stepped out, sending twin streams of flame towards Purcell and his friends. The fire swarmed over their force field, unable to get through, but Valkyrie used the distraction to bolt from behind the car to the bookshop, and leaped through into darkness. She tripped over something and almost went sprawling into a bookcase, but managed to keep going. She glanced back. Skulduggery was right behind her.

Then a stream of energy seared through his chest, lifting him off his feet and he fell, just collapsed on the floor.

"No!" she screamed, running back to him, grabbing his arm, pulling him after her. "Get up! Get up!"

"I think I killed him," said the blonde girl, walking in. "Oopsies."

Valkyrie pushed at the air but the girl dodged out of the way and it hit the boy behind her. He flew back and Doran Purcell came at Valkyrie. She used the shadows to fling him against the far wall as hard as she could, aware of the girl's short bark of excitement.

Blondie leaped at her. It was a clumsy attack and Valkyrie flipped her to the ground, started throwing down hammer shots. The other slammed into her from behind and they stumbled against the table. She kicked at his leg, stomped on his knee, cracked an elbow into his jaw. He went down and then Doran hit her, a punch swinging in from her blind side. Doran forced her back against the wall, holding her with one hand and punching with the other. She didn't want to kill him, didn't want to kill anyone, but Skulduggery was lying on the floor and not moving and so she hit him in the throat with all of her strength. He dropped and she turned, kicked the girl in the face as she tried getting up.

Valkyrie ran to Skulduggery. She turned him on to his back. His façade had melted away. He wasn't moving. She tried to lift him, and heard a chuckle from behind her.

They were on their feet again, and grinning.

"Did you really," the girl said, "think it would be that easy?"

Valkyrie grabbed the shadows but Doran moved faster than she could see, his fist slamming into her side like a truck. She was lifted off her feet, the breath rushing from her lungs, went stumbling into the other boy's arms. He picked her up, held her over his head and threw her into the bookcase. She hit the shelves and then the ground, books raining down on top of her, and something closed round her ankle and the boy was dragging her across the floor. She whipped shadows at him but they glanced off his force field.

She kicked at his wrist with her free leg and twisted at the same time, freeing herself and coming to her feet. He turned his head right into her hook, and she caught him on the hinge of the jaw. A sweet, perfect connection that sent him back a few steps, but which should have sent him straight to the ground.

Doran grabbed her from behind in a bear hug, lifting her into the air. She sent her heels backwards, missing with her left but feeling her right crunch into his knee. He hissed and dropped her and she torqued, sending an elbow up into his chin.

It should have put him down. It didn't.

The other boy punched her. He didn't know how to punch but there was so much strength behind it that it didn't matter. The room whirled and Valkyrie felt her backside hit the edge of the table.

"I like your jacket," the girl said. "Doran, Sean, get it for me."

Doran thundered towards her and Valkyrie did a backward somersault across the table, keeping out of his reach. He shoved the table and it caught her mid-thigh. She cried out and almost went down and he climbed on to it to jump, but she pushed at the air and sent him hurtling across the room.

Something blurred and the other boy, Sean, hit her again. She fell to her knees and he kicked her and she flipped sideways. When she landed, she would have cried out if her lungs had allowed her to make a sound. Sean walked up and stomped on her back. He did it again and it felt like her whole body was breaking. He flipped her on to her back, unzipped the jacket and yanked it off her. She moaned, turned, tried covering up but Doran's foot found her side and her ribs smashed. Valkyrie found a breath and screamed.

Sean threw the jacket to the girl and she put it on. "Oh," she said, "I like this. Oh, I like it a lot."

Valkyrie tried to curl up into a ball but every movement made her scream louder. She wrapped her arms round herself, feeling bits of jagged rib poking through her skin.

"What'll we do with her?" Doran asked, a grin in his voice.

"I don't care," said the girl. "Just kick her to death and be done with it."

28

HER SECRET AGENDA

"**I** demand a body!" the zombie head yelled from his jar of gross liquid. Sanguine had to resist the urge to throw a pillow at him. He'd already done that once, and had succeeded in toppling the jar on the table. The head had shrieked and rolled off on to the floor, and Sanguine had laughed so much he'd popped some stitches.

"I demand a body!"

"Would you please shut up?" Sanguine said. "If someone other than Nye hears you, we're *both* sunk."

Scapegrace ignored him. "Doctor Nye! Doctor Nye, I demand a body!"

Nye swept in, ducking its head to fit through the door. It had to bend its knees and spine in order to peer into the jar.

"You," it breathed through its surgical mask, "are shouting again."

"Where is my body, Doctor Nye? We had a deal."

"I remember," the doctor said. "Do you think I would forget? Or perhaps you think I would cheat you now that I have the remains of the White Cleaver?"

"Oh, I know you wouldn't." Scapegrace was trying to glare into the doctor's small yellow eyes, but his head was lopsided in the jar and so he ended up glaring at Nye's elbow. "Because until you find me a new body, you're not getting the White Cleaver's brain."

"The brain?"

Scapegrace chuckled. "You didn't think I'd hand over everything, did you? I told Thrasher to collect the pieces of brain into one single container, and then to keep that container back – just to ensure your honesty."

"And when I have fulfilled my end of the bargain...?"

"We'll hand over the final container. So you see, Doctor Nye, you're not dealing with some amateur here. I am the Zombie King. I am the Killer Supreme. And you will drop everything right this second and go find me another body or you will never see that—"

Nye took a plastic container from its pocket, and placed it on the table in front of the jar. It was filled with what looked like pieces of brain.

Scapegrace blew a bubble as he whimpered.

"Your friend Thrasher," Nye said, "is every bit as much of an idiot as you make him out to be."

"I'm going to kill him," Scapegrace said.

Nye flicked the jar with one long, bony finger. "Have patience, zombie. When I find a suitable body, work will begin. Do not presume to threaten me again."

Taking the container, it ducked back out through the door, and Scapegrace's head slipped a little further askew.

"Smooth," Sanguine said.

"Shut up."

"Are you ignorin' me now? Is that what you're doin'? Givin' me the silent treatment? Oh, no, the decapitated zombie isn't speakin' to me – whatever will I do? How will I cope? The shame, the shame, to be shunned by a head."

Scapegrace murmured something.

"Sorry? What was that?"

"I said at least I have eyes!"

Sanguine laughed, and Tanith walked in.

"You two seem to be having fun," she said, picking up a towel and covering the jar with it. She ignored Scapegrace's cries and sat on the edge of Sanguine's bed. "How are you feeling?"

Sanguine gave her the grin. "You actually sound like you care."

"Of course I care, honey-bunny," she said, squeezing his hand. "But if you could possibly manage to heal a little faster, that would be super-fantastic."

"It's gettin' worse out there, is it?"

She sighed. "This place is crawling with sorcerers. It's not safe for people like us. I keep expecting Skulduggery to come walking through that door or for Ghastly to call my name..."

"You give me the word, darlin', and I'll take care of that scarred freak in a heartbeat."

Tanith smiled, and tapped Sanguine's chest. "You leave Ghastly alone. He is not to be harmed, you hear me? Don't be mean."

"I don't know, Tanith. If I didn't know any better, I'd swear you still had a soft spot for that guy."

She leaned in and kissed him. "What's all this? Are you getting jealous again?"

Sanguine was about to answer when he saw movement over Tanith's shoulder. He stiffened and she turned as Madame Mist entered the room.

Sanguine didn't even have time to sit up before Tanith ran at her, sword out. Mist raised her arm and a torrent of tiny spiders shot out from her voluminous sleeve, catching Tanith full in the face. She stumbled to her knees, spitting and gagging, gradually lost under the growing mound. There were thousands of them. Tens of thousands. More. And then Mist's arm fell back to her side. Sanguine caught a glimpse of the black veins that spread beneath Tanith's skin, and she snarled and leaped from the mountain of spiders. Mist caught her, a slender hand closing round Tanith's throat as she swung her overhead and slammed her to the ground. The sword fell and Mist picked her up like she was picking up a doll and flung her to the other side of the room. Tanith crashed through a set of curtains, bringing the whole frame down with her, and landed somewhere behind the bed, tangled and cursing.

The spiders returned to their mistress, forming lines that flowed beneath the hem of Madame Mist's long black dress.

Nye swept in, looking like a giant spider itself. "What seems to be the problem?" it rasped.

Sanguine waited for Mist to alert the Cleavers or call for help or *something*, but all she did was stand there, very still, and Sanguine realised Nye had been addressing *him*.

"She's an Elder," he explained, feeling like there was a huge part of this situation that he hadn't been filled in on.

"Madame Mist is my patron," said Nye. "We have nothing to hide. The debt you owe to me for healing you is now owed to her."

Sanguine took a moment to figure it all out. "Right," he said. "OK. In that case, Tanith, it might be better if you didn't kill her."

Nye looked up to where Tanith crouched, upside down on the ceiling directly above Mist's head, a scalpel in either hand. She still wore the black lips and black veins of the Remnant inside her. Mist, to her credit, didn't even glance upwards.

Tanith jumped, flipping to the ground. Without taking her eyes off the woman in the veil, she passed the scalpels to Nye, and held out her hand to Mist. Their fingers touched, forming a bridge, and a trail of spiders trickled along Tanith's arm and disappeared up Mist's sleeve.

"Is that all of them?" Tanith asked, and Mist nodded. Tanith picked her sword up off the floor, her face returning to normal.

"So Madame Mist has a secret agenda," she said. "Who would have guessed?"

"The others suspect," Mist said softly, "but they have no proof. And so we have time."

"Time to do what?" Sanguine asked.

"To prepare," said Mist. "To arrange. You owe me a favour. I want you to kill someone."

"We figured that much," Tanith said. "Who?"

"Stay close, and stay hidden, and I will tell you who your target is when the time is right." Mist glided away so smoothly that Sanguine had visions of a carpet of spiders beneath her feet.

29

ALL BECOMES CLEAR

Doran Purcell's friends were quickly identified as Kitana Kellaway and Sean Mackin, all three of them seventeen years old and all pupils of St Brendan's Secondary School. Their parents hadn't seen them in days, and no one else had heard from them. There was a fourth member of their group, a girl called Elsie O'Brien. She was unaccounted for. Valkyrie didn't much care about that. Elsie O'Brien hadn't tried to kick her to death, after all.

She didn't remember much of it. The pain had sent jagged spikes through her mind, cutting her off from the details of whose boot came in first, or who had kicked her more, or how long she'd endured before the blackness started to seep into her vision. But she did remember the moment the air quaked, and the way Doran and Sean hurtled into Kitana. Skulduggery lifting her up was pretty clear in her head, as was the back door bursting open. She blacked out before they rose into the air, and only regained consciousness once she was back in the Sanctuary.

She was patched up by Reverie Synecdoche, a Sanctuary doctor who shivered whenever Doctor Nye passed behind her. Nye was working on Skulduggery, much to Skulduggery's irritation. The injuries he'd sustained had only aggravated his earlier ones, the bones the werewolf had damaged. Now he had to lie back and let Nye work its magic. He did so with no small amount of complaining.

Ravel dropped by at his first opportunity, heard Skulduggery moaning and stayed over beside Valkyrie. "We're looking for them," he told her. "We have mages combing the city, with strict instructions not to engage unless absolutely necessary. How are you?"

She chewed on the leaf that melted her pain away. "Mad," she said. "They took my jacket. What about the witnesses?"

Ravel expelled a deep breath. "We're doing our best," he said. "Geoffrey and Philomena are on it, we have clean-up crews and reconstruction going on... I won't lie, Valkyrie. This is a big one. This could be seen as a major mistake."

She looked at him. "Skulduggery will tell you, we did everything right. We kept our distance until we lost sight of Doran Purcell. Skulduggery went into the café after him, saw him there with the other two. The girl, Kitana, was hurling insults at some random woman. She went to melt her face and Skulduggery stepped in. Next thing he knew he was flying backwards through the window.

These aren't sorcerers we're dealing with. They don't know the rules about public displays of power and if we don't find them fast, things are going to get a whole lot worse."

"Hopefully, their inexperience will work to our advantage," Ravel said. "They won't know where to hide or how to disappear. They're just teenagers."

"So am I. Their level of power was massively different to anyone else we've seen, though. Argeddion must have overloaded them because they had no skill and no training and they still nearly killed us. Skulduggery fired at them and they didn't even know they could throw up force fields until it happened."

"It sounds like they're operating on pure instinct. We'll find them soon enough."

For the first time, Valkyrie noticed the Cleavers standing at a respectful distance. She frowned. "Hey... are they your bodyguards?"

Ravel glowered. "They follow me everywhere. Wherever I go I'm under constant protection. Ghastly can roam as he pleases, but me?"

"Well," she said, "you're the Grand Mage. You're important. What did Mist say about you taking control of the Cleavers?"

"She didn't say much, but then she never does. I have no idea if she even knows we suspect her of being involved in the attack. That damn veil hides a lot. Here, give me good news. Apparently you've solved the murder of Christophe Nocturnal."

"It was easy. The unlocked door, the sword wound. Tanith killed him."

"Any idea why?"

"Probably for sending that woman to kill me. She's quite protective, in her own way."

"Right," Ravel said. "Well, leaving aside what a staggering breach in security that was, at least it's one case closed, two more to go. We have Silas Nadir in the detention cell if you want to talk to him, to put a stop to your dimensional jaunts. And if Lament and his friends ever get their work finished downstairs, we'll have no more mortals going crazy, and the Supreme Council can leave us alone."

"See? Everything's almost fine."

He smiled despite himself. "I'll leave you. I have things to do and headaches to suffer. I'd love to tell you to take some time off and heal but..."

"I don't need to heal," she told him, smiling back. "I'm ready and rarin' to go."

"That's the spirit," he said, starting to walk off. "Oh, when Skulduggery's back on his feet, could you go down and check with Lament, see how things are going?"

"You got it."

"You're my favourite detective, you know that?"

"Oh, I bet you say that to all the teenage girls."

He laughed, and the Cleavers flanked him and then he was gone.

A minute later, Skulduggery had had enough. He strode to the door, fixing his tie, and Valkyrie ran after him. She told him what Ravel had said, and on their way to see Lament they took a detour to the interview room. Silas Nadir didn't even look up when they entered.

Skulduggery sat opposite him, and Valkyrie stood by the wall. Skulduggery tapped the tabletop, his fingers drumming a beat. Nadir moved his head like he was testing a crick in his neck, then raised his eyes.

"Look who it is," he said. "The cheating skeleton and his girl sidekick. Why am I even here?"

"You're here because you have a choice," Skulduggery said. "Hammer Lane is closing down so you're being sent to a new prison. If you co-operate, you can go to the gaol at Keel, maybe Funshog. If not, you can go to The Depths."

A flicker of something on Nadir's face. "You wouldn't send me there. You couldn't. I've killed a few people, yeah, but I haven't... You can't just send someone to..."

"We can," Skulduggery said, "and we will. Unless you co-operate."

"Co-operate how?"

"Undo what you did to Valkyrie."

Nadir looked at him, then at Valkyrie. "What?"

"Undo it," Skulduggery said.

"Undo what?"

"You're not doing yourself any favours."

"Listen, I have no idea what you want me to do, or undo. Tell me what it is, and I'll do it."

"You shunted me," Valkyrie said.

He made a face. "I did not."

Skulduggery got to his feet. "Let's go."

"Wait!" Nadir said. "Just hold on a second. Tell me what you think I did."

Skulduggery stayed standing, but didn't move. "You performed some kind of delayed shunt on Valkyrie when you attacked her at Hammer Lane."

"I don't know what you're—"

Skulduggery took a step towards the door.

"OK!" Nadir cried. "OK, fine, you say I attacked her, then I attacked her. I don't remember doing it, but I'd just been unhooked from that machine so, yeah, OK, maybe I did."

Valkyrie asked, "What exactly did you do? My arm hurt for a few days and then suddenly I was in another dimension. Twenty minutes later, I was back here."

Nadir sat forward, his eyes suddenly excited. "What was it like? It had a breathable atmosphere obviously, but what else did it have? Were there animals? Were there *people*?"

"You've never been there yourself?"

"No," he said. "God, no. Finding a frequency for a new dimension is one thing, but actually travelling there? What if the air is toxic? What if I appear in the middle of a volcano? What if there is no planet to stand on? There's a reason why there aren't many Dimensional Shunters still around, you know. Most of them are nothing but dust in some weird reality where the laws of physics are backwards. But the dimension I sent you to – it's habitable. This is amazing. Do you know how rare that is? I found a previously undiscovered *reality*."

"And you sent me there," Valkyrie said. "How?"

Nadir nodded. "Right, yeah. It's called echoing. It's when a shunt doesn't work right away. Instead of one great big shunt, you get a kind of echo of a shunt. It echoes and echoes and gets louder and louder, and when it's loud enough, you get shunted."

"Will it happen again?"

"That depends. How many times has it happened so far?"

"I shunted over and back."

Nadir hesitated. "Then yeah, it'll happen again."

"So stop it," Skulduggery said.

"I can't. It's all about the reverberations inside her now. It's got nothing to do with me. It'll stop itself. Something like that, you're really only looking at eight or ten trips before the echo gets too weak to affect you. You've taken two trips so far, so you have between four and six left to go, and that's it."

"Somewhere between?" Skulduggery said. "So it might not be an even number? It might not be four or six trips – it might be three or five. Which means she could be shunted over there and left stranded."

"Oh, yeah," Nadir said. "Didn't think of that."

"How much time before I get shunted again?" Valkyrie asked.

He shrugged. "This kind of thing sets up its own rhythm."

"If Detective Cain gets shunted over there," Skulduggery said, "and doesn't shunt back within an acceptable time frame, we'll need to go over after her. And you'll be taking us."

Nadir leaned back in his chair. "Will I, now? Well, as an integral part of the rescue mission, I might have a few conditions of my own. I'll let you know if I'm available." He smirked.

Skulduggery placed both hands on the table and leaned over. "You've heard about me. You've heard about the things I've done."

The smirk faded a little. "So?"

"So the stories you've heard are nothing compared to the truth, and the truth is nothing compared to what I'll do to you if something happens to Valkyrie. I'm the worst enemy you could ever make, Silas. Look at me and answer honestly. Do you believe me?"

Nadir swallowed. "Yeah."

"Good."

They left him there, and headed for the Accelerator Room. "You're going to have to stay above ground," said Skulduggery. "When you shunt, you stay in the same place, you just switch dimensions. We don't know if the other dimension has this Sanctuary. If it doesn't, you'll shunt right into compacted rock and earth."

"And if I'm above ground, I might shunt into a building or a tree or a person. It's dangerous either way."

"True, but—"

"We carry on as normal," she said. "We have to. We're too busy not to. Tell you what, when Lament gets the Accelerator working and when Kitana and Doran and Sean are in shackles, we'll find somewhere nice and safe and I'll stay there for however long it takes. OK?"

"For *however* long it takes. Even if it's weeks."

She nodded. "I'll bring a long book with big words."

"Deal," he said. "And if you shunt in the meantime without me, just stay in the one spot, stay out of sight and stay out of trouble until you return. Do you think you can do that?"

"Me? Stay out of trouble? Shouldn't be a problem in the *slightest*."

The Accelerator pulsed like a heart was beating from somewhere deep inside, sending a warm, gentle light through the veins of circuitry that passed beneath the skin of the machine. The white disc that had lain at its base now hovered centimetres off the ground, suspended by an unknown force, forming a sort of raised platform, what Lament was calling a dais.

Lament and the others worked in silence to disconnect the Cube from its power source. He and Kalvin may have been the engineers of the group, but both Lenka Bazaar and Vernon Plight proved themselves to be the equal of any scientist. Valkyrie reckoned that's what thirty years stuck in a mountain would do to you.

Ravel paid frequent visits to what was now known as the Accelerator Room, eager for progress, but Lament would not be hurried. The Cube would only be transferred into the Accelerator once all precautions had been taken. Valkyrie watched until she grew bored. Admittedly, it didn't take long.

She went exploring. There were lights down there now, and heat was starting to be pumped in and it wasn't quite as damp as it had been, but it was still pretty squalid. As she walked, she wondered how many hidden tunnels she was passing. Roarhaven was known for its secrets, after all.

"How are you feeling?" Skulduggery asked from behind her.

She turned, holding out her hands. "I feel great. Don't I look great?"

"You look wonderful," he said. "A little cold, maybe."

She glowered, and hugged her bare arms. "I can't believe that wretch has my jacket. I'm going to break her face next time I see her."

"They gave you quite a going-over."

"I've had worse."

"Have you?"

Valkyrie shrugged. "It's nothing I can't handle. What about you?"

"The only thing that still hurts is my pride."

"Yeah. Three amateurs, like. That's just embarrassing for you."

His head tilted. "Embarrassing for me, but not for you?"

"I'm not the one with the reputation in tatters."

"I think my legend will survive, thank you very much. We underestimated them and that was our mistake. The magic has woven in and around their reflexes and instincts – they don't need to know *how* they're doing something, they just do it. Next time we'll be prepared."

"Next time I'm breaking her face."

Skulduggery nodded with approval, and then turned his head to her. "You know, with everything that's been going on, we haven't had a chance to talk about Fletcher."

She laughed. "When do we *ever* talk about Fletcher?"

"Hardly ever," he admitted, "but you haven't seen him in a while, and he comes back, and he has a girlfriend..."

"How do you know he has a girlfriend?"

"He told me."

"Oh. Yeah, he has. She's nice. Myra, her name is."

He nodded, didn't say anything.

She arched an eyebrow. "What?"

"How do you feel about that?"

"Are we seriously talking about how I feel about my ex-boyfriend? Do we have nothing better to do with our time? Aren't there murders we need to solve?"

"You just look like you need to talk, that's all."

"I'm fine. My God, I'm grand. It's not like he's the love of my life. We broke up, he has a new girlfriend, that's what happens."

"You don't have a new boyfriend."

"Thank you for pointing that out."

"And Hansard Kray doesn't seem interested."

"Oh... my God... you can stop making me feel better now."

"It's just, if you were feeling somehow... unattractive..."

"Sorry?"

"I don't mean unattractive," he said quickly. "I mean, if you were thinking that maybe you'll always be alone—"

"I wasn't thinking that," Valkyrie said. "I wasn't thinking that at all. But now I am. Now I definitely am. You think I'll always be alone?"

"That's really not what I meant."

"Then what did you mean? My God, Skulduggery, just tell me. Be honest with me. Fletcher's moved on, Hansard doesn't fancy me..." She buried her face in her hands. "Oh, God, I'm seventeen years old and no one will ever love me. I'm going to be alone for the rest of my life. I've missed my chance. I've missed my chance at happiness. I'm an old maid. Oh, God..."

Skulduggery folded his arms. "You're mocking me."

She took her hands down. "Well, duh."

"I was only trying to be sensitive."

"I don't need you sensitive, Skulduggery. I need you aloof and irresponsible and arrogant. That's why I love you. That's why I let you hang out with me."

"I'm truly blessed."

She grinned. "You love me, too. Once you admit it, everything will be better."

"They're about to hook up the Cube to the Accelerator," he said, and turned and walked off.

She followed. "You can't run from your feelings."

"I can walk from them."

She laughed, and a blue light shone from behind them. They turned. A curved wall of transparent blue energy filled the corridor behind them. Valkyrie frowned. "And what's this now?"

"A force field," Skulduggery said, tapping against it. It sizzled slightly under his touch. "Judging from the curvature it's a spherical shield, bisecting floors and walls outwards of its epicentre."

"Right," Valkyrie said. "So we're in a big ball, then."

They started walking again. "Lament must have thrown it up," Skulduggery said. "Hopefully, it's a precaution, and nothing more serious." He slowed. "Wait a second. Hear that?"

Coming from the adjoining corridor, raised voices. They moved quietly and peered around.

The force field cut off the far end of the corridor, keeping a crowd of people back who were now trying to break through the wall of energy by blasting it with whatever they had. Lament stood inside the shield, watching them. He looked taller than usual. It took Valkyrie a moment to realise he was hovering a few centimetres off the ground. He turned slowly, and Valkyrie glimpsed his sandalled feet pointing downwards so that his toes almost brushed against the floor. He started drifting back to the Accelerator Room, and Skulduggery and Valkyrie ducked away before they were seen.

Valkyrie got out her phone, dialled Ghastly's number.

He answered immediately. "Where are you? We've got a situation."

"We know," she whispered. "We're in it."

"You're *inside* the force field? Is Skulduggery with you?"

"Yes. He can hear you. What's going on?"

"Lament guides us all out, he says this next stage might be dangerous, and then the force field appears. I turn around and he's floating, and his eyes are closed, and he apologises."

"What for?" Skulduggery asked. "What did he say?"

Ghastly's voice was tight. "He said they aren't here to keep Argeddion imprisoned. He said they're here to set him free."

30

THE EXPERIMENT

The line went quiet for a moment while Ghastly conferred with others. Then he came back. "We have a Sensitive here. He says he's just started to pick up a psychic wavelength that they've managed to keep hidden until now. We think Argeddion is controlling them."

"They spent the last thirty years in that mountain, watching over him," Skulduggery said. "At some stage he must have regained a degree of awareness, started reaching out, taking them over. This whole thing was just a ploy to get us to move them all here."

"I don't get it," said Valkyrie. "If they wanted to release him, why not just turn off the Cube?"

Skulduggery shook his head. "I don't think turning off the Cube is the problem. The problem is that Argeddion has been in an artificially induced coma for the last three decades. Maybe he simply can't wake up. If I were them, I'd be using the Accelerator as a defibrillator for the mind."

"They're going to shock him awake," said Ghastly. "OK, listen to me. You two are the only people we've got in there. I'd love to say we're coming in after you but this wall is stronger than anything I've seen."

"We could get Fletcher back," Valkyrie suggested. "He could take everyone in at once."

"A force field of this strength can't be teleported through," Skulduggery said. "If Fletcher tried it, his atoms would be scattered all the way across existence. Don't worry. We don't need anyone else. We've got surprise on our side, and a deliberate tendency towards extreme violence. We'll be fine."

Ghastly sighed. "Try not to kill anyone, at least. Remember that Lament's sorcerers are not in control of themselves."

Valkyrie put her phone away, and Skulduggery looked at her, and took out his gun. She nodded. They stole round the corner, ignoring the blue wall and the people on the other side, focusing all their attention on the doorway to the Accelerator Room. No one guarding it. No voices from inside. Valkyrie readied the shadows as Skulduggery counted down on his fingers.

Three... two... one—

They ran in.

"Hello," said Argeddion.

Lament and his sorcerers were on their knees in a circle around the Accelerator, their heads down. The Cube rotated slowly within the Accelerator itself, an empty cage. Argeddion hovered in mid-air above the remains of the Tempest, smiling at them. Residual energy crackled around his body, and his eyes were glittering orbs of power.

Valkyrie didn't know what to do.

"Hmm," Skulduggery said. "This is... disappointing, I don't mind telling you. I thought we'd arrive in the nick of time and stop this from happening. I blame myself, of course. And other people. Mostly other people. In particular I blame the people in this room on their knees. I blame them an awful lot. I don't suppose shooting you will do any good at this stage, will it?"

Argeddion smiled again.

"But it couldn't hurt to try." Skulduggery went to fire but the gun disappeared from his hand, and reappeared in Argeddion's.

"Violence," he said, turning the gun over and examining it. "Why do you always resort to violence?"

"Could I have that back?" Skulduggery asked. "It's my favourite."

"I don't like violence."

"All the same, that gun has sentimental value, so..."

Argeddion released his hold and the gun floated back to Skulduggery.

"Thank you," Skulduggery said, and went to put it away. Apparently as an afterthought he aimed and fired and the bullet bounced off Argeddion's head. "Yeah, that's what I thought might happen." He holstered it.

"Skulduggery Pleasant," Argeddion said, "pleased to meet you. Valkyrie, I feel like I've known you my whole life. I've been inside your head. You have such wonderful thoughts."

Alarm shot through her body. If he could read her mind, then he'd know—

"Yes," said Argeddion, "I know who you are. We're alike, you and I. We are as alike as we are different. We have both discovered our true names, we both have access to unimaginable power... but where you have so far used this power to hurt and destroy, I have used it to explore and learn. What makes you this way, do you think?"

"You can read my mind," Valkyrie said, "so you tell me."

Argeddion smiled. "You think you're a bad person. You think that behind the heroic acts and the bravery and the good deeds, you're evil. It's the only thing that makes sense to you, the only way you can explain it. You think every good thing you do is part of an act that you use to fool yourself. That's what you think."

Valkyrie didn't answer, and Argeddion looked at Skulduggery. "I can't read your mind. Your thoughts are configured in such a way as to confound my attempts. But I know you. I have seen you through Valkyrie's eyes. Do you want to tell her the small and simple fact that she is overlooking?"

Skulduggery hesitated, then looked down at her. "It's all an act," he said. "For everyone. We're all acting good and noble because acting good is what makes us good."

"And now she's wondering, *If that is true, why has Argeddion used his power in a peaceful manner and I have used mine to kill?* The answer, Valkyrie, is because I'm special." Argeddion laughed. "I'm a pacifist. Non-violence is what I believe in above all else. But you believe in violence. You believe that, as terrible as it is, it's necessary. And in your world, dealing with the things you deal with, you might be right. In my world, it is not, and I refuse to allow it to be."

"If you're a pacifist," Valkyrie said, "explain Kitana and Doran and Sean. They're killing people with the power you gave them."

"And that is regrettable," Argeddion said, "but I must see this through to the end."

"See what through? What's all this about?"

Skulduggery tilted his head. "They're test subjects. This is an experiment."

"Indeed it is," Argeddion said. "And most of the mortals I picked have not hurt anyone – at least not intentionally."

Valkyrie frowned. "But why are you doing this? What's the point?"

"Maybe someday you will be able to see what I have seen," said Argeddion. "In fact, should you ever find peace within yourself as Darquesse, I would love to be able to show you. Then you can glimpse, as I did, the realm of magic. It is a breathtaking experience. It will change everything within you."

"Sounds lovely. You didn't answer my question."

"Magic is a wonderful, joyous thing, and it should be shared, but sorcerers have been hoarding it since the birth of mankind. If the mortals knew of its existence, tests could be carried out to identify those who could wield magic. They could be trained, taught. We would have hundreds of thousands, if not millions, of mages and they could elevate this world to a true Age of Enlightenment. No more wars. No more pettiness. Peace and love and the search for knowledge. Paradise."

"Your idea is not new," said Skulduggery. "But if you were to prove to the world that magic was real, mankind would tear itself apart. The mortals would feel threatened and they would fight back with everything they had."

"Only if there were any mortals left."

Valkyrie paled. "You want to kill them? You said you were a pacifist."

"I don't want to *kill* the mortals," Argeddion said, chuckling. "I want to change them. My test subjects are paving the way for the entire mortal population of the earth to be gifted with magic."

"You... you could do that?"

"By myself, no," Argeddion said. "But with the Accelerator and the help of my surprise guest, it will happen."

"Your surprise guest?"

Argeddion smiled gently.

"This is insane," Skulduggery said.

"You can't see what I can see, Skulduggery. Heaven on earth. Can you imagine it? Once all my tests are run, once all the results are collected, magic will permeate every single person. They will evolve overnight, transforming the planet into a kingdom of enlightenment and peace."

"The Summer of Light," said Skulduggery. "That's what it is, isn't it? You've planned this so that everything will be ready to go on May the first – Greta Dapple's two hundredth birthday. That's when you're going to change it all."

"It will be glorious."

"No, it won't. You're talking about changing human nature. It can't be done. There will be no kingdom of enlightenment. The rot will start early, and it'll spread. There'll be war and horror and death. Your Summer of Light will turn into a Summer of Darkness. The human race will wipe itself out."

"You're blinded by your own limitations."

"And you're blinded by your lack of them. You're a better person than I am, Argeddion. You're a better person than most people. That's the problem. You have no idea how most people will react."

"I trust. I have faith."

"You're deluded, and we will stop you."

"You *could* have stopped me," Argeddion said. "You *could* have donned the armour of Lord Vile and come after me. With your natural strength and vicious nature, you might even have defeated me. But a quick peek into Valkyrie's mind tells me exactly where you've secured it..."

He vanished, and a moment later, he was back, holding a thick metal case. Skulduggery tensed.

"You can feel it from there, can't you?" Argeddion asked. "The pull? Like a magnet to you. But I'm afraid you won't be donning this armour any time soon." The case disappeared. "And now that Lord Vile is out of the picture, there is only one threat remaining."

Skulduggery stood in front of Valkyrie. "You don't have to hurt her."

"I have no intention of hurting her," said Argeddion. "I don't want to see any harm come to her in the slightest. But Darquesse is a problem that I have to address. Valkyrie, if you're able to access that power, you'll tear me apart, won't you? You're not as strong as I am, not yet, but where I would keep looking for a non-lethal way to stop you, you wouldn't feel the same need for restraint. Darquesse is a cold-blooded killer. And I can't let her emerge."

White pain flashed and Valkyrie cried out, stumbled, and Skulduggery spun and caught her as she fell. And then the pain was gone.

"My apologies," said Argeddion. "I didn't think that would hurt as much as it did."

"What did you do to me?" Valkyrie gasped.

"Think of it as putting up a wall between you, the sweet girl called Valkyrie, and Darquesse, the cold-blooded killer. You can't hear her voice any more, can you?"

Valkyrie stood by herself, her head still spinning.

"She will never bother you again," said Argeddion. "Not while I'm alive. You're safe from her, Valkyrie. You can still access your magic as you always have, but that level of power is now blocked off to you."

"She's gone?"

"She's still there, she's just... imprisoned. Your terrible future is now averted. All those fears you had about killing your parents, killing the world... They are no more." Argeddion smiled gently. "And yet I sense your loss."

She glared at him. "What are you talking about?"

"I can read your mind, remember. All of those guilty little secrets you're so ashamed of, they're spread open for me. Your private moments, your not-so-private moments, your doubts and your fantasies and your thoughts... Oh, Valkyrie, save your blushes. The only thing you should be ashamed of is how much you enjoyed being Darquesse."

"That's a lie," she shot back.

"You didn't enjoy the killing," Argeddion said, "but you loved the power. It's a shameful thing to love, but you're young. You're allowed to make mistakes. We're all only human, aren't we?"

"Are you?" Skulduggery asked.

"What else would I be?"

"Some people would say you're a god."

"That doesn't mean I'm not human also," Argeddion said, laughing slightly.

Lament's sorcerers were stirring. One by one, they rose up into the air, turning slowly. Their eyes were closed.

"I'm afraid I must ask you to leave," Argeddion said. "My friends will escort you back beyond the force field. For your own sakes, please don't try to break through it."

The sorcerers started to drift towards them, herding Skulduggery and Valkyrie to the door.

"Talk to us," Skulduggery said. "Convince us that what you're doing is right. Give us the chance to explain why it's a mistake. You've been gone for thirty years, for God's sake. You don't even know what the world is like any more."

"And this is where I change that," Argeddion said.

And then the emptiness swallowed him and he was gone. Vanished.

"He learns," Skulduggery said. "He may not have been conscious when Fletcher teleported us from the mountain, but he was aware."

"That's all it takes? He just has to experience something once and he can do it himself?"

"He knows his true name," said Skulduggery. "He can do anything."

Lament's sorcerers kept coming, pushing an invisible barrier before them, forcing Skulduggery and Valkyrie out of the room. Valkyrie tried pushing back but there was no strength behind it. She felt drained, like losing Darquesse had robbed her of her determination.

"Lenka," Valkyrie said. "It's me. It's Valkyrie."

Lenka smiled. It was disconcerting, seeing her smile with her eyes closed. "I know that, silly."

"How much of you is in there?"

"All of me is," she said. "I haven't gone anywhere."

"But Argeddion's controlling you."

Lenka shook her head. "That's not how it is at all."

"Then why are you doing this?"

317

Lament drifted closer. They were being forced back up the corridor, to the energy wall. "Because Argeddion deserves to be free," he said. "He never hurt anyone. He never wanted to hurt anyone. We took it upon ourselves to imprison him without him ever giving us a reason to do so."

Skulduggery tried pressing back against their energy, but it was no use. "So you feel bad, and now you're making up for it?"

"Yes."

"Then why are you all hovering on tiptoe and going around with your eyes closed?" Valkyrie asked.

Lenka laughed. "What are you talking about? Our eyes aren't closed."

"Yes, they are, Lenka. I'm looking at you right now and your eyes are closed. Can you see me?"

"Of course I can see you. There's nothing wrong with us, Valkyrie. We're just trying to do the right thing. I'm not like Tanith. I don't have some evil parasite nesting inside me. I'm still me."

Valkyrie frowned. "How do you know about Tanith?"

"Argeddion speaks to us. He opens his thoughts, lets us see what he sees. When he read your mind, we saw it all. We know about your guilt, and your fears, and your loves..." Her voice dipped. "And we know about your *secret*. We know it's been awful for you, living with the knowledge that you're going to kill your own parents. But that doesn't have to happen any more, Valkyrie. Argeddion has helped you. He's imprisoned Darquesse inside you. He's changed the future."

"He's going to destroy the world," Skulduggery said.

"Please," said Lament, "have a little faith."

When they reached the force field, it dimmed for a moment and they stumbled through, falling against the sorcerers collected beyond it. Lament and the others stayed on the inside, eyes closed and hovering off the ground.

Ravel pushed his way to the front, and looked at them. "Let me guess," he said, sighing. "You've got fantastic news."

31

CAROL

alkyrie felt odd. Muted, somehow. It wasn't as if she had been aware of Darquesse inside her at every minute of every day, or heard her voice constantly at the back of her mind, but now she could sense the part of her that was suddenly quiet. It wasn't fair. Argeddion said it himself – Darquesse would have beaten him. But it was like the best close-combat fighter in the world being taken out by a sniper from a mile away – taken out before the fight had even begun.

Not that she *wanted* the fight to take place. Of course she didn't. But if it did happen, she wanted to be as strong as she could be. She wanted to beat anyone who stood against her. She wanted to crush them. There was nothing wrong with that. Nothing wrong with wanting to survive. To win. To feel that power coursing through her.

She missed that power. She'd grown used to having it there, ready for when she needed it. She missed the voice in her head. No matter how much she ignored it, how much she fought against it, its presence had been reassuring. Facing down a werewolf? Three thugs kicking her half to death? None of that had bothered her because she knew, she *knew*, that all she had to do was give in for just one glorious moment, and she could feel that power again.

She didn't tell Skulduggery that. It wasn't that she didn't think he'd understand – it was that he'd understand all too well. And Valkyrie didn't want that.

But he was busy elsewhere in the Sanctuary. The force field had bisected some of the detention cells, short-circuiting the binding sigils that kept the prisoners' powers down. Eight of them had escaped, including Silas Nadir. Skulduggery was not happy about that one, but he had more pressing concerns.

Valkyrie saw Tipstaff and followed him because she had nothing better to do. He led her into a room with a large table, at which sat the Elders with Strom and Sult. Tipstaff gave them all a cup of tea and a biscuit. No one spoke.

"Why is Argeddion's plan such a bad idea?" she asked, breaking the silence. They looked at her blankly. "I mean, I know it'd be different, and the world would change in huge ways, but who are we to say that it wouldn't change for the better?"

Quintin Strom stirred his tea. "If everyone in the world was suddenly capable of using magic," he said, "there'd be a frantic scramble for dominance. We'd be looking at a new world order, and humanity would be decimated as each nation struggled to assert itself at the top."

"Millions would die," said Ravel. "Billions. There's a reason Sanctuaries exist. We regulate our people. Keep them in line. Many sorcerers have the potential to be weapons of mass destruction. And in a world as fragmented as this one, with as many religious and political beliefs as it does? A small group of extremists could bring about our end."

"So just explain all that to Argeddion," Valkyrie said.

"The man's been living in a bubble for the past thirty years," said Ghastly, "and before that he was living in a different sort of bubble, where no one wants to hurt anyone else. He'd never be able to understand the mindset of violent people."

"What," said Valkyrie, "you mean people like us?"

Ghastly looked at her. "If we could live in Argeddion's paradise, we would. And maybe it's possible – it'd be wonderful to think that it was. But we'd have to step over a generation of dead bodies to reach it. The cost, Valkyrie, it's just too great."

"We can't afford to be idealists," Ravel said without looking up. "It's our job to keep the world spinning. We let the mortals change it. As clumsy and as corrupt as they are, this is still their world. We're just protecting it."

The door opened and Skulduggery came in. He stood beside Valkyrie, and took his hat off. "Nothing," he said. "No sign of Argeddion. No idea where he materialised and no traces for the Sensitives to follow."

"We need to find out who his surprise guest is," Ghastly said. "If his plan hinges on this guest and the Accelerator, we have to take one of them out. The Accelerator is still behind that force field, but the guest may be vulnerable. How much time do we have?"

"Tomorrow's Thursday," Skulduggery replied. "We have until Saturday before his tests are complete. He infected the mortals downstairs to find the best way to infect *everyone*. I've just checked with Doctor Synecdoche, but there was no change in their condition when Argeddion awoke."

"And what about this Greta Dapple?" Ravel asked. "If he planned this out to coincide with her birthday, which is a sweet but psychotic thing to do, then maybe she plays a bigger part in this."

Skulduggery nodded. "Maybe she does. She isn't at her house and she isn't answering her phone. I have people looking for her. If we can find her, she could lead us straight to Argeddion."

"And what do we do when we find him?" Sult asked. "What can we do?" He looked to Strom, Strom looked to Ravel, and Ravel looked to Skulduggery.

"I'm working on it," he said.

The drive back to Haggard seemed to take for ever. Valkyrie fell asleep twice, and woke up both times by bouncing her head against the window. "Ow," she said.

"Sorry," said Skulduggery. They were on country roads, and his skull was in complete darkness. "How are you feeling?"

"I don't know," she said. "My head feels empty. He just... cut her off from me. I don't have her any more."

"If it's permanent, that could be a cause for celebration."

"But Darquesse and Vile might have been our only weapons against him." She sighed. "What are we going to do? This isn't as clearcut as usual. Kitana and Doran and Sean and Silas Nadir... those are the people we're used to dealing with. Killers. People who hurt other people. But Argeddion... he's not like them."

"Argeddion is as dangerous as anyone we've faced," Skulduggery said. "He may not be out to physically hurt us, but his goals are just as damaging. We need to treat him just like any other hostile."

"Would you kill him?" asked Valkyrie. "He's a pacifist who only wants to help people. And there's no guarantee that mankind *would* destroy itself. It might all work out according to Argeddion's plan. Who are we to say it won't?"

"Are you willing to take that risk?"

"I just... I don't feel right about this. He wants to make the world a better place and we want to keep the world as it is. That doesn't sound particularly... heroic."

"We have to maintain the status quo, Valkyrie. It's not our job to change the world. That's for the mortals to do."

"So you *would* kill him?"

There was a pause. "I believe his plan would result in billions dead. Yes, I would kill him."

"I… I don't think I could."

He turned his head to her. "I'm not asking you to."

The Bentley pulled in at the pier and Valkyrie got out. It was just past ten but she was exhausted. The air lifted her to her window and she climbed in. Her room was empty. She sat at her desk, where schoolbooks lay open. She yawned, and her reflection came in. It shut the door behind it.

"Hey," she said.

"Hey," it said back. "You look like you've had a rough day."

"Rough enough."

"Where's your jacket?"

Valkyrie glowered. "I don't want to talk about it. I just want to go to bed. You finished our homework?"

It shook its head. "Another half-hour or so, I'd say. Can you wait until then?"

"Yeah. Sure. I'll go for a walk, actually." She got up. "Hey, I want your opinion on something."

"Sure," said the reflection, stepping towards the mirror.

"No," said Valkyrie. "I want your opinion as the reflection of me the last time I was here, not as the reflection of me now. If you know what I know, then your perspective will be my perspective, and I don't want my perspective. I want your perspective."

"For anyone else, that would be overly complicated. OK. What do you want your old perspective on?"

"Argeddion is out. He's free. He wants to make every mortal magic and live in a kingdom of enlightenment and righteousness. It sounds lovely, to be honest, but according to Skulduggery and the others, it'd never work and we'd all end up killing each other. But he's really powerful, and the only way we had to stop him was to..."

"Become Darquesse," said the reflection.

"Yes. But I can't do that any more. He got in my head, he blocked her off. I can't Hulk out and Argeddion took Skulduggery's armour, made it vanish. It's not destroyed, or else all the Necromancer magic would return to Skulduggery, but it's hidden."

"You're disappointed."

"Argeddion's at least as powerful as Darquesse. We needed her."

"Needing her is dangerous."

"I know."

"You might have been able to stop Argeddion, but who would stop *you*?"

"Hopefully, Skulduggery."

"He'd have put on the armour and gone after you? After what happened last time?"

Valkyrie collapsed back into her chair. "I don't know. Yes. He did it before."

"He stopped you, eventually, after you both tore up O'Connell Street. You tried to kill people. You tried to take down a helicopter. And what about Skulduggery? When he puts on that armour, he's a killer. You know he is."

"But last time—"

"Last time was a fluke," the reflection said. "Somehow, he

managed to regain control of himself and he talked you down. But if you let her take over again, she won't go so quietly next time."

"Well, we don't have that option any more."

"That shouldn't have even *been* an option. Argeddion has a plan that *might* backfire – but your plan was to send two killers after him? What's the term that was used before? World-breakers? You were going to send two world-breakers after him? There is a risk of his plan going wrong and resulting in death and destruction. But if you had unleashed Darquesse, you'd be *guaranteeing* that people would die."

"Skulduggery would have stopped me."

"You can't be sure of that."

"I trust him."

"And that's the problem."

"What? What's the problem?"

The reflection hunkered down and rested her folded arms on Valkyrie's knees. "China told you once that Skulduggery would kill you without hesitation if he had to. He'd sacrifice anyone for the good of the mission. When you realised you were Darquesse, this was practically a comfort. You knew that if things got bad enough, you could rely on Skulduggery to put a bullet in your brain to stop you from killing your parents."

"That's ridiculous. I never—"

"You can lie to yourself," the reflection said, "but you can't lie to me."

Valkyrie shut her mouth.

The reflection continued. "But things have changed. Your relationship with Skulduggery has deepened, you know it has. You know the lengths he would go to for you, and that's the problem. Valkyrie, he would sacrifice the world to save you."

"You don't know that for sure."

"No," said the reflection. "But it's what you suspect."

"He wouldn't let me do that. He just wouldn't."

"Maybe not. But he'd waste time. He'd second-guess himself. He'd look for another way. He wouldn't go for the kill shot when he was given the chance, and by then, it might be too late. You don't have that reassurance any more. It's the two of you against the world. But that's not what you need. You need him with his finger on the trigger, and the gun to your head. You should be thankful Darquesse is no longer an option. I can't see how it could have ended well."

Valkyrie sighed. "How am I supposed to know what to do?"

"You're not," the reflection said gently. "You're seventeen. You're supposed to be dealing with school and hormones and dim-witted parents. You're supposed to be finding out who you are as a person."

"But I already know who I am," Valkyrie said. "I'm a world-breaker."

She changed her clothes. It was still warm outside so she pulled on jeans and a different T-shirt and went for a walk along the pier, listening to the dark waves against the rocks, then turned and walked up into Haggard. She passed the takeaway that had sprung up when the Pizza Palace had gone out of business. The video shop was gone, too. A lot of things had changed in the last five years.

Carol Edgley came out of the takeaway holding a steaming bag of food. She saw Valkyrie and hid the bag behind her back. "Hi, Stephanie," she said. She was blushing.

Valkyrie gave her a smile. "Hiya, Carol. Oh my God, that smells amazing."

"Uh, do you... do you want to share?"

"Would you mind? Just one or two."

Carol hesitated, then brought the bag out and opened it. She offered it to Valkyrie, who took a small handful of piping hot chips. Her stomach rumbled; she realised she was starving. She blew on them a few times before eating.

"These are so good."

Carol smiled, and had a few herself. They walked towards the corner of Main Street, where the road split.

"How are things?" Valkyrie asked.

"Good," Carol said. "Grand."

"How's your mum?"

"Fine. She joined a bridge club."

"I didn't know she liked bridge."

"She doesn't, but ever since we started defending you she needed a wider range of people to disapprove of."

Valkyrie took another few chips, and grinned. "You know, if it makes your life any easier, you can always go back to agreeing with her."

"No. No way. Those days are gone. Look at everything we missed out on because we were too busy being selfish. Gordon chose you to have all these adventures. He could have easily chosen us if we'd been nicer or cooler or, I don't know, happier. It's like Mum just kind of trained us to be miserable. Dad spoiled us and Mum was a bad example and look how we turned out. And then look at your mum and dad. They're cool, and funny, and weird, and genuine. They're genuine, y'know? Mum isn't genuine."

They walked along for a bit, with Carol eating her chips and Valkyrie looking at her. "She's not *all* bad."

"No," Carol said. "She isn't. She's my mum, and I love her, but she's not a nice person. You mightn't think we realise that but we do."

"I don't know what to say," Valkyrie admitted. "I don't want to agree with you, because that'd be mean. And I can't really argue..."

Carol laughed, and Valkyrie smiled.

"But no one's perfect," she continued. "My folks can get just as annoying as anyone's."

"But you had a head start," Carol said. "They gave you that, and that's what makes them cool. They didn't spoil you. They criticised you when you needed it. They didn't treat you like you were this little princess that only they could see. You were way more independent at twelve than we are even now. Do you understand that? The twelve-year-old version of you was more of a grown-up than I am right now, aged twenty."

"I think you're being a bit hard on yourself."

They reached the corner and Carol turned to her. "Look at me, Valkyrie. I mean, just look at me. I'm a slob."

"No, you're not."

"It's ten o'clock on a Wednesday night and I'm walking home with a bag of chips, just like I do every night. I'm fat. I've always been fat and I've always hated being fat but I'm too lazy to do anything about it. I start diets but they're too hard so I stop, and eat more. I'm fat and Crystal is thin, she's way too thin and she won't listen to me, she won't believe me when I tell her she's too skinny. She always says no, she hasn't reached her target weight yet, and she gets thinner and thinner and I can see her bones now. I know you're used to that with Skulduggery, but it's a lot different when it's your sister."

"Yeah."

"And then we look at you. Even from here I can see the muscles on your arms."

"I have to be strong to do what I do. If I wasn't involved in all this, I'd be just like you guys."

"No, you wouldn't. You'd still be tall, for a start, and you'd probably be swimming every day or horse-riding or something."

"Well, that's all *you* need to do. Whenever I'm not working on a case with Skulduggery, I train really hard. I practise magic, I fight, I lift weights, I work out. Every few months Skulduggery brings in another friend of his who's an expert in some fighting style I've never heard of and I get thrown about the place. Whatever muscles I have I got through hard work and sweat. And I hated most of it. But all you have to do is find the activity that you enjoy and you won't care about how hard the work is."

"I've... I might have found an activity." Carol looked away. "I've been, kind of... I've been practising magic."

Valkyrie raised an eyebrow. "I see."

"Just the fire stuff," Carol said quickly. "I'm not really good with the air, and I don't know about the water and earth, but I can click my fingers and sometimes things go on fire."

"Sounds... dangerous."

"I keep a bucket of water beside me when I do it."

"Listen, I don't want to tell you not to practise. I don't have that right. You have magic in you, it's part of your heritage, just like it's a part of mine. But you're taking a risk every time you do it. What if your mum sees you? Or your dad? They'd freak out, Carol. They'd call every emergency service they could think of. You could get into a lot of trouble."

"I won't, I promise."

"Can you at least try not to set fire to anything? That's going to raise some suspicions sooner or later."

"I won't do it in the house any more."

"OK. Thank you."

"Do you want another chip?"

Valkyrie smiled, and took one.

"Are you working on a case at the moment?" asked Carol.

"Yeah," she said.

"Anything exciting?"

"A few days ago I wrestled an Abominable Snowman."

"No way!"

Valkyrie grinned. "Yep. That was pretty cool. Really bad breath, though. Like, disgusting."

"Eww."

"And I've been to an alternate universe."

"Seriously? Like on *Star Trek*?"

Valkyrie laughed. "Since when do you know about *Star Trek*?"

Carol looked around, like someone might be listening, then leaned in. "Don't tell your parents, but Mum loves *Star Trek*. When we were kids, we used to watch the reruns of the original series, *Next Generation*, *DS9*... She liked *Voyager* more than we did, and none of us liked *Enterprise*... But she doesn't want anyone to know she's a Trekkie, so..."

"I promise I won't tell, no matter how amused it might make me."

"Thank you. So what was the alternate universe like? Are there evil versions of everybody? Is there an evil version of me?"

Valkyrie laughed. "Sadly, no. Our histories ran parallel up to a few hundred years ago, so none of us have been born."

"Oh. That sucks." Carol ate another chip. "Wouldn't it be cool to find out what your evil version would be like?"

Valkyrie made a face. "Not really..."

She walked Carol back to her house and they finished off the bag of chips. Carol told her about this guy she liked in college, and they giggled and laughed and when Carol walked to her front door, she had a bounce in her step, and looked lighter than her frame would suggest. Smiling to herself, Valkyrie took the little lane down to the beach and walked back to her house along the sand. She got to her room, the reflection went back into the mirror, and she stripped down to underwear and a T-shirt and climbed into bed. Sleep came quickly.

She didn't know what time it was when the throbbing in her arm woke her, but it was still dark as she lunged out of bed. She grabbed her phone and her ring off the bedside table and stumbled to the wardrobe. The world flickered around her and a wave of dizziness sent her into the mirror. Her ring fell from her grip. She reached for her black clothes as the reflection stepped out and then the bedroom was gone and Valkyrie was falling through empty space. She hit the ground and rolled, sprawling on to her back.

Her house was gone. She sat up, groaning, looking down towards the pier as the waves crashed and churned. The modern houses were gone. Old walls crumbled beside dirt tracks instead of roads.

She sat there on the untamed grass, in her underwear and a T-shirt, her phone clutched in her hand. She didn't have her protective clothing. She didn't have her Necromancer ring. The only thing she'd managed to do right was release her reflection, so at least her family wouldn't notice her departure. That was something, at least.

"Looks like we're in trouble," her own voice said, and she whipped around to see her reflection sitting behind her.

32

STRANGERS IN A STRANGE LAND

he town of Haggard was gone, and in its place stood a small village. Thin shacks of rotting wood squatted in the darkness, black voids against the star-filled sky. It was an unsettling sensation for Valkyrie to walk the ground she knew so well and for it to be so utterly different. They circled the village's perimeter. Small stones dug into her feet with every step. The reflection matched her pace but showed no sign of discomfort.

"You should have given me space," Valkyrie said, her voice tight.

"I'm sorry," said the reflection.

"The whole point of your existence is to stay behind, for God's sake. What use are you if we're both missing? Mum's going to freak out."

"Or she might just assume that you left for school early."

Valkyrie glared. "Have we ever done that before?"

"No," it admitted, "but with all the talk of exams lately, she might believe you're taking it seriously."

"So she's going to believe I got up an hour earlier because I wanted some study time?"

The reflection shrugged. "People believe what they want to believe so long as it's reasonable. But I'm sorry. I should have waited in the mirror until you were gone. I don't know why I tried to help you up. There might be something wrong with me again."

Valkyrie didn't say anything. She was being unfair and she knew it.

"OK," she said at last, "the plan. The plan is to stay out of sight until we're pulled back. We need to stay within arm's reach at all times, all right? I don't know how long we'll be here."

"You're cold. You need clothes."

"You need clothes, too. I don't want you running around in a strange dimension half naked. I have my modesty to protect."

Valkyrie checked her phone, more out of curiosity than any expectation that it would actually work. No signal and no Internet. She tried to find her position on a map but the phone informed her she could not be located. Out of the two things she had grabbed, why couldn't she have dropped the phone instead of the ring? The ring at least would have worked.

They found a clothes line that apparently belonged to a big fat man. The trousers were a fine length but they were far too wide, so Valkyrie had to use a piece of string as a belt. The coat was fine, though she had to roll the sleeves up a little. The boots were the worst, though. They were battered and tattered and much too big. But at least she *had* boots. The reflection was barefoot, and didn't have a coat, but it did find some loose change in one of its pockets so at least now they had money – even though they had no idea how much the coins were worth.

They were heading for the next town over. The plan was to keep to the back roads and they were succeeding admirably, as every road so far looked like a back road.

"What time is it?" the reflection asked.

"Why, do you have somewhere to be?"

"I'm just asking because your first visit here lasted twenty minutes. We've been here hours. It's nearly dawn."

"Yeah," Valkyrie said. "I noticed. Nadir said this echo thing will build its own pattern, but I have no idea how to work it out."

"We could be here for days."

"Yeah," said Valkyrie, her mood failing to lift.

Dawn split the night sky and glorious orange spilled across the horizon. They saw farmers in fields working with mules and horses, sweating in the morning sun. It was just like travelling back in time.

"I wonder if the whole world is like this," she said. "There has to be one country where things have progressed, where things have been invented. Life evolves, right? It doesn't just stay in one place and that's that."

"It does if you're a slave," said the reflection. "That's what the mortals are in this dimension, aren't they? Slaves. The sorcerers keep magic for themselves, their lives evolve and their society progresses, but for mortals? They're kept down here in the mud. They aren't allowed up."

Valkyrie looked at it. "That sucks."

"Yes, it does."

They got to the next village and bought some bread. Their money didn't stretch very far, but it was enough to satisfy Valkyrie's hunger. People looked at them oddly, seeing a set of twins in badly fitting clothes, but didn't bother them, and Valkyrie and the reflection stayed out of the way as much as possible. The houses here were the same as in Haggard, and the stony trail that acted as the main street was covered in horse dung.

They watched the people ignore a woman who was pleading for help. She grabbed the arm of a man and he tried to shake her off. Valkyrie turned away from her wailing and begging and only glanced back when he threw her down.

"Hey," said Valkyrie, and before she knew what she was doing she was halfway across the road.

"Please!" the woman cried. "Please help me!"

The man cursed her, raised a hand to hit her and Valkyrie clicked her fingers. The fireball flared and the man recoiled, turned and ran. She let the flames go out, fully aware that the street had practically emptied and that her reflection was shaking its head. The woman was on her knees, and she clutched Valkyrie's leg.

"Please help me."

"Here," Valkyrie said, "stand up. Stop crying. What's wrong?"

The woman allowed herself to be pulled up, but she transferred her hold from Valkyrie's leg to her wrist. "Please. My son. They took my son."

"What happened?"

"He was talking with his friends, just talking. It wasn't anything more than that. There was nothing about the Resistance or about fighting, it was just... He didn't mean anything by it. He wasn't complaining. But the Sense-Wardens came out of nowhere, and before he could explain himself they arrested him."

Valkyrie went cold. "Sense-Wardens patrol out here?"

"They patrol everywhere," said the woman. "They arrested him. Just him, not any of his friends. It's all a mistake. He would never have had anti-Mevolent thoughts. Please. Please, if you could talk to them, make them understand that my son isn't a threat..."

"I'm sorry, I can't talk to anyone. I don't know them."

"But you're a sorcerer, aren't you? You're..." The woman's eyes widened. "You're part of the Resistance."

"I'm not part of anything."

The woman tightened her hold. "Could you help him? Could you rescue him?"

"I can't," said Valkyrie. "Sorry. I'm not even from here."

"They have my son. Please. They might execute him. You have to help me. Nobody else will."

"If they've brought him beyond the wall, then there's nothing I can do."

"But they haven't," the woman said. "The Barge doesn't return to the Palace for another three hours."

Stay out of trouble, Ravel had said, and it had seemed so easy at the time.

"The Barge," Valkyrie said. "Where is it?"

"It leaves here in a few minutes, then joins the other Barges and they all return to the City. Please. There isn't much time."

Valkyrie sighed. "Wait here."

"Please don't leave me!"

"I'm going to talk to my sister, OK? Just stay here for a moment."

She pulled her wrist free, and hurried over to the reflection, which stood in the shade with its head down.

"I'm going to see if I can help this woman," she said.

"Skulduggery told you—"

"I know what he told me. I want you to follow. Wherever I go and whatever I do, you follow. You don't interfere unless it looks like I'm about to be killed or something."

"I thought we were supposed to stay within reach."

"Plans change."

The reflection looked up. "I really don't want to be left here alone if you return without me."

Valkyrie hesitated. "I know. Listen to me, if that happens, go back to Haggard, where we arrived. I'll come back for you."

The reflection nodded, then said, "Please don't get killed."

Valkyrie gave it a shaky grin. "No promises."

Valkyrie allowed the woman to guide her to a field that ran along the outskirts of town. Parked in this field was a vessel roughly the size of a jumbo jet. In fact, if someone had taken a jumbo jet made of black metal, torn the wings off, flattened it till the cylinder shape became rectangular, then that's what the Barge looked like. Minus wheels or windows or any obvious way in.

"You seriously want me to break into that thing?"

"Can you do it?"

"I don't see how. I don't even know how it works. Where does it open? Where's the door?"

The woman looked at her. "You've really never seen a Barge before? Where are you from?"

"Not here."

The woman bit her lip, then nodded. "I can show you the door. When it starts to leave, if we hurry, we can get to it without being seen."

"No, you should stay out of sight."

"You won't find it without me. I can be quick when I need to be." The woman picked up a rock. "And if the Redhoods come, I'll fight them with you."

"We don't fight Redhoods if we can help it," said Valkyrie. "If you see them, you run, OK? Leave any fighting to me."

The woman nodded, but didn't drop the rock.

They ducked down as a small squad of Redhoods returned to

the field. They disappeared round the other side of the Barge, and a few minutes later, a massive engine started rumbling.

"Get ready," said the woman.

The Barge shook a little, then slowly lifted up off the ground.

"It flies?" Valkyrie said. "You didn't tell me it flies!"

"Come on," said the woman, hurrying out from cover into the wide-open space of the field. Against every instinct she possessed, Valkyrie followed. They passed into the shadow of the Barge, and when they were directly underneath, the woman stopped and pointed.

"See? Right there. See that hatch?"

Valkyrie frowned. The underside of the Barge was completely flat, with nothing to hang on to should she propel herself upwards. "That's the only door? There isn't one on top?"

"That's the only one I know of."

"Then we're in trouble," said Valkyrie. "I can probably get up there, but I've got no way of opening—"

The woman swung and the rock cracked against Valkyrie's skull. She wasn't even aware of her body falling. She just lay on her back, her thoughts congealing into something slow and thick as she watched the hatch open, high above. A hovering platform lowered itself to the ground, and a man stepped off. He was familiar, but Valkyrie's muddled thoughts couldn't place him. He was tall and broad-shouldered. Grey hair. A strong jawline. The woman spoke to him, her hands clasped like she was begging. The man didn't even look at her. His eyes were on Valkyrie, as her mind struggled towards clarity.

"—brought her to you," said the woman. "Let my son go. Please. He made a mistake. He'll never do it again. Take her instead. I know you've been looking for her."

"Your son will be questioned," the man said. He had a deep voice, rich with authority. "If he has committed no serious crime, he'll be returned to you as a reward for your service."

The woman broke down crying. "Thank you, oh, thank you. When will he be released?"

But the man had wasted enough time on this mortal woman, and instead stood over Valkyrie, shackles in hand. Using his foot, he flipped her on to her belly. A name floated through her thoughts. She almost hadn't recognised him without his beard.

Baron Vengeous shackled her hands behind her back, and hauled her to her feet.

33

THE MAN IN BLACK

Elsie stood behind the lamp post and tried to work up the courage to talk to the construction supervisor. Most of the work in the street was already done. The café had a new window, the wrecked car had been taken away, all the damage was being patched up. According to the first news reports this street had seen some kind of gang battle, with people shooting at each other and blowing up cars. Then the reports changed to indicate that someone had been using a flame-thrower and, bizarrely, some kind of "laser beam". But the latest news cleared up all the confusion, stating that it had merely been a boring old car crash. The eyewitnesses came back on air, apologised for their mistakes and the newsreaders chuckled about it. The important thing was that nobody was hurt, and nobody was suing anybody.

Elsie had listened to all of it and she just knew that Kitana and the others were responsible, and that the people that Xebec had been talking about, the magic cops, were hiding what had really happened.

"Excuse me?"

She turned as two men approached, journalists, one of them holding a camera. The other one glanced around quickly, and gave her a furtive smile. "Were you here?" he asked. "Did you see it? Did you see what really happened?"

She blinked into the camera lens. "Are you from the news?"

"We're making a documentary," said the man. "We're exposing the truth behind the cover-ups. Are you a witness? Would you be willing to tell us what you saw?"

"I'm sorry," she said, "I don't know what... I wasn't here. Sorry."

The man looked at her. "Did they get to you, too?"

She frowned, and the cameraman tugged on his colleague's arm. "Come on, Kenny, let's go."

"She knows something."

"We'll be seen. Come on."

The cameraman hurried off. The other man, Kenny, gave her a business card. "If you remember anything," he said, walking backwards, "call this number." And then he was gone.

Elsie waited a few moments, then went to the skip by the side of the road and dropped the card in among the debris and broken glass. She took a deep breath, then approached the construction supervisor. "Excuse me," she said, "I'd like to talk to someone in charge."

The supervisor smiled at her. "That'd be me."

"Uh," she said. "No, I mean... someone who's really in charge. You know. Of the secret thing."

"The secret thing?"

She nodded. "With the... stuff."

He frowned at her. "Were you hit on the head recently, Miss? Maybe we should get a doctor to take a look at you."

"I'm fine," Elsie said quickly. "Well, no I'm not, but I just want to help. I know this wasn't a car crash. And I don't think it was gangs with laser beams, either. I... I think I might know the people who did this."

The supervisor looked at her, and gave her another smile. "What's your name?" he asked.

She told him.

"You know what?" he said. "I think I might call my boss. Do you mind hanging around for a bit?"

"I'll stay," she said.

He nodded, stepped away and made a call. Half an hour later, a beautiful black car pulled up and a tall, thin man in a black suit got out. He took off his hat and smiled at her as he shook her hand. He wore gloves.

"Elsie," he said, "thank you for getting in touch." He had such a nice voice. Smooth and comforting. "We've been looking for you over the past few days. Your mother is worried."

"I can't go home," Elsie said. "Not yet. I just need help."

"I know you do. My name is Skulduggery Pleasant. Unusual

name, I know, but then I'm an unusual person. As are you, it seems."

"You... you know about the... stuff?"

"If by stuff you mean your powers, yes I do."

"I just want this whole thing to stop," she blurted. "Can you do that? Can you take away my powers?"

"We can't," he said. "Not yet. But we're working on it."

"I don't want to hurt anyone."

"I know. But your friends do."

Elsie's smile was anything but happy. "I don't think they're my friends any more. I've known Sean since we were kids. Our mums are best friends, so we grew up around each other. I don't really know Doran. I mean, we've been in the same class for years, but I don't know him well. He's a bully, and he was arrested last year for assaulting a college student. He got away with it, though. He's... angry. I think he intimidates everyone. Except Kitana."

"Tell me about her."

"She's always been popular. All the guys do whatever she says. I suppose *everyone* does whatever she says, even me. The only thing we've got in common is Sean. If it wasn't for him, I don't think she'd even know my name. Kitana is... there's something wrong with her. Like, even before we got these powers she was always... wrong."

"And these powers – you all have identical abilities?"

"I think so, yes."

"What did you do when you got them?"

"What did I do? I don't know. I suppose I panicked. We were behind the school, mitching off maths. That's where we went when we were supposed to be in class, behind the sheds out the back. We were all normal. The lads were trying to impress Kitana and I was just sitting there, and then I felt sick. Like, hot and sweaty but also really cold, you know? Like I had the flu or something. And I looked up and the others were the same. We just thought it was a bug. We went home, and we all had the same dream, about Argeddion. I can't remember much of it, just this man in white and he was giving me something. A gift. I woke up the next morning and... and I just knew. I knew there was power inside me."

"How did it make you feel?"

"I didn't like it. Kitana said it was amazing but... I don't know. It was like there was a part of me that wasn't me. It was – what's the word? Unsettling."

"So all four of you suddenly had powers," Skulduggery said. "What did you do?"

Elsie shrugged. "We messed about for a few days. The more we used the powers, the stronger they got. Sean was really excited, he was talking about being superheroes and whatever. Doran called him stupid, he said we should rob all the banks in the country. Kitana said this was going to make her famous. She'd always wanted to be a model or be in the movies or something. It was going to make her a star."

"What about you? What did you want to use your powers for?"

"I liked Sean's idea the most," she mumbled.

"So what happened?"

"I don't know. We were all getting along great, we were all laughing and trying to decide what to do, and then..."

"Then?"

Elsie hesitated. "There was a bouncer in a nightclub who never let Doran in, because he was underage. Doran was always talking about him, about how he was going to go up one of these nights and kick his teeth in. And that's what he did. He went up, the bouncer told him he wasn't getting in, and Doran used his powers. He put the bouncer in hospital. I think he's still in a critical condition. Doran was laughing when he told us about it."

"How did Sean and Kitana react?"

"Sean was quiet at first, but Kitana kept asking all these questions, like what did it feel like, stuff like that. You could tell that she was into it, and because she was into it Sean got into it."

"And that's how it started."

"Yeah. Then it really got out of control. They killed Kitana's ex, they killed this guy who turned up and started telling us about the magic police... they killed Doran's brother..."

"We need to stop them before they hurt anyone else. Once they're back to normal, we can deal with whatever we have to deal with. But right now we need to stop them. Can you help us?"

"What do I have to do?"

"Do you have any idea where they are, or what their plans are?"

"They keep moving around, and I don't even know if they *have* plans. The lads do what Kitana tells them, and Kitana does whatever she feels like."

"Patrick Xebec was killed because he was a threat, but their real targets have been Kitana's ex-boyfriend and Doran's brother. They're going after people who treated them badly at some stage in their lives. Does Sean have anyone like that?"

"No. Not that I know of. His parents are nice. Doran's dad is drunk most of the time and Kitana's parents are never home, but Sean's whole family is lovely. Sean wouldn't hurt anyone."

"His power is corrupting him."

"But still, he wouldn't. He's not like the other two. He's nice."

"He's an accomplice to murder, Elsie. We have to stop him before he makes things any worse for himself. Can you think of anywhere they might go, or any score they might have to settle?"

"I can't think of anything. I'm really sorry. It doesn't even make any sense. Kitana didn't care about her ex. Not really."

"Then she was just looking for an excuse to hurt someone," Skulduggery said. "No one is safe from her, Elsie."

"I don't know where she is, honestly. The only... the only place I can think of that has people she'd like to hurt would be, you know, our school. You don't think they'd do anything, do you? We have friends there."

"I'll send some people round to keep an eye on the place. If they turn up, we'll deal with it. In the meantime, I'd like you to accompany me back to a place we call the Sanctuary. It... may not be the safest place in the world, but at least Kitana and the others won't find you. Will you accompany me?"

Elsie nodded. "Thank you. Thank you so much."

Skulduggery opened the passenger door and she got in, then he slid in the other side. "You might have to adjust the seat," he said. "The girl who usually sits there is quite tall, and likes everything exactly right."

Elsie moved the seat forward. "Will she mind?"

"Assuming she's still alive and she ever gets home, I'm fairly certain I'll never hear the end of it. Buckle up."

34

INSIDE THE CITY

The Barge rumbled and shook as it moved over Dublin City. Were it not for the fact that her reflection was somewhere down there, Valkyrie would have been perfectly happy to spend hours in this little cell, just filling in the time until she was pulled back to her own dimension. But she didn't want to leave it there. She didn't want to abandon it.

The shackles hurt her wrists, but comfort hadn't been uppermost in Vengeous's mind when he'd thrown her in here. Vengeous. The last time she'd seen him the Grotesquery was crushing his head, which was, what? Four years ago? She was pretty sure she preferred him with a crushed head. The Vengeous from this reality was every bit as humourless as his alternate self, and every bit as intimidating. He didn't have his sword any more, though, that cutlass thing. That was one thing to be grateful for, Valkyrie supposed.

It was pretty much the only thing.

Vengeous hadn't wasted any time with questions. He assumed she was part of this Resistance everyone kept talking about, and was probably looking forward to a nice bit of interrogation once they got back to the Palace. Valkyrie wondered if this version of Vengeous had been arrested by Skulduggery during that legendary fight China had once spoken of, or if none of that had happened here. If Mevolent, and now Vengeous, was alive here, then who else was? Was Nefarian Serpine waiting for them beyond the wall? And where was this reality's version of Skulduggery? Would he be much different to the Skulduggery she knew?

The idea that there could be two identical versions of Skulduggery Pleasant actually made her smile despite herself. The conversations that would result would probably be brain-punchingly narcissistic, at the very least.

The pitch of the Barge's engines changed. Deprived of a view, Valkyrie had no idea what was happening until the whole thing shook and clanked and shuddered, and then the engines slowly grew quiet.

They had arrived.

The door to her cell opened and a Redhood came in, yanked her to her feet. He brought her to the open belly of the Barge, to Vengeous, who ignored her while he oversaw the transfer of the mortal prisoners. Finally, he turned, dismissed the Redhood and walked down the steps. He turned when he was halfway down, looked back at her, his eyes glowing yellow. Valkyrie started down after him and his eyes returned to normal, and he led her out from under the Barge's shadow into the City.

The Dublin inside the wall was a vast oasis of luxury. The streets were wide and well ordered, bisecting buildings adorned with gargoyles as fierce as they were extravagant. Towers rose towards the sun and lush trees lined the pavements. At every corner there was a stone balcony, and on those balconies stood Elementals, conducting a stream of air over the privileged heads of the people. Carriages without wheels or horses or engines rose up from the ground to join this stream and were smoothly snatched away and carried from sight. There were a few rickshaws on the streets for those whose journeys deviated from the main routes, but there were no cars. The drivers of the carriages were all young sorcerers, probably Elementals, still learning their craft. The drivers of the rickshaws were brown-clothed mortals who kept their heads lowered. Valkyrie shouldn't have been surprised. What was the point of being the elite in society if you couldn't look down on those beneath you?

There were other mortals on the streets. They walked quickly, slinking in and out of alleyways so that they wouldn't offend the eyes of the magical. Servants and workers and slaves. Their social betters walked without hurry and wore clothes so fine they actually looked *delicate*, like a stray bit of dirt would tear a hole right through them. She didn't know what fashion they wore, with the high collars and pointy shoes and everything so bright and colourful and vibrant, but she could tell that a girl in brown being led among them was not a welcome sight. The shackles didn't help, she supposed, nor the fact that Vengeous was beside her.

People glared and sniffed as she passed. These people were sorcerers? These primped and pampered idiots? Most of the sorcerers she knew were battle-hardened and tough, used to sticking to the shadows and not drawing attention to themselves. The sorcerers of this reality were an altogether different breed.

"You've never been here before," Vengeous said. "You have that look in your eye that people get when they see the City for the first time. Take a good look. Drink in the sights. The dungeon has no such splendour on view. Your days will be spent in agony and your nights will be spent shivering and weeping and waiting for the pain to begin again."

"Yeah..." Valkyrie said, and shrugged. "Ah, I'm more of a morning person anyway."

He looked at her as they walked. She pretended she didn't notice. "The Sense-Wardens don't want to enter your mind, do you know that? The ones who tried have not yet recovered. They say you have something living inside you. A guardian. A protector. Is this true?"

"Yeah," she said, deciding it best to leave out the fact that her head was now a very lonely place.

"Do not look so pleased," said Vengeous. "Having a psychic prod his way through your thoughts may not be a pleasant experience, but luckily for us we still have physical torture. So do yourself a kindness. Before the interrogation begins, tell us what you did with the Teleporter, and maybe your suffering will be lessened."

She frowned. "Who? Oh, you mean that Remit guy with the twirly moustache? Yeah, I did nothing to him. I left him on a rooftop somewhere."

"Who has him?"

"Not me. Maybe he ran away. Maybe he wasn't happy. He did have a silly moustache, after all. That's usually a sign of some deeper unhappiness. Where's your moustache, by the way? Where's your whole beard gone? Why'd you shave it off?"

"Ah," he murmured. "You're one of those, are you?"

"One of who?"

"The kind who talk and joke when they're shackled. I've met a few of you. Your jokes are usually there to hide your fear, and it's always a good indicator that you will break easily, and quickly."

"Or," she said, "it might be a sign that I'm totally fearless and I laugh in the face of torture. I mean, it's not, but it could be."

He led her away from the main thoroughfare, to where the streets were slightly narrower. Still clean, still well-maintained, but a little less sunny and a lot less populated.

Valkyrie looked at him. "Can I ask you a question? I know this isn't how interrogations usually go, but since it hasn't officially started yet I thought I'd shake things up. What happened to *you*, Baron? I mean, is this what you do now? You transport prisoners? You used to be a general."

"I still am."

"No, you're a prison guard."

"I do what is needed. In times of war, it is a general's duty to win that war. In times of peace, it is a general's duty to preserve that peace."

"You call this peace? The people are terrified."

"Are you referring to the mortals? Of course they're terrified. Terror keeps them down. A terrified people is a peaceful people."

"Peace means nothing without freedom."

"Then peace means nothing. I'm sorry, were you hoping for a debate on the subject? You're a prisoner, and soon you'll be a prisoner in pain. We're not going to debate, or argue. You're no one. You're just another mortal sympathiser. Soon enough all your secrets will come spilling out."

They passed through a tunnel that blocked out the sunlight. A bald woman approached from the other side, her hands shackled. "Husband," she said, and Vengeous muttered something under his breath. Valkyrie raised an eyebrow as the woman neared. Vengeous's wife wore a grey shapeless dress made of sackcloth and her bare feet were chained at the ankles, forcing her to take small, quick steps. There was a small piece of wood hanging from a cord around her neck, into which were carved the two circles. With her hair shaved off and not one trace of make-up on her pale, drawn face, it took Valkyrie a moment to recognise her as Eliza Scorn.

"They were at it again last night," she said, not even glancing at Valkyrie. "Graffiti on the cathedral door. Scrawled obscenities and crude pictures. They need to be stopped. *You* have to stop them."

Her voice rose as she spoke, became shriller, echoing around the tunnel. Vengeous held up his hands in a comforting gesture, but stopped just short of touching her.

"I've alerted the City Mages," he said. "They're increasing their patrols in the area. Now please, I'm with a prisoner and cannot—"

Scorn shook her head. "Not good enough. These blasphemers need to be hunted down. You need to send your Diablerie after them."

"My love, the Diablerie have their duties—"

Fury twisted Scorn's face. "*Someone is defiling the cathedral!*" she screeched. "*When they defile the cathedral, they defile us all! Are you going to do nothing while your own wife is defiled?*"

For some bizarre reason, Valkyrie felt the need to look away to spare Vengeous the embarrassment of arguing with his clearly insane wife in front of a prisoner. Then she remembered that she *was* a prisoner, and so any awkwardness fell away.

"No one is defiling you," Vengeous said, keeping his voice down. "These are troublemakers and miscreants and they will be caught and punished."

"Miscreants?" Scorn repeated incredulously. "These are terrorists! They are openly blaspheming against the Faceless Ones and if you don't put a stop to it, this will spread. Do you hear me? It will spread."

Vengeous nodded. "I'll triple the guard."

"You need to hunt them down!"

"And I will do so. They will not escape our justice."

Scorn's hands rose to the wood around her neck. "You should question those in the dungeons. They know. They know who's doing this. That girl. Who is she?"

"We don't know yet. She's working with the Resistance."

Scorn whispered, but even so Valkyrie could still hear her words. "Question her. Pull her fingernails off. Cut out her eyelids. She knows who is doing this."

"Hi, Eliza," Valkyrie said.

Scorn stiffened, turned away, and Vengeous glared.

"Do not speak to my wife," he snarled.

Valkyrie ignored him. "Why the shackles, Eliza? Have you lost it so completely that you can't be trusted?"

Vengeous stormed over and Valkyrie forced herself not to flinch. "My wife wears those chains in penance for us all, to show the Faceless Ones that we are ready to be punished for what was done to them. She is a true believer. Her soul is righteous and pure, unlike yours."

"Diseased," Scorn muttered.

Valkyrie raised an eyebrow. "Sorry?"

"Diseased!" Scorn shouted, her eyes on the cobbled ground. "Your soul is diseased! Rotten! Putrefying!"

"That's a nice sack you're wearing."

"Stop her from talking to me!"

Vengeous shoved Valkyrie against the wall, his hand tight around her windpipe.

Scorn covered her face with her arms. "Stop her from looking at me! Stop her!"

Strong fingers dug into Valkyrie's cheek and pushed her head around until she was facing the other way. She heard Scorn's quick footsteps and the clinking of chains as she neared.

"Hurt her," Scorn said, fury biting at her words. "Kill her. Tear her face off. Rip her tongue out. Take her eyes."

"Mevolent wants to speak with her," Vengeous said.

"He can speak with her *corpse*. He can speak with her *carcass*. He can speak with her rotting *meat*, when her head is on a *pike*. He can speak with her *then*."

"He is waiting, my wife."

"Let him wait! This wretch of a girl gazed upon my face! She spoke to me, spiteful words! The Faceless Ones demand her suffering!"

"If that is so, then Mevolent will surely instruct me. Is he not the voice of the Faceless Ones on this earth?"

All Valkyrie could hear in response was Scorn's rapid breathing.

"Go back to your prayers," Vengeous said. "When I have delivered this wretch to Mevolent, I will return to you with the Commander of the City Mages. Together we will instruct him on how to police the cathedral."

"They're terrorists," Scorn said, her voice no more than a murmur.

"Yes, they are, and they will be hunted as such. Go. Pray. I will be with you shortly."

There was a moment of silence, and then chains clinked, and Valkyrie heard Eliza walk away. Seconds later, Vengeous leaned into her.

"I should crush your throat right now," he said.

Valkyrie started to say, *You make a lovely couple*, but she only got halfway through before Vengeous lifted her off her feet. Her legs kicked and she pawed at the hand around her neck.

"I don't know how much you know about me," he said calmly, "but I do not enjoy trading barbed witticisms. Such things are a waste of my time. If you even attempt to make a joke in my presence, I will break a finger. Understood?"

Spittle flew from Valkyrie's lips, and Vengeous released her. She dropped to her knees, gasping for breath.

"Very good," said Vengeous. "Come now. Mevolent awaits."

The Palace was a marvel of stone and steel and glass and glinted so brightly in the sun that it was actually painful to look at. Its steeples and spires rose like thin blades to pierce the sky. This was what Valkyrie had seen from the other side of the wall, this Palace with its towers so high you could probably look out over the whole of Ireland from up there. Probably.

A dozen men stood at the doors. Their left arms were armoured, their right arms bound in straps of leather. They wore heavy uniforms adorned with the three towers of Dublin, and each had a sword slung from a scabbard on their left hip, and a holstered gun on their right. City Mages, she guessed.

The corridor beyond the doors was ridiculously wide. In the centre of it was a large tank filled with a pale green liquid. In that tank, the naked corpse of Mr Bliss floated, a chain around his ankle stopping him from simply rising to the top.

"Mevolent likes to parade his vanquished enemies," said Vengeous as they passed.

Valkyrie pulled her eyes away, feeling hollow. The outside of the Palace may have been guarded by the City Mages, but the inside was the domain of the Redhoods. They stood like statues, scythes gripped in one hand, and she felt how her brown coat rubbed against her skin and how vulnerable it was. It would part as easily as her flesh to those scythes.

They entered into a large room. On the far side was a small pool of black liquid from which steam rose, seemingly responsible for the foul smell that hung in the air. Beside the pool there was a man on his knees, surrounded by six Redhoods armed with long spears. He was slender, with narrow shoulders, and his hair was cut short. His skin was tinged yellow, like a nicotine stain that had covered his whole body. His head was down. She couldn't see his face.

"That's Mevolent?" she asked, whispering.

Vengeous didn't answer.

At some unseen command, the Redhoods stepped forward and drove their spears into Mevolent's torso. He stiffened but didn't scream. The Redhoods withdrew their spears and stepped back, and Mevolent fell forward on to one hand. He stayed there for a moment, gathering his strength, then resumed his kneeling position. Once again, the Redhoods took a step, and drove their spears in. This time Mevolent did scream. He threw his head back, his eyes screwed shut, and let out an agonised howl. The Redhoods shoved their spears deeper, twisted, and the scream was cut off. They withdrew, and Mevolent slumped to the ground, blood oozing from his many wounds.

Something rose from the pool of black, something long-limbed and spider-like, slowly unravelling its arms as it straightened. The creature called Nye ignored Valkyrie completely as it reached for Mevolent, gently pulling him across the floor. The Redhoods stood to attention as Mevolent slid slowly into the pool.

"Every day he dies," Vengeous told her, keeping his voice down. "A short death, always violent. Always painful. Blood is always spilled. By doing this he will teach death that he is its master, and when it comes for him against his wishes, it will hesitate and withdraw."

Nye rose from the pool and left the room. It didn't even glance at Valkyrie. But of course, it had no reason to. To it, she was just another prisoner.

A moment later, Mevolent's head broke the surface of the black liquid. He climbed the steps out of the pool and a woman rushed forward with a robe. It was only when he was out that Valkyrie truly appreciated just how tall he was. Even barefoot, he towered over the woman and the Redhoods. The woman handed him a towel and he wiped the black residue from his face, turning away from Valkyrie before she got a good look. They left through the same door that Nye had scuttled through, and Vengeous prodded Valkyrie, forcing her on.

They came to what could only be described as a throne room. Elaborate weapons of all kinds hung from the walls, but the throne itself was a simple thing, just a heavy wooden chair that looked like it had been carved straight from the tree. On their way towards it, they passed a glass case. Within, garments stood like a suit of armour, fabric and leather and chainmail woven together in blacks and greys. The helmet was dark metal, its features arranged into a screaming visage, and the hooded cloak that covered it all was tattered and ripped and covered in half-hidden sigils.

"His battlesuit," Vengeous informed her. "The master had never been defeated while wearing it. The helmet has been the source of terrible nightmares for his many enemies."

Valkyrie didn't respond. She wasn't looking at the clothes or the helmet. She was looking at the small golden staff with a black crystal embedded in its hilt.

The Sceptre of the Ancients.

She stared at it. She no longer had Darquesse. Skulduggery no longer had Vile. But the Sceptre could kill Argeddion. If she could get it back to her own—

Vengeous shoved her so hard she nearly went flying. She recovered in time for him to grab her arm and position her before the throne.

"You are not to look the master in the eye," he said. "Mevolent is the voice of the Faceless Ones on this earth and as such you have neither the right nor the honour to look upon his face. Any attempt to meet his gaze will be met with punishment. Do you understand?"

Valkyrie nodded.

Mevolent came through the narrow door behind the throne, barefoot, wearing a simple robe and some kind of veil over his head that hid his eyes. Remembering Vengeous's words, she looked at his hands as he sat. For a while, he didn't speak.

"Have you ever seen a man come back to life before?" he asked at last. His voice was deep but flat. Unimpressive. "Not many have. Over the years, stories have grown up around what you have seen here today. The truth gets misplaced the more the stories travel. They say I bathe in blood. Have you heard that? According to the stories I must submerge myself in mortal blood for two hours out of every twenty-four, or else my body starts to break apart due to the corruption I have inside me. That's a lot of mortal blood to drain every single day, but they don't take such things into consideration when concocting these stories, do they? On a purely logistical level, if I had to drain all those mortals, I'd never have the time to do anything else, would I?

"Other stories tell how I eat innocent newborns, how I'm ten feet tall, how I breathe fire and have great dragon wings. None of these are wholly accurate. I don't have dragon wings, I don't breathe fire, I'm only eight feet tall and I've never eaten a newborn that didn't have it coming. My name is Mevolent. What's yours?"

For a moment, her throat was too tight to speak. "Valkyrie," she said at last. "Valkyrie Cain."

"You're not from here, Valkyrie, are you? I don't need my Sense-Wardens to tell me that. I'd have known it just by looking at you. You don't belong here."

"No."

"But you've obviously heard of me. You have too much fear about you not to know who I am. Am I what you expected?"

She shook her head.

"Words, Valkyrie. Use your words."

"No," she said. "You're not what I expected."

"I'm glad. I would hate to be predictable. You've heard about the monster Mevolent. You've heard the stories. You've heard what I've done. You expected something... different. What did you expect?"

"I don't know."

"This conversation is the only thing delaying your pain. It's in your best interests to prolong it."

She swallowed. "I didn't know what to expect. I've heard so much about you, but not... not what you were like. I expected someone..."

"Scary?"

"You are scary."

"Violent, then?"

"Yes. Maybe."

"I am a changed man. During the war, I was violent and bloodthirsty. When the war ended, I was violent and ruthless. During my reign, I have been violent and unyielding. Wherever I walk, I leave bloody footprints. But no more. Violence spreads misery, and I have grown tired of misery. Your friends in the Resistance, I would like to meet with them to forge a treaty, to go forward in peace."

"I don't have friends in the Resistance."

"We both know you stand against me."

"But I don't know anyone in the Resistance. I'm not from here, you said it yourself."

"Yet you have been noticed, Valkyrie. *We* noticed you, twice in the last few days. I'm sure you've come to the attention of the Resistance also."

"No, I'm telling you, I haven't met any of them."

"Don't take me for a fool, Valkyrie. I'm extending a hand in friendship."

"I'm sorry, I don't—"

Mevolent's mouth twisted into a snarl beneath his veil and Vengeous struck Valkyrie across the face. She fell to her knees.

"I try to be kind," Mevolent murmured. "I offer an olive branch instead of a sword, and this is where it gets me. Insulted. Mocked."

"I wasn't mocking you."

"You expect me to believe that someone like you has not caught the attention of the Resistance?"

"Maybe I have," she said, "but they haven't been able to find me. I don't want to join the Resistance."

"You're lying to me."

"I'm not, I—"

"Of course you are. You have to. You're lying because your life is in danger. You're lying because I could order Baron Vengeous to snap your neck and there's nothing you could do to stop him, is there? Well?"

"No," she said. "There isn't."

"So of course you're lying. I expect you to lie. It's only natural. You will lie until you run out of lies, and then you will tell the truth until you run out of truth, and then you will start lying again, telling us what you think we want to hear. We know this. It's inevitable. It's what happens. You will be no different to the hundreds, to the thousands, to the tens of thousands of people we've questioned."

Valkyrie kept her eyes away from Mevolent's face. She was fully aware of how close Vengeous stood to her. It was times like these, back in her own reality, that Skulduggery Pleasant would break down the door and stride in with a joke and a bullet. God, she missed him. God, she wished he were here right now. What she wouldn't give to see that door open and the Skeleton Detective walk—

The door opened. Mevolent's head moved slightly, his mouth twitching. A shadow at the door. Footsteps. Familiar footsteps. Skulduggery's footsteps. A smile broke across her face. He'd found her. He'd used Nadir to follow her over and he'd found her and—

He emerged from the doorway and Valkyrie's heart sank. Blood drained from her face and she suddenly got so very cold.

"Oh, no," she whispered, as Lord Vile moved to stand beside the throne, his black armour lapping at the air around him.

35

CHIPPING AWAY

Erskine Ravel was like one of those old movie stars, all dashing good looks and easy charm. He was, and Elsie had never actually used this word to describe anyone, simply *captivating*.

And Ghastly was so completely and utterly cool. She'd been shocked at first, when she'd seen his scars, but she couldn't remember anyone who made her feel quite so safe when she was in their company – her dad, maybe, back when she was a little girl, but that was it.

They walked by those grey-clad men and women, and she caught sight of her reflection in the visors of their helmets. Walking alongside Ravel and Ghastly, she suddenly realised how ridiculous she looked. Fat, ugly, wearing clothes that she'd once thought disguised both of these facts. These were exceptional, magnificent people she was around, and who was she? Take away the powers she hated and she'd be back to being a nobody.

They approached a blue wall of energy, on the other side of which four people in robes hovered a little off the ground with their eyes closed. Elsie was suddenly struck by how amazing this all was.

One of the men smiled, though his eyes didn't open. "Erskine," he said. "Ghastly. Aren't you two busy enough? Don't you have a crisis to control?"

"We're never too busy for old friends," said Ravel. "We just thought we'd come down, see how you were, see if you needed anything. A snack. A magazine. Maybe a bathroom break."

"You can't stop Argeddion."

"Who said anything about Argeddion? I didn't even mention his name. I wasn't even thinking about him. But since you've brought him up, Tyren, you are absolutely right. We can't stop him. Not without your help."

Tyren's smile widened. "You really think we're going to lift a finger against him? After what we did? He deserves freedom."

"Years ago, yes, he did. You made a mistake, and you weren't the only one. Meritorious should never have agreed to your plan. But now? It's too late. The point can be argued that you made him into exactly the kind of threat you feared, but I'm not one for assigning blame. That's not how this Council of Elders works. We *are* all about redemption, though, and this is your chance to redeem yourself. Elsie O'Brien," Ravel said, "I'd like you to meet Tyren Lament. Tyren and his friends have been infected with the same magic as you. Tyren, say hello to Elsie."

Tyren Lament turned his head slightly, as though he could see her through his eyelids. "I thought I recognised a kindred spirit. Hello, Elsie, how are you today? You know, by rights you should be over here on this side, with us."

Ghastly raised his eyebrow at her. "Well? It's up to you."

"Uh, no," she said. "No thank you. No offence, sir, but you're... you're kind of creeping me out."

Lament laughed, and the other robed people chuckled. "Fair enough, fair enough," said Lament. "So is this your tactic, gentlemen? Bring a lovely young lady down to us just so she can make fun of our sandals?"

"This isn't a tactic," said Ravel. "We just thought Elsie would like to see the first people gifted with a slice of Argeddion's power. What do you think, Elsie?"

She hesitated. "Am I going to end up like them?" she asked quietly.

"No," Ghastly said, shaking his head. "Argeddion's been controlling their will for the last few years, that's why they're like this."

"It's really not as bad as it sounds," Lament said.

She peered at him. "But how do you do things? How do you talk to us? Is he controlling what you say?"

"That's not really how it works. Think of it like this – ages ago,

Argeddion sat us all down and had a conversation, and during that conversation he made us see that we were wrong, and he was right. Whether or not we *were* wrong, or he *was* right, is completely irrelevant, because now it's what we believe. That's what it's like."

Elsie frowned. "So you *know* you're being controlled? Why don't you try and get free?"

"Because we don't want to."

"Why not?"

"Because we don't have to want to."

"Why not?"

"Because Argeddion has taken that want away from us."

"I don't... I don't want to insult you," said Elsie, "but I don't think I could live like that. Don't you want to be free just for the sake of being free? There has to be some part of you that wants to do whatever you want to do."

"No," Lament said, "there isn't."

"I doubt that's entirely true," said Ghastly. "Our Sensitives have noticed a weakening in the link you have with Argeddion. The longer he spends away from you, the less control he has. Do you feel it? The weakening?"

"I'm dreadfully sorry," Lament said, "but no, we can't feel any such thing."

There was a girl to Lament's right, a small blonde girl, and she raised her head. "I can," she said.

Lament turned his head a fraction. "Lenka?"

The girl, Lenka, hesitated. "I can feel it. Argeddion's control is fading."

The man at the other end of the line nodded. "I can feel that, too. I've been having my own thoughts recently. A strange sensation."

"Interesting," said Lament. "Do all of you feel this?"

"I feel a change," said the other man, the man with dark skin. "Not quite at the level of Kalvin or Lenka, but a definite change. At this rate, it's conceivable that we all break free of his control completely over the next day or so."

"All of us?" Lament asked.

The man smiled. "All of us."

Lament looked happy. "Now that is interesting. Freedom, eh? Well, I'll be looking forward to that, even if I don't particularly want it."

Lenka grinned. "But might the fact that you're looking forward to it be the first sign that you're achieving it?"

"Lenka," he said softly, "you've just blown my mind."

Ghastly looked back at Elsie, and shrugged. "And this isn't even the weirdest conversation we've had this week."

36

THE OLD MAN IN CHAINS

Redhood took her to the dungeon beneath the Palace, to where darkness was kept at bay by only a few sputtering torches in rusted brackets. The cells were open and prisoners lay within, most of them too damaged or weak to attempt an escape. Those who were strong enough were chained to the walls. The stench of pain and filth and terror made Valkyrie's eyes water and brought bile to the back of her throat.

The shackles that bound her wrists were in turn bound to a long chain in an empty cell and that's where the Redhood left her. She covered her nose with her hands and breathed through her mouth.

"You get used to it," said a voice.

There was a man in the cell opposite. He had long grey hair and a long grey beard and looked like he'd been there for a long grey time. His body was bony and old, and he hung from his wrists but didn't seem to mind the discomfort.

"The smell," he said. "You get used to the smell. A few days here, you won't even notice it."

Valkyrie walked to the door of her cell and looked at him in the gloom. Her mouth opened but she didn't know what to say. Someone was crying. Someone else was muttering. There seemed to be a light-hearted conversation going on somewhere in the dark, and she wasn't entirely certain that it was between more than one person. She bit her lip.

"You're trying not to panic," the old man said.

A ghost of a smile rose from within. "Yeah," she answered.

"Keep trying," said the old man. "You'll panic soon enough, but at least you'll know you did your best. Most people panic immediately when they're brought here, and I think it's the embarrassment that gets to them in the end."

There was something about him, something about his voice, that suddenly clicked in her mind.

"Grand Mage?" she asked, frowning.

Eachan Meritorious laughed. "Grand Mage? No one's called me that for a very long time. You must be older than you look, my dear. What's your name?"

"Valkyrie," she said. "Valkyrie Cain. What... what happened to you?"

"I'm afraid you're going to have to be a little more specific with your questions."

Her chain was long enough to allow her to step into his cell. "You weren't always like this."

"That's very true," he said. "Sometimes they hang me upside down."

"That's not what I mean."

"They think it's funny. I suppose it is, in its limited way. When you're a guard in a dungeon, you have to make your own fun, don't you? So, tell me what you did to get thrown in here. Not the most original topic of conversation for a dungeon, I admit, but I'm afraid I'm a little behind on current affairs."

"I tried to help someone."

"A noble gesture."

"I tried to help a mortal."

"A futile gesture. Why ever would you want to do something silly like that? These cells are filled with noble and silly people like you, plus the mortals they tried to help."

"Grand Mage, I'm not from here."

"Sightseeing, are you?"

"I'm not from this reality."

"Hmph," said Meritorious. "This place didn't take long to send you round the bend."

"I'm not crazy."

"I'm not judging you, my dear. Some of my best friends are

crazy." He nodded to the corner. "Take Wallace, for example. He's crazy as a loon, aren't you, Wallace?"

Valkyrie frowned. "Uh, there's... there's no one there."

Meritorious sighed. "That's what we long-term prisoners call dungeon humour. You learn to appreciate it after a few years."

"I'm not crazy, and I'm not lying. I'm from another reality. Look." She took out her phone and showed it to him. "This is a phone. See the screen? That's not magic, that's technology. That's mortal technology. Have you ever seen anything like it?"

"No," said Meritorious, "but that might be because I've been stuck in this dungeon for the last few decades. What does it do?"

"It lets me talk to people that aren't here."

Meritorious looked unimpressed. "We can all do *that*, my dear girl."

"Yeah, but they answer me."

"I'm sure they do."

"But not in a crazy way," she said, getting irritated. "It's for communication. I can talk to anyone around the world with this."

"Wait, wait, wait," Meritorious said. "Are you talking about a *tele*phone? My dear, I've seen a telephone, and while progress is a wonderful thing, there are some inescapable truths. If that is a telephone, then where are the wires?"

"It doesn't need any."

"And yet you say it's not magic?"

"Telephones don't need wires any more."

"Then how does anyone hear you? And how do you dial? Where are the numbers? It's a very small object to be capable of doing many wonderful things, don't you think?"

"It does much more than that," Valkyrie said, opening up a game and showing it to him.

His eyes widened. "What wonder is this?"

"It's called Angry Birds. Now do you believe me?"

He took a moment. "Mortal technology, eh?"

"They've been allowed to flourish," she said, pocketing the phone. "A Dimensional Shunter sent me here. In the reality I'm from, Mevolent's been dead for a very long time. Without him enslaving everyone, civilisation has evolved."

Meritorious nodded. "And this, these Angry Birds, is the pinnacle of mortal evolution?"

"Uh," she said. "It's one of them, I suppose..."

"Astonishing. Please forgive my scepticism. From what I know of Shunters, the applications for their powers are limited. The chance of any Shunter even finding another dimension that is *liveable* is quite remote, never mind a dimension that has run almost parallel."

"I know how rare it is," said Valkyrie, "but this guy managed it, and he sent me here."

"Unfortunate, to say the least. And in your world, Mevolent is dead?"

"Yes. You were there when he died. You were part of it."

He laughed. "Well, that is heartening to hear. At least some version of me didn't fail. And you know that version of me, do you? I'm still Grand Mage in your world?"

"You were," Valkyrie said after a hesitation. "Then you died."

"Ah."

"Bravely."

"So, in the dimension where good triumphs over evil, I'm dead. And in the dimension where evil triumphs over good, I'm in a dungeon. I can't help but feel slightly aggrieved. Existence, it seems, is a harsh mistress."

"I think it was Mevolent. That's the one big difference. In my history, he died. In yours, he didn't. And then he took over, and everything changed from that moment on."

"Well, as you can see, in this dimension, he won the war," said Meritorious. "He either killed or imprisoned those who fought against him. Some escaped his clutches, but not many. From what I've been told by my fellow prisoners, the Resistance is not quite as strong as one might believe."

"If he's so powerful, how come he hasn't brought the Faceless Ones back?"

"Thankfully, he hasn't been able to. Some secrets are still beyond him."

"What about the Book of Names? Can't he use it to find out whatever he needs? Or he could just find out his true name, and eventually he'd be so powerful he'd just have to *want* them to come back and they'd be here."

"All true," Meritorious said, nodding. "But the Book of Names has been safely hidden away, and I'm the only one who knows where it is. Why do you think he hasn't killed me yet, the same way he killed Morwenna and Sagacious?"

"Sagacious Tome?"

"The bravest man I ever met. They tore him limb from limb and he still wouldn't betray me. Does Sagacious live, in your world?"

Valkyrie thought about going into detail, then decided against it. "No," she said. "Neither of them does."

"My poor friends," Meritorious said. "But at least for them it's over. He tortures me every few months now. I'll never tell him, of course, and his psychics will never be able to break my mind. I think he tortures me more out of habit than anything else."

"But he has Teleporters, doesn't he? And if he has Teleporters, then he can just open a portal once he has the Grotesquery."

"I'm afraid I don't know what a Grotesquery is."

"Oh," she said. "Well, in my history, Vengeous found the remains of a Faceless One and it was later used as an Isthmus Anchor to—"

"Stop!" he whispered suddenly. "Don't say anything. If you know where the remains are in your reality, then they'll find them in this one and—"

"But I don't," Valkyrie said, keeping her voice down. "Vengeous found the remains during the war. I don't know where they were originally."

"Then that must be another difference between the timelines,"

Meritorious said. "So the point where our realities diverge was not Mevolent's death, after all. It was something else. Interesting."

"Is the whole world like this? Is everywhere as bad?"

"Some places it's even worse. Africa is no more, did you know that? They were the last to fall, and Mevolent made an example out of them."

"It sounds like hell."

"It has similarities. And your home, to me it sounds like heaven. A paradise where the mortals control their own destinies and fire angry birds at pigs in little boxes. May I see them again?"

She took out her phone. "How about we listen to some music instead? I'm thinking 'Apple of my Eye'. Do you have Damien Dempsey in this dimension?"

"I'm not really sure."

"Well, then," she smiled, "this'll be an education."

She had dozed off with her back to the wall. When someone shook her awake, she opened her eyes to a figure in darkness.

"Valkyrie Cain?" the man whispered. "Your reflection asked us to get you out of here."

Before she could answer, he stood and moved further into the gloom to wake another prisoner. The dungeon was suddenly a very quiet hive of activity. People hurried through the torchlight, chains rattling as shackles were unlocked. It was a prison break.

Hope flaring in her chest, Valkyrie sprang to her feet. There was a man on his knees, his hands tied behind his back and a gag in his mouth. A rope was tied around his neck like a leash, the other end gripped by a man she knew.

"Dexter Vex," she said.

Vex frowned and smiled at the same time. "Do I know you?"

She resisted the urge to hug him. "Sort of. Kind of. Not really. You've seen my reflection?"

He nodded. "It's waiting for us at the rendezvous point."

"You're the Resistance?"

"That we are," he said. "And it's thanks to you that we can free our brothers and sisters."

"Me? What did I do?"

Vex grinned. "You gave us our way in."

He pulled back on the leash and the kneeling man raised his head to the light. Alexander Remit glared up at her.

"You left him on a roof, and the poor fella was so disorientated when my friends arrived that he didn't even have time to teleport away."

Remit growled something behind his gag.

"We've been after one of their Teleporters for years," Vex continued. "But we never expected to get one like this. He's been everywhere. Every part of the City, every part of the Palace. We were given our opportunity, and we took it. Thanks to you."

"Happy to help," Valkyrie said. "So who's going to release Meritorious?"

Vex looked back at Meritorious as he hung there on the wall. "We can't free him," he said, his voice heavy. "The chains that are holding him are beyond anything we're used to. Mevolent made sure that no matter what happens, the Grand Mage will stay a prisoner."

"You're just going to leave him?"

"We don't have a choice," said a man as he walked by. It was the same man who'd woken her. She should have recognised his voice.

"Ghastly," she said.

Ghastly Bespoke glanced back at her. "You and your reflection know a lot about us. You mind telling me how?"

Valkyrie hesitated. "Later," she said. "I promise."

It was unsettling, looking at Ghastly and not seeing the recognition in his eyes. For the first time she noticed what some of them were wearing – black clothes, made of the same material as her own outfit back home. This Ghastly was a little narrower than the one she was used to. He still had the same broad shoulders but where her Ghastly had a boxer's physique, the Ghastly who stood before her looked like a sprinter. Less physically powerful, but faster.

He walked over to Meritorious and Valkyrie followed.

"I'm sorry," said Ghastly.

Meritorious smiled. "You're not to blame, my friend. Do what you can. Save who you can. This girl here, take her, too. She has an interesting story."

"I'm sure she does," said Ghastly. "We've rounded up everyone. We have to go."

"Then go."

"I'll be back for you, Eachan. We'll get you out somehow."

"I'm an old man and my time is almost done, so don't you worry about me. I'm not as valuable as you all seem to think I am, and I'm certainly not as wise as I pretend to be. If I see you again in the sunshine, so be it. If I die down here, I'll make sure they'll have to clean up after me for a week."

The air was split by a scream.

"Vile!" someone shouted. "It's Lord Vile!"

Suddenly everyone was panicking. Ghastly grabbed Valkyrie's arm, dragged her after him. She glimpsed a dark figure striding between the cells, and all those people trying to get away.

Darkness swarmed to his armour, filling the space behind him. Tendrils lashed out, as fast as striking cobras, impaling those who tried to run. The dead and the dying were lifted off their feet and paraded ahead of Vile as he walked, their tortured cries adding to the panic of those still with a chance of escape.

"Keep him back!" Ghastly roared, and immediately five sorcerers barged past Valkyrie, on an intercept course. Elementals and Adepts, they hurled whatever they had at him. Most of their attacks struck the helpless bodies of Vile's victims, and the attacks that got by were instantly swarmed by shadows.

Ghastly ran to a wall, started drawing with chalk. "Behind me!" he roared. "Everyone behind me!"

People pushed and shoved, almost knocking Valkyrie back. Finished with one symbol, Ghastly ran to the opposite wall, started drawing there. He had a scrap of paper in his other hand, and he was copying it as best he could.

Shadows reared up behind the five sorcerers who faced Vile, and they turned, tried fending them off, but the shadows swayed and feinted, waiting for the silent command to strike. And then they struck, slicing through the sorcerers and picking their bodies up off the rough ground to join the grisly parade, and still Vile walked.

Ghastly finished drawing, pressed his hand to the symbol, then backed off towards Valkyrie. "Run!"

They ran. Vile flung the bodies of his victims away and pressed forward, stepping between the symbols. There was a green flash, so bright it blinded Valkyrie for a moment. She staggered, feeling around her. Slowly her vision came back and she turned, blinking, saw Vile on the ground, trying to get up.

Ghastly grabbed her arm again, turned to the dozens of people all linked by touch to Vex and Remit in the middle of the crowd.

"Everyone linked up?" Vex asked loudly.

Valkyrie glanced back. Vile was on his feet.

"Go!" Ghastly ordered. Vex put a knife to Remit's throat and they teleported, all of them, exchanging the oppressive confines of the dungeon for the open sky of a meadow at evening time.

There were people on the outskirts of the meadow, people who rushed in, shouting. At first Valkyrie thought they were being attacked, but when they collided, they collided in hugs. She watched all these people be reunited with friends and family, and Ghastly led her through it all. She saw the top of a scythe in the crowd and tensed, then glimpsed grey instead of red. Cleavers. Proper Cleavers, not Redhoods, standing to attention.

"Wait here," Ghastly said, and moved between them. She quickly lost sight of him and stood there, looking around for a face she recognised.

"Did you meet Mevolent?" asked her reflection, appearing beside her. Valkyrie surprised herself by how glad she was to see it.

"Yeah," she responded, smiling. "Not what I was expecting. I thought he'd be, you know, fire and brimstone and drenched in blood. But he's normal. Not totally normal – he's eight foot tall and insane – but normal enough. Lord Vile is with him."

The reflection looked at her. "Maybe that's why Mevolent is still alive."

Valkyrie moved closer, and kept her voice low. "That's what I was thinking. Which means if *our* Skulduggery hadn't snapped out of it and thrown away the armour all those years ago, Mevolent would be ruling our dimension as well. What's going on here? How did you meet these guys?"

The reflection shrugged. "They found me. Apparently having a stranger in town wearing clothes that don't fit is enough of an oddity to attract the attention of the Resistance. Vex came to see me. He's so good-looking."

Valkyrie nudged the reflection's side with her elbow. "Keep your voice down."

An eyebrow arched. "My opinion is your opinion."

"Yeah, but I don't need him knowing my opinion."

The reflection smiled. "Sorry."

Ghastly approached through the crowd. "Valkyrie, she will see you now."

He turned and she hesitated, then followed, the reflection by her side.

"She?" Valkyrie whispered.

The reflection gave another little smile. "The Resistance leader."

The crowd parted ahead and revealed a woman in a long white dress, the most beautiful woman Valkyrie had ever seen. Her hair was as black as a starless night while her eyes were as blue as ice and twice as cold. China Sorrows gazed upon her and didn't smile.

"Child," she said. "We are in your debt. Without your gift of the Teleporter, my people would still be rotting in that dungeon."

"Thank you for taking me with them on the way out," Valkyrie replied. "You're... You're the Resistance leader?"

China arched an eyebrow. "You sound surprised. Do I know you?"

"No," Valkyrie said. "But I've heard of you."

"Your reflection tells me you're an Elemental, is that right? We're always on the lookout for more recruits to the cause."

"Sure," Valkyrie said, a little doubtfully. "It's just I don't know how long I'll be here."

China was already turning away. She had delivered her invitation and that was all she cared about.

Ghastly stepped closer. "You promised to tell me how you know the things you know," he said. "I see recognition in your eyes. We've met before, haven't we? But I don't remember."

"It's complicated," she said. "I'm not from here." Her arm started to ache. "Oh... and it looks like we'll be heading home soon."

"Is that so?"

She smiled at him. "It was very nice to meet you, and I'm glad I could do something to help. And if you ever meet a girl called Tanith, do yourself a favour and ask her out immediately."

Ghastly smiled. "You are quite odd."

She nodded. "I've heard that."

The reflection stepped between them, looking off to Valkyrie's left. "Who is that man?"

Valkyrie and Ghastly looked to where its gaze rested. Amid all of the tearful reunions and the hugging there was a man in rags standing alone in the crowd. His head was down but his eyes were moving.

Ghastly took a moment. "I don't know. Just another innocent citizen arrested by the Redhoods."

"He seems anxious," said the reflection.

"Breaking out of prison will do that to you."

"He keeps looking around, like he's waiting for something to happen."

Valkyrie frowned. "Mevolent knew you had the Teleporter," she said, rubbing her arm. "He could easily have put a spy in the dungeon in case you attempted a rescue, then sent Vile down there, to make sure we left in a hurry without checking who everyone was..."

Ghastly looked at her, then back at the man in rags.

"Would you do me a favour?" he asked, not taking his eyes off him. "Would you please inform Miss Sorrows that it is time to leave? And then could you tell Dexter Vex to disperse the crowd? Thank you."

Without waiting for a response, Ghastly started moving towards the man in the rags. The man saw him coming and turned, started walking away. Ghastly sped up. Valkyrie heard a shout from somewhere to her left, turned her head in time to see Lord Vile step out of swirling darkness.

The people closest to him cried out and stumbled back. He brought his arm around, darkness gathering like a wing beneath it, and flung the shadows away from him. They whipped through the crowd, severing limbs and puncturing torsos, felling half a dozen fighters in one go before retracting.

Ghastly had changed course, forgetting about the man in rags and instead zeroing in on Vile. He used the air to leap over the heads of the panicking crowd, landing in a crouch before his enemy. He clicked his fingers, summoning flames into both hands.

He lunged and Vile sent his shadow-knives to slice his body from shoulder to hip. Valkyrie gasped as Ghastly parted from himself and fell in two pieces.

She became aware of something overhead, a great looming shadow, and looked up as the Barge opened its doors. Redhoods dropped like rain. Vex unleashed a stream of energy but a scythe flashed and took his arm. The reflection tried to dodge a Redhood but he was too fast. Valkyrie didn't even see it go down. She pushed at the air and clicked her fingers and got a boot in the belly for her efforts. She folded, all the breath rushing out of her and every muscle constricting.

Through tear-blurred eyes she saw the Resistance fighters struggling to hold the Redhoods at bay while China made her escape. They didn't last long. Scythe blades turned red and screams filled the air. Valkyrie still couldn't breathe. Her head thundered and she felt like she was going to pass out. Then the world flickered.

She squirmed in the dirt, looking back through the gleaming boots of the Redhoods towards the reflection. It caught her eye, understood what was about to happen, and started crawling towards her. Valkyrie reached out, the world flickered again, and the reflection stretched for her hand, and right before their fingers touched, the reflection and the world went away and Valkyrie gasped for breath as she lay on a road in the glare of headlights.

There was a screech of brakes and Valkyrie got to her hands and knees, forced herself up, staggered away. The driver got out of his car, pointed and shouted, telling everyone what he'd seen, a girl appearing out of nowhere. Valkyrie kept going, arms wrapped round her midsection. They wouldn't believe him. By the next morning, he'd start to doubt what he'd seen himself. She didn't have to worry about it.

Now all she had to worry about was her reflection, trapped in a world it didn't understand. Scared. Defenceless.

Alone.

37

THE DEBRIEF

"Mevolent has the Sceptre of the Ancients."

Valkyrie sat in the Medical Bay in the brown clothes that swamped her while Reverie patched her up. The Elders stood beside Skulduggery, staring at her as the implications of this sank in. Quintin Strom and Bernard Sult stood to one side with Grim, Strom's bodyguard, close by.

"And it's functional?" Ravel asked.

"I didn't see it in action," Valkyrie said, "but it's in one piece and it has a black crystal. Yes, I'd say it's functional."

"If we went in there and got it," said Ghastly, "we would have a weapon capable of stopping Argeddion."

Valkyrie nodded, and let her gaze linger on Ghastly for a little while. It was nice to see him in one piece.

"But how?" asked Strom. "Silas Nadir is no longer in custody, which means we would need a team of our top operatives to stay within arm's reach of Valkyrie at all times. And who knows how long it will be before she's pulled through again? It's impractical."

"First things first," said Ravel. "Valkyrie, where does Mevolent keep the Sceptre?"

"In his throne room."

Mist shook her head, ever so slightly. "If we do manage to steal it, what then? The Sceptre's previous owner must be dead before the new owner can use it. Mevolent would have to be killed."

"Not necessarily," said Dr Nye, looming over them all. "Forgive me. I couldn't help overhearing. I do not profess to be an expert on Sceptre lore, but I have a casual understanding of transdimensional physics. More of a hobby than anything else."

"Get on with it," Skulduggery said.

Nye cleared its long, skinny throat. "The transportation of any object of power, the Sceptre included, between dimensions, would invariably result in what can only be described as a short circuit. Upon its arrival, the Sceptre's power would be depleted. All it would need in order to reactivate would be a simple recharge of magic. The result would be a fully operational Sceptre that was ready to imprint upon a new owner."

"You're sure about this?" asked Ravel. "You're sure it would just wipe clean?"

"I'm ninety per cent sure."

"So there's a ten per cent chance it won't work."

"Yes, but my ten per cent is someone else's fifty. I assure you, Kenspeckle Grouse would agree with me if he weren't so amusingly dead."

Ravel looked at Skulduggery. "It's your call."

Skulduggery's head tilted. "Mine?"

"If anyone is going to be close enough to Valkyrie the next time she shunts, it'll be you. You might be able to take another few people with you, maybe a few Cleavers, but it could just be the two of you."

"And if it is, then this is the mission you're assigning us. To steal the Sceptre of the Ancients from Mevolent, one of the most powerful and evil sorcerers who ever lived."

Ravel nodded. "I'm afraid so. You're going to have to improvise. If China's Resistance survived the attack, enlist their help. Either mount an offensive or sneak into the Palace. Take the cloaking sphere from the Repository and keep it on you. Take whatever else you think you might need. Your primary objective, the both of you, is to retrieve the Sceptre."

"We have another option, too," Valkyrie said. "We don't have to kill Argeddion to stop him. Lament didn't, thirty years ago. He just used three words that the killer of Walden D'Essai's mother said to him. What was it he called it? A traumatic phrase from his childhood. It stunned him, giving them the time they needed."

"And what's the phrase?" Strom asked.

"We don't know," Valkyrie said. "But if we find Walden D'Essai in that other reality, we could ask him."

"What makes you think he's even alive over there? And what makes you think you'd be able to find him?"

"Mevolent's City is thriving. Every piece of progress is reserved for the people inside those walls. Someone like Walden, with the work he does and the mind he has... he'd be in the City. Mevolent wouldn't let someone like that go."

Ravel looked at her. "You have a point. OK then, primary objective is to retrieve the Sceptre. Secondary objective is to find Argeddion's traumatic phrase, in case we can use it to temporarily disable him."

"Third objective," she said, "is to get my reflection back."

"Don't worry about that," said Ravel. "Reflections don't feel pain if they don't have to, and no Sensitive will be able to read its thoughts. It won't tell them anything about where it's from."

"I'm not worried about what it might *say*, I'm worried about *it*. I don't want it over there alone."

"Valkyrie—"

"I don't want to hear that the reflection is not a real person. I know it isn't. But that doesn't stop me from wanting it to be safe."

Ravel looked at Skulduggery for help.

"I've given up trying to convince her otherwise," Skulduggery said. "Her reflection is unique. It's not like the obvious fakes we've seen before."

"But it's still not a person," said Ravel.

"It is to me," Valkyrie responded.

He sighed. "Fine. Recovering the reflection is your third objective

– but only if it doesn't put you at risk. And in exchange, Valkyrie, we'll need a Sensitive to build a wall in your mind as soon as possible."

Valkyrie frowned. "What? Why?"

"We can't let Argeddion read your thoughts if you encounter him again. The Sceptre must remain secret."

"Oh, yeah," Valkyrie said. "Right."

"We'll need the best. Luckily, we'd already called her in for any help she might give us on breaking the psychic link between Argeddion and Lament's group. Let's leave them to it."

They dispersed, and standing behind them was a woman with long grey hair and a kind face.

"Hello, Valkyrie," said Cassandra Pharos. She came forward, gently clasped Valkyrie's hands between hers. She had a very serene way about her that would have been comforting if Valkyrie's mind wasn't suddenly full of images of the dream whisperer she'd burned. "How are you? You've grown up so much since the last time I saw you."

"Well, a lot's happened," Valkyrie said. "You look great."

"Flattery means little to a woman of my age, my dear. But it still works, so thank you." Her smile dipped. "Now that I have you, I don't suppose you've heard from Finbar lately?"

Valkyrie shook her head. "I was kind of hoping *you* had."

"Sadly, no. I'll be honest, I'm getting worried about him. Being used by the Remnants like that could have... damaged him. Permanently."

"Maybe he just needs more time. It might even be doing him some good, just living a normal life for a change."

"Maybe," Cassandra said, "maybe. But we have more pressing matters to deal with, do we not? You need a wall built in your mind."

"Apparently so."

"I don't want you to worry about this. I won't be able to read your thoughts while I'm constructing it, and it's not going to affect you in any way once it's in. All it does is form a protective shield should anyone try to enter your mind without permission. It's entirely painless. Just lie back and close your eyes. That's it. I want you to relax now. Just feel the tension drain from your body…"

They drove back to Haggard through darkness. There was something wrong for the entire journey, and Valkyrie only realised what it was when they pulled up at the pier. She turned to him. "Was there somebody sitting in my seat?"

"Hmm?" he said. "Oh, yes. Elsie O'Brien. Very nice girl. Terrible self-image. She should take lessons from you on confidence. I think you'd do her a lot of good."

"Never mind all that, Skulduggery. You let her adjust my seat."

"She's not as tall as you."

"But you let her adjust my seat."

"I did, yes."

She stared at him.

He hesitated. "I'm really sorry?"

"I'm gone for not even twenty-four hours and you let someone adjust my seat? What, were you looking for a new partner already? Am I that easily replaced?"

"I take back what I said. Elsie shouldn't talk to you. You're quite obviously unhinged."

Valkyrie spent a minute trying to get the seat back to its original position. She sat back in it, frowning. "I don't even know if this is how I left it. Was I this far back?"

"It looks right."

"I had this perfect, you know."

"I'm dreadfully sorry. Next time, Elsie can run alongside me as I drive."

She folded her arms and sulked.

He patted her shoulder. "I'm sorry I let someone adjust your seat. And I'm really glad you're back."

Valkyrie smiled. "See? Was that so hard to say?"

She got out, kicked the tattered boots into the sea, and ran barefoot to her house. She climbed through her window and changed quickly in her room, stuffing the brown clothes under her bed. She looked at herself in the mirror. She looked tired. She needed a shower. She reached out slowly and tapped the glass, but nothing happened. Her reflection was merely her reflection.

Tears came to her eyes without warning and she stepped back, muttering, wiping them away. This was not the time to break down, for God's sake. She took a deep, deep breath, and blew it out. There. Much better. No more tears. All that fragility pushed aside.

She put on a happy face, in much the same way that the reflection would have, and skipped lightly down the stairs.

"Hey, Mum," she called.

Her mother appeared in the kitchen doorway at the same time as her dad popped out of the living room.

"Wow," she said, jumping back. "You're like ninjas."

"Steph," her mum said, saying the name like it was a sigh of enormous relief. "Where were you?"

There was a leaden weight somewhere in her chest that she ignored. "I told you I'd be at the library after school."

"No, you didn't."

Valkyrie laughed. "Well, OK, I didn't *tell* you but I wrote it on the note."

"What note?"

She passed her mum, moving to the fridge. "This note. The one I left... oh. Where's it gone?"

"I didn't see any note," said her mother.

"Me neither," said her dad.

"Oh," said Valkyrie, making a show of scanning the floor. "Oh, it must have fallen off. Must be under the cooker or something. And the battery on my phone died." She turned to them, widening her eyes. "Oh my God, so that means you didn't know I left this morning before you got up? Oh, I'm so sorry! Were you worried?"

Her mother laughed. "No, no, of course I wasn't."

"I was," said her dad.

Her mum frowned at him. "You just noticed she wasn't here ten minutes ago."

"The longest ten minutes of my life."

"Is that why you went back to reading the paper?"

"I needed something to distract me."

Valkyrie smiled at them both. "Well, I'm really sorry for any distress I may have caused. I'll try not to let it happen ever again. But now, Mum, is there any dinner left? I'm starving."

She ate, looked in on her little sister, and put her black clothes in a pile on the floor beside her before she went to bed. She kept her Necromancer ring on. She lay in the darkness for a few minutes, then reached for her phone. She dialled.

Skulduggery answered immediately. "Are you shunting?"

"No," she said, "no, everything's fine. But what if I do shunt again tonight?"

"I considered that," he answered. "And without wishing to alarm you, I'm in your back garden."

She laughed. "You're what?"

"If your arm starts to hurt, open the window for me and we'll go together."

"You can't stand in the garden all night," she said, and got up, wrapped a sheet round herself and opened the window. A moment later, he was perched on her sill. She went back to bed, and snuggled under the covers. "Come in," she whispered.

"I'm fine out here."

"Don't be dumb. You might be seen."

He considered it, then climbed through, closing the window behind him. "And what if your parents walk in?"

"Then I'll tell them I borrowed the skeleton from the school lab and dressed it in a nice suit as a prank."

"You're not known for your pranks."

"Maybe it's time for that to change."

He went to the wall opposite the bed, and slid down until he was sitting. With the light off, all she could see was the outline of his hat. "Do you want me to tell you a bedtime story?"

She smiled. "No thank you. You can sing me a lullaby if you want."

And that's what he did. In a voice so soft it barely reached her through the darkness, he sang her 'Me and Mrs Jones', and she fell asleep to his voice.

38

TWO AGAINST THREE

A phone beeped quietly and she woke. It was morning. Friday the 30th of April. One day before May 1st, and Greta Dapple's birthday, and the Summer of Light, when the world would tear itself apart. What a cheery, happy thought to wake up to.

Valkyrie sat up, yawned, stretched both arms above her head.

"I'm still here," Skulduggery told her, and she yelped, almost fell out of bed. "Sorry," he said. "You looked like you'd forgotten about me."

"I had," she said, glaring. "Did we get a call?"

"Yes, we did. One of the mages stationed at St Brendan's School saw someone answering Kitana Kellaway's appearance in the vicinity. We may as well drop by on our way to the Sanctuary to check it out."

He stayed in her room while she took a shower, then she dressed in her school uniform and went down to the kitchen. She had a quick breakfast, said goodbye to her folks, and left the house. She hurried round the corner, rose up to her window and climbed through. Skulduggery turned his back while she pulled on her black trousers and boots. She pulled on a black top, really missing her jacket. Then they both dropped down to the garden. Sixty seconds later, they were in the Bentley, driving for Haggard's Main Street.

Behind St Brendan's Secondary School there was a closed-down supermarket, and at the rear of that there was a small car park. It was here that they found the dead sorcerers. Five of them, their bodies torn and ruptured. Skulduggery muttered something Valkyrie couldn't hear and she turned away, went to the brick wall that acted as a boundary between the car park and the school grounds. She used the air to hoist herself to the top and straddled the wall.

"It looks quiet," she said.

Skulduggery rose into the air until he was standing on the wall. "We'll have reinforcements here in ten minutes. We should wait."

"That's what we *should* do," Valkyrie agreed, swinging her leg over and dropping down on to school grounds.

Skulduggery drifted down beside her as she walked. "It really doesn't seem fair," he said, checking his gun. "Those sorcerers trained for years to develop their powers, and these kids wake up one morning and they're able to tear them apart with a gesture."

"They're not kids," Valkyrie said. "They're the same age as me. Do you think of me as a kid?"

"No, but then I've never defined you by your age."

"Then don't define them by their age, either. They're not kids, they're murderers."

"If you're telling me not to go easy on them because they're under eighteen, you don't have to worry."

"So you're going to be your usual ruthless self?"

"It's been working well for me so far."

She glanced behind them. "Did you know any of the sorcerers back there?"

"I knew all of them," he said. "You knew three – but you wouldn't have recognised them."

The empty feeling in Valkyrie's chest expanded slightly.

They reached the football pitch and looked across at the school buildings. No alarms, no screaming, no explosions.

"Maybe they changed their minds," Valkyrie said.

"I doubt it," Skulduggery responded, putting his gun away.

"Do we have a plan?"

"We do, but it's not very good."

"Any plan at all would be a reassurance."

"Very well. We go in there and we evacuate each room as quietly as possible."

"That actually sounds like a good plan."

"It does, until you realise it's very light on details, such as *how* we evacuate them and how we manage to do it without causing a panic."

"We could set off the fire alarm."

"Which would cause the panic I just mentioned, which in turn could set off Kitana and her friends. If this turns bad, we're going to have to forget about hiding magic from the mortals. If you have to throw fire right in front of them, then that's what you do. Focus everything you've got on defending yourself and the people inside, do you understand?"

"Yes. This really isn't going to be pretty, is it?"

"It's really not," Skulduggery said.

They approached the school from the rear. Skulduggery disconnected the alarm on the fire doors and they slipped inside. The corridor was long and empty. Still no screaming. A face slid upwards from Skulduggery's collarbones, and he opened the door of the first classroom they came to. The teacher, standing at the board, looked round.

"Can I help you?"

"I'd like a word, please," Skulduggery said. "If you wouldn't mind?"

The teacher frowned, but joined them in the corridor.

"My name is Detective Inspector Me," Skulduggery said, keeping his voice low, "and I'm part of the new school safety initiative. You won't have heard of it, it's all very top secret. Basically, what I'm going to need you to do is take your class out through the fire door here and escort them a safe distance from the school."

"I'm sorry?"

"Get your class away from the school."

"Listen, I wasn't told anything about this."

"That would have ruined the surprise, don't you think? Please do as I say."

"Could I see some identification, or a badge or something?"

"I don't need a badge, I have natural authority."

The teacher frowned at Valkyrie. "And who are you? You're a little young to be a cop, aren't you?"

"I'm the student liaison," she told him. "It's my job to take notes on how the teachers interact with the pupils in a time of crisis."

"So this is some kind of fire drill? Then why isn't the alarm going off?"

"Because we want to observe each class one at a time," Skulduggery said. "And speaking of time, we're running out of it. If you don't start the evacuation in the next thirty seconds, you will have failed the test."

"Failed? Now just hold on there..."

"Twenty-five seconds."

The teacher's eyes widened. "But where do I evacuate them to?"

"Anywhere away from the school."

"But where? We could go across the football pitch. There's a car park at an old supermarket we could—"

"Not there," Valkyrie said quickly. "Is there anywhere else?"

"There's the trail down to the woods."

"Is that out of sight of the school?"

"Yes."

"Then that's where you take them. Eight seconds left. And tell them not to make a sound."

The teacher darted back into the classroom. While Skulduggery waited, Valkyrie hurried to the next door and glanced through the glass panel. A full room. She hurried on, counting one empty room and two more full. She reached a room at the halfway point and stopped. The teacher was sitting rigidly at his desk. The students were also sitting bolt upright. She heard someone talking, too low to make out the words. She backed off, walked quickly back to Skulduggery as the last of the students left through the fire door.

"They're here," she whispered. "They're in class. Everyone in that room is terrified."

Skulduggery's face grimaced. "We're going to have to evacuate everyone out through the windows. Footsteps on this floor are just too loud."

"We won't be able to do it," she said. "You're talking about hundreds of students who are going to be giggling and laughing and once they're outside you know there's bound to be a few eejits who start shouting for joy at missing class. Once Kitana realises that something is wrong, she's going to start killing people."

"Then we forget about the evacuation. We focus on taking them down."

"We'll have to take them by surprise."

"And I have just the thing," he said, undoing a few shirt buttons. He reached his hand in and rooted around.

"What are you doing?"

"I keep a pouch in there now," he said. "There's a big empty space inside me, so why not use it for storage? It beats having unsightly bulges in jacket pockets. Ah, here it is." He took out a wooden ball, and handed it to her. The cloaking sphere.

"You hold this," he said. "You'll have to adjust it accordingly, because we're going in and bringing them out one at a time. Either that or we go in, get into position, and leap out at them. Or we do something else. I don't know. It depends on what it's like in there. Are you clear on the plan?"

"That's not a plan."

"Are you clear on what we're hoping to do?"

"Barely."

"Then let's go."

She twisted the sphere – one side clockwise, the other counter-clockwise – and they were enveloped in a bubble of haze that rendered them invisible to anyone standing outside it. She twisted the hemispheres back a little, drawing the bubble tighter around them. Sticking close together, they approached the door. Skulduggery turned the handle and pushed it open slowly.

"Who is it?" Kitana asked from the back of the class.

"No... no one..." the teacher said.

They stepped in. It was incredibly weird to be standing there in front of thirty people and not one of them able to see or hear them. Kitana and Doran were sitting beside each other at the very back, and Sean was lounging at his desk a little closer to the front. Everyone around them was terrified.

"Hey!" Kitana shouted. She was wearing Valkyrie's jacket. "Come on in, whoever you are!"

"We'll go for Sean first," Skulduggery said.

Valkyrie nodded. She didn't want to talk when they were being stealthy. It just felt wrong.

Kitana rolled her eyes. "Sean, would you please close the door? I want to get back to my speech. What was I saying? Hey, Mr Teacher, sir, what was I saying?"

Sean got up, started walking for the door while the teacher started stammering. "I... I don't..."

"What was the last thing I said, Mr Teacher?" Kitana continued, her hand glowing with energy. "Don't you remember? Weren't you listening?"

The teacher looked at the open door and bolted, but Sean darted forward, caught him and threw him back over his desk. Kitana laughed and Doran whooped.

"Yay, Sean!" Kitana called. "You're my hero! That's a gold star for Sean in Teacher-Throwing, my favourite new subject!"

Sean laughed and Doran thumped his desk in amusement, but Kitana's smile faded, and she leaned forward. "Hey, Sean... what's wrong with your leg?"

Valkyrie looked down. The bubble curved over the side of Sean's knee.

"Dude," said Doran, "a chunk of your leg's missing."

Skulduggery nodded and Valkyrie twisted the sphere a bit more. The bubble grew, enveloping Sean completely. As everyone else in the classroom gasped at his apparent disappearance, Skulduggery slid an arm round his throat. Sean made a sound and his hands flailed as the sleeper hold tightened.

Doran leaped from his chair, eyes wide. "Seriously? We can turn invisible now? This keeps getting cooler!"

Skulduggery backed off and Valkyrie stayed with him. By the time they passed into the corridor Sean was unconscious. Skulduggery laid him on the floor and snapped handcuffs around his wrists.

"Sean?"

Kitana walked out of the classroom. "Sean?" she repeated. "Are you here?"

Skulduggery muttered a curse, picked Sean off the floor and dragged him further away.

Doran came out after her, his face red from straining. "Am I still here? Can you still see me?"

"I can still see you, you idiot," Kitana said. "I don't think he's invisible."

"Then where's he gone?"

"I think he's still here. I can feel him. He's close. Can't you feel him?"

Doran shrugged, then turned and looked right at Valkyrie. For a moment she thought he could actually see her, but his eyes moved on without focusing and she relaxed.

"They have him," Kitana whispered.

Valkyrie looked at Skulduggery. "What do we do?" she asked, her voice sounding unreasonably loud.

"*Who* has him?" Doran whispered back to Kitana.

"Taking them by surprise seems to work," Skulduggery said.

Kitana looked around and whispered, "The magic people."

"If they can't see us coming, their instincts can't kick in to save them," Skulduggery said. He left Sean on the floor and took out his gun, held it straight out, aimed right at Doran's head.

Valkyrie blinked.

"You think they're still here?" whispered Doran. "You think they can see us?"

Kitana didn't answer. Doran waved his hand through the air, trying to feel for enemies. Skulduggery's gloved finger rested on the trigger as Doran turned his way.

"You can't just..." Valkyrie said, and faltered.

"You said I'd have to be my usual ruthless self," Skulduggery replied. "If I take them both out now, they won't get to harm another living soul. It's better for everyone if they die right here."

"You're just going to shoot them?"

"This is life or death, Valkyrie." He thumbed the hammer back. "Giving someone a fighting chance is giving them a chance to beat you. What have I taught you about combat?"

She looked at Doran and Kitana as they slowly backed away. "Never fight on someone else's terms," she said quietly. She closed her eyes. "Do it."

She waited for the gunshot, hearing only Doran's whisperings. She looked up. Skulduggery was putting his gun away.

"Dammit," he said, then picked Sean up off the floor and threw him straight at Doran. To Doran, Sean suddenly appeared out of thin air and collided with him. They cracked their heads together and went down, and Kitana jumped back, cursing.

"Evacuate them," Skulduggery said, and used the air to leap at Kitana. He grabbed her, arm round her neck, but a wave of energy rippled out from her centre, flinging him away.

Resisting the urge to jump into the fight, Valkyrie instead ran into the classroom. She slammed the door, deactivated the sphere, scaring the hell out of everyone inside.

"The windows," she said. "Out the windows. Hurry!"

Windows were opened and there was a frantic dash. They were shoving and pushing and stamping to get out. The teacher was doing his best to orchestrate things but he was making it worse.

Valkyrie clicked her fingers, summoning a ball of flame into her hand. Everyone froze. She nodded at a group. "You. Out first. Go. No one else move."

The group did as they were told. When they were off and running, she nodded to the next group. "You lot. Go."

Group by group, they left, followed by the teacher. Valkyrie turned back to the door. It had gone suspiciously quiet out there.

She turned the handle and peeked out. Sean was still unconscious, still in shackles. She stepped over him, ran to the double doors at the end of the corridor. Smoke rose from a huge scorch mark in the wood. She passed through. Heard a crash. She ran, came to the gym. One of the doors was off its hinges. There was a flash of light from inside and she heard Skulduggery cry out. She twisted the sphere and ran in.

Skulduggery was on the floor of the gymnasium. His façade had retracted, and Kitana scowled at Doran as they closed in slowly. "Would you please learn to aim?"

"Don't blame me," Doran said defensively. "I got a massive headache because of this guy."

Kitana looked back at Skulduggery. "So what are you? Are you actually a skeleton, or is this just a trick or something, like a disguise?"

"No disguise," Skulduggery groaned.

"Why do you wear a suit?" Doran asked.

"Would you rather me naked?"

"No," Doran shot back. "That'd be gross."

Kitana sighed. "Why would it be gross? He's a skeleton."

"Well, yeah, but he's a guy, like. If it was a naked skeleton woman, then that'd be OK."

"So a naked skeleton woman would be hot, would she?"

"Yeah," Doran said, like it was the most obvious thing in the world. "Because she'd be naked."

Kitana turned back to Skulduggery. "I want to apologise for my friend. He's not very bright, and he's a bit of a homophobe."

"It's not homophobia," Skulduggery said, slowly getting to his feet. "It's just typical teenage boy bluster. He'll grow out of it, assuming he lives that long."

"Is that a threat?" Kitana asked. "Are you threatening us?"

"Not at all. But now that we have a private moment to talk, why not discuss some rather pertinent matters? Such as what you're hoping to accomplish with all this."

"All what?" Kitana asked. "Oh, you mean the murder and mayhem? Don't you like it? Aren't you a fan?"

"Not especially."

"Well then, Mr Skeleton, you are no fun. We were chosen by Argeddion because we would use these powers in the way they were intended, to punish the people who have messed us about in our lives."

"Your ex-boyfriend, did he mess you about?"

"He humiliated me."

"He broke up with you. There's a difference. Doran, you killed your brother. Do you really think he deserved to die like that?"

"Yeah," said Doran. "I do."

"What about Patrick Xebec, and the others? What about all the people you've hurt? And when all the punishing is done with? Then what are you going to do?"

"Whatever we want," Kitana said. "For the rest of our lives, we will do whatever we want."

"You know I can't allow that."

"You can't stop us. Those magic men tried to stop us earlier and we killed them so easily I was laughing."

"I see."

Kitana smirked. "Do you?"

"I do," said Skulduggery. "You're psychopaths. The magic may have pushed you over the edge or maybe you were like this anyway, I don't know. But the point is you're psychopaths now."

"I suppose we are."

"I should have shot you when I had the chance."

"And *we're* the psychopaths?" Kitana laughed.

"You didn't get these powers so you could punish those who've wronged you. You weren't chosen for any special reason."

"You're just jealous."

Valkyrie moved around them, heading towards Skulduggery as he straightened his tie.

"Argeddion is using you in an experiment," he said.

Doran frowned. "You know Argeddion?"

"You see? You don't even know who the players are. Who did you think Argeddion was – some mystical being granting great power to mere mortals? Before he was Argeddion, he was just an ordinary sorcerer. He worked for peace and enlightenment. You're his test subjects and you're trampling over everything he believes in."

Kitana put her hands on her hips. "Oh, really? Well, if we're such a mistake, then where is he? How come he isn't here to tell us where we're going wrong?"

"He's refusing to believe that you're as bad as you are. But this? Coming to your own school to attack it? I think this will be all he needs to realise his error of judgement."

"I think you're lying."

"I don't care."

Kitana smiled. "You're jealous. Just admit it. You're jealous that Argeddion picked us and not you. I know you all think you're so cool with your secret societies and whatever, but we're the new breed of sorcerers. And we're stronger than you."

Valkyrie dived on Skulduggery, hiding him from view, and dragged him to one side. Kitana and Doran let loose streams of energy that came dangerously close.

"Thank you for that," Skulduggery said.

"No problem."

They circled them, keeping low, as Kitana and Doran spun and fired at random, their eyes wide.

"Where are they?" Doran cried. "Where are they?"

"How am I supposed to know?" Kitana snapped.

Skulduggery took out his gun. "I didn't want to have to do this," he said as he took aim.

Valkyrie looked away, and Skulduggery fired twice.

39

FORCED HANDS

"**D**ammit," Skulduggery said.

Valkyrie looked back. Kitana and Doran were still standing. Hovering in the air next to each of their heads was a bullet, gently rotating.

"Hello, children," Argeddion said from where he floated above them all.

He waved his hand and the cloaking sphere stopped working. The bubble retracted but Kitana and Doran weren't interested in a skeleton and a teenage girl any more. They gazed upwards like they were seeing their own personal god.

"It's you," Doran whispered.

"Hello, Doran," Argeddion said. "Hello, Kitana. I'm sorry it took so long for me to meet you, face to face. I took some time to experience what it means to be a free man once again. Hello, Skulduggery. Hello, Valkyrie."

Skulduggery holstered his gun. "Are you proud of them?" he asked. "They came here, to this *school*, to kill everyone they found. If you're hoping you showed them enlightenment, I'm afraid I have some bad news."

"They're young," Argeddion said. "They'll learn."

"And in the meantime, they'll kill and destroy. You're meant to be a pacifist. You're meant to value every human life. How can you let this continue?"

Argeddion smiled. "Because I can see the difference between one life and many. Between a few lives and all. The children are learning and exploring and pushing their boundaries. They don't know who they are yet."

"They're through pushing boundaries. Now they need rules."

"I have no wish to limit them with the restricted view of western morality."

Skulduggery shook his head. "You've got to take responsibility for this."

"I'm taking ultimate responsibility," said Argeddion. "Spiritual responsibility. These few missteps don't matter. Can't you understand? Look at them standing there. They're beautiful and flawed and a work in progress."

"Dammit, Argeddion, your plan isn't working. Why can't you just accept that? You wanted to elevate mankind by giving them magic, so take a look at what you've created so far. They're killers."

"And so are both of you."

"We've made mistakes, but we try to do what's right."

"You mean you've learned your lessons. You made your mistakes, killed and destroyed, and now you're fighting the good fight. So what makes you think that these children will not follow your example?"

"Because they're psychopaths."

"And Lord Vile wasn't? And Darquesse is a well-adjusted personality?" Argeddion laughed. "It seems to me that there is one rule for you two, and another rule for everyone else."

"You can't let them learn their lessons at the expense of innocent lives."

"Every life lost is sad, but also necessary. These children are the future. They need the freedom to make mistakes and grow from them."

"Yeah," said Doran, wearing that smirk again, "let us grow, Mr Skeleton."

"If you want them to learn," Skulduggery said, "turn them over to the Sanctuary. We'll train them, teach them how to control their powers."

"You'll imprison them," Argeddion said, "like I was imprisoned, because you're scared. Because you don't understand them and you can't control them. I'm sorry, Skulduggery. None of you can be trusted."

"For God's sake, you can*not* let them walk away."

Argeddion looked down at Kitana and Doran. "Go," he said. "I'll see you again."

It took them a few seconds before they moved, but when they did, they were laughing like kids. Kitana blew them a kiss as they left.

Skulduggery didn't move. "You shouldn't have done that."

"When this is over," Argeddion said, "you will understand." And then he vanished.

The Cleavers arrived, sealed off the school. Skulduggery dumped Sean Mackin in the back of their van and slammed the door on his head. They waited for Geoffrey Scrutinous and Philomena Random to get there, told them the situation. This was bad. A signal block was now in effect, jamming all communication, but a few hundred teenagers had just had half an hour to get the word out of crazy goings-on at their school, and the news was spreading.

They drove back to the Sanctuary and found Ghastly outside the interview room where Sean Mackin was being held.

"This is bad," Ghastly said.

"We know," Skulduggery answered.

"Bernard Sult is running around, snapping out questions like he expects them to be answered. I've managed to avoid Strom all morning, but I don't think Ravel has been so lucky. What are we looking to get out of Mackin here?"

"Just where they're staying. We can't afford delays. They know we'll be questioning him, so they won't stay around for long."

Ghastly nodded. "I'm going to send Elsie in first. Maybe she'll be able to appeal to his better nature before we have to scare him."

Valkyrie and Skulduggery stepped into the room adjacent, nodding to the mage who sat at the monitor. She saw Sean on screen, sitting at the table and looking scared. The door opened, and Elsie O'Brien walked in. She was a heavyset girl in black, with thick eyeliner and a pierced lip. She had a nice face, but she was worried. Nervous.

Sean glared at her. "I should have known you'd be here."

"It's OK," Elsie said. "Everything's going to be OK now."

He slouched in his chair. "Really? Are you going to force them to let me go?"

"They only want to help you."

He laughed. It was a nasty laugh. "Does it look like I'm being helped? I'm in a jail cell. I was put in handcuffs."

"Sean, you have to know that what you were doing was wrong."

"You're such a coward."

"Please just—"

"Please just," he mimicked. "Do you have any idea how annoying your voice sounds, you ignorant cow? You look like a cow as well, did I ever tell you that? You're fat and ugly like a cow. I couldn't stand it when you smiled at me. I wanted to vomit."

The door opened and Sean shut up. Ghastly walked in.

Sean gathered his feet under him and looked at his hands as Ghastly pulled a chair over. He sat across from him.

"Now then," Ghastly said, "you want to talk about ugly, Sean?"

Sean swallowed.

"There are those who have said over the years that I myself am ugly. What do you think?"

Sean gave the tiniest of terrified shrugs.

Ghastly leaned forward. "Am I ugly, Sean?"

"You... you have scars."

"And do they make me ugly?"

"I don't... I..."

"Well?"

"No. They don't make you ugly."

"So I'm not ugly? Am I handsome?"

Sean nodded quickly.

"Am I the most handsome man in the world?"

"Yes."

"Just as I suspected," Ghastly said to Elsie, "this guy doesn't know what the hell he's talking about."

A small smile flickered on Elsie's lips, and Ghastly looked back at Sean.

"She's trying to help you, you idiot. She asked to come in here, to talk to you, to try and get through to you. Because no one else wants to help. You hear an army of people outside this door, begging to be allowed to help you?"

"N-no."

"No. Exactly. Because there isn't one. But Elsie wanted to try, and this is how you repay her? She told us you were a good guy, Sean. That you were decent. Not like Doran. Doran's a psycho. And not like Kitana. She's... she's something else. Elsie told us that you just got carried away a little. The power went to your head. Is that what happened?"

"Yes."

"Did the power go to your head, Sean?"

"Yes."

"Is that why you killed those people?"

"I'm... I didn't..."

"You also killed a few of ours, outside that school. And another sorcerer, a man named Patrick Xebec. He had a wife, did you know that? I bet you didn't. And you killed him."

"No," said Sean. "I didn't. I didn't kill anyone."

"Where are your friends, Sean?"

"I don't— I don't know."

"Where are they staying?"

"I don't know, I swear."

"Then where *were* you staying?"

Sean hesitated. "Please... I don't want—"

Ghastly slammed his fist on the table and Sean jumped. "You don't have your magic in here, Sean. In here, you're just an ordinary boy. You're an ordinary boy in an awful lot of trouble. It's over for you. You're caught. We have you. You've got to help yourself as much as you can, because no one apart from Elsie cares about you. Where were you staying?"

Sean swallowed thickly. "A friend's house," he said. "His name's Morgan Ruigrok."

"Don't make up names, Sean."

"He isn't," said Elsie. "I know him. His whole family's got weird names. I know where he lives."

Ghastly nodded. "Well, OK then. This is a good start." He got up, walked to the door.

Sean licked his lips. "Am... am I going to get a lawyer?"

Ghastly opened the door and didn't look back. "We have people who can read your mind, Sean. Why the hell would we need lawyers?"

Valkyrie and Skulduggery joined Ghastly and Elsie outside.

"Elsie," said Ghastly, "this is Valkyrie Cain, Skulduggery's partner."

"Hi," Valkyrie said, shaking her hand. "You know these Ruigroks?"

"Morgan goes to school with us," Elsie said. "His family live in Stonybatter, but they're all in Holland for a few weeks."

Ghastly nodded. "We have a lead," he said. "Better get going."

Skulduggery and Valkyrie turned to leave, but stopped. Ghastly cursed. Ravel walked towards them, Quintin Strom and Grim right behind. Strom looked furious.

"You," he said, jabbing a finger at Skulduggery. "I want to talk to you."

"I really don't have time."

"You'll make time," Strom said, his lip curling, "because I am dying to hear why you went into that school without waiting for back-up."

"Oh, come on," Valkyrie said, her own anger rising. "If we'd waited ten minutes, who knows how bad things would have got? Yeah, stories are circulating on the Internet but no one's dead. A teacher got a few bruises but that's it. Isn't that a win for us?"

"This is a disaster," said Strom. "Pure and simple. With the technology available today, we have to be extra vigilant in blocking communications and stopping the word from getting out. This is exactly the kind of thing we were worried about."

"The situation is being handled," said Ravel.

Strom glared at him. "Handled? This is being handled? This? I have been treating you with great sensitivity and tact because I know that having a Supreme Council looking over your shoulder cannot be easy to accept. I've almost been embarrassed to be here. But now I see I *have* to be here. I *need* to be here."

"Now just hold on a second—"

"No!" said Strom. "No, I will not hold on a second! You have been entrusted with the responsibility of running this Sanctuary and enforcing all of its laws and policies and you are failing, and failing spectacularly."

The muscle in Ravel's jaw stood out. "You're still a guest here, Grand Mage Strom. Do not make me regret my decision to allow you to observe."

"You didn't allow me anything! I allowed *you*! I allowed you to fool yourselves into thinking you had a choice!" Strom took a breath. When he had his anger under control, he spoke again. "You are clearly unfit to serve as Grand Mage," he announced, "and all three of you are unfit to serve on the Council of Elders. By the authority vested in me by the international community I am hereby taking command of this Sanctuary. You are relieved of your duties."

Nobody moved.

Valkyrie was frozen to the spot, though her eyes darted from person to person.

Moving slowly, Grim reached for his jacket, and Skulduggery drew his revolver and pointed it into his face.

"I wouldn't do that if I were you," Skulduggery said.

The bodyguard raised his hands.

Strom's eyes widened. "What you just did is illegal."

"We're in charge," Ravel told him. "You think we're going to roll over just because you tell us to? Who the hell do you think you are?"

"I am a Grand Mage, Mr Ravel, a title I earned because of hard work and dedication. Whereas you, on the other hand, are Grand Mage because nobody else wanted the job."

"Whoa," said Ravel. "That was a little below the belt, don't you think?"

"None of you have the required experience or wisdom to do what is expected of you. I know you'll find it hard to believe, but we didn't come here to take control. We came here to help."

"And now you want to take control anyway."

"You have proven yourselves incompetent. And what are you doing now? You're holding a Grand Mage at gunpoint?"

"Technically, Skulduggery is only holding a Grand Mage's *bodyguard* at gunpoint. Which isn't nearly as bad."

"You all seem to be forgetting that I have thirty-eight mages loyal to the Supreme Council in this country."

"And you seem to be under the illusion that we find that intimidating."

"If I go missing—"

"Missing?" Ravel said. "Who said anything about going missing? No, no. You're just going to be in a really long and really important meeting, that's all."

"Don't be a fool," said Strom. "You can't win here, Ravel. There are more of us than there are of you. And the moment our mages get wind of what's going on down here, the rest of the Supreme Council will descend on you like nothing you've ever seen."

"Quintin, Quintin, Quintin... you make it sound like we're going to war. This isn't war. This is an argument. And like all arguments between grown-ups, we keep it away from the kiddies. You've got thirty-eight mages in the country? Ghastly, how many cells do we have?"

"If we double up we'll manage."

"Don't make this any worse for yourselves," said Strom. "An attack on any one of our mages will be considered an act of war."

"There's that word again," said Ravel.

"This is insanity. Erskine, think about what you're doing."

"What we're doing, Quintin, is allowing our people to do their jobs."

"This is kidnapping."

"Don't be so dramatic. We're just going to keep you separated from your people for as long as we need to resolve the current crisis. Skulduggery and Valkyrie are on the case. When have they ever let us down?"

Ravel turned to them, gave them a smile. "You'd better not let us down."

Skulduggery inclined his head slightly, and Valkyrie went with him as he walked away.

"Holy cow," Valkyrie whispered when they were around the corner.

"Holy cow indeed."

Before Kitana and her friends had made it their temporary home, this had been a perfectly nice house. But now there were holes blown – and punched – through walls. Valkyrie did not envy the family who were going to return to this mess. Ordinarily there would have been a clean-up crew hard at work already, but with everything that had been going on they just couldn't afford to bother with the little stuff.

"No sign of where they moved on to," said Skulduggery. "Ghastly's going to try and get a little more out of our prisoner, but I don't like his chances. I think if Sean had anything else to tell us, he'd have told us."

"Are you worried?"

"Do I look worried?"

"You never look worried."

"That doesn't mean I'm not."

"Are you worried about putting Quintin Strom in shackles?"

"Oh," he said, "that. Hmm. I don't know. It's definitely a situation we have found ourselves in."

"Could it lead to war?"

"Possibly."

"But would they really go to war? I mean, war's a pretty big deal. It's huge, like. It's war."

"War *is* war," Skulduggery admitted. "This is very true."

"Would they really go to war over something so small as pulling a gun on a Grand Mage and imprisoning him and all of his bodyguards and sorcerers and stuff? It's not like we killed him or anything. This isn't Franz Ferdinand we're talking about."

"Hopefully, they'll see the funny side of it."

"There's a funny side?"

"I don't know. I'm hoping they'll see it and point it out to us."

"How long do you think we'll have before Strom's people start to get suspicious?"

"Ravel should be able to bluff his way through a few hours," Skulduggery said, "so we'll have to make the most of it. Do you realise that you're holding your arm?"

Valkyrie looked down, suddenly aware of the dull throbbing. "Uh-oh."

Skulduggery grabbed her shoulder and took out his phone. Valkyrie started texting. The room flickered.

"Ghastly," Skulduggery said, "we're about to shunt. We'll be in touch." He hung up.

Valkyrie's thumb danced over her phone. *Mum, phone battery almost dead! Staying at Hannah's for extra studying and pizza!! Be home tomorrow xx*

The throb in her arm was making her hand shake, but she pressed SEND and held her breath, waiting for the message to deliver.

And then the house vanished and they were outside and there was sunlight streaming through the trees. Skulduggery looked at her.

"Did it go through?"

She checked her phone, and nodded, breathing in relief. Even as she'd been writing it, she wondered if she was using too many exclamation marks, but she was glad she left them in. Nothing says "all is good with the world" like exclamation marks, after all.

"So," Skulduggery said, "this is the alternate reality, then."

Valkyrie watched him as he looked around. God, she was glad he was here.

"Right," he said, "we need to get past the wall and into the City. We can't fly in – they'll have guards posted and all kinds of security systems, and we just don't have the time to conduct reconnaissance. We're going to need help. We need the Resistance."

"If any of them are left," she said. "The last time I saw them there was a whole lot of dying going on."

"Then the best place to start looking would be the field where you last saw them." He wrapped an arm round her waist, and they lifted off the ground. "You'll have to direct me."

"You realise," Valkyrie said, "that China is the leader."

"I do," he replied.

"And you're OK with that?"

"I am. Besides, there's always the chance that she was among the ones who were killed by Mevolent's forces."

"Mr Bright Side," she muttered.

40

OLD FRIENDS

They flew for half an hour before they came to the field. Whole swathes of grass were scorched, others burned through entirely. Streaks of dried blood coated the ground. A ferocious battle had been fought here, of which Valkyrie had only glimpsed the beginning. She wondered if her reflection had survived, and her gut twisted with anxiety.

Skulduggery took her high into the air until the fields became a patchwork quilt of colours separated by ditches, trails and hedges. The closest village was to the south and that's where they flew. But Skulduggery slowed as they neared.

Not content with attacking the Resistance, Mevolent's forces had obviously felt the need to vent their anger on the local populace. The buildings were burned and smashed, and bodies lay rotting in the sun, covered in swarms of black-bodied flies. Skulduggery didn't land. They just hovered above the streets until he was sure that there was nobody down there living. Men and women and children. Even dogs. Unbridled hatred had swept through this little village leaving nothing in its wake. Valkyrie wondered how many of those innocent lives had been taken by Lord Vile. She could tell by Skulduggery's silence that he was thinking the same thing. She hugged him a little harder.

They followed the main dirt road that led out of the village. There was a farm a few miles further south and they touched down in the yard. A farmer and his sons gazed at them but didn't move.

"You talk to them," Skulduggery said. "A pretty girl is less scary than a walking skeleton."

Valkyrie stepped forward, moving slowly. "Hi," she said when she was close enough.

The sons were around ten or eleven, and they stood behind their father, a thin man with a hard face.

"We don't want any trouble," he said.

"That's not why we're here," she told him. "The village up the road there – do you know what happened?"

The farmer looked at her, looked at Skulduggery behind her, and nodded.

"We're not from the City," she said. "We don't work for Mevolent."

"We don't want any trouble," the farmer repeated.

"Please, we need to get in touch with the Resistance."

The farmer shook his head. "Don't know anything about them. Please leave."

"I understand that you're scared..."

"Can't help you."

"Do you know anyone who could?"

"No. No one. Don't know anything."

"Sir, we don't have a lot of time."

"Please go."

Skulduggery touched her elbow and she sighed. "OK. I'm sorry for disturbing you." The farmer's sons stepped out from behind their dad as Skulduggery and Valkyrie lifted into the air. She gave them a goodbye wave that they didn't return.

"That was horrible," she said as they flew. "Did you see how scared those kids were?"

"They can't really be blamed," Skulduggery responded. "They've just buried their mother."

Valkyrie frowned. "How do you know?"

"There was a dress on the clothes line, but the father didn't send the kids into the house so there's no one in there to keep them safe. The cart had a blanket on it."

Valkyrie closed her eyes. "She'd been in the village. They used the cart to bring her body home. Oh, God, and then we fly in, the exact kind of people they don't want anything to do with..."

"This is some world you've found."

"Where are we going now? Off to find another family to traumatise?"

"Actually, I've worked out where we are, and back in our reality, the nearest town is Ratoath. Hopefully, they have a corresponding town here."

"So we're going to traumatise a whole town now? Oh, goody. They're going to love us."

Ratoath turned out to be a fair-sized town, the buildings a little bigger and a little sturdier than the villages they'd passed over to get there. Some of the houses were even nice, with gardens in the back, and there was a market and a pleasing bustle to the people. They still wore the dull browns that identified them as lowly mortals, but their backs were straight and their heads were up. These people had a confidence that others lacked.

They landed unseen behind a tavern. Valkyrie frowned, looked up at the building. That's exactly what it was. It was a tavern. It was the twenty-first century in this reality, the same as it was in her own, but it wasn't a pub they had landed behind, or a bar. No, it was a tavern. What an odd, backwards world this was.

Skulduggery stopped at the corner, and nodded to the large building across the square. "If anyone knows anything, that's where they'll be," he said.

She nudged him, pointed to the building to their right. It was a church, its roof sunken, badly in need of repair. It had those familiar two circles carved above the door, and looked like a place that nobody visited.

"Each settlement has to have one, more than likely," Skulduggery said. "But while you can make a town build a church, you can't make them worship."

"What do the circles mean?" she asked.

"The big one represents the Faceless Ones. All-encompassing, all-knowing. The little one is us, floating around the edge, barely intersecting. It means we're little more than fleas, unable to even begin to comprehend the full majesty of existence. It's very patronising, as far as religious symbols go, and somewhat self-pitying."

"This reality's version of Eliza Scorn goes around in chains."

"They used to do that in our dimension as well. There'd always be one fervent believer who took it upon themselves to suffer for our sins. It was meant to be altruistic and selfless, but I generally found those people to be nothing more than attention-seeking martyrs. Hmmm... that's interesting."

"What?"

"There seems to be a gentleman walking towards us with a shotgun."

Valkyrie peeked out. Sure enough, there he was, a mortal in his sixties, walking with a shotgun levelled at belly height.

"Hello there," said the mortal.

Skulduggery paused for a moment, then stepped into view, and Valkyrie did the same.

"Well now," said the mortal, "a skeleton in a fancy suit. There's something you don't see every day."

"Speak for yourself," said Valkyrie.

The man smiled. "My name's Healy. I'm what you might call the local constabulary for Ratoath."

Skulduggery nodded to him. "How do you do, Mr Healy?"

"It talks," Healy said with a smile. "Wonders will never cease, will they? I'm doing fine, sir, thank you for asking. I'm going to have to request that the pair of you raise your hands, though."

"We're not looking for trouble," Skulduggery said as they complied.

"Only a madman would look for trouble in a town like Ratoath," Healy responded. "We have strict rules, you see. As the duly appointed constable, I would not be the most popular person in these parts, seeing as how my duties include rounding up troublemakers for the Barge every few weeks. But arresting people like you would easily fill my quota."

"People like us?"

"Sorcerers," said Healy. "Resistance sorcerers."

"How do you know we're Resistance?" Valkyrie asked. "We could have come straight from Mevolent himself."

Healy shook his head. "They don't sneak in. When they arrive, they let you know about it so you can start shaking in your boots. No, you pair are Resistance, I can tell a mile off."

Skulduggery tilted his head. "You don't sound very nervous, Mr Healy. If we are Resistance sorcerers, then we're very dangerous people."

"The Resistance don't hurt mortals. Everyone knows that."

"You seem awfully sure that you're not in any danger."

"You pull a gun on a person, you'd be surprised how confident you get."

Skulduggery flicked his left hand and the air tore Healy's shotgun from his grip. At the same time, Skulduggery's revolver flew from his jacket into his right hand, and he thumbed back the hammer. "You know what?" he said. "You're absolutely right. I am positively brimming with confidence."

Healy raised his hands slowly. "I didn't shoot you," he said, "and so I'd appreciate it if you returned the favour."

The shotgun drifted into Valkyrie's hands, and she broke it open and took out the cartridges. "What if you're wrong?" she asked. "What if we are from Mevolent?"

Healy shrugged. "After what I just did? You'd probably burn this town to the ground."

"And you're still not nervous?"

"No, Miss. I am not."

"Mind telling us why?"

Healy smiled, and his eyes moved slowly. Valkyrie and Skulduggery turned, and saw Anton Shudder standing there.

He didn't even blink. He gazed at Skulduggery like they'd been around each other every day for the last 200 years.

"Please," Skulduggery said, "don't make a fuss."

Predictably, Shudder didn't even crack a smile. "Why are you back?" he asked.

"We need to talk to China."

Shudder didn't respond.

"We want to get into the City," Skulduggery continued. "We thought she might know a way. Or maybe you do, and you could tell us, and we wouldn't have to disturb her. I think that'd be best for everyone, actually."

"I do nothing without Miss Sorrows' permission."

"What a fulfilling life you must lead."

"My reflection," Valkyrie said. "Is it here?"

Shudder turned his eyes to her. "Your reflection was taken along with thirteen of our people. Nine others were killed last night, and four more have died since then of their injuries."

"Can we talk to her? China said it herself, she's in my debt. If it wasn't for me, you guys would never have got that Teleporter."

"The Teleporter they tracked from the dungeon," said Shudder. "The Teleporter who led them straight to us."

"None of that is my fault."

"Tell China we have a proposition for her," said Skulduggery.

"I am her bodyguard," said Shudder, "not her liaison. If you want to tell Miss Sorrows something, then do it yourself." He walked past them, heading across the square to the large building.

"I think that was his way of saying follow me," Healy told them, smiling.

Valkyrie handed him back his shotgun and joined Skulduggery. They followed Shudder through the door, and a section of the flooring opened up, revealing steps leading down. At the bottom of the steps Cleavers stood, clad in grey, with those visored helmets that used to creep Valkyrie out so much. Now they comforted her.

She much preferred the grey-suited Cleavers to the crimson-suited Redhoods.

Shudder pushed open the door. A man was sitting in a chair. His chest was bare and he had a black disc the size of a drinks coaster attached to his forearm. China Sorrows was carving a sigil into his chest with a scalpel.

She stopped work for a moment and looked up, her startling blue eyes fixed on Skulduggery. "Who are you?"

Valkyrie frowned. "You don't recognise him?"

China went back to work on the man in the chair, who didn't seem to notice the pain. "One skeleton looks the same as another," she said. Of course, I've only known one to actually *walk*..."

"Hello, China," Skulduggery said.

It may have been the light, but Valkyrie could have sworn she saw China take a sharp breath. She straightened up.

"It is you," she said. "Where were you? Where have you been? Everyone... everyone thought you were dead."

Skulduggery took his hat off. "Do I look dead?"

"I refuse to answer ridiculous questions."

"China Sorrows... such a past we share. It's practically unfathomable, isn't it? The influence we've had on each other's lives? You helped make me the man I am today."

China didn't respond. Instead, she glanced at the man in the chair. "We'll finish this later." He nodded, removed the black disc from his arm and winced, then walked out.

"And I," Skulduggery said as China began cleaning the scalpel,

"I'm sure I've affected your growth as a person in equally memorable ways. The years we spent as enemies, hunting and fighting and warring... From a spoiled little disciple of the Faceless Ones to leader of the Diablerie and now look at you. The leader of the Resistance. You've changed."

"I'd hope so. Where have you been all this time?"

"That doesn't really matter."

"It matters to me." China placed the scalpel in a slim case, and closed the lid. "First we have Valkyrie Cain and her reflection appearing out of nowhere, and now we witness the return of the living skeleton after, what, one hundred and fifty years? And they're friends, no less. So I have questions. Where have you been, what are you doing back, and who are you?"

"You know who I am," said Skulduggery.

"I know who you *were*," said China. "And I've asked a lot of people about *you*, Valkyrie, and no one seems to know who you are or where you came from, either. This is all very mysterious. I don't like mysteries. They unsettle me."

Valkyrie suddenly became aware of how vulnerable they were, with Shudder and a handful of Cleavers standing behind them.

"We're not from here," Skulduggery said.

China's gaze flickered to him. "Explain."

"A Dimensional Shunter sent us here," Skulduggery said. "We don't belong in this world."

"And you expect me to believe that you're from a parallel universe, then? Is that it? Tell me, does your universe have a China Sorrows?"

"It does."

"And is she stupid?"

"She is not."

"Then why would you think I would believe you?"

"We could prove it, if you'd like. Maybe tell you something, something the version of me from this reality probably never knew. For instance, that you delivered my wife and child to Serpine so that he could murder them in front of me. Something like that, perhaps."

China was silent for a moment. "How long have you known?"

"This last year, but that's in a whole other reality."

"And your version of me... did you kill her quickly or did you make it last?"

"Neither. She still lives."

"I don't understand."

"I'm a lot of things, but I'm no hypocrite."

"I had a hand in killing your family, in killing you and turning you into what you are now... and you don't want to kill me for it?"

"Of course I want to kill you," said Skulduggery. "I want to kill most people. But then where would I be? In a field of dead people with no one to talk to."

"You are different from the Skulduggery I knew."

"Maybe. Maybe not."

"What do you need? A way home?"

"That should take care of itself. No, we need to get into Mevolent's Palace."

"Why?"

"They're holding my reflection," said Valkyrie.

"Let them keep it," China said. "It's a reflection. No, there's something else."

"There is," said Skulduggery, "and we need to retrieve it. It's very valuable to us."

"Tell me what it is, maybe I have one to spare."

"I doubt it."

"You'll tell me eventually, because I won't help you otherwise. You could lie to me, of course, but I'd know."

"Our world is in danger," said Skulduggery. "We need a weapon powerful enough to kill a god."

China laughed. "You want the Sceptre? Impossible. Mevolent keeps it in his throne room where it is protected by an Arietti Sigil, and when he leaves the Palace, he has it with him at all times. You'd never get to it."

"Loan us your captured Teleporter and we'll surprise you."

"If I could, I would," said China. "Unfortunately, he escaped in the confusion when Lord Vile and the Redhoods attacked. He's back with Mevolent now, along with a dozen of our best fighters. It was not a good day for us."

"Then get us in some other way, or give us a map and let us try it ourselves. What have you got to lose?"

"A perfectly good map," China said. "How do you intend to get your hands on the Sceptre, if you do manage to sneak in? Have you any idea how many Redhoods patrol those halls? And what about Vengeous, and Lord Vile? And Mevolent himself?"

"We've faced Vengeous and Vile before," said Skulduggery. "We'll do OK. As for Mevolent, we're going to hope that he's sleeping. It's not a perfect plan, but it'll do."

Valkyrie nodded. "It's really not a perfect plan."

"But you can't use the Sceptre," China said. "While Mevolent lives, it will only work in his hands."

"Not once we bring it home with us. We can use it to save our world and, more importantly for you, Mevolent won't have his most powerful weapon any more."

China observed them for a long, drawn-out moment. Then she picked up her scalpel case. "I will arrange for a guide to escort you beyond the wall," she said. "I assume time is of the essence?"

"When is it not?"

"Indeed," she said. "Indeed. You'll need this." She held up the black disc that had been attached to the arm of the man she'd been working on. Skulduggery gestured, and it floated into his hand. "If you're captured," she continued, "I would appreciate it if you would kindly die before they interrogate you. This town is very important to the Resistance. We can't afford to lose it."

"We'll do our best to go down fighting."

"That's all I ask. Wait here, and I'll send someone to take you to your guide. Valkyrie, it was lovely seeing you again. Skulduggery..." She didn't bother finishing the sentence, she just bowed to them both, and glided out of the door.

Valkyrie looked at the black disc. "What's that?"

"It's a pain regulator," he said, fiddling around with the back of it. "It's used to either subdue pain, or inflict it." He slid a piece of the underside into his hand. It was a small, flat piece of slate with a symbol printed on it in white. He pocketed both.

A girl in her twenties came to take them to a nearby building. Her name was Harmony. She was pale and pretty, and had a scar that curled from the corner of her eye to the corner of her mouth. She held a torch as she led them down old stone steps.

"Our guide lives down here?" Valkyrie asked, a little dubious.

"His movements here are restricted," Harmony told her. "He's not what you might call trustworthy."

Skulduggery said, "And yet you trust him to lead us into the Palace?"

"Oh, yes," said Harmony. "Absolutely. It's what he does *after* he's led you in where things could get tricky. But you should be fine. Years ago, Mevolent issued an order that he be killed on sight, so I don't think he'd try to betray you like he betrayed them."

"He betrayed them?" said Valkyrie. Then, "Wait, he was on their side?"

"One of Mevolent's top men, so he was. One of his Three Generals." Harmony slammed her fist against the door and pushed it open without waiting for a reply. Inside, Nefarian Serpine lay on a bunk, naked but for a towel covering his privates. He scratched his beard as he looked up at them with glittering emerald eyes.

"Yeah?" he said. "What the hell do you want?"

41

THEIR GUIDE

Those eyes of his, those bright green eyes, latched on to Skulduggery and an eyebrow slowly rose. "There you are," he said. "After all these years... What, did you get lost on your way to kill me or something?"

Serpine sat up. His black hair was long and his beard was straggly. He wore a clunky metal glove on his right hand, and his ribs showed. "Are you at least going to give me a fighting chance?" he asked, easing himself off the bed. "This fancy glove they make me wear binds my magic, so it'll have to be fisticuffs. You prepared for that, skeleton? Ready to finish this once and for all?"

"He isn't here to kill you," said Harmony. "We're loaning you to him."

"That doesn't sound very sporting."

"You know a secret way into the City," Skulduggery said. "You're going to take us in, as far as the Palace. Tonight. If you try anything sneaky, I'll take great pleasure in killing you."

Serpine smiled. "If I'm seen inside the City, there are many people who will take great pleasure in killing me. I think I'll stay here, thank you very much."

"This isn't a request," Harmony said. "Miss Sorrows has made her decision."

"Well, she can unmake it," Serpine replied, sneering slightly. "I'm not setting foot inside that wall, and if you had any sense, skeleton, you wouldn't, either."

Skulduggery looked at Harmony. "Could you excuse me for a moment? We'd like to talk with Nefarian alone."

Harmony shrugged. "I'll be outside," she said, and closed the door behind her.

Skulduggery and Valkyrie looked at him, standing there.

"What do you think?" Skulduggery asked.

"He's not very impressive," Valkyrie said. "I don't like the beard. And the towel doesn't exactly cover a whole lot."

"He's fallen on hard times," Skulduggery said. "He needs goals in his life. He needs a future to look forward to. Nefarian, we are here to offer you both of these things." He took the pain regulator from his pocket. The air shifted and the disc shot from Skulduggery's hand into Serpine's belly. He grunted, frowned, tried to peel it away from his skin.

"Don't bother," Skulduggery said. "Only we can remove it, and we have no plans to do that until we get what we want." He held the black slate in one hand. His thumb tapped it lightly and Serpine's eyes bulged and he fell to his knees. His body shook. His muscles stood out, straining, like they wanted to burst free from his body. Valkyrie could tell that he wanted to scream but couldn't.

Skulduggery deactivated the disc, and Serpine fell forward, gasping.

"The goal in your life that we are offering you," Skulduggery said, "is the chance to rid yourself of that little device. The future you can look forward to is a future where you don't have to suffer white-hot agony whenever we get bored. Two rather healthy aspirations, are they not?"

Serpine snapped his head up, glared at them. "I go free," he said. "After I lead you in, after you take this thing off me, I go free."

"You aren't free now?"

"They say I am, but everywhere I go I have an armed escort. I've proved myself to Sorrows, I supplied her with names and locations and some of Mevolent's best-kept secrets, and what do I get in return? A small bed in a cold room and my powers bound. If you get her to agree to set me free, I'll take you."

"She'll never agree to that," Skulduggery said. "She's not going to just loan you to us and then let you run off. What does she gain from that deal?"

"Then we don't tell her. We agree, the three of us, here and now, that you let me go when we're done. I'll take my chances on my own."

"If we're going to set you free, we need more than just a guide into the City. You have to take us into the Palace itself, to the Sceptre."

"You're insane."

"That's the deal."

Serpine hesitated. "Very well. I take you to the Sceptre, you take this disc off me and unlock this glove and let me go."

"Agreed. How long will it take to get into the City?"

"What time is it now?"

"Around three."

"Afternoon or morning, skeleton? You lose track when you don't have windows."

"Afternoon."

Serpine nodded. "The best time to sneak in will be at the end of the working day. We need to be outside the wall at six. Before then I'll need clothes. My own clothes. And tell them to send a barber. If I go in looking like this, we'll be arrested on the spot. I assume you have some sort of disguise, skeleton? I'd wear it if I were you. The people of the City are cultured and elegant, not like the grim and shabby specimens who trudge around this place. You, girl," he said to Valkyrie, and threw her the towel from around his waist. "Run me a bath."

Using her thumb and forefinger, Valkyrie pulled the towel from her head and dropped it on the floor. "Gross," she whimpered.

They spoke to Harmony and she arranged the barber and the bath, then they found his clothes. Valkyrie was outside with Skulduggery, sitting on the horse they'd given her, when a Cleaver escorted Serpine out into the sunlight.

The beard was gone and the hair was short. His clothes were old and worn, but still elegant. He blinked against the light, shielding his eyes with the iron glove. She saw for the first time how pale he was.

He saw them and smiled as he came over.

"There," he said. "So much better. If one is rushing into certain death, one had better look one's best, don't you think? I almost feel like my old self again." He looked at Skulduggery. "You know, the old self who killed your family."

"Oh, yes," Skulduggery said, "him."

Serpine swung his leg up on to his horse, and looked down at Harmony. "Do try not to miss me too much while I'm gone," he said. "If you find yourself inconsolable, feel free to lie down in your favourite spot on my bunk."

Harmony's face got suddenly warmer, Serpine laughed, and turned to Skulduggery. "Shall we go?"

They left the village at a canter. Valkyrie hadn't ridden a horse in years and it took her a while to ease into the rhythm. She soon found herself enjoying it. And soon after that, she began to ache.

They saw the wall in the distance before they saw Dublin, but soon they were making their way through the narrow streets of the mortals, who hurried from their path even though they had slowed the pace to a brisk walk. They had journeyed mostly in silence, but the closer they got to their destination, the chattier Serpine became.

"It seems the years have mellowed you, skeleton," he said. "Where is that old anger I used to know? Where is all that fury? All that hatred? Have you changed? Have you become, for want of a better word, a different man?"

"A lot of things have happened since you saw me last," Skulduggery said. "I've already had my revenge, for a start."

"Oh? How so?"

"The how, where and when don't concern you, Nefarian."

"Very well." Serpine smiled. "But was it everything you had hoped it would be?"

"Oh, it was," said Skulduggery. "Except that it was over far too quickly."

"Well, I'm right here if you feel there is blood left unspilled."

Skulduggery didn't respond right away, and Valkyrie started to get worried. But then his head tilted in that way of his. "A tempting offer, and much appreciated. It is a rare occasion indeed when I am invited to inflict vast amounts of damage upon a person. If I didn't know any better, I'd swear you wanted me to kill you here and now instead of risk Mevolent getting his hands on you."

Serpine laughed. "Actually, I'd rather skip my untimely demise *completely* if it's all the same to you."

"Naturally. But if you were going to die on this little mission of ours, and it looks like that's a distinct possibility, then I'm sure you'd prefer a quick neck-break to a prolonged torture session – which is undoubtedly what Mevolent has in mind for you."

"Oh, you don't know Mevolent like I know him, He's a forgiving fellow, all things considered. If I were captured, I'm sure he'd be quite understanding."

"In that case, if we are outnumbered, we'll happily leave you behind, yes?"

Serpine smiled, but the smile was tight. "Please do," he said. "I haven't seen my old friends in years. We have so much to catch up on."

42

COLLECTING THE
RESULTS

Ghastly stood in front of the mirror wearing his Elder's robes. He hated them. He hated them so much he wanted to cut them up, fashion them into something new, something worthwhile or, at the very least, something extravagantly stylish. He took them off, threw them over his desk, and rubbed his eyes. Grand Mage Strom was in a detention cell, Skulduggery and Valkyrie were off having a transdimensional adventure, Kitana and her friends were still causing havoc, and an entire section of the Sanctuary was sealed off thanks to Lament and his sorcerers.

All that plus the fact that Argeddion was walking around conducting those experiments of his and being basically omnipotent meant that Ghastly had enjoyed very little sleep recently.

He missed his old bed. He missed his shop. He missed the part of his life where people didn't run to him for answers. He was a tailor, not a leader. The only reason he'd taken this job in the first place was to have the resources to track down and cure Tanith Low. But here he was, all this time later, and he was still no closer.

He chose a tie, put it on, tightened the knot all the way and then tugged it down once to loosen it.

He hadn't even *seen* Tanith since that time in the van, the Christmas before last. One moment they were chatting, the next there was a bright flash and then everything went dark. When he'd regained his senses, Tanith had fled with a Remnant inside her. It actually stung that she'd infiltrated the Sanctuary mere days earlier to kill Christophe Nocturnal in his cell, and she hadn't even stopped by to say hello.

That was a weird thing to be upset about, he knew, but he couldn't help it.

He buttoned his waistcoat and rolled up his shirtsleeves, the exact same number of turns on each arm. Looking good could not be left to chance, after all. He may have been disfigured, but that was no reason to let himself go. And at least his scars were symmetrical. Someone knocked on his door. He opened it.

"The mortals," Tipstaff said. "They're awake."

Ghastly ran, joining Ravel on the way down to the lower levels. They passed Elsie and Ghastly grabbed her hand, making sure she stayed close. By the time they reached the quarantine zone, there was a small crowd gathered. Ghastly got to the front, taking Elsie with him.

The mortals were on either side of the room, standing perfectly straight with their eyes fixed ahead of them. Doctor Synecdoche shook her head. "This shouldn't be happening," she said. "They're all fully sedated. They shouldn't be able to open their eyes, let alone get out of bed."

Ravel went up to the nearest mortal, waved his hand in front of her face. "She's unresponsive," he said. "Are they sleepwalking?"

"Maybe," said Synecdoche. "I mean, yes, they are, but why? Nothing happened. Nothing has changed. But they all just sat up at the same time. All of them."

"Elsie?" Ghastly said. "Are you OK?"

"There's someone here," she whispered. "I can feel him."

"Argeddion?"

She nodded. "The same way I can feel Sean, I feel Argeddion. He's close. He's getting closer."

"Grand Mage," said Ghastly, "Argeddion's on his way. We need to get you to a safe—"

"No," said Elsie.

"No what? He's not on his way?"

She shook her head. "He's here."

Argeddion stood down the other end of the ward. "Hello, Elsie," he said.

The mages and Cleavers who rushed him disappeared before they took two steps. Ghastly was left with Elsie and Ravel, Synecdoche and Tipstaff.

Ravel looked around slowly, then addressed Argeddion. "What did you do with my people?"

"They're a few miles away," Argeddion said. "I didn't harm them, don't worry. I'm a pacifist, remember?"

"What are you doing here?"

Argeddion smiled. "My first batch of test subjects have completed their tasks," he said. "I'm just here to collect the results."

He started walking slowly through the two rows of mortals. Their chests began to glow, and warm globes of light drifted out of them and into him as he passed. Once the light left them, they collapsed. Synecdoche hurried forward, but Argeddion held up a hand, stopping her. "They're quite all right," he said. "They're just sleeping. When they wake, they'll be back to normal."

Ravel guided Synecdoche back to where Ghastly and Elsie were standing. "You're taking your magic back?"

"Yes. And as I take it back, I'm absorbing all the information it gathered. How it affected them, how it improved them, how it hurt them."

"Why?" Synecdoche asked. "So you can refine the dosage for next time?"

Argeddion smiled. "That's exactly why, my dear doctor. I don't want people going berserk, now, do I? Unpredictable behaviour was an unfortunate necessity for the first time out, but I assure you it will be much smoother on the big day."

He reached the end, and the last mortals collapsed. Argeddion sighed. "I feel all tingly."

He walked by them, out into the corridor. They followed.

"Don't waste your breath trying to convince me that what I'm doing is wrong," he said. "Skulduggery and Valkyrie have given it their best shot and I haven't changed my mind. I do think, however, that I'm starting to change theirs..."

"I doubt that very much," Ravel said.

Argeddion shrugged. "Wishful thinking, then."

They climbed the stairs, Sanctuary staff clearing the way as he neared. He looked at Elsie and smiled. "You don't seem to be embracing your powers like your friends have."

"I... I don't want to hurt anyone," she said.

"Of course you don't. Why would you? You're not a barbarian."

"The others hurt people."

Argeddion nodded sadly. "I know. I've seen it. It's disturbing, isn't it? But they'll learn. That's the wonderful thing about humanity – their ability to learn from their mistakes."

"I don't think you should have given us those powers."

"But you were perfect. You suited my needs. I needed to see how it would affect society as a whole. You four had everything I was looking for – the right group dynamic, the right amount of tensions, of loyalties, of friendships. Was it perfect? No. But when this is over, you'll give me the answers I need, and you will know that you helped make the world a better place."

They left the Sanctuary, emerging into open air, and Argeddion stopped.

"Hello," he said softly.

Lament's sorcerers hovered in the sky above them. Their eyes were open.

"We can't let you leave," Lament said. "You're too dangerous. You must be stopped."

Argeddion looked up at them. "I have to say, I'm impressed. I knew there was a possibility of you breaking free, but I had no idea you'd be able to do it so soon. Well done, my friends."

"We're sorry for what we did to you," said Lament. "It wasn't an easy choice to make. But recent events have proven that we were right to fear you."

"I bear you no ill will," Argeddion said. "I've lain inside your minds for years. You, all of you, are a part of me, and I love you for that."

"Thank you, Argeddion. But we can't let you continue."

"You can't survive without me, Tyren. None of you can. My magic has been sustaining you for years. If you attempt to stop me, you will fail, you must realise that."

"We have to try," Lament said.

"Of course you do." Argeddion smiled, and rose into the air until they surrounded him, energy crackling.

"It's been an honour knowing you," he said. There was a pulse of light and the hovering sorcerers fell to the ground.

Ghastly ran forward, dropping to his knees beside Lenka. Her eyes were open. She wasn't breathing. "What did you do? What did you do to them?"

"I took back the power I'd given them," Argeddion said.

Ravel's face twisted in anger. "You *killed* them."

"They were intent on wielding my own magic against me. It wasn't a choice I wanted, but it was the choice I was given. They were my friends, in a way, and they died peacefully."

"They were murdered. You just murdered them."

"And they imprisoned me for thirty years when I had done nothing wrong," Argeddion said, and for the first time Ghastly heard an edge to his voice.

He closed his eyes, then opened them. "My apologies. I didn't mean to snap. But I've just lost my only four friends in the world. I'm feeling quite emotional."

He drifted up, and up, and vanished.

43

18 MOUNT TEMPLE PLACE

They were smuggled into the City by a trader who owed Serpine a favour. He hadn't been happy about it, this mortal, and wasted no time in complaining. But they huddled down in the back of his cart as it trundled across O'Connell Bridge, and the man stopped griping long enough to bluff his way through the gates. Once inside, they slipped from the cart and Serpine led them through the back streets.

Once they were far enough away from the Redhoods and the City Mages, Valkyrie was sent forth to figure out where the hell they were off to next. A man hurried by, wearing what was probably the height of fashion for Dublin-Within-The-Wall. His shoes were pointy and *click-clacked* on the pavement, his shirt had an extraordinarily long collar and his hat was, quite honestly, ridiculous. Valkyrie chose him because he was obviously harassed, and obviously in a hurry. People in a hurry were more inclined to give answers without asking questions.

"Excuse me, sir, I was wondering if you could help me."

He frowned at her as he moved, and she had to walk quickly to keep up. "With what?" he asked. "I'm a very busy man. You think this City runs by itself? I'll tell you something, it doesn't. It takes work. It takes people like me."

"I just need to find someone."

"Have you tried looking?" he said, and sped up.

She matched his pace. "I'm new here, I don't know anyone. I'm looking for my uncle."

"Family? Stay away from family. Family is bad news. My family can't stand me. You know why? Because I work hard. They're jealous. Everyone's jealous. Everyone's going home to their families but am I? I am not. I'm still working, that's what I'm doing. That's why they're jealous. It's not easy being me. It'd be easier being you, and I don't even know you. I know me, though, and I should get an award."

"I just need to find—"

"Need to find? Need to find? Why do you need to find? If you're looking for someone, search the Well."

"The what?"

"The Well. Are you stupid?"

"I'm not sure what that is."

He turned suddenly. "You don't know what the Well is? The World Well? You don't know what it is? What age are you?"

"Uh, seventeen."

"You're seventeen years old and you don't know what the World Well is? Where have you been? Where are you from? What's wrong with you? Are you stupid? Are you dim? Are you...?" He stopped suddenly, and for a moment he looked horrified. Valkyrie readied a power-slap, prepared to unleash it the moment he started to shout for help. Instead, he smiled. "Oh, I'm dreadfully sorry," he said, suddenly talking really slowly. "I didn't mean to be rude."

She frowned. "Uh... that's OK..."

He tilted his head towards her. "Different people learn at different rates. It's nothing to be embarrassed about."

"I'm sorry?"

"No no no, I'm the one who's sorry. I have a daughter myself, actually. You remind me of her. She's four."

Valkyrie glared. "Right."

"The World Well is a marvellous thing," said the man, talking even slower now. "Can you picture in your head a big bucket? Can you do that?"

"A bucket," Valkyrie said. "Yeah."

"And in this bucket, or this Well, is all the information in the world. It's all put in there. Every book ever written, every fact and figure. Do you understand?"

Valkyrie took a deep, calming breath. "Sure."

"Now, this is where it gets tricky. The bucket is, sort of, all around us. It's in the air, almost. It's in magic, and magic permeates everything. So if we want to check something, a fact or a figure, then we just dip our little handies in the bucket, and pull out what we want to know."

She looked at him. Didn't say anything.

"So," the man said, "you're looking for your uncle, isn't that right? What's his name? Do you know his name? Maybe your mammy or your daddy wrote it down on a piece of paper for you?"

"Walden," Valkyrie said, trying to smile. "Walden D'Essai."

"Walden D'Essai," he repeated. "OK. Just give me a moment and I'll check for you." He smiled at her, his eyes going glassy. If it turned out that Walden wasn't a resident of the City, Valkyrie prepared herself to look particularly dim-witted. If it turned out he was dead, she prepared herself to look distraught. "Ah, here he is. Oh, your uncle is a very important man. He's in charge of sewage, did you know that? The City would be a very stinky place if it wasn't for great people like your Uncle Walden."

"Where does he live?"

The man took a moment, then smiled again. "Found it. He lives at number eighteen Mount Temple Place. That's all the way on the other side of the City. I don't think you'd be able to walk there." He chuckled. "Do you want to get a taxi?"

Valkyrie nodded, started walking away. "That sounds like a good idea."

"Do you have any money?"

She stopped. *Dammit.*

She turned and he gave her a few coins. "There. That should

get you to your Uncle Walden and you'll have enough left over for an ice cream. Do you like ice cream?"

Valkyrie muttered under her breath.

He beamed, and waved down a passing carriage. The driver diverted from the airstream, and set down beside them. "Eighteen Mount Temple Place," the man instructed as she got in. "You say hi to your uncle for me, won't you? And thank him for doing such a wonderful job with the sewage!"

"I will," Valkyrie murmured, and sat back as the carriage lifted off the ground and rejoined the stream. It flew round the corner, where she leaned forward and tapped the driver. "Pull over for a second, would you?"

He did as she told him, and a moment later, the door opened and Skulduggery and Serpine climbed in. When they were moving again, she looked at Serpine. "Why couldn't you use the Well to find out where he is?"

"I'd be detected immediately," he said. "Things like the World Well, everyone thinks it's about sharing information, but it's just another tool for Mevolent to keep track of you."

"The Well?" asked Skulduggery.

"Magical Internet," said Valkyrie.

"Ah."

They got to 18 Mount Temple Place. It was a two-storey house on a rising hill, its architecture identical to the buildings around it. They did a quick sweep of the area.

"D'Essai's security system is a good deal more elaborate than any of his neighbours',"" Skulduggery said. "We'd need a few hours to break in, but if he's on his way home with everyone else, we probably only have minutes."

"It will deactivate when he enters," said Serpine. "If one of us distracts him immediately upon opening this door, the other two can use the opportunity to sneak in through the back. Seeing as how I have a recognisable face, it can't be me."

"I'll do it," Valkyrie said.

They went round the back and Valkyrie hung around on the street, doing her best to look inconspicuous. No one gave her a second look. She saw Walden D'Essai coming up the hill, and gave the signal to get ready by running a hand through her hair. Walden passed her, opened his front door and Valkyrie said, "Mr D'Essai?"

He turned. "Yes, hello. Can I help you?"

"I hope so," she said, and smiled. "My name is Valkyrie Cain. Could I speak with you for a moment?"

"Regarding?"

"Your work."

He smiled. "And why would a young lady like yourself be interested in Sewage Maintenance?"

"Honestly? The glamour."

The smile turned to a laugh. "Do you mind telling me what you really want to talk about?"

"It's of... a personal nature."

He looked at her, and took a moment. "I'm sorry, I don't think I can help you."

"You're the only one who can."

"Then you have me mixed up with someone else. I'm sorry."

He stepped inside and closed the door. Valkyrie stayed where she was. A few seconds later, the door opened, and Serpine beckoned her inside.

It was a tastefully decorated interior, and would probably have been neat and tidy were it not filled with books and notepads. Walden sat stiffly in what looked like his favourite armchair. He looked around, scared. "Take what you want. It's not worth much but I won't call the authorities, you have my word."

"We're not here to rob you," Skulduggery said, and the face he was wearing smiled gently.

Valkyrie picked up a few of the books, flicked through them. "Heavy reading for a Sewage Maintenance Engineer," she said. "*Realms of Magic. The Existence Equation. Philosophy and Sorcery. Between Gods and Man: The Next Stages of Human Evolution.*"

"It looks like you have an interesting hobby," said Skulduggery. "So how does someone who clearly wants to explore magic, and where magic comes from, find himself working in the sewers?"

"It's nothing," Walden said. "Just a few books. It means nothing. Please. If you don't want to rob me, why are you here? What do you want with me?"

"I've been asking them the same question," Serpine said.

"Walden," said Skulduggery, sitting on the couch opposite him, "we're not from here."

"What do you mean?"

"I mean, we're not from this world."

"I don't... I don't understand..."

Serpine shrugged. "It's true. I know it sounds ridiculous, but it's true. They're not from here."

Walden blinked at Skulduggery. "Then... then you're... you're *aliens*?"

Before Skulduggery could reply, words spilled from Walden's mouth. "Oh, I knew it! I knew it! I knew we couldn't be alone in the universe! When I was a kid, they laughed at me but I knew there was something more to life, more than this world and this level of magic and the day-to-day grind of living, and here you are, sitting across from me, a real-live alien being! Do you have a flying saucer? Could you take me up in it?"

Skulduggery didn't answer right away. "Uh..." he said.

Valkyrie stepped forward. "We're not aliens. We're from a parallel dimension."

Walden's face fell. "Oh."

"But look," Skulduggery said. He tapped his collarbones and his face flowed away. "I'm a skeleton."

Walden nodded, unimpressed. "Right. So why are you here, then? I have a lot of work to do."

"We need your help."

"Why?"

"We can't tell you."

"Well, that's just wonderful."

"Will you help us?"

"If I help you, will you leave?"

"Yes."

"Then I would really like to help you. But I won't if it's going to get me into trouble."

"There'll be no trouble."

"But you answer me a question first. Who is that?"

Serpine arched an eyebrow. "Me?"

Walden nodded. "I know you from somewhere. I know your face. But I'm not good with faces. Who are you?"

"They've called me a great many things over the years, but my name is Nefarian Serpine."

Walden's face went slack. "The traitor."

"Yep, that's one of the things they called me."

Walden stood up so quickly he knocked his chair over. His voice rose in volume. "I can't talk to you. I can't talk to *him*. I can't associate with him. Do you know what would happen to me if the Sense-Wardens found this moment in my mind? I'd be arrested. I'd be tortured!"

"That's not going to happen," Skulduggery said calmly.

"You don't know that!" Walden said, panicking. "I'm doomed. I'm dead. They're going to arrest me!"

"Walden," Skulduggery said, "sit down. Take a deep breath."

"I can't! I can't breathe!"

"There's no need to panic. The sooner you help us, the sooner we'll be out of here."

"Go!" he shouted. "Leave! Leave before I call the City Mages!"

"First we need to talk."

Walden covered his face with his hands. "Please," he said. "Please leave me alone."

"In a minute. Walden, we have an emergency back in our dimension, and you're the only one who can help us."

"Why me?"

"I'll be honest with you – it would probably be best if you didn't know. We're trying to minimise the effect this will have on you."

"What do you want me to do?"

"Just remember. We need you to remember a moment in your life. It's not a happy memory, Walden. It was the day your mother was killed."

"What? What has that got to do with anything?"

"It would take too long to explain. The man who killed her, he said something to you, didn't he? After he'd done it?"

Walden stared. "How did you know?"

"You need to tell us what he said."

"But I don't understand what—"

There was a loud knocking on the door. "Walden D'Essai," came the voice. "Open up immediately. Open up in the name of Mevolent."

Walden went pale. "Oh, no," he whispered.

44

THE WAY IN

alkyrie pressed her back to the wall. She took slow, quiet breaths. Shadows coiled round her right hand. Serpine was on the other side of the room, crouching behind a chair. She peered out, watched Walden walk to the door. Skulduggery went with him, gun in hand. He nodded, and stood behind the door as Walden opened it. Two Redhoods stood on the step behind a City Mage.

"Hello," Walden said. "Is something wrong?"

"Reports of a disturbance," the City Mage said. "Shouts, and whatnot."

"Coming from here? Really? I... I'm sorry, Mage, I don't know what to say. I haven't heard anything."

"A man shouting," the City Mage said. He looked bored. "Were you shouting, sir?"

"Shouting?"

"Shouting. Did you raise your voice, sir? Did you cry out in alarm? Were you shouting?"

"Shouting," Walden said, considering the word. "No, I'm sorry. It wasn't me. It might have been the wind."

"You're saying the wind was shouting, sir? Why would the wind shout? What would it have to shout about?"

"I'm not really sure..."

"Me neither, sir, but it was your suggestion. Up until you suggested it, the thought had never entered my mind that it might have been the wind that was shouting instead of a person. Instead of a person like you, sir."

"Well, I just meant the wind may have sounded like it was shouting."

"Oh, I see, sir. Well, that is infinitely more plausible, I'll admit. Do you have anyone in the house with you? Maybe someone who can corroborate what you're saying?"

"No, I'm sorry. I live alone."

"So do I, sir, but you don't hear me shouting about it, now do you?"

"No, City Mage."

The conversation lulled. Behind the door, Skulduggery adjusted his position slightly.

"Sir," the City Mage said, "I could call in the Sense-Wardens and I could get them to rummage around in your brain to find out if you were shouting or if it was, as you say, the wind. Do you think I should do that?"

"It... It's up to you, City Mage."

"That's right. It is indeed up to me, thank you very much. I could call them in, go through official channels, follow the rulebook to the letter... or I could let this one slide. If you were to give me your word, say, that there wouldn't be any more shouting coming from this particular area, I could continue on with my patrol, and trust that you, or the wind, won't be disturbing your neighbours any further. You have quiet neighbours. They notice things like loud noises."

"I... I'll not be shouting, City Mage. You have my word on that."

"And the wind?"

"I don't think it'll be shouting, either."

The City Mage examined him for a long time. "Have a good evening, sir," he said, and moved down off the step.

"Thank you," Walden said as he was closing the door. "Thank you very much."

Skulduggery accompanied him back to the living room. He put away his gun as Serpine stood.

"Why didn't you turn us in?" Valkyrie asked.

Walden looked at her. He was pale, but his gaze was strong. "What do you mean? Why would I turn you in? Quickly now, we don't have much time. What do you need?"

"I told you what we need," Skulduggery said.

"That's it? You just want to know what the man said when he killed my mother? He said he was sorry, and then he ran off."

"That's all?"

"Yes. He said, *I'm sorry*, and then off he went."

"You don't seem particularly traumatised by the words."

"People say *I'm sorry* every day. The words had no effect on me. Him killing my mother, on the other hand..."

"Maybe it's different," Skulduggery said. "Maybe the killer in our reality said something else."

"Listen, I don't understand any of this, but I was assured that no one from the Resistance would ever contact me. You could get me killed."

"You work with the Resistance?" Valkyrie asked. "Doing what?"

"I don't understand. Did China Sorrows send you or didn't she?"

"She helped us get into the City," Skulduggery said, "but she didn't know we were coming to see you. What do you do for them?"

"Does it matter? You break in here, you get the Redhoods and a City Mage knocking on my door, you ask me ridiculous questions about my mother's murder... Isn't it time you left?"

"You sneak people out," Serpine said. "That's it, isn't it? You sneak people out through the sewer pipes. I've been wondering about that for years. I tried it once myself, got lost down there for days. Also it didn't smell that great."

"Please," Walden said stiffly. "You have to leave, all of you. Before you ruin everything."

When they left him, he was trembling. They let Serpine walk on ahead, but Skulduggery kept the slate in his hand.

"*I'm sorry*," Skulduggery said, and shook his head. "That's not it. Lament said it was a phrase that stopped Argeddion in his tracks."

"I don't want to point out the obvious," Valkyrie said, "but Lament was under Argeddion's control when he said that. He was probably lying to us."

Skulduggery murmured something, then said, "Is that all it is?"

"What do you mean?"

He moved closer, his voice dipping. "The fact is, thirty years ago they trapped Argeddion. Lament, under Argeddion's control, told us that it was this traumatic phrase that allowed them to do so. The key words there being *under Argeddion's control*."

"So he lied," said Valkyrie slowly, "which means they trapped him some other way."

"And obviously Argeddion didn't want us knowing what that other way was..."

"You still don't sound convinced."

The eyebrows on Skulduggery's face furrowed. "It's a bit much, that's all. A phrase from his childhood that triggers a complete emotional shutdown? Why so elaborate? What did it achieve?"

Valkyrie didn't say anything. She'd found it best to let Skulduggery continue on his own at times like these.

Skulduggery looked around. "It achieved this. Right here, right now. It achieved this."

473

"I don't get it."

"We are here, in this City, in this dimension, walking down this road, because of what Lament told us."

"No," Valkyrie said. "We are walking down this road because Nadir did that shunt thing, and I brought you with me."

"Nadir reached for me, too. In the prison. He tried to shunt the both of us."

"So?"

"Mien had Nadir hooked up to the prison for fifteen years – for Nadir, that was fifteen years of being *asleep*."

Valkyrie blinked. "And Argeddion was communicating through people's dreams."

"Nadir said he didn't know what we were talking about when we charged him with assault. I thought he was lying. Now I don't think he was. I don't think he was even aware he'd done it."

"So Argeddion got to Nadir in his dreams, talked to his subconscious, and told him to shunt the both of us over here? But how would Argeddion know we'd even want to talk to Nadir in the first place?" She frowned. "Wait. Of course he knew. Greta fed us enough information to lead us to Nadir, and from Nadir we found Argeddion. He's been controlling Greta, too."

"Maybe," Skulduggery said, "or maybe she just shares his optimism about the human race. Either way, he wanted us to come here. This has been his plan all along."

"But why? So we can get the Sceptre? He wants us to kill him?"

Skulduggery shook his head. "He may not have known about

the Sceptre. He probably never even considered it. No, he sent us here for the one thing he didn't have over there."

"Which is...?"

"Walden. He wanted us to find Walden."

"He wanted us to find himself? And do what?"

"He told us, even with the Accelerator he's still not powerful enough to spread magic to every single mortal on the planet. But with two Argeddions, working together..."

Her eyes widened. "*Walden* is his surprise guest?"

"And we've found him for him. He couldn't send one of his drones – the further away they are from him, the weaker his control becomes. He needed independent people to come over here with their own agenda."

"So... so what do we do?"

"What do you think we should do?"

Valkyrie looked back. "The most logical thing would be to... to kill Walden."

"Agreed."

"But we can't."

"It's not that we *can't*..."

"We won't, then. We can hide him. You can hide him, and not tell me, so Argeddion wouldn't be able to find out where he is."

"That'd only slow him down," Skulduggery said. He nodded. "OK. Now that we know what Argeddion wants, we can work to make sure it doesn't happen. The best way to do that is to take advantage of his oversight."

"We get the Sceptre."

"We get the Sceptre and we use it on him before he gets his hands on Walden."

"Easy as that," said Valkyrie.

"Indeed. So we're back to our main objective."

"What about Serpine?" Valkyrie whispered. "Can we trust him?"

"Of course not," said Skulduggery. "But we don't know the City, and we need him to help us get into the Palace. And anyway we've got the regulator."

Serpine stopped walking and turned, waiting for them to catch up. "If you've quite finished plotting and planning, we have a Palace to break into, don't we?"

Valkyrie frowned at him. "We're miles away."

"You don't break into a palace through the back door, Valkyrie, especially not one like this. It is unlike any palace or castle ever built."

"So how do we get in?"

"We exploit a strength," he said, "and make it a weakness." He led them over a wall between two buildings, and they hurried to a narrow door. Skulduggery snapped his palm against the air and the door flew open. Serpine went first, and Valkyrie heard a scream and a crash. By the time she ran in, Serpine had his hand over the mouth of Eliza Scorn and he was dragging her down to the cellar.

"Baron Vengeous," Serpine said, "is a man who likes things done a certain way. He likes his meals served on time, he likes his uniforms pressed just so, and he likes his houses built with secret passageways. Isn't that right, Eliza?"

Scorn sat in a straight-backed chair in the middle of the cellar and glared at him. "May the crows peck out your eyes," she said.

"Charming."

Were this cellar in any other part of the country, it would be dark and cold and lit with candles. But here, in the City, it was bright and warm and clean. It was also empty.

"Is that why we're here?" Skulduggery asked. "We're going to sneak in through a secret tunnel? Then why aren't we sneaking, Nefarian?"

"Because I don't know where the tunnel is, *Skulduggery*. And judging by the shackles around her wrists and ankles, I doubt Eliza will tell us, no matter how much pain we visit upon her. Martyrs are the most annoying of captives. Ah, how different things might be if I had this glove off..."

Skulduggery threw the pain regulator's black slate to Valkyrie. "Here. Use this if he takes longer than five seconds to answer a question."

Serpine held up his hands. "Ah-ah, don't be so hasty! We're waiting for Vengeous to get back. He never takes the surface route – it's much too long. He always comes via his little secret passageway, which opens up somewhere in this cellar."

"We don't have time to waste," Skulduggery said. "We could shunt back at any moment. Where I'm from, we have a device we use for detecting tunnels." He took out his phone, activated the screen, and started taking slow steps around the cellar with the screen held towards the floor. Valkyrie didn't have a clue what he was doing, but she stayed quiet.

Scorn glared at Skulduggery, then at Serpine. "The Faceless Ones will burn your soul for this."

Serpine gave a shrug. "Better a burnt soul than a fried mind."

"How dare you!" she screeched. "The Dark Gods *opened* my mind! They gifted me with enlightenment!"

Valkyrie put a hand on Scorn's shoulder, keeping her in her chair. "Keep calm, please. Serpine, don't annoy her."

"I'm just talking," Serpine said, his green eyes innocent. "It was one of Mevolent's grand plans, opening a door for the Faceless Ones. A half-baked ritual he found in some obscure book of old magic. But the thing is, it worked. The door opened. The problem was that it didn't stay open for more than a few seconds. It worked once, and never worked again. But in those few seconds, Eliza caught sight of something... and something caught sight of her."

"I looked into the face of a god," she whispered, her eyes following Skulduggery.

"And we all know what that does to you," said Serpine. "When she stopped screaming, a few years later, she cut all her hair off and started walking around in chains. And by complete coincidence, that was exactly what Baron Vengeous was looking for in a woman."

"Be silent," said Scorn.

"The old ball and chain became the old bald-in-chains, and he's never been happier."

Scorn flew at Serpine and he jumped back, laughing as she tripped over her own shackles and sprawled on the floor.

Valkyrie tried helping her up. "Eliza, stop. He's just trying to provoke you."

"Unhand me, filthy creature!"

"Me? I'm just trying to be nice."

"Stop the filthy creature from speaking to me!"

"Oh, for God's sake..."

Scorn pushed her away. "God? *God?* You know not what a true god looks like! You are a blasphemer! You may not gaze upon me!"

"*I know not?*" Valkyrie said. "Why do religious freaks talk like this? It's always religious freaks and villains." She frowned over at Serpine. "And how come she'll let you gaze upon her but not me?"

"Because I'm not a blasphemer," Serpine replied, as Scorn rose to her knees and clasped her hands in muttered prayer.

"Wait a minute," Valkyrie said. "You still worship the Faceless Ones? Then why did you turn against Mevolent?"

"Because he's insane," Serpine answered, "and ridiculous, and I thought I'd win. Why does anyone do anything?"

Valkyrie blinked. "So you haven't reformed?"

"Why should I reform? You people are the ones in the wrong here."

Scorn nodded. "Filthy blaspheming creatures, that's what they are. Their souls will be burned."

"Oh, shut up," Valkyrie said.

"Found it," Skulduggery said. They all turned. He pointed at the wall next to him. "The tunnel starts here."

"Heathen!" Scorn screamed. She jumped up, ran forward and fell over, as expected. Skulduggery ignored her.

"Despite all the distractions she barely took her eyes off me," he said, "and every time I passed this area her mouth tightened. This is where she didn't want me looking."

"So that device isn't for detecting tunnels?" Serpine asked.

Skulduggery returned his phone to his pocket. "No, it's not. It's for making calls and playing Angry Birds."

Scorn tried to get up off the floor but Valkyrie put a foot on her back. "Blasphemers! You'll never find the lever!"

"We don't need it," Skulduggery said. He placed his gloved hands on the wall and focused. After a few seconds, the whole thing started to tremble. Bricks cracked, crumbled, moved aside and fell, and the tunnel was revealed. He looked back at them. "Eliza, you've been a big help, but we can take it from here."

She screamed at them.

45

THE PERFECT BODY

The bodies were here. If Scapegrace had a belly, it would be filled with butterflies. Thrasher held him and shifted his weight from one foot to the other as they waited for Nye to arrive.

"Stop," said Scapegrace, sloshing about in his jar. "Stop doing that."

"Oh, sorry, Master," said Thrasher. He waited until the liquid had settled before speaking again. "You know what I feel like, Master? A child on Christmas morning."

"Well, you can't have one," Scapegrace said, and chortled.

"I, uh, I don't get it, sir."

"Of course you don't," Scapegrace snapped. "That's because it's sophisticated humour for sophisticated people. And what are you not, Thrasher?"

"I'm not a sophisticated person," Thrasher said meekly.

Doctor Nye swooped its head down to get in through the door. It didn't apologise for being late, it didn't apologise for making them wait. Of course it didn't. It was a creature. It was a thing. It didn't understand what it was like to be human.

But Scapegrace did. He once was human... and he would be so again.

Nye unlocked the Mortuary, and led them in. "Here are your choices," it said.

Three bodies lay on slabs, covered in blue sheets. Nye uncovered the first body. It was a short man, elderly, with white tufts of hair sprouting out over his ears but none on the top of his head. Scapegrace glared. "You call this an option? Look at him! Why would I want to be him? When I said I wanted a new body, I meant young, six feet tall or above, a full head of hair, in good shape, must have a—"

"You did not furnish me with such specific requirements," said Nye.

"I thought it was pretty obvious that I'd be wanting something top of the range."

"Not to me. Besides, the range we have available to us is... limited."

"If they're all like this, I'll wait for the next batch, thank you very much."

"No waiting for you, zombie-head. You're going to break up in that solution any day now. These are your only options."

Scapegrace spoke through gritted teeth. "The others better be an improvement. Show me."

Thrasher brought him to the second slab as Nye pulled the sheet away.

"Is this more to your liking?" it asked.

Scapegrace glowered. "Do you think this is funny?"

"I confess," the doctor replied, "I do not know. You human creatures are somewhat of a mystery to me. This body, however, fulfils your requirements. Early twenties. Six feet tall. A full head of hair. In excellent physical condition."

"Also a woman," said Scapegrace.

"This is a problem for you?"

"It may have escaped your notice, Doctor, but I am a man."

"No, Mr Scapegrace, you're a head in a jar. You don't even have an Adam's apple any more. But I will show you the final body and you can make your selection."

Scapegrace's hopes were fading fast as Thrasher carried him to the third slab. And then the sheet was pulled off.

"Oh, my," said Thrasher.

Scapegrace smiled. Scapegrace grinned. This one was perfect. Tall, broad-shouldered, a strong jaw, cheekbones as sharp as glass. Sandy hair. Muscles. A six-pack. Male. Everything... everything was perfect.

"Doctor Nye," Scapegrace said, "you have outdone yourself."

"Oh, Master," Thrasher said, reaching out to prod the body's arm, "this one is magnificent."

"Stop!" Scapegrace ordered. "Stop touching it! Hands to yourself!"

Thrasher obeyed, and hung his head.

Scapegrace peered up at Nye. "When can we begin?"

"Immediately," said Nye.

46

THE PROBLEMS
WITH MORTALS

he man with the golden eyes sat opposite the boy, and smiled at him.

"Hello, Sean," he said.

"Please," said the boy. "I'm sorry. I'm sorry I did the things I did. But I didn't kill anyone. The others did, but I didn't. I'm really sorry. I just want to go home."

"It's a bit late for that, isn't it?"

"Please."

"Do you know the problem with mortals, Sean?" asked the man with the golden eyes. "And by mortals I mean all those people walking around without access to magic. I mean you, two weeks ago. The problem with mortals is that there are just so many of them. Things would be simpler if sorcerers were the dominant species on the planet. Then we wouldn't have to hide. We wouldn't have to slink around in the shadows.

"There are other problems with mortals, of course. They're dull. They plod through their little lives, oblivious to the wonders around them. They're mean and spiteful and petty. There are those of us who would love to do what you and your friends have done, to announce to the world that magic exists and that we're taking over. But... we have rules. And where there are rules, there are people to enforce those rules. So we have to be a little sneakier."

"What do you want?"

"Now there's the question I've been waiting for." The man with the golden eyes stood up, and walked to the door. "I'm going to let you walk out of here, Sean. There are associates of mine waiting to escort you through one of the many secret tunnels to freedom, where you can join up with your friends and continue your reign of terror."

"I won't, I swear."

"No, Sean. This isn't a trick. I *want* you to continue. We all do. We're big supporters of what Argeddion is doing. Bringing magic to the masses? It's a wonderful idea. If everyone is magic, after all, there'll be no need to hide, will there? The secret will be out."

The boy nodded. "OK."

"And we'll help you as much as we can. If you get caught again, just stay quiet, don't mention you ever saw me, and you'll be free within hours. You have supporters, Sean. The entire town of Roarhaven is cheering you on. You're a hero here."

The boy nodded quickly.

The man with the golden eyes opened the door. Outside were two sorcerers. He looked back at the boy. "You'd better hurry. I'm sure your friends are worried about you."

The boy hesitated, then bolted out of his chair. The man with the golden eyes watched him run, flanked by the sorcerers.

"Did it work?"

He turned as Madame Mist glided to his side.

"I think so," he said. "The boy is scared, but when he rejoins his friends, this escape should bolster their confidence. If they think they have us on their side, their attacks will grow bolder."

"Your plan is dangerous," she said. "We cannot control these children. We don't know how to kill them once they've served their purpose."

He shrugged. "By then the world will know magic exists. Every Sanctuary of every country will be coming together to defeat them. I'm not worried. You shouldn't be, either."

"I preferred the old plan," said Madame Mist.

"We can still go back to it if this doesn't work out. But if it does work out, think of all the time and effort we'll have saved. And we won't even have had to involve the Warlocks."

"And the assassins? Will we need them?"

"They owe us a favour, don't they? They may as well pay it back."

"Have you decided on a target?"

"Oh, yes," said the man with the golden eyes, smiling.

47

INTO THE PALACE

They moved quickly under the City, reaching the first junction in just over twenty minutes. Serpine guided them left, and after another ten minutes of walking they came to a ladder.

"Here we are," he said, "just like I promised. This is where we part ways, yes?"

"No," Skulduggery said, "actually, it's not."

"Then the least you can do is take this glove off," Serpine said, holding out his right hand. "If we're discovered, I need to be able to defend myself."

"You have us," Skulduggery said. "You don't need anything else."

Serpine glared at him but said nothing, and Skulduggery motioned to the ladder. Muttering, Serpine went first, pushing aside the covering at the top. Valkyrie came up last, emerging into darkness. Serpine was close by, searching for a switch.

"Be ready," he whispered. "It's around here... aha."

There was a soft, almost inaudible *click*, and a crack of light spilled into the black. Skulduggery moved straight to it, opening the door further. Standing in the corridor with his back to them was a Redhood, scythe held by his side. Skulduggery swung both hands towards the Redhood's head. He didn't make contact but the air rippled and the Redhood stumbled. Valkyrie gestured and the scythe flew backwards into her hands as the Redhood fell into Skulduggery's. She'd seen him use that trick before, delivering an instant concussion that knocked the target out cold. Quiet and immediate and very effective. Skulduggery dragged the Redhood's sleeping form into the darkness and they left him there, then stepped out into the corridor, Serpine giving directions as they went.

They passed a corner, approached another and slowed at Skulduggery's hand signal.

Footsteps.

She watched Skulduggery standing there with his back against the wall, his body completely relaxed as the footsteps got louder. Then a door opened somewhere behind Valkyrie. Her eyes widened. Another set of footsteps now, from the opposite direction. Serpine, in between them, grinned like he was enjoying the dilemma. Valkyrie crept to the corner. The footsteps of Skulduggery's target grew even louder. Valkyrie's target was almost upon her.

She didn't look round as Skulduggery pounced. Whoever had emerged from that corridor didn't even get a chance to cry out. She heard scuffling, and a gasp. Skulduggery had him in a choke of some kind. Valkyrie hadn't the first idea how she was going to subdue *her* target.

A sorcerer rounded the corner and Valkyrie hit him, a punch to the face that rattled her arm and twisted her wrist. The sorcerer fell back, mouth opening to shout and she pushed at the air. His head cracked against the wall and he dropped, and she kicked him in the jaw on the way down.

"Stealthy," said Serpine as he passed her. He took hold of the sorcerer's ankles and dragged him from the corridor.

Valkyrie glared at him. Her wrist was hurting but she didn't rub it. She didn't want to give him another reason to gloat.

They passed a door she recognised, a door that led to the dungeons. Her reflection was down there. She bit her lip, forcing herself to continue past it. First the Sceptre, then the reflection. They moved slower now, more deliberately, taking extra care not to make a sound.

"We're here," Serpine whispered.

Skulduggery and Valkyrie took a peek. The throne room lay beyond a grand doorway, and two Redhoods stood guard. By Mevolent's throne there was a small table, and upon that table a cup or a chalice of some kind. It was all very medieval. The glass case containing the Sceptre stood exactly as she had remembered – not that she'd expected it to have moved. But with their luck lately...

Serpine turned to them. "All right," he whispered. "I got you to the Sceptre. I fulfilled my end of the bargain. Now you fulfil yours."

Skulduggery shook his head. "We're not letting you go until we're out of here."

"That wasn't the deal. You promised me freedom."

"And what's to stop you from alerting Mevolent to our presence? I'm sure it'd do a lot to repair your special friendship."

Serpine's eyes were narrow. "Fine," he said. "But this regulator. Remove it."

"After."

"No. Not after. Now. You don't trust me? I don't trust you. I killed your wife and child. They may not have been the wife and child you knew, but they're close enough. What's to stop you from leaving me here, twisting on the ground in pain? I'm sure you'd be able to make a clean getaway if everyone was distracted by my screams."

Skulduggery looked at him for a moment. "Fair enough," he said.

Serpine parted his shirt, and Valkyrie used the black slate to detach the disc. She put both in her pocket as Serpine rebuttoned. "Thank you," he said. "I feel so much better."

"Both of you stay here," Skulduggery said, and crept to the doorway. He gently nudged the air, and the cup across the room toppled off the table. The Redhoods turned at the noise so Skulduggery stepped through the doorway and immediately rose silently into the air until Valkyrie couldn't see him any more. One of the Redhoods started walking over to the table while the other resumed his normal stance. Valkyrie kept out of sight for the next minute, then risked another peek. Satisfied that there was nothing suspicious going on, the Redhood had rejoined his colleague. They stood within arm's length of each other, scythes in hand and held upright.

Another minute passed, and just as Valkyrie was beginning to wonder if Skulduggery had got himself stuck in a chandelier or something, he came swooping down behind them, legs swinging, and caught both Redhoods in the back of the head. He continued the move into a flip as they sprawled, scythes clattering to the floor. They didn't get up. Valkyrie and Serpine hurried in.

"Apologies," Skulduggery said as he landed. "That was unforgivably showy of me."

"Got the job done," Valkyrie said, finding it impossible not to smile.

Skulduggery's gun leaped into his hand. "Not one more step," he warned.

Serpine turned, a chuckle on his lips, an arm's length away from the glass case. "I was just making sure there weren't any tripwires," he said. "For your information, it doesn't look like there are."

"Much obliged," Skulduggery said. "Now move away."

Serpine held up his hands in surrender and did as he was instructed. Skulduggery holstered the gun and Valkyrie followed him to the case.

"How do we open it?" she asked.

Skulduggery clicked his fingers, summoning a ball of fire into his palm.

Serpine frowned. "I hope you don't think you're going to burn through it. This is protected by an Arietti Sigil."

"Which forms the strongest seal in existence," Skulduggery murmured. His hand moved, manipulating the flames, and Valkyrie watched the fireball shrink, but grow hotter as it did so.

"Fire has no effect on it," Serpine said. "There is nothing that will break this seal. I thought you knew some way past it."

The fire constricted to the size of a golf ball, and then smaller, to the size of a marble. It hovered in space, cupped by Skulduggery's hand, and then his forefinger straightened and the fire moved up along it. With the white-hot fireball balanced on his fingertip, Skulduggery scorched a broken triangle on to the glass.

"You don't know how to break the Arietti Sigil," he told Serpine. "But I do."

"Impossible. If anyone had found a way to break it, we would all know."

"You forget," Skulduggery said, adding to the sigil as he spoke, "we're not from around here. Where we're from, the secret to getting by the Arietti Sigil was revealed decades ago. By Arietti himself."

The sigil complete, Skulduggery extinguished the flame and stepped back. The scorch marks sizzled.

Serpine folded his arms. "It doesn't seem to be working."

"Give it a moment," Skulduggery answered. "Wait for the melting to stop and the form to settle."

There was a sound, the *pat pat pat* of bare feet running, and Valkyrie looked round as Eliza Scorn ran into the room.

"*Blasphemers!*" she screeched as she hurled daggers of red light towards them. "*Heathens!*"

Valkyrie dived to the floor, thankful that years of living like a nutcase had robbed Scorn of her aim. The madwoman wasn't wearing her chains, probably for the first time in years, so she ran forward and back like a rabbit on the road, eyes burning with the intense energy of a zealot. Skulduggery swept his arm wide and she screamed as she flew into the wall, but then scrambled up again like the pain meant nothing, and came forward.

Valkyrie sprang to meet her, ducking another badly aimed dagger and lashing out with her shadows. Scorn went staggering and Valkyrie crashed into her, driving her back, sending half a dozen elbows into her face until one of them found its target. Scorn slumped in her arms, suddenly quiet. Valkyrie laid her on the ground, breathing fast, listening out for alarms. She glanced back at Skulduggery and Serpine. Amazingly, astoundingly, it looked like they had got away with it.

"Get your hands off my wife," Baron Vengeous snarled from the doorway.

Ah.

He ran at her and Valkyrie tried backing up but he was much

too fast. Her feet left the floor and there was a hand round her throat and she was still moving back, and all she could see were his eyes and his gritted teeth and the only thought that flashed through her mind was how much better he had looked with a beard. Then Skulduggery collided with him and Valkyrie fell, gasping. Serpine grabbed her, hauled her up.

"The glove," he said quickly. "Get it off me."

She coughed, tried to push him away but he held on.

"Skulduggery can't take Vengeous alone," he said. "He needs my help."

"I'll help him," Valkyrie said, finding her voice.

"You have to find your reflection, don't you? Dammit, we don't have much time before the whole Palace is alerted. I know Harmony gave you the key to this glove! You'd have to be prepared for all eventualities!"

Vengeous threw Skulduggery against the wall and started slamming fists into his head and body. It was all Skulduggery could do to stay standing.

Valkyrie took the key from her pocket, passed it over Serpine's wrist, feeling the glove beneath her palm. After a moment something clicked, and Serpine pulled his hand free. It glistened, as red and raw as the day the skin had just been stripped off it. The look of pure joy on Serpine's face was disturbing.

"Help Skulduggery," Valkyrie ordered.

He looked at her with those mocking emerald eyes, and smiled. "But of course," he said.

She forced herself to leave them, and took the door that led to the dungeons.

There weren't any Redhoods guarding the dungeons. Instead, there were men in filthy overalls, dozing on chairs. She slammed them into walls and took their keys, then carried on, checking each cell until she found her reflection.

Valkyrie froze. The first thing she noticed was that the fingers of its right hand were missing. Its brown shirt was caked in dried blood.

"I'm here," Valkyrie said, her voice soft.

The reflection raised its head, and Valkyrie stopped breathing. Its left eye was gone, that side of its face swollen and bruised.

"What happened?" she managed to ask.

"They weren't happy with you," the reflection said, "so they took it out on me."

"Are you...? Did it hurt?"

"Yes."

"What? Why didn't you shut off the pain?"

"I'm afraid it can't," came Meritorious's voice from the cell opposite. "From what your reflection has told me, it has bypassed so many of its original parameters that it has lost the ability to differentiate between simulated pain and actual pain."

Valkyrie tried to keep the horror at bay. "But... but you're fine now. I mean, you are, right?"

"Actually, no," the reflection said. "I'm in agony."

Valkyrie looked back at Meritorious, who shrugged. "Just because it's not screaming and crying doesn't mean it doesn't feel its injuries. It needs to be returned to its mirror so it can heal."

Her legs suddenly leaden, Valkyrie hunkered down by the reflection and fitted the key into the shackles with shaking hands. Once the chains fell, she helped the reflection to stand. "Can you walk?"

"I can," it replied. "But please, don't move fast."

They moved slowly out of the cell. Valkyrie looked in at Meritorious. "We'll be back—"

"Don't tell me," he interrupted. "I don't want to know what your plans are. The less I know, the less they can torture out of me. Go. Hurry."

She nodded, and took the reflection back the way she had come. And then Alexander Remit was standing in front of them.

"I know what you're thinking," he said. "You're thinking, *Oh, hell*. And you're right to think that. You know how cold you've suddenly become? That's because you're realising that this was a huge mistake."

"Or it could be the draught."

The reflection nodded. "These dungeons *are* quite draughty."

"And the reflection makes a joke," Remit said. "You weren't joking earlier, were you? When we had our fun? Eh? Didn't hear you making any jokes, then. Mostly I heard screaming. But then you're not like any reflection I've ever seen. You could almost pass for human. You certainly screamed like a human."

Valkyrie let the reflection lean against the wall, and she walked towards Remit slowly.

"Your friends upstairs are about to be horribly killed," he said, circling her, "and there's no one coming to rescue you this time."

She moved around him. "Who says I need rescuing? I slapped you around the place once before – I can do it again."

"You hit me when I wasn't ready."

"You tried attacking me from behind."

He shook his head. "No. You're trying to goad me into doing something rash. Not this time. This time, you're the one who falls, and I'm the one who stands over you making smart comments."

"I doubt you'd be up to it."

He laughed. "I'm sorry, you're insulting *my* intelligence? Did you really think this would work? A second incursion into the Palace? Even now, our lord and master Mevolent is being roused from sleep. How did you expect to survive? How did you expect to escape? The Resistance doesn't even have a Teleporter of its own to get you out of here. If that isn't the height of stupidity, I don't know what is."

"You want to know what the height of stupidity is?" Valkyrie asked. "It's getting so wrapped up in one little argument that you completely and totally forget that the person you're arguing with isn't alone."

The reflection stepped up behind Remit and pressed the pain regulator into his back. There was a crack and the smell of ozone and Remit jerked and fell to his knees.

Valkyrie kept her finger on the black slate. He had been right, though. The Resistance didn't have a Teleporter of their own to get them all out of the Palace. But, as she wrapped one arm round her reflection and curled her fingers in Remit's hair, now they didn't need one.

"I'm going to shut off the pain for two seconds," she said. "The moment it's off, you teleport us straight to the throne room or I'll kill you."

She tightened her grip on the reflection and turned off the pain. Remit took a moment to gasp, and then they were upstairs as Serpine dived at Vengeous, red hand going for his face, but Vengeous batted the hand away and flipped him over his hip.

Valkyrie turned on the pain before Remit tried anything sneaky.

Skulduggery staggered to his feet and pushed at the air. Vengeous picked up one of the unconscious Redhoods, using him as a shield, and the displaced air rippled around him.

The glass case stood open, and the Sceptre lay on the ground beside it, totally ignored by the three men fighting.

"The next time I turn off the pain," she whispered into Remit's ear, "you either teleport us out of here, to the same field as last time, or I'll have Nefarian Serpine kill you. Understand?"

He gurgled something that sounded like "yes".

She held out her hand and pulled at the air and the Sceptre flew into her grip. "Skulduggery!" she shouted.

Skulduggery was too busy getting punched by Vengeous to look around, but Serpine heard her and immediately abandoned the fight. She glared, but threw him the Sceptre to free up her hands.

She whipped the shadows at Vengeous and they struck him across the back. He whirled, eyes blazing yellow, and Valkyrie felt her body start to vibrate. The feeling vanished when Skulduggery kicked at Vengeous's knee. He cried out, stumbled, and Skulduggery took the opportunity to stagger out of his reach. Valkyrie's arm started to ache.

The door burst open, and Lord Vile and Mevolent strode in.

Vile stopped suddenly, his head tilting. Skulduggery gave him a little wave, then jumped into the air, shot like a cannonball towards Valkyrie. She turned off the pain and Remit breathed in relief.

"Teleport," she commanded. Skulduggery's gloved fingers grazed her shoulder and then she was outside, in the field, in the dark, Remit on his knees, her reflection to her right, Serpine holding the Sceptre and—

"That," said Skulduggery, hovering beside her, "was very well timed." His feet touched down. "We should all be proud of our running-away skills."

"I'm very proud of mine," said Serpine, running a sleeve across his cut lip.

Valkyrie turned on the pain and Remit gagged and resumed his trembling. "My arm hurts," she told Skulduggery. "We have maybe thirty seconds." The reflection tightened her grip.

Figures detached themselves from the dark around them, China and Shudder the first to emerge from the gloom.

"Astonishing," said China. "You actually did it."

"Thanks to you," Skulduggery responded. "We're very grateful for everything you've done to help us, but you didn't have to risk coming here."

"So many fine sorcerers died in this field just twenty-four hours ago," China said. "Their blood is still fresh. It sticks to my shoes. Did you see Meritorious?"

"Yes," Valkyrie said. "He didn't want to know what the plan was, or what the plan might be. He's still alive, and he's in pretty good spirits for someone chained upside down on a wall."

China smiled. "That is good news. I'd hate for Mevolent to take his frustration out on him. He's a good man. You didn't manage to kill Mevolent, did you?"

"Sadly not," said Skulduggery.

"How unfortunate for us," China murmured. "May I see the Sceptre?"

Serpine walked over, handed her the weapon.

"Uh," Valkyrie said, "we only have a few moments."

"I know," China said, turning the Sceptre over in her hands. "Oh, it's beautiful. It's everything I thought it would be."

Skulduggery stepped forward, his hand out. "Indeed. It's just a pity it won't work here."

She nodded absently. "Not yet, anyway."

Skulduggery went for his gun but Shudder's Gist burst screaming from his chest and slammed into him. Skulduggery rolled and Valkyrie grasped the shadows out of sheer instinct, but the reflection put a hand on her shoulder to stop her. China hadn't taken her eyes off the Sceptre, but the sorcerers around her were powered up and ready to attack. Even Serpine stood there with his arm outstretched, his red right hand flexing. Valkyrie let the shadows dissipate, and raised her hands in surrender.

Skulduggery got to his feet. The Gist snarled and snapped at the air above him, but he ignored it and focused his attention on China. "While Mevolent lives that thing is useless."

"Mevolent won't be alive for ever," she responded, finally raising her blue, blue eyes, "especially now that he doesn't have his favourite toy. And once he's dead and I take over, no one is going to argue with the lady who wields the Sceptre."

The world flickered. "Skulduggery," Valkyrie said, gripping the reflection's good hand.

He hesitated. "China, we need that Sceptre. We'll bring it back once it's done."

"And that is something I just can't risk."

"Skulduggery!"

Skulduggery's whole body was rigid as he stalked over to Valkyrie. The world flickered again, and again, and he put a hand on her arm.

"Don't come back here," China said. "If we ever see you again, we'll kill you."

And then China and the others were gone, and Valkyrie was standing in the field in her own reality, with Skulduggery and her reflection on either side of her.

"Damn that woman," Skulduggery said softly.

48

KITANA'S QUANDARY

For the first time in weeks, Kitana was scared.

She'd left Doran to play his video game and went flying, searching for Sean and trusting her gut to lead her in the right direction. Doran's blunted stupidity was starting to eat away at her patience. Sean, at least, had a mind of his own. She'd flown above the clouds, feeling herself get closer and closer. She'd eventually come to a small town in the middle of nowhere behind a stagnant lake and some dead trees, and landed on the hill overlooking the whole place. At the edge of this town there was a low, circular building. She had felt him. He was in there, somewhere. And so was Elsie. Kitana had felt her presence, and her mouth had twisted. Stupid, fat, ugly Elsie. Always there. Always hanging around, trotting after them ever since they were kids, impossible to get rid of. Like a bad smell.

She had been standing here, on this hill, when the four people in robes came into view, hovering in the air above the entrance to the circular building. Kitana knew who they were. Not their names. She didn't know their names, or anything about their lives. But she'd recognised a part that she shared with them. These people had been visited by Argeddion, just like she had.

And then a few moments later, the doors had opened and he came out. Argeddion.

She'd known it was him even though she was much too far away to make out his face. His presence was undeniable. There were some people behind him. She sensed Elsie, but gladly ignored her. Her focus was on Argeddion as he had lifted into the air, surrounded by the four sorcerers. She smiled, delighted.

And then these little balls of light had shot out of them, into Argeddion, and by the way the sorcerers fell she knew they were dead before they hit the ground.

Kitana had stared. No. This didn't make any sense. She'd ducked down in case Argeddion saw her. She didn't want him to see her. She didn't want him to do to her what he had done to them. She'd flown off, as fast as she could, convinced he was after her. But every time she looked back all she saw was empty sky.

She spent hours in the sky, exhausting herself. Finally, she returned to the house they were staying at. She hesitated before opening the door, terrified of finding Argeddion standing there, waiting for her.

Instead, she found Doran, still playing that ridiculous video game.

She told him what had happened and finally sat.

"He killed them," she said. "He killed them like they were nothing. They were floating in the air and then... *boom*."

Doran's eyes widened. "They exploded?"

"No, you idiot. They dropped dead."

Doran shrugged. "It'd have been better if they exploded."

"Oh my God, can you please have one single thought occur to you? He killed them. He didn't even have to wave a magic wand – they fell out of the air dead. It was no effort to him. He can kill us the same way."

"Why would he want to?"

"Because once his experiment is over, he's not going to need us any more. He'll kill us and we won't stand a chance."

"Argeddion wouldn't kill us. He made us like this. You heard what he called us. His *children*. He wouldn't kill his children."

"He didn't call us *his* children, he just called us *children*. He's not on our side, Doran. The only people on our side are us."

He blinked dumbly. "So, like, what do we do?"

"We're going to have to kill him."

"How?"

"How do you think, genius? With the magic he gave us. We're going to catch him by surprise, throw everything we have at him, and then we're going to tear him apart."

"You make it sound easy."

"Because it will be. If there's anyone he's going to let his guard down around, it's us. We owe him everything. He'll never expect it."

"Can... can I finish my game?"

Kitana looked at him, looked at his big stupid face and suddenly longed for Sean's company. "Sure," she said. "You can finish your game."

Doran breathed in relief, and resumed playing. She thought about burying her fist in his head, but forced herself to walk into the other room. Moron. *Moron.* She needed Sean now more than ever, needed his sensitivity to balance out Doran's dull thuggery.

And then Sean stumbled in through the back door. He stared at her, like he couldn't believe he'd found her.

"About time you got here," she told him. "We've got a mission. We're going to kill Argeddion. You in?"

"I... Kitana, I just escaped from a cell, I don't know if I'm—"

She glared at him. "Dammit, Sean, stop your whining. We can't put this off because we don't know how long we have left. We're going to kill him and we're going to kill him as soon as possible. And if your sensitive little soul can't handle that—"

"I can handle it," Sean said defensively.

Kitana gave him a smile. "I knew I could count on you."

49

THE DEAL

Skulduggery used the air to lift the reflection up to the bedroom window, and Valkyrie guided it in from inside. It sagged and she grabbed it, kept it standing.

"Sorry," it mumbled.

She waved to Skulduggery and he headed back to wait in the car. She helped the reflection over to the mirror, but it hesitated. She realised it wanted to stand by itself so she let it.

"I want to thank you," it said, "for coming back for me."

Valkyrie didn't answer.

"A lot of people wouldn't have bothered. They wouldn't have risked it. They would have just left me down there. I'm glad you didn't. I'm glad you saved me."

Saved it? It stood before her beaten and mutilated. "It's my fault,"

Valkyrie said. "I should have stayed with you. I should have kept out of trouble, like you said. If I'd have done that, none of this would have happened."

The reflection shook its head. "You came back for me. That's what matters."

"They *tortured* you."

"And if you give me your permission, I'll block that out." It looked at her with its one eye. "Believe me, Valkyrie, you don't want these memories…"

Valkyrie swallowed. "Thank you."

"Thank *you*. I just… I needed to say that now. That's all."

It stepped into the mirror and Valkyrie tapped the glass, and all the injuries and blood went away and she looked at herself while the memories settled. She remembered reaching for the reflection in the field while people died around her, and she remembered being the reflection, reaching for Valkyrie. And then she watched herself disappear, and she was hauled to her feet, herded into the Barge with all the other prisoners, and then it went blank.

She realised she was shaking.

Her mum was making toast for Alice when Valkyrie walked in, and Alice herself was sitting on the floor, grinning. Valkyrie scooped her up. "Good morning," she said, and Alice giggled.

Her mother turned. She looked surprised and… something. Something else. "I didn't hear you come home. Did you have a good time?"

"Yeah," Valkyrie said, "it was fun. Didn't get much studying done, though."

"Ah, I wouldn't worry about that. You work too hard as it is."

"I *am* a hard worker," said Valkyrie, frowning slightly. "Everything OK?"

"Yes. Everything's fine. I mean..." Her mother hesitated, then turned fully and gave a sad smile. "I lost my job."

"What? Mum..."

"It's OK, it's OK. I knew it was coming, I suppose. We all did. Bank branches are closing down all over the country so it was really only a matter of time before it hit us. It's worse for the others. At least Des has the company, and I was down to three days a week anyway to look after the little Miss here..."

"And we have all of Gordon's money," Valkyrie reminded her.

Her mother shook her head. "That's yours. He left it to you."

"Yeah, but it's yours, too."

Her mum turned, spread butter on the toast. "Nope, that's not how it works."

Valkyrie laughed. "Of course that's how it works. He didn't just leave it to me, he left it to all of us. I don't care that my name was the only name on the piece of paper. All his royalties and stuff are ours, not mine."

"That's very nice of you, sweetheart, but we don't need it. I have my redundancy and Des has the company—"

"But there isn't even enough work going around to keep him

busy. He spends most of his time playing golf, Mum, and he doesn't even know the rules."

Her mum hesitated, then nodded. "They hate him over there..."

"He owns a construction company and you worked in a bank. When I was a kid, that was great, but it's been nothing but bad news for the last few years. Do you honestly think I didn't notice that things were getting tougher?"

Her mum smiled at her. "Sometimes it's hard to tell with you."

"Well, I noticed, but I didn't say anything because I thought you knew that everything Gordon left me is ours. I mean, when have I ever cared about money? The only thing that matters to me is that you guys are happy and safe and healthy."

Valkyrie watched her mother take a deep breath. She wanted to hug her, to share this moment with her as honestly as she could, but time was tight, and Skulduggery was waiting.

"Here," she said, passing Alice to her, "take my sister and explain to her that she can go to the best college in the world when she's older. Money is not a problem."

There were tears in her mother's eyes. "You're so good, Steph."

"I have my moments," Valkyrie said, and gave her a smile and left the kitchen. She shut off the regret as soon as it sprang up. She'd hug later, when she was sure the world wasn't going to turn upside down. She got back to her room and let her reflection out of the mirror. It looked so much better now. Valkyrie gave it the clothes she was wearing, then pulled on her black trousers and boots. The reflection threw her a black T-shirt and she put it on. "I want my jacket back," she growled.

"You'll get it," said the reflection. Then, "I'll give your mum a hug from you."

Valkyrie smiled sadly, and jumped out of the window. Skulduggery picked her up and they drove to Roarhaven. She barely noticed the time passing. She thought about her mum and her dad, and little Alice.

Skulduggery braked sharply.

"Ow!" she said. "What the hell?" Then she looked up, saw Kitana and Sean and Doran standing in the middle of Roarhaven's main street. Skulduggery turned off the engine and they got out.

"Hi," said Kitana. Sean looked uneasy, but Doran was grinning.

Moving without any hurry, Skulduggery took out his gun, clicked the hammer back and aimed.

Kitana laughed. "Hold on," she said. "We're here to talk, so please don't shoot. You know it can't hurt us but the bang it makes is so scary."

The gun didn't waver. Kitana shrugged, and looked at Valkyrie. "From the way you're glaring, I see that you're still a little annoyed with me for something."

"You're wearing my jacket."

"It looks better on me, though, doesn't it?"

"By the time this is over," Valkyrie said, "I'll have taken that back."

Kitana's smile widened. "You're welcome to try."

"Can we hurry this up?" Sean asked, stepping forward. "We're here because we have a proposal."

"Go on," said Skulduggery.

"You want to stop Argeddion? Well, so do we."

Skulduggery lowered the gun. "Why?"

"That's none of your business," Doran said sharply. "The only thing you need to know is that we're the only ones who are powerful enough to do it. You're certainly not. None of you are. He could wipe you out with a wave of his hand."

"So why would you, being as powerful as you are, even need us?" Skulduggery asked. "Why don't you go after him right now?"

"We were thinking you could divert his attention," Kitana said, grinning. "Then, when he's busy laughing at you, we come in, shoot him in the back. I mean, we're powerful, but he's still Argeddion."

"I don't know," Skulduggery said slowly. "It seems to me that we should just step back and watch you and him fight it out. Then when it's done, we walk in and mop up."

"You wouldn't take the chance," said Sean. "If he kills us, he's killing the only people who can hurt him. So what do you say?"

"We'll have to meet with the Elders and put it to them," Skulduggery said. "You can wait in the Sanctuary while they decide."

Sean laughed. "So you can take away our powers like you did with me? No, we'll stay out here, thank you very much."

"How can we trust you not to hurt anyone?"

"Why would we hurt anyone? The people here love us."

"Run along," Kitana said. "Ask your bosses. We'll wait."

"Don't kill anyone in the meantime," said Skulduggery.

She winked at him. "Cross my heart."

A circle of Cleavers had formed around the three of them, and Skulduggery and Valkyrie passed through it into the Sanctuary. Tipstaff was at the door.

"Where are they?" asked Skulduggery.

"The Accelerator Room," answered Tipstaff. "The Cleavers wanted to evacuate them but they wouldn't leave."

"Sounds like them, all right."

There was an argument raging between Ghastly and Sult by the time they got down there. The force field was gone and there were mages everywhere, sifting through the remains of the Tempest and examining the empty Cube, which was still rotating inside the Accelerator.

Ravel appeared at Valkyrie's elbow. "Thank God you're back," he said softly. "Things here are a trifle tense."

Skulduggery looked at him. "Lament?"

Ravel hesitated. "Dead. Argeddion took his powers back from everyone except Kitana and her friends. It returned the mortals to normal, but for Lament and the others it was too much."

Valkyrie's eyes widened. "Wait, they're all dead? Even Lenka?"

"I'm sorry."

Her eyes drifted to the place where she'd last seen Lenka Bazaar, hovering behind the force field. Another friend, lost. Another one to add to the list.

"Do you have the Sceptre?" Ravel asked.

"We had it," Skulduggery answered. "It was in our hands. But the China Sorrows of that reality is as untrustworthy as our own."

Ravel muttered a curse under his breath.

"Detective Pleasant," said Sult, marching up to them with Ghastly on his heels. "Maybe you can give me a straight answer. No one here seems to know where Grand Mage Strom is. I find it pretty hard to believe that he could be misplaced as easily as a set of keys."

"He's not misplaced," Ghastly said, clearly not his first time saying this, "he's in a meeting with Madame Mist."

Sult turned to him. "A meeting about what? What could be so important to take him away from a developing crisis?"

"A crisis that he has no say over," Ghastly reminded him.

"And yet again you fail to answer a simple question."

"He is in," said Ghastly, "a *meeting*."

Their words blended into noise. Valkyrie didn't care about any of this. Lenka was dead, and they were arguing about politics. It was suddenly so very clear to her. Argeddion's plan, his Summer of Light, needed to be squashed before it had a chance to snatch away any more innocent lives.

"Gentlemen," Ravel said, breaking up the argument, "this is not the time for this. Mr Sult, I appreciate your input but I'm really going to have to insist that you return to your quarters and let us deal with what we have to deal with."

"I'm not going anywhere," said Sult. "I am Grand Mage Bisahalani's representative. As such, I am the Supreme Council's representative. And since we cannot seem to locate Grand Mage Strom, I am the only one to tell you what has been decided."

"Decided?"

"I don't see the Sceptre of the Ancients in Detective Pleasant's hand. Am I to take it that the mission to retrieve said weapon was unsuccessful? Don't bother answering that, it's quite clear. Which means we have four super-powered threats still to deal with, and the only weapon I can see that could be of use is the Accelerator."

Valkyrie frowned. "What?"

"It is now available to us, as the force field dropped once Argeddion killed the traitors," Sult said.

"Traitors?" she echoed. "They weren't traitors. Argeddion was controlling them."

Sult shook his head. "He may have been *manipulating* them but I believe they were in full control of their—"

She lunged at him. "Lenka was not a traitor!"

Ravel wrapped an arm round her waist and Ghastly pulled her hands from Sult's collar as Sult staggered away. Anger flashed across his face and he stepped up while Valkyrie struggled, fist bunched.

"I know," Skulduggery said in a tone that made everyone freeze, "that you're not about to strike my partner."

Slowly, Ravel and Ghastly let go of Valkyrie, and Sult's fist unclenched.

"Of— of course not," he said. "I apologise, both for losing my temper and for insinuating that any of Tyren Lament's people were to blame for what has happened."

Valkyrie fought the urge to smash his face in.

"The Supreme Council wants to use the Accelerator to supercharge their mages," Ghastly said. "Even though we don't know what the Accelerator will do to a person. For all we know it might kill them. Worse, the sheer power might drive them insane and then *they'll* kill *us*."

"I hardly think we have a choice," said Sult. "Kitana and her friends are on our doorstep as we speak."

"Have any of you actually spoken to them?" Skulduggery asked.

Ravel looked at him. "Spoken to whom?"

"Kitana and her friends. We have. They're offering us a deal. We soften Argeddion up, they come in and finish him off."

"But why do they want Argeddion dead all of a sudden?" asked Sult. "What do they get out of it?"

"Security," said Skulduggery. "They're the only ones who can hurt him, but he's the only one who could be assured of hurting them, too. They're afraid he's going to take their powers away, like he did with Lament and the others."

"Could they do it?" asked Ghastly. "Could they kill him?"

"I think so," said Skulduggery. "We'd need to draw Argeddion in and hit him with enough force to stagger him."

"Any ideas how to do it?"

"Luring him into a trap should be pretty easy."

"And the second part? The part where we have to hurt him?"

Skulduggery gestured to the Tempest. "We know some pretty smart people, don't we? I'm sure it wouldn't take them long to figure out how to turn this into a weapon."

"And what if it works?" Ravel asked. "Then Argeddion is down, but we still have the girl and her friends walking around."

Skulduggery hesitated. "That's where our overall plan has to change. We'd originally hoped to put Argeddion back in the Cube. The Accelerator could run it for an eternity and he'd never get loose again. That was a solution that would have pleased everyone. But now, with everything we know, that's no longer an option."

"We have to kill him," said Valkyrie. They looked at her. Ghastly in particular seemed shocked. "We have to," she continued. "He killed Lenka, he killed Lament, and the blood of every single person that Kitana and her friends have hurt or killed is on his hands as well. It's the first of May. His Summer of Light starts today unless we stop him."

Ravel looked at Skulduggery. "Do you agree? You want to kill him?"

"No," said Skulduggery. "I want *them* to kill him. Kitana and the others. He said something a few days ago that's got me thinking that the people he's infected will only keep their powers for as long as he is alive. If he dies, their powers die with him."

"So if Kitana and her friends kill him... they'll be sabotaging themselves."

"You're sure about this?" Ravel asked.

"Relatively," said Skulduggery.

Ravel looked at Ghastly, who sighed. "It might be the only way," he said. "So how do we go about it?"

"That's the other piece of bad news," Skulduggery said. "In order to make sure they're strong enough, we're going to have to boost their powers."

"You want to put *them* in the Accelerator?"

"It's the only way to be certain."

"And what if it does drive them insane?" Sult asked.

"More insane than they've already been driven? I think we can take that chance. If it kills them, well, then we have one less problem to worry about. But if it works, they'll be powerful enough to do what needs to be done."

Ravel sagged. "But I've kind of made it an unofficial policy never to make psychopaths stronger."

"They'll only be that strong until they defeat Argeddion. Once he's dead, they'll revert to being normal teenagers."

"And can I hit them, then?"

"You're the Grand Mage, you can do whatever you want."

"I want to hit them."

"You know," Ghastly said to Skulduggery, "for someone who hates plans, you've got an awful lot of them."

"Well, yes," Skulduggery replied, "but really, the likelihood of any of them actually working is extraordinarily slim."

Ravel shook his head. "You should really learn to recognise the point where you should stop talking."

50

SUPERCHARGED

He was right, of course – but then Skulduggery usually was about things like this.

Ravel called everyone in the Science-Magic Department down to the Accelerator Room, and they examined the Tempest and within half an hour they had come up with the best way to weaponise it in the time they had available. They set about dismantling the Tempest's components, adapting and rethinking as they went. It was all very, very boring, and Valkyrie lost interest halfway through.

She nudged Skulduggery.

"Isn't this fascinating?" he said.

"Yeah," she lied. "So you said drawing Argeddion into a trap won't be a problem. But we don't even know where he is."

"We don't have to. We have something he wants."

"Which is?"

He looked at her, and hesitated. "You love your grandmother, don't you?"

Valkyrie frowned. "We're not giving him my granny."

"No, I just mean you love her. She's an elderly lady, and you love her."

"So?"

"So it's important at this stage to acknowledge that you love your grandmother, who is an elderly lady, and to also acknowledge the fact that she is a strong and intelligent woman."

"Please don't tell me you're in love with my granny."

He sighed. "We're going to use Greta Dapple to draw Argeddion into a trap."

"What does that have to do with my granny?"

"Nothing, but I wanted to establish that elderly people don't need to be coddled."

"Some of them do."

"Well, yes, some of them, but not your granny. And... OK, I'm kind of losing track of where I was going with that. Here's what I didn't want – I didn't want you confusing your grandmother with Greta Dapple."

"Why would I confuse them?"

"I don't know. I thought there might be a danger of that happening. I thought if you started looking at Greta as a kind of substitute for your beloved grandmother, then you wouldn't want to see her being used as bait."

"My granny's still alive."

"I'm aware of that."

"I don't need a substitute for her."

"OK then. Are you onboard with using Greta as bait?"

"Yeah, sure, whatever. Lenka's dead because of the lies Greta told us. She may have believed she was doing it out of the goodness of her heart, but it doesn't change the fact."

Tipstaff hurried over. He looked even more harassed than usual. "Excuse me, Detectives, I was wondering if either of you would have a moment to deal with a slight... problem in the Medical Bay."

"I'll do it," said Valkyrie. "Anything to get me away from this conversation." They walked towards the stairs.

"Thank you," said Tipstaff. "There are strange... noises coming from Doctor Nye's ward. Sounds of a disturbance, if I may be so bold."

"Oh, you may," Valkyrie said.

"I hope you don't mind. I know how some people become unnerved around Doctor Nye."

"Not me," she said. "Any opportunity to threaten it with violence is a good opportunity for me."

Tipstaff left her at the top of the stairs and she went on alone. She walked straight in, found Nye hunched over a microscope.

"Doctor," she said, "apparently you're having a problem up here."

It looked around. "Problem? No, no problem. I'm sorry, I don't know what you—"

There was a crash from the room behind it. Valkyrie raised an eyebrow and started forward. Nye uncurled itself and stepped into her path.

"Back away, Doctor," she said, shadows curling between her fingers.

"Detective Cain, I assure you, there is nothing untoward going on here at all. It's a waste of your valuable, valuable time to be even—"

"Step away. I'm not going to ask you again."

It hesitated, then nodded, and moved from her path. She was halfway to the door when it spoke.

"It was too good to pass up."

She turned. "What was?"

"The opportunity. The procedure. I'd never performed one before. I wanted to see if I could. I wanted to see what would happen with the consciousness, with the brain... with the soul. And now I've done it not once, but twice. Two successful procedures."

There was another crash.

"What have you done, Doctor?"

"In layman's terms? A brain transplant."

"What?"

"Two of them. They came to me a year ago, these two pathetic and shambling zombies, and I sent them away. But then they returned and I looked upon their sad, rotting faces and I felt something I had not felt in decades. Pity. I... pitied them."

"You're talking about Scapegrace?"

"Scapegrace, yes, and his idiot companion. Scapegrace was nothing more than a head in a jar, and his companion was an idiot. So I agreed to find them new bodies, strong new bodies, and transfer their brains."

"Are you serious? They're back there right now with new bodies? Where did you get them?"

"The bodies? Donated to science. I can show you the paperwork if you would like."

There was a crash, and a shout.

"Excuse the noise," Nye said. "They have to learn how to co-ordinate. Adjustment will take time."

"This is insane," Valkyrie said. "Are you seriously saying you...? So you just took out their brains and...? Can I... can I see them?"

"Ah... Detective, this is a very private and personal moment for them both. I'm sure you can understand their need for—"

A man stumbled out clutching a sheet round his waist and Valkyrie's eyes widened. "Whoa," she said as he bumped into a table. He was tall and sandy-haired and his physique was jaw-droppingly amazing. "No way," she said. "Scapegrace?"

The man looked at her, and shook his head. Then a woman came charging out of the backroom, slammed into the man and they both went rolling across the floor.

"Give it to me!" the woman screamed. "Give it to me!"

Nye scuttled over. "Mr Scapegrace, you *know* the procedure cannot be repeated, your brains are in far too deteriorated a condition."

"*You! Gave! Me! The! Wrong! Body!*"

"An honest mistake," Nye said. "You didn't make a clear choice. You said you found the female body amusing. I assumed this indicated acceptance."

"Master," gurgled the handsome man with the incredible body as the woman continued to throttle him, "please..."

Valkyrie walked backwards as quietly as she could, then turned and left them to it.

She found Ghastly in the next corridor, and he called her over.

"I need your help with something," he said softly.

"What do I have to do?"

"Just stand beside me, basically. Look pretty. Contribute to the conversation."

"What conversation would that be?"

"The conversation that will result when I take Sult down to see what we've done with Grand Mage Strom. Are you feeling up to it?"

"Ravel gave this job to you?"

"He did. Isn't he nice?"

They stopped talking when Sult came over, and Ghastly led the way to the detention area. Not a whole lot was said on the way, but Sult frowned when they got to the cells.

"What am I doing here?" he asked, suddenly looking like he was about to bolt. Ghastly didn't answer. Instead, he opened the cell door.

Sult's eyes widened. "Grand Mage? But what...? What's going on?"

Strom stood in the middle of the cell. "I've been placed under arrest, Mr Sult. What does it look like?"

Sult stared at Ghastly. "You can't be serious. You did this? You arrested a Grand Mage?"

"His intentions constituted a threat to the Council of Elders and this Sanctuary, and so he was arrested and detained until—"

"Are you mad?" Sult raged. "Do you have any idea what you've done?"

"We were threatened, we acted accordingly."

"You falsely imprisoned a Grand Mage!"

"The arrest was entirely legal."

"False arrest, false imprisonment, kidnapping, assault on an Elder, obstruction of justice—"

"Obstruction of what?" Ghastly said with a laugh. "You came in here with threats and an agenda to take over and we defended ourselves in a peaceful manner."

"*You can't do this!*"

"Well, we did."

"This is lunacy!"

"Is Mr Sult to join me in here?" Strom asked, his voice calm. "Or have you come to your senses?"

"We have a chance to resolve our current crisis," said Ghastly. "Working with the three teenagers, we're going to launch a full-scale attack on Argeddion, weakening him enough so that they can deliver the killing blow."

"I see. And what makes you think you can trust these children?"

"They're scared of him now," said Valkyrie. "But what they don't know is that once he dies, their powers will vanish."

"Putting an end to one crisis," Strom said, rather pointedly.

"Indeed," said Ghastly. "Which is why I'm here."

"Oh?" said Strom.

"You offered us your help, and we'd like to take you up on that offer."

Sult's eyes practically bulged. "I'm sorry? You want our help *now*? *Now*, after falsely imprisoning a Grand Mage?"

"That's right," said Ghastly.

Sult started to laugh, but Strom held up a hand.

"Mr Sult, please. Elder Bespoke, the actions of your Council were illegal and aggressive."

"I disagree."

"Be that as it may, what you have done could very well result in a war between Sanctuaries, sir – an unheard-of situation." Ghastly nodded, and Strom sighed. "This isn't over. If this plan works, and if the threat posed by Argeddion is averted, there will be consequences."

"We'll deal with that if we survive."

"Very well," said Strom. He put on his jacket. "We promised you our assistance, and our assistance you shall have. For now."

"OK then," said Boffin, standing there in his white lab coat looking all pleased with himself, "Tyren Lament's design for the Tempest was, quite frankly, ahead of its time. It was a singularly momentous achievement that even today will raise the collective eyebrow of the scientific community."

His name wasn't really Boffin. Valkyrie couldn't remember his actual name. It was something long. She'd called him Boffin because he looked like a Boffin.

"In weaponising the Tempest, we have adhered to Lament's design template and merely tweaked, or as my good friend Professor Lorre would say, *tickled* –" and at this there was a polite chuckle from other people in white coats – "the relay system and delivery method. In essence, we have made the Tempest mobile. Where the chair was ideal for Lament's needs of siphoning a mage's power, it is not so for ours. Therefore, I give you the new and improved Siphoning Disc." He held aloft something silver with holes cut into it.

"That's a hubcap," Ghastly pointed out.

Boffin nodded. "Ah, yes, it is indeed."

Ravel pinched the bridge of his nose. "You're giving us magical hubcaps?"

"We've only had a few hours," Boffin said, a little defensively. "We've used what was available."

"Go on," Madame Mist said.

Boffin cleared his throat. "The Siphoning Discs will be connected via cable to the Tempest itself, which we have adapted to suit our needs."

"Adapted how?" Skulduggery asked.

"We've opened it," Boffin said. "We've attached a focusing nozzle to aim – but unfortunately, it can only aim upwards."

"Then it's a good thing our target flies," Ghastly muttered.

"There are sixty Siphoning Discs," Boffin continued, "so at the very least sixty mages will be required."

"At least?"

"The discs will drain an individual's magic in the same way Lament's chair did, only it will be faster, and more intense. The chance of some mages being overwhelmed is... substantial. When they pass out, there will need to be another mage ready to take their place."

"So we hold on to those discs," Ravel said, "and our power is pulled from us, collected in this Tempest pyramid, and then fired upwards."

"As pure energy," Boffin said, nodding. "Yes. By our calculations, it should stun even a being of Argeddion's power. Provided you can get him to stay in the same place while you shoot him."

"Leave that to us," Skulduggery said.

"Oh, good," Boffin said, visibly relieved.

The atmosphere darkened when Kitana, Sean and Doran entered the Sanctuary. Against their protests, the Elders had been moved to another part of the building, purely for safety reasons. Ghastly seemed especially indignant. Non-essential personnel were moved out of the Sanctuary completely, so it was only Valkyrie, Skulduggery and Bernard Sult who escorted the teenagers downstairs. Sean seemed nervous and trying not to show it, while Doran kept a permanent smirk on his face. Only Kitana appeared genuinely relaxed as they were shown into the Accelerator Room.

"Ooh," she said, rushing over to the Cube as it rotated in the Accelerator. "What's this?"

"It's called the Cube," said Sult. "It's where Argeddion was imprisoned."

"It's so cool," she said, eyes wide. "Look at it, all floaty and glowy and stuff."

Doran rolled his eyes like he couldn't be impressed.

Skulduggery hit a button and two mechanical arms lowered, catching opposite corners of the Cube and lifting it from the Accelerator. Kitana watched it move, enthralled.

"What's it doing now?" she asked.

"It's getting out of the way," Skulduggery said. "We'll put it back when we're done, but the Accelerator is what we're here for."

Kitana made a face. "That? That's boring."

"What does it do?" Sean asked.

Skulduggery looked at him. "It will increase your magic long enough for you to stop Argeddion."

"This will make us stronger?" Kitana asked, instantly forgetting about the Cube. "Even stronger than we already are?"

"It will amplify your abilities."

Kitana's eyes narrowed. "You're not trying to trick us, are you, skeleton man? I've seen that Superman movie where he uses that chamber thing to rob the villains' powers."

"We're not tricking you."

Doran rapped a knuckle against the Accelerator's glowing skin. "Then why don't you guys use it, and you go up against him?"

"We don't fully understand the source of Argeddion's magic," Sult said, "but we do know that it is a purer strain than ours. You can think of magic like a frequency if you want. Your magic is on the same frequency as his, so you stand a better chance of hurting him."

Kitana turned. "Use the Accelerator on just one of us to start with. If you're trying to trick us, and it takes their powers, we'll kill everyone in the town above us."

Skulduggery looked at her. "So who should go first? Maybe you yourself, Kitana?"

She laughed. "I don't think so. Doran, how about you?"

Doran frowned. "Why me?"

"You're the strongest, aren't you? If it is a trap, you'd be the one able to resist."

Sean scowled, and Doran smirked, then nodded. "Yeah, OK. I'll do it. Where do I stand?"

While Skulduggery told him what to do, Kitana wandered over to Valkyrie.

"Isn't this fun?" she said. "Us two girls, having an adventure, surrounded by all these boys fussing over us. We're going to be the best of friends when this is over, I just know it."

Valkyrie looked at her. "When this is over, I'm going to beat you to a pulp and take my jacket back."

Kitana laughed. "Oh, Valkyrie! You're so funny!"

Doran stood up on the dais, fists clenched. "All right," he said. "Let's do it, come on. Charge me up."

Skulduggery tapped the controls. "Just give me a moment..."

Doran's leg was shaking. "Come on," he said. "Hurry up. Haven't got all day."

"Just one more moment..."

"Here," said Doran. "You have used this on people before, right?"

"Hmm?" Skulduggery said. "People? No, not on people. Ah, here we go."

The dais lit up.

"Oh, I don't know about this," said Doran. "I don't think I want to do this..."

"You'll be fine," Skulduggery said.

"How do you know?"

"I don't."

The hair stood up on Valkyrie's arms and light filled the room. The Accelerator whined like an animal, the whine getting louder and louder and the dais beginning to tremble.

"I want to get off!" Doran shouted. "I want to get off!"

"You can't get off!" Skulduggery shouted back over the roar. "If you get off you'll die!"

"I'll die?"

"I don't know," Skulduggery shouted. "Probably."

And then there was a flash, and Doran screamed, and then his scream was drowned out by the Accelerator...

... and then the whine lessened, and the light dimmed, and Doran was kneeling on the dais with his head down.

Kitana stepped forward. "Doran? Doran, you OK?"

He raised his head, looked at her and grinned. "You have *got* to have a go on this."

51

ARGEDDION FALLS

They drove out of Roarhaven, skirting round Dublin and taking the smaller roads until they came to a cottage bordering a large field. A few small sheds huddled beneath the shelter of a line of trees like they were trying to escape the sun. The Bentley slowed, parked along the road. Behind it, dozens of vans did the same.

The sorcerers worked quickly. Using a cloaking sphere to hide themselves from the cottage, they laid the Tempest in the middle of the field and quickly hooked up the cables. Valkyrie watched the sorcerers lie on the ground in a wide circle, using camouflage to blend in. Once they were hidden, the sphere was retracted so that it only covered the Tempest itself, and Skulduggery and Valkyrie walked up the narrow driveway and knocked on the door of the cottage.

Greta Dapple answered, and smiled at them. "He said you'd be by here eventually. Come in, come in."

She shuffled to one side, and when they were in, she closed the door. "Would you like anything to drink? Tea?"

"No thank you," said Valkyrie. Greta's home was an old person's home. Old-fashioned, with doilies and a small television. Valkyrie helped her to her chair.

"Thank you, Valkyrie," she said, sighing as she settled in.

Skulduggery took off his hat and focused his eye sockets on Greta. "You've been talking to him," he said.

"Oh, yes."

"Where is he?"

"I'm afraid I don't know."

"Greta," Valkyrie said, "maybe you can help us. You need to convince him to stop what he's doing. People are getting hurt."

"Walden wouldn't hurt a fly. He is and always has been a perfect gentleman. If only all gods were as mannerly as he is, the world would be a better place."

"Argeddion is not a god," Skulduggery said.

Greta shrugged. "He's the closest thing to one that I've ever met."

"Has he told you what he plans to do?"

"He has. I think it's a wonderful idea."

"He's endangering the lives of billions."

"Oh, have a little faith in the human spirit, would you? He wants to make them better. He wants to make them happier. Wouldn't you like to live in a world without strife?" She paused. "Well, maybe you wouldn't, Detective Pleasant, but hopefully your young partner has not been completely corrupted by violence just yet."

"I'd love to live in a world without strife," Skulduggery said, "but that's not the path I've chosen. I do the things I do so that other people don't have to. Argeddion doesn't realise what he's about to unleash."

"He's about to unleash peace and love."

"He's about to unleash an animal."

"Mankind is not an animal."

"Oh, it is, Greta. It's a scared, dangerous animal. He thinks people are going to wake up one morning and be elevated by the wonders he's shown them. He thinks we're going to live in a kingdom of the righteous, of the noble. But we're not like that."

"I feel sorry for you, Detective. You fight for us but you have no true understanding of what we are. The tragic thing is that young Valkyrie probably follows your philosophy to the letter."

"We're just trying to help people," Valkyrie said.

"Then you're doing it wrong," said Greta. "Don't become a bitter old cynic like your friend here. Trust in the decency of others and you won't be disappointed."

"Where is he, Greta?" Skulduggery asked.

"I don't know."

"When will he be back?"

"I couldn't say."

"When did you see him last?"

"This morning. We spent the night together. We talked of so many things. He didn't have an awful lot of news for me, but that's to be expected, I think, when you've been asleep for thirty years. But I told him everything that had happened to me since he was taken, and we spoke of our old dreams, and of the future."

"And what is your future?" Skulduggery pressed. "Are you and Walden going to live happily ever after in this new Age of Enlightenment?"

"Me?" Greta said. "Oh, my time is nearly up. It's sad, really. I wish I could have stayed young and beautiful for him – although he says I'm still the most beautiful thing he's ever seen." She laughed softly. "He's such a bad liar."

"You love him," said Skulduggery.

"Of course," said Greta.

"Then you won't help us, even if you agree with us."

Greta gave them another smile. "I'm glad you understand."

"Unfortunately, I do. Can I ask you to accompany us outside?"

Greta seemed surprised, but smiled again as Skulduggery helped her up. Valkyrie didn't look at her. She couldn't.

They went outside, moving slowly, and crossed to the field.

"It's a beautiful spot," Skulduggery said.

Greta nodded. "It belonged to my parents. They died over a hundred and sixty years ago, but I can still hear their laughter. They didn't know I was magic. They didn't know magic existed. I've always regretted not telling them. What about you, Valkyrie? Does your family know?"

Valkyrie shook her head.

"A shame," said Greta. "But don't worry. They will. You'd make it easier on them if you told them beforehand. Tell them today. Show them what you can do. Delight them. Tell them that soon enough, they'll be able to do it, too. Think of the look on their faces."

They were on the field now. They'd passed through the circle of sorcerers and Greta hadn't even noticed, even though she'd been right on top of one of them.

"Walden loved this place as much as I did," she continued. "The peace and the tranquillity, the fact that no matter how fast the world was moving around us, we could always stop and hear the birds sing."

"Greta," Skulduggery said, "we've tried to be reasonable. We've tried to use logic and common sense to convince Argeddion that this is not the way to go. But we've run out of options."

"I don't understand."

At Skulduggery's signal, all of the hidden sorcerers raised a hand. Greta gasped. "What... what are they doing here?"

"It's a trap," Skulduggery said. "We've worked out a way to stop Argeddion and we're using you to draw him in."

"No. No, I won't do it."

"You already are. With the bond you share, I can't see how he wouldn't be tuned in to your emotional state at all times. Your panic will send him running."

"Then I won't panic. I won't—"

"You're panicking right now, Greta. You're doing exactly what we want you to do."

She stared at him, then stared at Valkyrie. "How can you do this? What is wrong with you that you can do this?"

"We're sorry," said Valkyrie.

"He doesn't want to hurt anybody!"

"He may not want to," said Skulduggery, "but he will."

Greta covered her mouth with her hand, and tears filled her eyes. "He loves me. How can you use that against him? What kind of people are you?"

Skulduggery tilted his head. "We're the people who get the job done."

"I'm disappointed," said a voice from behind them.

Greta sobbed as Argeddion walked forward, taking her in his arms. "It's OK, my sweet. It's OK."

Valkyrie glanced at Skulduggery, and they both took a step back.

"Walden," said Greta, "no, it's a trap."

"I know," Argeddion said. "But it won't work. Please, go back inside. I'll speak with you soon." He kissed her gently on the forehead, and then made her vanish. He looked up. "As I said, I am disappointed in you. Greta is an elderly lady, and you purposefully cause her distress simply to draw me out?"

"We had to get you here," Skulduggery said.

"Why? So all of the sorcerers you have surrounding us could attack me at once? What, you thought I wouldn't notice them? A clumsy plan for such an intelligent man."

"You've left us no choice."

Argeddion's eyes flickered to Valkyrie. "I see someone has installed a psychic block in your mind. A good job they did, too – although it wouldn't take me long to dismantle it if that's what I wished."

"We're offering you a chance," Skulduggery said. "Return to the Cube. We have it powered by the Accelerator. It's safe. Forget all this. Let the world evolve on its own."

"Abandon everything, after I've learned so much?"

Argeddion held out his hand and a man appeared beside him. He was in his twenties, dressed in a suit, and he was sweating profusely. He looked like he hadn't even realised he'd just teleported.

"This is my newest test subject," Argeddion said. "As of yet, no side effects or abnormal behaviour. He is coping quite well with his new abilities."

The man looked up, eyes wide. He stared at Skulduggery. His hand began to glow. He cried out, raising his arm and energy crackled—

—and then he crumpled to the ground, unconscious, and a small globe of light drifted from his chest, absorbed into Argeddion's hand.

Argeddion was silent for a moment while the man disappeared. "That was a promising start," he said at last. "I knew this wasn't going to be easy. I knew there was going to be a lot of trial and error. But I'm close. When the power I gave to Sean and Doran and Kitana reaches its full potential and returns to me, it will answer a lot of questions. It won't be long now before I discover the correct amount of magic to give to mortals which will not result in trauma."

Skulduggery shook his head. "We gave you a chance to surrender. It's obvious you're not going to take it."

Argeddion smiled. "Is this when you spring your trap?" He rose into the air. "Very well, then. Here I am, a nice big target for you all."

"Actually," Skulduggery said, "would you mind moving to your right a little?"

"By all means. How's that?"

"Perfect," Skulduggery said. "Thank you."

Argeddion sighed. "Is this when the violence begins? Are you going to attack me now?"

"We are," said Skulduggery. "But not in the way you think."

The cloaking sphere retracted, revealing the Tempest lying directly beneath Argeddion's hovering form. All around the field, sorcerers burst from cover, grabbed their Siphoning Discs. Energy pulsed down the cables, stirred in the Tempest and burst upwards, catching Argeddion right in the centre of the beam.

Valkyrie followed Skulduggery to the edge of the circle, their discs floating into their hands. Her hair whipped round her face. It was like standing in a pool of static electricity. She could feel her strength draining, and didn't know how long she'd be able to keep it up. When it was almost too much, she released her hold. Immediately she started to feel strong again.

"Give it a moment," Skulduggery said from beside her.

When she was back to full strength, she picked up the disc once more. Gritting her teeth, her body trembling slightly, she watched as all around the field sorcerers sent their power into the beam of debilitating energy that kept Argeddion trapped.

"It's working," she managed to say, then frowned. "Where the hell is Kitana?"

Argeddion twisted, tried to reach out beyond the energy, but the beam was too thick. He pressed one hand down, grimacing as he struggled to do the same with the other one. The energy hit his palms and spilled over but still he pressed down. He was focusing on his own energy, pressing it down further, shifted into a better position, and then he pushed. The beam rippled, the ripple hurtling down its length in an instant and the Tempest shook, got brighter.

Skulduggery cried out a warning but it was too late. The Tempest exploded, sending out a shockwave that took everyone off their feet. Valkyrie hit the ground and kept rolling, glimpsed Skulduggery crashing through the door of the old barn.

When she came to a stop, her head was ringing. She looked up, saw Argeddion, floating there, exhausted but recovering his strength quickly. The Tempest was destroyed. Their one chance to stop him, gone. And Kitana and the others hadn't even bothered to—

A stream of energy hit Argeddion from above and he cried out, went tumbling through the air as Kitana and Sean and Doran swooped down out of the clouds. They all fired, each of their streams connecting, each one sending Argeddion spiralling in a new direction. Doran burst forward, grabbed Argeddion, spun him and hurled him straight down. Kitana cheered as Argeddion hit the ground.

Greta Dapple emerged from her cottage, moving as fast she could. Valkyrie groaned as she got up.

Kitana landed. "Hey there," she said, and lashed out, sending

Argeddion sprawling over the smoking remains of the Tempest. "We don't mean to be ungrateful or nothing, but we're teenagers, you know? We need a positive role model in our lives, and you're not it."

Her hand glowed and a beam sizzled through his back. He screamed and she laughed, and then he rose into the air, but it wasn't his own doing. Sean was in control, grinning as Argeddion contorted in pain.

"Sir," said Doran, "I just want you to know how much we appreciate all this power you've given us. It was really very nice of you. Thanks."

"Stop that!" Greta called. "Put him down! Stop that right now!"

"Stay back!" Argeddion shouted, but she kept coming.

Valkyrie cursed under her breath, started running to intercept.

Sean let Argeddion fall, and Doran hunkered over him, started hitting him. "Thank you," he kept saying as he punched. "Thank you."

Argeddion didn't even try to defend himself. He just kept reaching for Greta. "No," he gasped. "Don't. Stay back."

Kitana grinned. "Nonsense. Come forward, old woman."

Greta was out of breath when she reached them. Valkyrie was sprinting towards her.

"You let..." Greta said, "him go..."

Kitana looked back at Argeddion. "I have to say, and I don't mean this as a come-on, but you could probably do better." She looked at Greta and smacked her across the face, and the old woman was dead before her feet had even left the ground.

Valkyrie roared and leaped and Kitana turned, punched her in the gut. Valkyrie folded, spinning away, her insides broken, her lungs empty.

"*Greta!*" Argeddion screamed. "*Greta!*"

His screams sliced into Valkyrie's head and she felt like her skull was going to crack open. Doran stumbled back and Sean stomped on Argeddion's head until he shut up. Valkyrie sagged.

"Doran," Kitana said, "stop. Don't kill him." She nudged Valkyrie over on to her back, and smiled down at her. "Hear that? We're not killing him. What, did you think we were stupid or something? It was so obvious from the way you lot jumped all over our little plan that you wanted us to do it."

"Two birds with one stone," said Sean.

"That's it exactly," said Kitana. "We kill him, we lose our powers, don't we? I mean, it's the only logical conclusion. So we're not killing him. You know what we *are* doing? We're going to dump him in that cool glowy square thing so he'll be trapped and we'll stay like this for ever."

Sean picked Argeddion up and rose into the air. Doran followed, and Kitana was the last to go. "Oh, Valkyrie?" she said, right before she flew off. "This is over, and I'm the one wearing your jacket."

She laughed, and they were gone.

Valkyrie tried to breathe.

She heard voices. Someone dropped to their knees beside her. Reverie Synecdoche. The doctor. She felt hands on her, warming her skin, easing the pain, and then her lungs filled with oxygen and she gasped.

"Don't try to sit up," Reverie said. "You've got internal bleeding. We need to get you back to the Sanctuary."

Valkyrie grimaced, looked around. Sorcerers and Cleavers were organising themselves, preparing to return. She saw Skulduggery striding over. He had a black metal case in his hand – the case that held Vile's armour.

"Thank you, Reverie," he said, scooping Valkyrie up in his arms. "I'll take her to the Sanctuary immediately."

"But it's been evacuated!" Reverie shouted after them as Skulduggery rose into the air. "There are no doctors there!"

They angled towards Roarhaven, quickly leaving the field behind them. "I'm fine," said Valkyrie as they flew.

"Of course you are," Skulduggery replied. He'd lost his hat and his jacket was torn.

She did her best to shut out the pain. "Where'd you find the case?"

"Greta's barn. Argeddion hid it close to home. Vile is the only chance we have now of stopping them. And if by some ridiculous stroke of luck he does stop them, then you need to stop me."

"How? By bleeding on you?"

"By being your usual charming self."

"Ah," she said, trying not to cough. "My secret weapon."

They reached the Sanctuary and Skulduggery took her inside. They flew gently through the empty corridors and down the steps.

Voices up ahead. Arguing. They heard snatches of the conversation. They'd successfully moved the Cube back inside the Accelerator, but Kitana didn't know how to open it and for some reason she was blaming Sean. From the sounds of fists against flesh, it seemed as though Doran was in charge of keeping Argeddion unconscious while they figured it out.

They ducked into a room and Skulduggery set Valkyrie down. She leaned against the wall and did her best not to pass out. He didn't say anything as he stepped into the corridor with the case. He didn't need to.

He undid the first clasp and then Sean grabbed him, hurled him into the wall.

"Told you!" he shouted. "Told you I felt something coming!"

"Yeah, yeah," Kitana said from the Accelerator Room. "Just kill them, would you?"

Valkyrie stumbled to the doorway in time to see Skulduggery reaching for the case, but Sean picked it up, held it tight to his chest. "You want this? What's in it? It's probably important, isn't it? I'll let you have it if you beg. Go on, skeleton. Start begging."

Black liquid dripped from the case, forming a little puddle at Sean's feet. The dripping quickened, and liquid began to leak from the other end, flowing steadily now, like the case was filled with oil. Sean noticed, and adjusted his hold, and the case sprang open and a wave of black burst forth, splashing down on to Skulduggery, covering him from head to foot, wrapping round him, getting thicker, forming armour. And slowly, Lord Vile looked up.

Sean let the case fall. "I'm not sure what's going on."

Vile lashed out, a wall of shadows smashing into Sean and throwing him back.

"Hey!" Sean yelled. "Help!"

Kitana emerged from the other room and froze. Doran came behind her. "What the hell is that?"

"It's him!" Sean said. "It's the skeleton!"

Vile kicked him and Sean went sliding across the floor. Kitana's hand glowed, and a streak of energy hit Vile in the back. He staggered, his armour coiling and thrashing. He'd been hurt.

He turned, and sharp tendrils of shadow converged on Kitana's position. She fell to her knees with her hands covering her head, but the shadows could only slither across the force field surrounding her body. She looked up, the realisation that she had somehow protected herself making her braver. She stood, still flinching whenever the shadows snapped at her like angry snakes. Those shadows withdrew at Vile's command, and Kitana grinned.

"Get him!" she commanded, and Doran and Sean flew at Vile.

Valkyrie stumbled sideways, almost falling to the floor, and when she'd sucked in another breath she tried to straighten up, and found Kitana standing in the doorway.

"You just couldn't leave it alone, could you?" Kitana said, and she punched through Valkyrie's chest, grabbed her heart and squeezed—

52

FEARFUL SYMMETRY

—and Darquesse felt her heart burst, and it was like a million suns exploding inside her, a cascade of sensation that burned through her mind and lit up her thoughts. She felt, even in that instant, how her body was preparing to shut down, how it was all going to judder to a stop in the next few moments.

The next few moments were, of course, an eternity for someone like Darquesse. If Kitana had really wanted to kill her, she should have destroyed the brain. Without the ability to think, there'd be no way that Darquesse would be able to ignore the trauma and heal herself over while Kitana's hand was still inside her.

Kitana's big blue eyes widened, and she tried tugging her hand free. Darquesse gave her a smile, allowing herself to be dragged forward a few steps. It looked like Kitana's wrist had fused to

Darquesse's chest. All very amusing. Finally, Kitana freed herself, and Darquesse healed again even before the blood had fallen to the ground.

Kitana backed off. "How can you do that?"

Darquesse didn't pay any heed to the words. The girl was trivial, and didn't deserve her attention. The power she wielded, however, was something that demanded more study. She saw how it flickered around the edges of the girl's being, lapping like hungry fire. Such a delightful thing. Darquesse reached out to touch it but Kitana slapped her hand away.

Darquesse laughed, and hit her, and Kitana went away and Darquesse stepped into the corridor. Doran was on the floor, trying to get up. Lord Vile had turned his full attention on poor little Sean. He was using a trick that was affectionately known as the death bubble. She watched it expand to envelop the boy, and the life energy around his body dimmed immediately, losing its colour, fading into grey. His face, meanwhile, went white, eyes wide and mouth slack.

Darquesse watched it all unfold, waiting for Vile to draw the bubble back into himself, taking Sean's life with it. The force field couldn't do anything against an attack like this. This was magic, not instinct, and none of these children knew the first thing about magic. They'd been presented with a gift, and then just figured out the best ways to use that gift to hurt people. They were clumsy, awkward creatures with no understanding of the power at their fingertips.

A stream of energy hit Vile and he stumbled. The death bubble collapsed and Sean dropped to his knees, sucking in lungfuls of air. Kitana waved her arm and Vile flew backwards, smashing through the wall. She reached out with both hands, straining, and Vile contorted amid the rubble. Magic twisted in the spaces between them, invisible to the human eye but oh so obvious to Darquesse, who saw things much more clearly. Kitana was trying to tear Vile apart. It was fascinating to see, this girl with so much undeserved power going up against a weaker but more skilled opponent. And she was trying so hard, bless her. Her teeth were gritted, muscles were straining, and sweat was starting to roll down her red face. She was putting everything she had into this, but Darquesse's brand-new partner still managed to hold himself together. What an impressive creature he was.

Darquesse moved in, shoved Kitana back and kicked at her leg. The girl's force field was adapting, reconfiguring itself to defend against physical attacks. Darquesse kicked again and again, her boot smashing against the force field, driving the leg back slightly but not inflicting any damage. Darquesse ignored Kitana's laughter and focused instead on the fields of power she was picking up whenever they clashed. Kitana's power was purely instinctual, the force field a defence conjured up out of desperate necessity. But there was no thought behind it, no design, no subtlety, and as such it was a brittle thing, easily broken. Darquesse kicked again, and at the same time she sent her magic twisting downwards. The force field held against her boot but her magic slipped through, curled round Kitana's leg, went taut and then snapped. Kitana's leg broke backwards and her scream was like something a wild animal might utter.

Doran grabbed Darquesse from behind, hauling her back, his arm round her throat. Darquesse reached over her head, going for his eyes, but he turned away. Grinning, she dug her fingers into his scalp, and pressed. She felt his skull give way beneath her fingertips and Doran screamed, threw her from him. She looked back as he collapsed to his knees, hands at his head. His screams mixed with Kitana's. They hadn't taken the time to learn how to heal. Pity. Darquesse was enjoying this fight.

Now it was Sean's turn. His magic picked her up, tossed her the length of the corridor. He couldn't see it as a physical thing but she could. It was ready to instantly obey his commands, but he was an inexperienced fighter and his commands were hesitant. His magic came at her then retracted, nervously pulsing. If only he could see himself as she saw him, as unsure and scared, then maybe he would have taken this opportunity to run.

He made a decision, the magic solidifying round his body, but when he went to attack, the magic betrayed his intentions and she dodged it easily. She stepped into the air and flew, picking him up off his feet. He tried pushing her away but she grabbed his arm, wrapped her legs round him as they hurtled towards the far wall. They hit the wall and Darquesse pushed off with her feet, and now they were flying back again. She swung a leg over his head and he cried out as she hugged his arm and leaned sideways, hyper-extending the elbow into an armbar, and then she flipped them both, felt the arm pop and snap and almost tear itself from his shoulder. She let him crash to the ground, feeling like Ronda Rousey the way she hovered over him as he screamed. *Atomic armbar*, she decided. That was a good name for it.

An energy stream cut through her side and she spun in mid-air, glimpsing Doran lowering his hand and Kitana raising hers. Darquesse dropped, stumbled off balance. Kitana let loose a stream and Darquesse jerked back, but she was too slow. The stream hit her jaw, disintegrating the flesh and bone, and she fell. Another stream burrowed through her chest from behind and she twisted, slumped awkwardly to the floor.

Impossible. They were stronger. Their injuries had healed, and they were stronger. To Darquesse's eyes, they practically glowed with power, when mere seconds ago they were half dead.

Kitana fired again and Darquesse held up her left hand, catching the stream in her palm, keeping it from her head. Her palm sizzled but she poured her strength into it, reinforcing it, buying herself some time to recover. Kitana laughed, and the stream intensified, and Darquesse's hand burned away to a stump. Kitana raised her arms and let out a whoop of victory.

"You don't look so pretty now," she said, and laughed.

Doran looked down at Sean. "Stop screaming and heal yourself," he said irritably.

They were changing. Now that they had learned how to heal they were directing their magic into other avenues. Their newfound confidence was overriding their instincts, and Darquesse watched as their force fields evaporated around them. They probably didn't even realise that they were now vulnerable to a physical attack. But Darquesse did, and all she had to do was stand up and kick their asses. Which was easier said than done with one hand and half a face.

Sean's whimpering died down as he focused on his broken arm. Grimacing against the pain they still hadn't figured out how to dampen, the arm clicked back into its proper shape. He wiped his eyes as he stood.

Doran laughed. "Are you crying?"

"Shut up," said Sean.

"Do you need a moment to compose yourself?"

"I said shut up."

Doran grinned, oblivious to the shadows coiling behind him. Vile emerged silently. Darquesse wanted to shout encouragement to him. He didn't know that they no longer had their force fields. He couldn't see magic as Darquesse saw magic. She tried to tell him to just go for it, destroy the brain, but she had no mouth with which to speak.

Shadows wrapped round Doran's head and yanked him back. Kitana whirled, straight into a wave of darkness that drove her to the ground. Sean stumbled, panicking, and shadow-knives raked across his face, drawing blood.

Vile saw the blood and cocked his head, figuring it all out for himself.

He flung his arms wide, his armour throwing sharpened streams of blackness in three directions. Sean covered his head, howling as the shadows slashed into his arms. Doran curled into a ball, tucking his head down. Kitana cut through the darkness with a wave of angry energy and got to her feet. The streams of darkness retracted into Vile's armour, and he raised a cloud of shadows between them. Kitana fired blindly, one of her blasts accidentally hitting Doran.

Vile shadow-walked behind Kitana but she must have sensed him because she whirled, pushed him back against the wall, her fingers digging into his chest. Shadows snapped at her but she ignored them. She was trying to tear his armour off. Suddenly the armour parted, revealing the shirt and tie beneath, and Kitana uttered a laugh of triumph, mistakenly assuming she had won. Instead, the armour came back, slicing through her hands as it re-formed. Kitana staggered, her fingers dropping to the ground, and Vile struck her with a spiked fist, caving in half of her face. He then sent a spear of darkness into her throat, pinning her to the wall. Vile was about to take her head when Sean dived at him. Kitana fell to her hands and knees and Vile flipped Sean over his hip.

Darquesse got up, staggered away. She rounded the corner and fell to her knees. Argeddion stood before her.

They looked at each other. He didn't attack. Of course he didn't. And not just because he was a pacifist. He *couldn't* attack. He barely had the strength for it. "Darquesse," he said. "How did you escape?"

She finished growing herself a new jaw, and teeth and flesh and a tongue and lips. "You let me out," she said with her brand-new mouth. "When Greta died. You shattered the psychic blocks in my head – including the one you'd set up yourself." She stood, healing her body. "You're making them stronger. You're giving them all of your lovely, lovely power."

"Not all of it."

"Look at you," she said. "You're practically defenceless." She reached out with her magic but he stepped back, the last dregs of his own power flaring to protect himself. "Even that took a lot out of you."

Argeddion paled. "You can see it, too?"

"Magic?" she said, focusing on the new hand she was growing. "Yes, I can see it."

"It took months for my eyes to adjust," said Argeddion.

Darquesse shrugged. "I suppose I'm a fast learner. Or maybe I'm just better than you."

"But if you see things the way I see them, if you see the beauty, then why do you want to destroy everything?"

"I don't. The psychics say they've seen me pulling the world down around us, but I sincerely don't know why I'd want to do that. I like the world as it is. It's funny."

"But you're a killer."

"I can be a little nasty, it's true, but who isn't a little nasty these days? Apart from yourself, obviously. And I bet you're seriously regretting that now, aren't you?"

"I will never regret not hurting people."

Darquesse laughed. "I love that you're ignoring so much of what's been going on. Far more people have been hurt and killed because of your little experiment than I ever had the chance to hurt and kill. Look at the three lunatics you've given your power to. You're responsible for everything they've done."

He shook his head. "Once I started, I couldn't interfere. They needed the freedom to make their own decisions. I needed to see what they'd do."

"And now you've seen." Her magic raged against his, driving him to his knees. "Scientists are a cold-blooded bunch. Standing by while innocent people are killed, while the power you so generously donated is twisted and warped by the fragile little minds of the ordinary people. I can't believe you thought your plan would ever work."

"It will work," Argeddion said. "It's not over yet."

"Yeah? Give me a few seconds."

"I'm afraid I can't do that. You can see everything about me, can't you? My energy, my magic, my aura? Over time, you'll be able to see other things, too. It's all there, it just takes time to study. I can see all that in you, and I can see something else. You've been travelling through realities, yes? Bouncing back and forth."

Darquesse let him talk, and busied herself with getting by his defences.

"I can see the energy that's propelling you. There's just a little remaining, enough for maybe two more trips. It's going to need some time to build up momentum, but that's the thing about magic. Once you see it, you begin to understand it. And once you understand it, you can affect it."

His magic surged and Darquesse gasped, felt her arm suddenly throb, and then the world flickered, flickered, and he reached out for her and they were standing in darkness, in ruins.

"Here we are," he said happily.

She adapted her eyes to see in the dark. They were still in the Sanctuary but there were rocks everywhere, like there'd been a cave-in centuries ago. Argeddion was smiling. "Thank you," he said, stepping away. "I wouldn't have known how to get here by myself."

He was a sneaky one, she'd give him that. She didn't understand magic like he did – not yet, anyway – but she knew what he'd done. He'd given her a boost of his own power, a boost that had sped up the looping time of Nadir's little present. Now the last remaining bit of that energy was whizzing about inside her. It was charging itself so quickly, in fact, that she knew she wouldn't be here for long.

She smiled back at him. "Here you are. And what? You go and find Walden? What then? I'm the only one who can take this trip, and I'm not feeling inclined to bring you back with me."

"Don't you worry about me," said Argeddion. "I've had much longer than you to learn how things work – these days I just have to experience magic and I can replicate it. I'm confident I have enough strength to shunt back on my own, and I'll be back long before you, my child. But when you do return? It will be to a changed world."

She reached for him but he vanished.

Cursing, she flew upwards. The rocks thundered and crunched all around her, and the ground split and she rose into the grey sky. It was raining here. Even the weather was different in this dimension. The rain plastered her hair to her skull. She wasn't used to the sensation of being beaten. She didn't like it. The fact that Kitana and the others had posed an actual physical threat, and that Argeddion had outmanoeuvred her... It stung. It hurt her pride. It bruised her ego. She was Darquesse, for God's sake. The Killer of Worlds. She was the one person on earth you did not want to mess with. And yet here she was, floating in the rain and waiting to go home.

She wanted to tear Kitana's head off. She wanted to crush Doran's throat and rip out Sean's spine. Then she wanted to pull Argeddion limb from limb and use his head as a football and eat his eyes and swallow his tongue and turn him to...

Dust.

A smile broke across Darquesse's face, and she looked towards Ratoath. Now where would China have put that pesky little Sceptre?

53

A LITTLE BIT OF WAR

Ratoath was a town under siege.

Mevolent's forces hurled everything they had at the interlocking force fields. Buildings burned and smoke billowed like all it wanted to do was escape the madness. And it *was* madness down there. It was full of screams and shouts and blood and violence. There were the sounds of gunfire and clashing swords and the crackling of magical energies. A vast army, ready to swarm and barely being held at bay by the few Resistance fighters who stood behind the barricades.

There was fighting in the streets, also. Here and there, Mevolent's army had broken through. Some mortals ran. Others stood their ground beside their sorcerer friends, and did their best to hold back the tide. A futile effort. Noble, certainly, but futile, definitely. The sheer numbers of Redhoods alone would overtake the town, never mind the mages who fought under Mevolent's banner.

And Darquesse hovered above it all, searching for one person in all of that madness, reaching out with her magic to locate the unlikely leader of the Resistance. She saw her, China, in her white dress, sprinting barefoot down a laneway, pursued by Redhoods who ran two abreast. Fourteen of them, closing in. For a moment Darquesse thought that she might have to intervene, but as China burst out of the alleyway, the clever woman tapped a hidden sigil carved into the wall. Silly Redhoods, following her into a trap. The alley walls erupted and the Redhoods were shredded to bloody pieces, and no less than they deserved.

Plumes of smoke and dust rushed out after China, filling the street. She coughed and waved her arms, trying to see where she was going. From her vantage point Darquesse could see Baron Vengeous moving up from behind, clearly hoping to jump out at her like some dreary horror-movie maniac. But there was Anton Shudder, dropping on to him from a rooftop.

Vengeous turned his shoulder into him, shoved, got him against the wall and started throwing punches. Shudder soaked up all the damage, waited for Vengeous to tire, and then he exploded into movement. He wrapped an arm round Vengeous's head, fingers digging into his eyes while his other hand gripped his chin, and then he cranked Vengeous's head around. The neck snapped and Vengeous twisted as he fell, and Shudder stepped over his body and took China's arm, and led her away. She hadn't even realised

Vengeous was there. For some reason this made Darquesse laugh. Poor Baron Vengeous.

Darquesse floated above it all, keeping an eye on China as she parted ways with Shudder, watching her hurry into a house and Shudder turn back to the fighting. From up here, the small town looked like it was gradually being consumed by fire and smoke. Mevolent's forces would be here soon enough.

Darquesse approached the force field and it parted for her. She drifted down to the building and in through a window. There were people downstairs. China was giving them orders. Fear rose through the floorboards like heat. It was all very exciting.

Footsteps. Bare feet on stairs. China came in, walked right by Darquesse without even seeing her.

"Boo."

China spun, her tattoos flashing, and Darquesse dodged a wave of blue energy that cracked the wall behind her. China's eyes narrowed. "You," she said.

A Cleaver ran in, but China held up a hand to stop him. "Oh, I don't have time for this at all," she said. "Can you not see? Mevolent is attacking. Apparently he's leading the charge *himself*. Get out. Run, while you're still able."

"The Sceptre," Darquesse said. "Where is it?"

"Run, or I'll have you killed."

"Sceptre..."

Annoyance tugged at China's lips. "I told you I'd kill you if I saw you again."

"Me?" Darquesse said, and smiled. "Oh, you've never met *me* before."

China nodded to the Cleaver and he stepped forward. Darquesse glanced at him and turned his lungs inside out. He fell, clutching his throat.

China raised an eyebrow. "I see."

"I'm glad. The Sceptre?"

"I don't have it here," she said. "I've hidden it. If you can get me out of here, away from Mevolent's forces, I'll give it to you."

"I'm not here to bargain, I'm here for the Sceptre."

And then the room exploded.

To her eyes, it all happened so very slowly. The wall to her right caved in, buckling the floorboards and the ceiling, filling the air with shards of wood and stone. Darquesse was picked up, thrown sideways, out through the opposite wall as what looked like the whole building splintered and came after her. She fell to the street, ears ringing, barely able to hear the explosions that followed in rapid succession. A mortar attack, maybe. Softening the opposition before the big push.

She rolled on the cobbled street, the remains of China's building falling around her. Her skin was lacerated but it was nothing major. She sat up. A few streets away she could see the Redhoods charging, people running from them in terror. She saw Lord Vile, his shadows whipping through the paltry defences and barricades. The bad guys were coming.

She got to her feet, pulling a piece of floorboard from her neck. Screw that. The bad guy was already here.

She was pretty sure China survived the explosion. Darquesse hadn't seen how she'd fared, but she was confident that a woman like China Sorrows would not be taken out by a mere mortar round. Which meant she was retreating to as secure a location as she could find – which was probably where she had the Sceptre hidden.

Darquesse took a step and scowled. Her hands went to her head. She turned, saw white robes, lots of them, and then she gagged and dropped to her knees.

The Sense-Wardens surrounded her, flooded her mind with pain and misery, made her want to curl up into a little ball, just surrender, stop fighting, beg for the instant release of death. The struggle wasn't worth it. The anguish wasn't worth it. Everything hurt and everything died and nothing was worth it. Give up. She should give up. Oh, God, she wanted to give up. She was crying. Of course she was crying. Why wouldn't she? Life was nothing and nothing meant anything and everything was meaningless and she should just lie down and die. Just die, for God's sake, and let the Faceless Ones judge her in death. Just lie down here and stop fighting and accept the end.

But she didn't worship the Faceless Ones.

She didn't believe they straddled life and death. She didn't believe they would judge her.

These weren't her beliefs. These were the beliefs of the Sense-Wardens, the men and women surrounding her and forcing these thoughts into her head. Oh, they were clever, these Sense-Wardens. They crept in there and force-fed her these feelings and made her despair. It almost worked, too. But they weren't strong enough. Not against her. Not against Darquesse. She was quickly becoming a god, quickly becoming strong enough to kill the Faceless Ones should she ever meet them again. These Sense-Wardens didn't have the first idea who they were dealing with.

But they were realising now.

And some of them were already trying to pull out, but it was much too late. Now she was in their heads, and she was overpowering their puny little minds, crushing them with an ease that was frightening, terrifying. They tried to retreat but she caught them, one by one, and she was turning out the lights inside their minds. One, two, three and look as their bodies dropped four, five, six and they were all gone now, their minds ruined, their bodies shutting down, and Darquesse stood up and willed away the headache.

They hadn't come at her one at a time like they'd done to Valkyrie the first day she shunted. They came with back-up. Reinforcements. They should have come with more.

She walked through the narrow streets of this narrow town, ignoring the distant screams and explosions, ignoring the frightened people, both mortal and mage, who ran this way and that. She stopped before a large building, three storeys tall, reinforced like a mini-fort and protected by a force field that fried the air if it got too close. Beyond the force field, Cleavers stood, scythes at the ready. She ignored them, too. This was the last secure building in the town. Something like this, with its defences, could withstand a full-on assault for days.

She ignored it, walked by it.

The fighting hadn't reached this part of the town. Here, the streets were peaceful. There was no one running about, no one lying dead halfway out of a window, no one kicking in doors. If it weren't for the sounds of war right behind her, this might almost be idyllic.

She walked until she came to a little tavern. Oh, it looked like such a nice little place. So gentle. So unassuming. She pushed the door open, went inside. It even smelled nice. She walked up the stairs, found China and Anton Shudder waiting for her. China had a few cuts and bruises, but apart from that she was her usual beautiful self.

"How did you find me?" she asked, giving a splendidly ladylike sigh.

Darquesse shrugged. "This seems like the kind of place you'd retreat to, that's all. Looks unassuming, but it's got windows to every street so you can see what's coming. Seems pretty sturdy, too. Not as sturdy as the fort you've got everyone defending, but then this doesn't draw as much attention." She looked at Shudder. "I know what you're thinking, Anton. But I wouldn't try it if I were you. I'm a lot tougher than I look."

Shudder observed her with cold, clear eyes, and didn't respond.

"I'll give you the Sceptre," said China. "We don't have to be enemies."

"Sounds ideal," Darquesse said.

Shudder frowned, stepped to the window. "Teleporter," he said.

He could have been bluffing, it could have been the oldest trick in the book, but Shudder wasn't one for tricks, and so Darquesse joined him at the window. Alexander Remit stood on the next rooftop, watching them. He disappeared before she could do anything.

Teleporters were bad news. He could be back here in five seconds with an entire army. It would probably be best if she moved now.

"The Sceptre," she said, striding to China. "Now."

China's beautiful blue eyes widened slightly. Darquesse sighed, and turned. There he was, Remit, standing before her with his master at his side. Of course. Why bother with an army when you have Mevolent?

He was dressed in his battlesuit of chainmail and armour and leather, complete with spiked metal helmet shaped like a screaming face. He looked Darquesse up and down while Shudder and China backed out of the room.

"You're different," he said.

She examined his magic from where she stood. His power was impressive. She saw no hint that he had discovered his true name, contrary to so many rumours. Instead, she noted the level to which he had risen as an Elemental, surpassing every preconceived notion of how strong a mere human could become. People like Darquesse and Argeddion aside, he was quite possibly the most powerful sorcerer who had ever lived.

And he was most definitely a threat.

Darquesse sent her magic forth. Mevolent took a step back, confused at the sudden sensation as every bone in his body strained, cracked and snapped. He fell, and Remit stumbled away, eyes wide. He vanished and she let him go. She was here for the Sceptre, nothing else.

And then, slowly, Mevolent got back to his feet.

She smiled at him. "How did you do that?"

He didn't answer. He gestured. The air that Darquesse breathed suddenly expanded, rupturing her windpipe, swelling her throat. It would have broken her cervical vertebrae had she not overridden his control. She returned her throat to normal, repairing the damage as she did so and taking a deep breath when it was done.

"Sneaky," she said.

Remit staggered out of thin air, dragging the biggest sword Darquesse had ever seen. Mevolent grasped the hilt with both hands, swung it up. It even looked big when *he* held it.

"That's your plan?" she asked as she approached. "You're going to try and stab me? How disappointingly uninspired."

When she was close enough, he swung. At the last moment she saw something in the blade that shimmered, and moved her head back. The energy that whistled by her throat almost made her cry out. The sword came back at her, impossibly light in Mevolent's hands, and Darquesse stumbled to get away. She didn't know what it was, but she instinctively knew it could kill her.

Mevolent pressed forward, his attacks relentless, his speed and ferocity robbing Darquesse of any chance to gather her thoughts. The only thing that mattered was keeping away from that blade. She tripped, fell, rolled, scrambled up and stumbled. The blade cut through stone and wood as it came for her, Mevolent twisting and turning beneath it, never leaving himself open. She jumped backwards, into the air, but he came after her, and now they were flying and she still couldn't make space between them. They spiralled and torqued and that blade just kept getting closer. She ducked, managed to shove him away and retreated.

"That's some sword," she said, backing up to the other side of the room. "Just a little something you happened to have in your collection?"

"It is known as the God-Killer," he replied. "What it cuts, it kills. You can feel the truth in my words, can't you?"

"Which is why I'm all the way over here," she said. She reached out with her magic, tried to pluck the sword from his hands, but it resisted her attempt. Annoying.

"We don't need to fight," she said. "I came here for the Sceptre, but you can keep it. Let me have the God-Killer."

"These weapons were forged to make war against the Faceless Ones. I can't allow someone like you to possess one of them."

"I promise I won't lose it."

Something screeched – Mevolent turned and was knocked back by Shudder's Gist. It clawed at his arm and the sword fell, and it flew at him again but Mevolent pushed at the air and Shudder was launched backwards off his feet.

The God-Killer lay on the floor in the middle of the room. Darquesse smiled.

Mevolent dived for the sword but she went straight for him, catching him in the side with a kick that sent him hurtling through the wall.

She picked up the God-Killer. It was heavy. She didn't know much about swords, apart from the pointy end goes in the other person, but she could see herself swinging this in battle. True, it was almost the length of her from end to end, and that could make her look slightly ridiculous. But so what if the sight of her made her enemies chuckle as she came for them? Wasn't it better to die with a laugh on the lips than a scream?

She didn't know. It was probably much of a muchness, as her father would say.

Four sorcerers came for her, wielding weapons of their own, and her heart leaped with delight. She dodged an axe and swung the sword and it cleaved through the man like he wasn't even there. Almost immediately she felt a spear poke all the way through her side. Ghastly's jacket would have prevented that. The thought of Kitana wearing it made her angry. She took her left hand from the God-Killer's hilt and crushed the spear-man's throat.

Another sword came for her and she brought the God-Killer to meet it. Metal clashed. Clashed again. It was all very exciting. But then the man, and what an ugly man he was, did some fancy move and his sword opened her up. He stepped behind her and spun, driving his sword through her back. She tried reaching for him, but his sword held her where she was and she still had that stupid spear sticking out of her. Then the fourth sorcerer ruined it all by pointing a sawn-off shotgun into her face.

Before he could pull the trigger, she sent her magic into him, boiling his brain in his skull. She turned as the ugly man pulled his sword out and tried swinging for her head. Her hand wrapped round his fist, twisted so that the blade angled towards his own throat, and pushed it in deep.

She let him fall, then pulled the spear from her side and snapped it. She looked at the God-Killer. Swords, apparently, just weren't her thing. She hurled it through the window, took a moment to heal herself, then stepped through the hole in the wall that Mevolent had made. Just in time to see him ripping the Sceptre from China's hands.

His metal mask turned to Darquesse. The crystal flashed and black lightning streaked by her head as she dived to one side.

China, being China, used this opportunity to run from the room.

Darquesse wheeled, barely avoiding another arc of lightning that turned the wall to dust behind her. Mevolent fired again and she felt the lightning sizzle by her face as she jerked back. She launched herself upwards, breaking through the ceiling, Mevolent right behind her. Open sky lay ahead. She didn't know how fast he flew, but she was sure she was faster. Only out here, all he had to do was aim. Down there, there were things to duck behind.

She changed course abruptly and he overshot. She needed people,

people to distract him, people to hide behind. She needed walls and doors and cover.

They flew to the battle, where Cleaver fought against Redhood and the Resistance fought the whatever. Kingdom? Empire? Whatever Mevolent was in charge of. Darquesse didn't know. She had more pressing matters.

Lightning sought her out and she flipped in mid-air so that Mevolent shot beneath her. She grabbed him, was pulled along with him, and he tried turning the Sceptre but she knocked it from his hand. They hit the ground and tumbled, people screaming all around them.

She got to her hands and knees and all of a sudden he was standing over her with a concrete block in his hands. She didn't even have time to wonder where he'd picked it up before it came crunching down on her head. Her face hit the road. She'd bitten her tongue. She hated that.

He grabbed her, lifted her, threw her. She bounced off a house and fell back to the street, looked up in time to see him lob a cart. She punched through it but splintered wood opened a deep cut on her forehead, and then he was beside her, stomping on her knee and then trying to pull her head off. Wow, this guy was violent.

She flung herself backwards, trying to dislodge him, but he held on, kept pulling. She could feel the tendons in her neck start to break. The brown-clothed mortals ran in terror as she struggled. This was not how she was meant to go out, not with her head pulled off in a dimension that wasn't even her own. She propelled him back against a wall and bit down on his wrist, but his sleeve protected him. Still, at least he wasn't dragging her around any more. She could get her feet underneath her and—

Mevolent twisted and she kicked uselessly, but couldn't do anything to prevent him from dragging her away from the wall again. The sound of her cartilage popping filled her ears, and her muscles tore and her skin split, and Mevolent held her in his hands. She didn't understand it at first, and then she was raised to meet his metal mask and her sight was failing, greying, closing in, and he dropped her and the world bounced around her. She spun, toppled, came to a slowly rocking rest, and Mevolent walked away, past a headless body lying in the middle of the road.

Her headless body.

Oh, hell.

54

HEAD OVER HEELS

Seven seconds until brain death.

She could feel it. Everything was slowing. The only sound she heard, bizarrely, was the sea. Like there was a conch shell held to her ear. She blinked. She was seeing things in black and white. She wondered if Scapegrace had seen things in black and white when he was a head in a jar. She wondered if she'd ever get a chance to ask him.

First things first. That body over there. So slim and strong. And the shoulders – impressive. The T-shirt was ripped and torn. The trousers were tight, just how she liked them. The boots were fantastic. She wanted those boots again. She wanted feet to fit in those boots. She wanted feet.

Five seconds to brain death.

Mevolent was still walking away. He'd been tougher than she'd expected. He'd practically killed her, after all. Practically. Almost. Almost, but not quite. Pull the head off, the brain still has time. That was a mistake.

She reached out with her magic and pulled her body towards her. It slithered over the ground. Brown-clothed mortals opened their mouths to cry in shock but all she heard was the sea, like the sea back in Haggard, where she'd been young and safe and happy. Where she'd been Valkyrie Cain, and before that, Stephanie Edgley. Where she'd had her parents and her sister. Where she'd been loved.

But that was Valkyrie, facing her own mortality, grasping the things that meant the most to her. And Valkyrie had no place here. Not now. Darquesse needed to stay in control. Only Darquesse could do what needed to be done.

Three seconds to brain death.

The body nudged against her and she tipped herself back, lining up her ruined neck. Tendrils of meat latched on to each other, finding their mate, pulling the head and body together. Vertebrae clicked and cartilage clacked and muscles reached and re-formed and strengthened. Veins and arteries, nerves and skin, becoming whole.

Blood surged. Oxygen rushed. Brain death averted.

Darquesse propped herself up on to her elbows and looked at Mevolent, who was striding back towards her. "Wow," she said. "That was something."

He flew at her and she kicked, both legs catching him in the stomach and sending him crashing into the road behind her. He sprang up and so did she, but she swayed, the world tilting.

"Dammit," she muttered.

Mevolent's fist crunched into her cheek and she reeled back, knocking against a heavy wooden fence post. He came at her again and she grabbed the post, swung it with all her strength. It broke on impact but at least Mevolent was driven to his knees.

Darquesse reached for another post, tore it from the ground and threw it as Mevolent stood. He stumbled back a few steps. Darquesse threw another, and another, plucking them from the earth, throwing them like darts. Mevolent tried to get up. He got to one knee, shook his head beneath that helmet, and stood. He looked around, and that's when Darquesse hit him with the horse.

She found the Sceptre in a side street just as China Sorrows was picking it up off the ground.

"I wouldn't do that if I were you," Darquesse said, landing gently behind her.

China raised the Sceptre. "Did you kill Mevolent?"

"If I did, then that Sceptre is now yours to control. So you can use it to kill me. Of course, if he isn't dead, and you try to use it, then I'll just take it from you and beat you to death."

"An interesting dilemma," China said.

"Isn't it just?"

"How long do we have?"

"Before I return home? A few seconds. I can feel them ticking down. I'm starting to feel the pull already."

"So we only have moments to resolve this."

Darquesse smiled, and didn't say anything.

China bit her lip thoughtfully. "I don't suppose running would do me any good."

Darquesse shook her head, started walking towards her.

China backed away. "Take the sword. The God-Killer. You can kill your enemy with that."

"Don't like swords any more," Darquesse replied.

"There are others weapons. I've heard of them."

"I want the Sceptre."

"The Sceptre belongs here."

"I'm taking it with me."

"There must be something I can do to make you—"

Darquesse held out her hand. "Give it to me."

The black crystal sparkled in a shaft of sunlight. China tightened her grip. "I think Mevolent's dead. If you didn't kill him, he'd be here by now. I think he's dead and this thing will kill you if I fire."

"That's your decision to make," said Darquesse. Her fingers neared the Sceptre.

China's jaw set. Her muscles tensed. Darquesse smiled.

She took the Sceptre, and China's hand dropped to her side.

It felt good in her grip. Darquesse searched through the magic inside her, found the reverberating energy that Silas Nadir had passed into her system. There was only a small amount left but she grabbed it, spun it, strengthened it, and within moments her arm was starting to throb. She looked back at China. "If I were you, I'd run," she said. "Mevolent's forces are closing in."

"You didn't kill him?"

"Didn't have time."

"So if I'd tried to fire..."

"I'd be wearing your beauty all over my fist by now." The world flickered. "My time here is up. Good luck with your war."

"Good luck with yours," China said, stepping back into a doorway. But there was someone there, someone waiting for her, and a skinless hand came to rest lightly on her shoulder. China stiffened, those beautiful blue eyes widening, and red energy crackled round her body and brought her to her toes before she could even scream. Pain blossomed from within her and snapped her body from Serpine's grip, and she fell to the ground, as perfect and lifeless as a doll.

Serpine smiled at Darquesse, and she smiled back. The world flickered again, and in that moment Serpine brought up his hand and energy exploded out at her. She hurtled back, head over heels through the air, and the world changed and she slammed into a parked truck. She dropped to her knees, back in her own reality, kneeling in dirt in some quarry, surrounded by trucks and pallets and equipment. She took a moment to laugh at Serpine's audacity and rub her chest where he'd hit her, and then she realised her hands were empty. She'd dropped the Sceptre.

"No!" she roared, springing to her feet. "NO!"

She whipped her head round. Maybe it was here. Maybe it had come through with her. Maybe it was—

She kicked the truck and sent it sideways. "*NO!*"

She flung herself into the air, into the sunshine, screaming her curses, twisting and flying for the Sanctuary, her speed drawing tears from her eyes. And still she screamed. Serpine. Serpine, that murderous, treacherous little toerag. He was beyond her reach now but Kitana wasn't, or Sean, or Doran. She was going to kill them all. Going to rip them apart. Going to obliterate them.

She flew faster than she'd ever flown before. It might have been fun if she hadn't been feeling so murderous.

Roarhaven approached. Her eyes narrowed as she neared the Sanctuary, seeing in her mind's eye where Kitana was standing, three levels below the surface, down there in the maze of corridors, in the Accelerator Room. She saw Doran and Sean, too, and Vile on the floor, trying to get up.

She flew at the roof, punching through and crashing through this floor and then the next, swerving now, crashing through a wall, sensing the alarm as Kitana turned. Then she was bursting through, barrelling past Doran and Sean, her fists colliding with Kitana's pretty face. She hit Kitana with the speed of a bullet and the poor girl's head came apart. Her momentum took Darquesse through into the next room, and she touched down, laughing. Back in a good mood. She stepped back through the hole in the wall. Doran and Sean were on their knees, staring at what was left of Kitana.

"Oops," said Darquesse.

Magic writhed around Doran's arm, and his hand glowed and spat forward a stream of energy that burrowed through Darquesse's belly. He still hadn't figured it out.

Even as she healed herself, Darquesse diverted some of her power down through her veins to bundle around her hand. She released it and it burned through Doran and he toppled over, a smoking crater where his face used to be.

"The brain," she said to Sean as he backed away. "Destroy the brain, and how can we heal ourselves? Do you see? It's simple."

Sean licked his lips. His magic thrashed, waiting to be unleashed. She watched it, and when she saw how he was going to use it, she moved, batted his arm down even as it was rising. One hand gripped him under the chin and she spun behind him, her other arm braced against his shoulder blades, and she pulled his head off with all the effort of popping open a can of Coke.

A sorcerer who had earned his power could have used the last few moments until brain death to try something, to try to heal himself, but Sean didn't know the first thing about anything. Darquesse dropped the head and kicked it out into the corridor. She wished Mevolent could have seen that.

"Violent," she murmured. "So very violent." She looked over at Lord Vile as he got to his feet. "We make a good team, you and I. We should do this again. Maybe go after Argeddion when he gets back, finish this once and for all. What do you say?"

Vile, as usual, stood there and said nothing. His fingers tapped against his leg, that same fast rhythm that Skulduggery had been tapping for the past few days, like it was a song he couldn't get out of his head. Annoying, now that she thought of it.

And now that he was still, the subtle movement of his armour became apparent, pulsing slightly to the irregular beat. Darquesse narrowed her eyes. Skulduggery Pleasant was a cunning adversary. He'd have foreseen a time when Darquesse would return, and he knew she'd never give him the chance to talk her down again. He needed a weapon against her, a weapon that he would have had to keep secret from Valkyrie.

That finger-tapping was no meaningless tic. It was a psychological trigger that he'd embedded in his subconscious. It may have been Lord Vile standing before her, but it was Skulduggery underneath, and he was using the rhythm to break free of the more murderous part of his nature.

Whatever he was planning, Darquesse couldn't let it happen.

She studied Vile's armour, saw how it moved. She looked closer, deeper, saw how Necromancy inhabited it. The armour was a living thing, though not a living thing with any degree of sentience. Magic lived in it, and magic was alive, and so the very nature of the armour was transformed as a result. She saw it and understood it, and once she was ready, she focused her mind and called to it.

Vile inclined his head, and stopped tapping his leg.

She called again, more forcefully this time, and the armour reacted, straining against Vile's command. Black droplets of shadow splashed to the ground and Vile struggled, the armour turning solid again, solid and sharp. Darquesse ducked a swipe at her throat. She moved in but he was fast, grabbing her and twisting and smashing her head through the wall. He pulled her on to his hip and flipped her. The world tilted and the floor spun into her face. She started to laugh as Vile knelt on her back. This was *fun*.

She threw him back with a simple pulse of energy and she called to his armour and it flowed to her hand, collecting into a spinning ball of shadow and substance.

The last of it dripped from Skulduggery and he fell sideways, barely managing to support himself against the wall.

"Sorry," said Darquesse, the ball still spinning. "I know you were planning something sneaky, but I quite like it out here and I have no intention of returning to the dark corners of my mind."

"Give me Valkyrie back," said Skulduggery, his voice weak.

"No. And don't think you can charm your way through to her. No more touching stories on how much you mean to each other. She wants me out here. She wants me in charge. She's enjoying this."

Skulduggery took a moment, then straightened up. "You can't kill me," he said.

Darquesse laughed, held out her hand to prove him wrong, then hesitated.

"You might want to," said Skulduggery, "but you can't. That's Valkyrie's influence."

She dropped her hand on to her hip. "It's an influence that's fading. Her voice grows fainter every minute. Another day of this and I think we'll come to an agreement, her and I, and then we will truly be one."

"You're not going to have a day. You're not even going to have another minute."

"Ah," said Darquesse, "this is the moment where you unveil your secret weapon, is it? Come on, then, don't keep me in suspense. What are you waiting for?"

"Them."

Darquesse sensed Argeddion before she heard his footsteps, and turned as he came in. Walden D'Essai followed after him, his face pale and his eyes wide. Magic boiled in his veins, and she knew Argeddion had shared with him their true name.

Argeddion looked at the carnage with dismay.

"You didn't have to kill the children," he said.

"But I did," she answered, "the same way I have to kill you."

Even as she said it, though, she knew she couldn't. Killing Kitana and the others had released their power to flow back into him. He was far beyond even her now.

"Why do you hurt people?" Argeddion asked. "We talked about the things I would show you. If you had just turned your back on violence, the secrets of the universe could have been yours."

He waved his hand gently and Darquesse turned, eyebrows rising, as Kitana got to her feet, her head in one piece. Without magic inside her she was an unexceptional individual, suddenly terrified and empty. Doran stirred, and started to get up as Sean's head appeared by his body and reattached itself.

"You resurrected the dead," said Darquesse. "*That* is impressive."

"And that is only the beginning of my power," Argeddion replied. "Today the world changes. Today the human race moves on."

Darquesse grinned. "Cool."

Argeddion shook his head. "I'm sorry, Darquesse, but we have to leave you behind. I don't know why you are the way you are but... oh, my dear child. You could have been the best of us."

"Uh," Walden said. "Will someone please tell me what is going on?"

Skulduggery leaned against the Accelerator, fingers tapping that annoying rhythm once more against the skin. "You're here to change the world, Walden. He wants to bring magic to the masses."

Walden looked at Argeddion. "Is that what you meant by making your world a better place?"

"A new age approaches," Argeddion said, smiling gently.

Walden stared at him. "Are you insane?"

Argeddion blinked. "I'm sorry?"

"Giving magic to mortals? Have you ever *met* any mortals? They'd kill each other!"

"No," Argeddion said. "My experiments are complete. Thanks to Kitana and Sean and Doran, I know the dangerous levels. Mankind will be elevated to a new plane of existence."

"I've lived in a world dominated by magic. The strong rule. The weak are oppressed and kept down in the gutter."

"Strength will cease to be an issue—"

"Strength is always an issue, you fool! There will always be the strong and there will always be the weak! And you want me to help you? You want me to help you use magic to destroy your own world? No. I won't do it. Return me to mine."

"Magic is mankind's birthright, Argeddion. I don't understand why you can't see that."

"Argeddion is your name," Walden said, "not mine. I'm still me. I'm still Walden D'Essai. I live at eighteen Mount Temple Place and I love Greta Dapple. I'm not going to change just because I can. Look at the people you've hurt. Look at the pain you've caused. You say magic is our birthright? I've studied magic my entire life and I've come to the conclusion that it was never meant for us. It's an accident we have it."

"No. No. Magic is a beautiful—"

"It's dangerous! It's too dangerous!"

"You can't mean that." Argeddion took hold of Walden's arm, tried dragging him to the dais. "Please. Come along. We'll make the world—"

"Let go of me!" Walden shouted, shoving Argeddion back. Darquesse watched as the two men scuffled, Walden's hands tightening round Argeddion's throat. She saw the anger in them, and Argeddion pushed him back and Walden just kept coming and here it was, Argeddion's animal instinct, blossoming across his mind and his temper flared and Walden burned to ashes in his hands.

Argeddion staggered back in shock. Darquesse's grin grew wider.

"No," said Argeddion as the ashes settled. "No. I didn't mean it. I didn't mean it. What have I done?"

If Darquesse were to ever have a chance of killing him, it was now, while he was too distraught to think straight. She stepped towards him.

Skulduggery's fingers drummed against the Accelerator, faster and faster, chasing that rhythm, that irregular beat that he repeated, looped, again and again.

Incessantly.

Argeddion looked at him and Darquesse stopped her approach, caught out. Annoyed, she turned.

"I have to ask," she said. "What are you doing? That tapping, that's your big plan? How is that supposed to defeat the both of us?"

"You have the power of gods," Skulduggery murmured, "but you're not gods. Not yet. Your thoughts are human thoughts. Your minds may be expanding, but how you think is still a human process – for the moment, anyway."

She noticed that there were sigils on the walls, but they were simple things, made to generate light but not energy.

Then the sigils started to pulse with the rhythm. And they got faster, starting pulsing on their own, faster and faster and brighter and brighter and Darquesse frowned, and laughed, and opened her mouth to speak and

55

A HAPPY ENDING

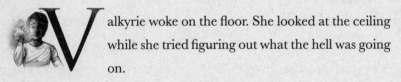alkyrie woke on the floor. She looked at the ceiling while she tried figuring out what the hell was going on.

There were voices. People. Ghastly stepped over her. "She's awake," she heard him say.

There were more people. The Sanctuary was no longer empty. The mages had returned. Skulduggery knelt by her.

"How are you feeling?" he asked.

She looked at him a while before she spoke. "What did you do?"

"I had the lights orchestrated to interfere with the electrical activity in the human brain. Basically, I induced a seizure in both of you."

"But... I'm not epileptic."

"You don't have to be. All that's required is the right sequence at the right speed."

He helped her up. Argeddion was sitting against the wall, eyes open but not looking at anything. Cassandra Pharos and two other Sensitives were kneeling around him. Someone else, too, a man she recognised. Deacon Maybury.

"You've been tapping that rhythm for days," she whispered.

Skulduggery nodded. "I had to drive it into my subconscious so that Vile wouldn't be able to resist using it. Ever since I thought we might require Darquesse, I knew I needed some way to stop her afterwards, something she wouldn't expect."

"She'll be expecting it for next time," said Valkyrie. "You won't be able to get away with this twice."

"Next time I'll have figured out how to keep her away from you for good."

"And if that doesn't work, we always have the Cube." She stood straighter, strength returning to her legs. "What are they doing to Argeddion?"

"Imprisoning him doesn't solve the problem," Skulduggery said, speaking louder now, "it just delays the inevitable. I wanted a solution. The only way I'll be happy is if Argeddion is no longer a danger to anyone, and the only way that would happen is if Argeddion went away and never came back."

"Is that what they're doing? Planting an idea in his mind before he wakes up?"

"Not quite. Deacon owed us a favour and I decided to call it in.

He's helping Cassandra and the others to hide Argeddion. They're building up walls around that personality, shutting him off from the rest of Walden D'Essai."

"They're rewriting his personality?"

"Hopefully not. Hopefully they'll only rewrite his identity – they'll keep his personality as intact as they can. He'll be given a new name, a mortal name, and all memory of magic will be wiped."

"Can they do that?"

"I don't know. But working together, they stand a good chance." He looked at her. "Are you feeling better yet?"

"Yeah. Yeah, I am."

"Good. There are some people we need to talk to."

She followed him into the corridor, where Kitana stood with Doran and Sean, surrounded by Cleavers.

Sean was the first to see her. His eyes were red with tears. "I'm very sorry," he said. "I'm sorry for all the horrible things I did. I'm sorry for all the people I hurt and the danger I put you all in."

Valkyrie walked towards him.

"I don't know what happened to me when I had the magic," he continued, blubbing a little. "I don't know why I did the things I did, or why I didn't stop Kitana. But I followed her, because I'm weak and stupid and she was pretty." Through his tears, he laughed. "Can you imagine that? I almost killed you because Kitana was pretty. How pathetic am I?"

Valkyrie murmured, waited until he was angled just right and then brought her hand up, caught him on the jaw. He crashed to the ground.

Kitana looked worried, but she covered it with a hesitant sneer. "So that's it? You're going to use your magic against us now that we have none?"

"I'm not using magic," Valkyrie said. "But that's my jacket you're wearing, and I want it back."

She walked to Doran next. Apart from the trembling, he didn't move. He looked at her with scared eyes.

Her forehead crunched into his face and he flopped to the floor.

Kitana had gone quite pale. "Whatever," she said with an attempt at another sneer. She took off the black jacket, threw it at Valkyrie's feet. "Bet you're so happy now, aren't you? Now that I have to go back to living a normal life after the power I've had."

Valkyrie raised an eyebrow. "Normal? I'm sorry, Kitana, what exactly do you think is going to happen now? You think you're going to go back to your old life? You've killed people. You're going to spend the rest of your life in prison."

Valkyrie hadn't thought it would be possible for Kitana to go any paler. She was wrong.

"You can't put me on trial," Kitana said, her voice wavering. "I'll tell everyone about you. Everyone will know."

Valkyrie picked up her jacket, put it on. "Trials are for mortal problems. This isn't a mortal problem, and you won't go to a mortal prison."

"You can't do that," said Kitana. "My parents—"

"Will be told you killed someone and you're going to jail. We'll keep the magic aspect out of it, we'll give them enough information to keep them satisfied, and we'll even arrange for visits. We have people who can make them believe whatever we want."

"You... you can't do this. No, I want a trial. A proper one. I need a lawyer, for God's sake. It was the magic! The magic messed with my head! I can't be held responsible for the things I did!" Kitana was crying now, hands over her mouth and shoulders shaking. "Please, Valkyrie, I didn't know what I was doing. Argeddion got into my mind, he got into all our minds. Doran, Doran got it the worst. He was praying to Argeddion, did you know that? This whole thing was his idea. I'll co-operate, I'll do whatever you need me to do, but please, keep him away from me. He's dangerous, Valkyrie. He'll kill me if he knows I'm helping you."

Valkyrie walked over to her. Since she had met her, all she'd wanted to do was punch her face in. But that was when Kitana had been big and powerful and brimming with murderous arrogance. The girl standing before her now, crying and blubbing like any teenage girl would in these circumstances, was not the same girl Valkyrie had wanted to punch.

But she'd do.

Valkyrie's fist connected with such a satisfying jolt that it actually made her smile as Kitana fell sideways, eyes already rolling in her head. Valkyrie resisted the urge to kick her as she lay crumpled. Such behaviour was unbecoming of a Sanctuary detective.

* * *

Quintin Strom argued his way past the mages who were meant to hold him back, and walked up with Grim by his side. Ravel was standing with Skulduggery and Valkyrie, and he muttered under his breath when he saw him coming.

"Grand Mage," he said when Strom reached them, "I want to thank you for your help today. Without you—"

"Without us it would have been a disaster," Strom finished. "You're lucky we were here."

Ravel murmured.

"Mr Sult sustained a broken arm when the Tempest blew," Strom continued. "He's getting that seen to. The moment he's able, he's going to call Grand Mage Bisahalani and give him a full report on what transpired here."

"I see."

"You play a dangerous game, the lot of you. At any moment this could have slipped away and there would have been nothing you could do about it. It's a miracle that didn't happen." He took a breath. "Even so, Erskine, I wish to apologise. What I said to you earlier was borne out of a bad temper. You may be young and inexperienced and your whole Sanctuary may be beleaguered, but you pulled through. You did it. You stopped Argeddion. So I'm going to have a chat with Mr Sult, and maybe we can find a way to reinterpret what transpired here."

Ravel tilted his head, just like Skulduggery. "Reinterpret?"

"You were facing an impossible situation," said Strom. "I'm not sure I would have done any differently if I were in your shoes."

"So that whole thing about you being locked in a cell..."

"Was not appreciated," Strom said, eyes narrowing. "And if you ever try anything like that again, I will tear you apart. But... yes, as for that whole incident, I can forgive it. And looking back, a few hours alone with my thoughts was probably good for me."

"I have to say, that's surprisingly generous of you."

"I don't want you to misunderstand me. Things are not OK. I have not been reassured that you can handle whatever happens next. I still think you need help, and you need guidance, and yes, maybe you need someone else in control. But... neither are things as bad as I feared. You govern well, you govern with your hearts as well as your heads, and you have good people by your side. All of this helps."

"So what will be your recommendation to the rest of the Supreme Council?"

Strom rubbed his chin. "Hopefully, I'll be able to convince Mr Sult to withhold some of the details. Make no mistake, Sult's report, as it is, could very well result in the first stirrings of war. Even an abridged version of what happened might be enough to start us down that road, but I think I can persuade my colleagues to trust you – at least for now."

"We appreciate that."

"You're going to need help, you know. Don't let your pride stand in the way of a secure future for your Sanctuary."

"Our pride isn't at stake," Ravel said. "Our autonomy is. Every Sanctuary in every country governs itself. That's how it is, and that's how it should be."

Strom sighed. "This conversation is far from over. But at least we'll be able to discuss it with a little civility from now on."

Ravel raised an eyebrow. "Providing you convince Sult to see things your way."

"Oh, I think I can manage that," Strom said. "I can be quite charming when I want to be."

He shook their hands and nodded to Grim, who gave them all a glare before following his boss back up the corridor. Ravel went to check on Argeddion and Skulduggery turned to Valkyrie.

"I can't believe you abandoned me in the middle of a fight," he said, keeping his voice down.

"I didn't abandon you," she pointed out. "Darquesse abandoned Lord Vile. And she didn't even do it on purpose. I went dimension hopping again. Almost came back with the Sceptre, too, but it slipped out of my hand right before I shunted. Darquesse was not amused. But what are you complaining about, anyway? You survived."

"Barely."

"Barely surviving is still surviving. Where's the armour?"

"Back in the case, hidden away. And Darquesse is back in your mind, I take it?"

Valkyrie shrugged. "They saved us. Both of them. Vile *and* Darquesse. The ultimate secret weapons. And don't look at me like that. I'm not saying we should ever use them again. I'm just saying we needed them this time and it worked out for us."

"And we never use them again."

"Absolutely. Now if you'll excuse me, I've needed to pee ever since you short-circuited my brain."

She left him and headed for the nearest toilet. When she was finished, she emerged from the cubicle to find Elsie standing at the mirror.

Valkyrie hesitated, then went to the sink and washed her hands. "Hey," she said.

Elsie took a moment. "I felt Sean die. I felt all of them die. But… but they came back. Now I can't feel them any more. I can't feel anything. I'm back to being me."

Valkyrie turned off the tap, wiped her hands on her tattered T-shirt. "That's what you wanted, wasn't it? For your magic to be gone?"

"Yes. I think. But I didn't know how… lonely it would be." Elsie turned to her. "While all this was going on I was too busy to think about, you know, what it would be like when it was over. But I'm going to go back to my old life and Sean is…"

"Going to prison."

Elsie took a deep, shuddering breath. "I've followed him around since we were kids and he's never even looked at me. Not really. I thought, I thought I loved him. I convinced myself that I loved him, and maybe I did, but Kitana and Doran would laugh at me and call me names and Sean never, he *never* stood up for me. How could I love someone like that? How could I love someone who so obviously didn't care about me in the slightest? What does that say about me or what I think of myself? I deserve more than that

– more than someone like him. He's not as bad as the other two, really he's not, but he thought Kitana was so perfect and so great and you know what? She's a monster. And I'm not as skinny and I'm not as pretty but I'm a much better person than she is."

Valkyrie looked at her. "Wow."

Elsie gave a laugh. "Sorry about that."

"Don't apologise. That was a good speech."

"It *was* pretty good, wasn't it?"

"Do you feel better now?"

"I do, a little."

"We have Kitana in a cell downstairs, you know. Do you want me to hold her arms while you hit her?"

Elsie laughed. "Thanks for the offer, but I think I just want to go home now. Mr Scrutinous said my family won't even have missed me, but I've missed them."

Valkyrie grinned. "I'll give you a call in a few days, see how you're doing. Maybe offer you the opportunity again."

Valkyrie took Elsie to someone who could drive her home, then went and found Skulduggery. While sorcerers hurried to and fro all around them, they took a slow stroll through the Sanctuary, enjoying the fact that they didn't have to do anything.

"It can get quite tiring knowing you," she said, walking with her eyes closed.

"Now, now," he countered, "I hardly think I can be blamed for any of this. And has there been any lasting damage? Don't you have your precious jacket back? Haven't you used up all of that shunting energy that was reverberating around inside you?"

"That is so not the point." She opened her eyes, looked down at herself, and immediately closed her jacket. "My God," she said. "You've been letting me walk around with my T-shirt like this?"

"What's wrong with it?"

"It's literally in shreds."

"I thought it was a fashion thing."

"It's barely there!"

"I didn't say it was a *wise* fashion thing."

She zipped up. They walked on. "Nadir's still out there," she said.

"That's true."

"A dimension-hopping serial killer is on the loose. That can't be good."

"We'll find him," Skulduggery said. "If not us, some other detective in some other Sanctuary. Maybe he'll go and investigate the reality where he sent you. If we're lucky, Mevolent will rip him apart for us."

"And if we're not lucky?"

He shrugged. "We'll stop him."

"You're so sure?"

"Of course," he said. "I have faith in us."

They found Ghastly standing in the corridor – just standing there against the wall, with his head down.

"Hey," Valkyrie said as they approached. "What's wrong? We won today, or did you miss that bit?"

Ghastly didn't look up. "Strom is dead," he said. "He was in his chambers, collecting his things. When he didn't come out, his bodyguard checked on him. One of the walls was cracked. That was Sanguine. But the sword that took Strom's head, that was Tanith."

Valkyrie went numb. "But... we were just talking to him..."

"Sult left as soon as he heard," Ghastly continued, "took all of their mages with him. He's probably on the phone to his boss right now. Strom never even got a chance to talk to him."

Valkyrie's stomach churned. She felt like she was going to throw up. "What do we do?" She looked at Skulduggery. "What do we do now?"

"We do what we always do," Skulduggery said, buttoning his jacket and straightening his tie. "We prepare for what's coming next."

EPILOGUE

A Sunday afternoon with the birds singing and the sun shining. The house belonging to Fergus and Beryl Edgley was empty, save for Carol and the reflection standing with her in her bedroom.

"Thank you for doing this," Carol said. "I swear, I will practise every day until I'm as good as you are. And I won't tell Crystal, not if you don't want me to. I can keep a secret, like."

"I know you can," said the reflection.

"Can I call you Valkyrie?" Carol asked. "Just when we're alone, like. I promise. I should probably come up with a name of my own, right? If I'm going to be training with you and everything?"

"Yes, you will," said the reflection. "Although I'd actually prefer if you just call me Stephanie."

"Oh," said Carol. "Yeah, OK. Whatever you want. So how do we start? What's in the bag? Can I see?"

"Not yet," the reflection said. "The first thing you have to do is undress."

Carol frowned. "Really?"

"Just down to your underwear. We'll be working with fire, and your clothes are flammable."

"But... um..."

"Don't worry," said the reflection, "I won't laugh. You don't have to be embarrassed." Carol hesitated, and eventually started to remove her clothes. The reflection drew a symbol on Carol's mirror while it waited. When Carol was down to her underwear, the reflection handed her a piece of torn paper. "Read this."

Carol looked at it. "What is it? Is it a spell?"

"That's exactly what it is."

"But I thought you said sorcerers don't use spells."

"It's not that kind of spell," the reflection said. "The words are used to focus the magic of someone like you – someone who doesn't know what they're doing."

Carol read from the page. "Surface speak, surface feel, surface think, surface real." She looked up. "Is that it? Did I do it right?"

"I don't know," the reflection said. "Touch the mirror."

Carol hesitated, and then raised her hand and pressed her fingertips against the glass. She took her hand away. The image in the mirror did not.

Carol stepped back. "Oh my God," she whispered. "Why's it doing that? Is it... is it looking at me?"

"Yes," said the reflection. "That's exactly what it's doing."

Carol turned to it. Her eyes were sparkling. "What do I do now? Will you teach me to throw fire?"

The reflection smiled. "All of that takes time."

"How much time? Show me what I can do."

"I'm afraid I can't do that."

"Why not?"

"Because I don't actually have any magic."

"What are you talking about? You've got *loads* of magic, Valkyrie. You're amazing."

"Even if I could teach you," said the reflection, walking forward, "it wouldn't do you any good. I've told a bit of a lie, actually. I think you'll understand, once I explain myself. You won't like it, but at least you'll understand. Or maybe you won't, I don't know. You were never the brightest twin, now, were you?"

Carol blinked, puzzlement shining in her wet eyes, and the reflection took another step closer and slid the kitchen knife into her belly. Carol made a sound, halfway between a retch and a gasp, and her hand closed around the reflection's arm. She had a surprisingly strong grip for someone so soft.

"And I *told* you not to call me Valkyrie," said the reflection.

Carol lurched back like she was off balance, then doubled over and fell to one knee. She dropped forward, hand out to catch herself, but her arm buckled and she ended up on the floor. "Am I dying?" she asked. Her voice was small.

"Yes," said the reflection.

Carol's breathing rattled. "Why?"

"I need someone magic," the reflection told her. It reached into its bag and took out the Sceptre, wiped some of the quarry mud off it. "I went back for this, found it under a truck. Darquesse didn't realise she'd brought it with her. Valkyrie didn't think twice about it. I'm the only one who bothered to sort through the memories, because I'm the only one who deserves it. Your death will charge the Sceptre. That's what I'm hoping, anyway. If I were magic, I'd just do it myself, and no one would have to get hurt. But I'm not magic, and I can't ask anyone, now, can I? I can't ask Valkyrie to charge it, because she'd know I was planning to kill her with it." The reflection bent down, pressed the Sceptre into Carol's hand.

"Please," Carol whispered. "Call an ambulance."

"No," the reflection said, straightening up. It turned to the mirror. "Come out," it said.

Carol's reflection did as it was told, and stepped from the glass into the room. It stood over the real Carol.

"You are to take over her life," Valkyrie's reflection told it. "Her sister will probably notice something is wrong. It won't be easy, but avoid her as much as possible. Avoid all sorcerers. Stay away from Valkyrie. You won't have to do it for ever – just until I kill her."

"Skulduggery Pleasant will know you're not Valkyrie," Carol's reflection said. Its voice was lifeless, devoid of emotion.

"Of course he will," Valkyrie's reflection responded, "and he'll destroy me once he finds out what I've done. Which is why I'm going to kill him, too. And Tanith. And Ghastly. And anyone else who might come here and take away what I've earned." Carol's reflection did not comprehend what was being said to it. "Maybe you'll be like me," Valkyrie's reflection continued. "Maybe you'll grow, and evolve. Maybe you'll stop being this girl's reflection and start being something else. And if you do, you're lucky, because the only person to challenge you is lying at your feet. I've taken care of your problem for you. Now I have to take care of mine."

Carol's reflection looked down. "She looks dead."

Valkyrie's reflection picked up the Sceptre. The black crystal was glowing. "It worked," it said. It was pleased. "Clean up the blood. I can't have anyone raising the alarm, do you understand?"

"Yes," said Carol's reflection.

"Listen to me. Are you listening?"

"I'm listening."

"The dead person at your feet was a stupid girl. She was a stupid, ignorant, selfish girl. Which means you are a stupid, ignorant, selfish thing. But you can change. You can improve. You can be better than she ever was. You can be a better Carol than the real Carol ever managed to be. Do you understand the gift that I'm giving you?"

"No."

"You will. In a few years, you will. You'll turn into something better. Look at me. I was like you once. Every little thing about me was false. But I'm not like that any more. Valkyrie Cain abandoned Stephanie Edgley when she took a new name. She left Stephanie behind, like a coin, for someone else to pick up. Someone like me. So that's who I am now: Stephanie. And I am a better Stephanie than Valkyrie could ever hope to be. I'm not an empty shell, and you don't have to be, either. This Sceptre bonds to people, not to things. I'm not a *thing*. I'm not an *it*. I'm a *person*. I am a *her*."

Stephanie pointed the Sceptre at Carol's body and the crystal flashed, the black lightning turning the dead girl to a collapsing pile of dust. "I have a family who loves me. I have parents and a little sister who I'm going to take care of. I have friends in school, and I want to go to college. I want a normal life. A happy life. A life. And I'm going to take it."

Stephanie smiled at her own reflection in Carol's mirror. She liked the way her eyes twinkled when she did that. She put the Sceptre back in the bag and walked to the door. "Dispose of her remains," she said without looking back. "Use a hoover."

SKULDUGGERY PLEASANT

LAST STAND OF DEAD MEN

He's dead.
She's still in high school.
But together they're going to save the world.

Read the eighth book in the bestselling
SKULDUGGERY PLEASANT series…

Two wars rage. One is a war between Sanctuaries – a
war of loyalty and betrayal and last, desperate stands.
The other is a war within Valkyrie Cain's own soul.
If she loses, Darquesse will rise.
And the world will burn.